FATE OF PERFECTION

ALSO BY K.F. BREENE

The Warrior Chronicles Series

Chosen
Hunted
Shadow Lands
Invasion
Siege
Freedom (coming soon)

Darkness Series

Into the Darkness
Braving the Elements
On a Razor's Edge
Demons
The Council
Shadow Watcher
Jonas
Charles

FATE OF PERFECTION

K.F. BREENE

Text copyright © 2016 by Hazy Dawn Press, Inc.
All rights reserved.

Published by 47North, Seattle

www.apub.com

Amazon, the Amazon logo, and 47North are trademarks of Amazon.com, Inc., or its affiliates.

ISBN-13: 9781503940680
ISBN-10: 1503940683

Cover design by M. S. Corley

Printed in the United States of America

Chapter 1

"We're ready for you, miss."

Millicent glanced away from her idea board. Mr. Arnet, her subordinate, stood rigid with downcast eyes, waiting. She glanced at the time. "My demands have been met with regards to the tests?" she asked.

His Adam's apple bobbed as he gulped. "Yes, miss. They acquiesced to your . . . requests."

"Good." Stepping back from the glowing screens, she swiped her hand through the air in front of her documents, using the movement of her body heat to issue a command. The documents scattered, filing themselves back into their respective folders. "And the weapons?"

"Are laid out for you, miss. As requested."

She waited for Mr. Arnet to back out of the way before she stepped forward. Two of the Moxidone conglomerate guards waited beyond, looking at the ground respectfully. Without a word, she stalked through the department, going over the various commands she'd need to practice with the new suit. Mr. Arnet followed behind, and two more staffers joined him at the door leading into the weapons bay.

"What's the news from the other conglomerates, Mr. Arnet?" Millicent asked as they approached two men sitting in metal chairs.

Their hands were bent behind their backs and obviously secured. Rope tied their ankles to the chair legs. Muscles bulged on their large frames and surly expressions accompanied hateful stares.

"Just that Gregon Corp. is boasting a new, completely secure firewall. It protects their upper-level staffers." Mr. Arnet slowed as they approached a small table with a hologram pod sitting on top. "They've tested it thoroughly. Their systems specialist seems . . . smug."

Millicent sniffed as she palmed the table, bringing up the hologram and then the console. After tapping in her code, her program sprang into the glow. "Having Curve huggers test your program is about as useful as accessing the mainframe through a burned-out screen. That's just laziness. They should've contracted me to test it."

"It's said that their programmer has complete confidence. From what I hear, she said she didn't need your—Moxidone's—double check."

Millicent arched an eyebrow. "She doesn't think I can get through, is that what you're saying, Mr. Arnet?"

"Yes, miss," he said quietly. "That is what I've heard."

Millicent looked over her prison program without seeing it, hearing the unspoken challenge by the programmer in the other conglomerate. There was only one person in the world as good as Millicent when it came to programming. Millicent and this other woman were constantly at war in a passive-aggressive sort of way. Being that they worked for competing conglomerates, they'd only communicated via notes when contracted to review each other's work. And those notes were always a list of failures.

And now this woman was throwing the gauntlet, basically telling the world that she was better than Millicent. This was Gregon Corp.'s attempt to get the code tested for free, Millicent had no doubt.

Still . . . the wall would have to be torn down. That was a given.

"I'll expect more information by the end of the day," Millicent said in a flat tone. "Now, let's test, shall we? Where are the weapons?"

"Over here, miss." Mr. Arnet motioned her over to a case along the far wall. After glancing at the test subjects, still tied to their chairs, he placed his palm on the scanner and then stepped out of the way. The metal cover slid aside, revealing four guns resting on velvet.

Gun—right, Millicent thought.

A lightweight metal pole extended from the right sleeve of her suit, with a catch on the end. She chose the five-shot, a small gun that was great in close combat. After hooking it in place, she gave the command for her suit's mechanism to pull it back in and secure the weaponry.

"Yes," she said, moving her arm to learn the feel of the added weight. "Noticeable, but an improvement. Let's hope the mechanism is improved as well. Are the test subjects wearing bulletproof plates?"

"Yes, miss. Unless you repeat fire, the plates should hold."

She nodded without comment. Most staffers in her position wouldn't be concerned with killing. In fact, they'd probably aim to. The fact that it made her uncomfortable was an emotional gray area, and something she couldn't advertise.

Gun—left.

A pole extended from the other sleeve, with a larger catch. Being right-handed and faster on that side, she often chose a larger, heavier gun for her left hand. It was a handicap she was familiar with, and now strengthened with firepower. The left wasn't as fast, but it made a bigger impact.

"Knife, miss?" Mr. Arnet glanced at the row of knives, ranging from pocket-sized to incredibly daunting.

"This suit is only equipped for two guns."

"Yes, miss." Mr. Arnet backed away.

Millicent reassumed her position in front of the hologram. She accessed the implants of the test subjects. "I will be uploading the program in four . . . three . . . two . . ."

One of the test subjects flexed and shook. His jaw clenched, and fire sparked in his eyes. The other grunted, but didn't move. Hate flashed through his gaze.

"Interesting . . ." Millicent looked over the individual's stats. "The upload seems to have created a mild electric shock. Seems quite painful. I'll have to amend that, or we'll get pushback on the update."

"Yes, miss." Mr. Arnet and the other staffers took to their screens along the wall to make notes, not that she'd need them. The alterations would be easy.

"I will now set the parameters of the new imprisonment program. These men had previously been incarcerated, is that right?" Millicent altered the settings as she waited for Mr. Arnet's response.

"Yes, miss. Murderers, both. Fairly gruesome. They will be recycled when we no longer have need of them."

"Yes, of course." Millicent surveyed their corded muscles and long limbs. They looked powerful, and if they'd committed a violent crime, they were certainly unhinged. It appeared the conglomerate had taken her threat seriously and was allowing her the training she required. *Good.*

Finishing with the settings, she uploaded those as well, pleased when the smaller update didn't cause the same stiffening. Next she stepped away. Without a word, one guard wheeled the table to the side and the other stepped up next to her.

"More room, please. I'll be fine, I assure you." Millicent glanced behind to make sure the guard increased his distance. "Mr. Arnet?"

"We're ready, miss."

"Execute the program in test subject B. Monitor his stats."

"Yes, miss," Mr. Arnet said. The other staffers bent toward their screens.

The man who had shaken during the update clenched his jaw. His face turned red, and frustration bled into his eyes. "Undo his bonds, please," she said. Her pulse started to pound. A burst of perspiration coated her forehead.

Here we go.

A guard did as instructed and then took out a gun before stepping away. He sighted on the test subject, whose face shone with sweat. Muscles flexed along the subject's body.

"Stats, Mr. Arnet," Millicent said, struggling to keep the anxiety out of her voice.

"Pain sensors are flaring," Mr. Arnet yelled, as though he were under fire. "He's not fighting them very hard."

"He has a tiny bit of muscle play," one of the other staffers said.

Millicent flexed and unflexed her fingers. Her breath came fast. Still, nothing happened.

A bead of sweat dripped down the side of the subject's face. Then his muscles went lax and fear overcame the frustration in his eyes.

"Update," she said, knowing the answer.

"It held." Mr. Arnet sighed with a smile. He wiped his forehead. "You did it, miss. It works."

"It works on weak individuals," Millicent said softly, now staring at the other subject. He stared back, his gaze teeming with cold determination and violence. "Bind subject B, and let's get ready for subject A."

"Yes, miss." Mr. Arnet bent to his screen. She almost didn't hear him say, "One more."

"We're ready, miss," Mr. Arnet said, braced. The guard stepped away after securing subject B.

"Execute," Millicent said.

The subject's brow lowered over his eyes. Confusion and then irritation stole over his expression. Millicent stopped herself from taking a step back. She knew that look. He'd fight the program. And given his size and background, he'd probably win.

"Release his bonds," Millicent said, working to keep her voice even. "Be careful."

The way the guard jerked away after undoing the subject's hands was telling.

Here we go again. Millicent thought, *Heels.*

The spikes in her heels elongated, raising her up. The plates would stop the razor tip from penetrating his body. Hopefully. Or else this would be over very quickly.

Silence stole over the bay. The subject did not move. Did not even flex.

"Update," Millicent barked, her pulse rushing in her ears.

"Placid," Mr. Arnet said. "Not fighting."

"Do I need to make you fight?" Millicent asked the subject.

A glimmer sparkled in his eyes. Humor.

His sudden flex made Millicent jerk. With a human roar, the subject's face went red and his muscles strained against the invisible bonds created by the program and his implant. Struggling, he stood.

"He's breaking through," Mr. Arnet yelled in a high-pitched voice. "The program won't hold."

"Hmm," Millicent said, sidetracked by her desire to solve the technical problem.

"Miss—"

It was the only warning she got. And the only one she needed.

The man rushed her, shedding her program's attempts to keep him contained like an oversized coat. She dodged his hammy fist, stepped, and kicked. Her spike jabbed his side, putting a dent in the practice suit.

He punched at her again. She dodged and then jumped into a scissor kick—no sense jumping the huge man. It wouldn't do any good.

Her foot struck his chest this time. He staggered backward.

Two quick steps, another jump, and she thrust her heel into his sternum with all her weight behind it.

Gun—right.

His breath exited his body with a pained grunt. Her heel tangled in the suit plate as the gun silently and quickly filled her hand. She unhooked it from the pole as gravity dragged her body to the ground. She yanked her foot free, tearing the suit. Blood poured out of the hole she'd made in the man's body.

Clearly the practice suits weren't as good as the weapons she'd designed.

Twisting and then jumping up, she braced herself with her gun out, not sure how much damage she'd done. Her finger rested on the cool metal of the trigger.

The man staggered toward her before stumbling off course. Pain bled through his expression, and his hand grabbed at the new hole in his chest. He looked down in confusion before the strength went out of his legs.

Her gut twisted, but she kept the uncomfortable feeling from her face as she straightened up and rehooked the gun.

Gun—right, disengage.

"Guards," Millicent said, her tone flat and her heart clattering behind her ribs.

The guards sprang into action, making for the subject as she turned toward the weapons bay. With a studiedly neutral expression, she waited for Mr. Arnet to assist her in putting the guns away, ignoring his shaking hands and pale face. After she was finished, Millicent turned to go back to work. She had fixes to make on this latest program.

"Miss?"

She turned with a quirked eyebrow, not trusting her voice just yet. Mr. Arnet pointed at her shoes.

"Yes, of course." *Heels—disengage,* she thought. And then sighed when they failed to perform. "They tend to malfunction when my adrenaline is up from fighting." Millicent tsked. "Another issue to resolve."

"Yes, miss," Mr. Arnet mumbled, following closely behind her.

She didn't spare a look at the subjects. The conglomerate wouldn't expect her to. She would, however, need to hack into the system to check the implant's recording of her vitals after the shock of stabbing him. She wagered there would be some telling information that she didn't want to surface. It might undo all she'd worked so hard to build.

Chapter 2

A slamming door reverberated off the walls like a shotgun blast.

Trent McAllister jumped. With the pad of his finger, he wiped away a drip of sweat. A figure emerged in the hallway. Then two figures.

It was time.

Back snapping straight, he stood next to his idea board and prepared for the single most important meeting of his life. He tried to ignore the uncomfortable shaking in his extremities as more sweat dribbled down his brow.

"Mr. McAllister is right over here, sir." Trent's boss, Ms. Hutchins, let her hand drift in Trent's general location.

With an irritated snort, Mr. White stalled in his determined stride and glanced Trent's way. "Yes, of course."

As they came to a stop in front of Trent, Ms. Hutchins looked off toward the other work pods in the dimly lit, hushed space, organized in straight lines spanning the large floor. Screens glowed a faint blue, illuminating faces staring in focused concentration. All except for those who knew the director was hanging around. *They* were staring in Mr. White's direction with wide eyes.

"His is the intriguing idea behind our current project," Ms. Hutchins said. "The report is on your desk, I believe."

"Yes, of course." Mr. White gave Trent his full hard-eyed attention. "You've finally come up with a way to increase the percentage of brain use, correct?"

Trent moved his lips, but instead of words, only an embarrassing croak tumbled out of his mouth. He cleared his throat as Mr. White glanced at his wrist screen. Glowing red numbers appeared along Mr. White's skin. Time was running out.

"Yes, sir, in a way," Trent said in a shaking voice. "Working with the lab, I've engineered a chemical compound that should work seamlessly with fetal development in the womb—"

"Oh, now wait a minute." Mr. White leaned back and held up a thin hand with gnarled knuckles. "The womb?" He looked at Ms. Hutchins. "You're talking about affecting the *natural* creative projects? I don't remember reading that in my report—"

"It's the only way," Trent rushed to say, taking a wobbly step forward. His stomach clenched as both bosses turned to stare at him with tight lips and a warning in their eyes. "Excuse me for interrupting, sir. But yes, it can only be done with natural creation. My goal is simply to enhance the female's body during a few key phases of brain development in the fetus. Possibly nothing will happen. Indeed, that would be the worst-case scenario—besides the hit to our budget. But I suspect that the chemical reaction during creation, starting from roughly week six, will stimulate brain function in a few areas. The percentage of increase will be minimal, but the *ways* in which we'll expand the brain's capability are exciting."

"And what exciting ways might that be?" Mr. White shifted his weight and cocked his head.

"Yes." Trent tapped the air in front of his screen and then pulled up a document. He pointed at the structure of the chemical compound he'd devised, careful to stay outside the heat registers so the image didn't wobble off the screen. "Right now we can program certain electronic devices to respond when we *think* the commands. Our implants are intermediary devices. They read the brain waves we've previously taught them, enhance those brain waves to react with the device, which then physically performs the action. It saves time and effort. Naturally, some people are more suited for this, and those individuals get a higher level of . . . cooperation, but everyone with an implant can effectively learn these strategies to some degree. The problem is, these commands, and the accompanying actions, are mostly rudimentary. It's limited to one- or two-word commands. *Go. Stop.* That sort of thing. So we're hoping to expand the capability."

Mr. White's brow scrunched up. "But some people can work with thought commands without an implant. The tech is still supposed to work . . ."

"Yes, sir. Ah . . ." Trent wiped away sweat. "Technically, yes, the best and strongest minds can still think commands without an implant. But the results are anything but impressive. They have to be very close to the tech, and focus ten times harder. Only the very brightest can guarantee accuracy with all the crisscrossing of . . ." He clasped his hands to keep from waving them around. Waving wasn't helping him come up with words. "Data. Or, you know . . ." He reclasped his hands to stop himself from waving them again. "Interference from all the wireless systems in place . . ."

Mr. White blinked a few times before scratching his nose in what could only be irritation. This wasn't going well. "My field of expertise isn't organic matter," he said. "Break this down for me differently. What is the end goal?"

"Oh. The end goal. Yes, sir. I should've started with that, maybe." Trent offered a smile. It wasn't returned. "I'm trying to further the human capacity for hands-free command. I'm trying—my goal is to make complex commands not only plausible, but more effective, and with a larger array of electronics. I'm trying to expand on a good thing." His laughter wasn't contagious, it seemed.

Mr. White's jaw clenched. He looked at Ms. Hutchins. "It seems to me our time and budget would be better spent working on the electronics and not on our extremely expensive assets."

"He is below the Curve in communications," Ms. Hutchins said in a disapproving scowl. "It's a failing that holds him back." Trent shifted uncomfortably. "We hope to remove the need for an implant in these matters. We'd still issue an implant for tracking and controlling purposes, of course, not to mention the plethora of other applications, but activating one's wrist screen, interfacing with consoles—all would be organic with the new generations, with exponentially increased results."

"I see." Mr. White's gaze homed in on Trent's idea board. He squinted, and a crease worked between his brow. "And why natural births? Why not just test this compound on the lab-born assets? That seems more cost-effective, and they are in greater supply. If something were to go wrong, it wouldn't be as grievous."

"Well, you see," Trent said, trying to collect his thoughts, "in the Enlightened Ages, when we adopted the outside-womb incubation, we started choosing which characteristics and attributes each baby would inherit. We always chose the best attributes—still do, of course. We want the best for our children, after all. I don't know about you, but *I'm* happier with a strong heart, good eyesight—"

Ms. Hutchins cleared her throat suggestively.

"But," Trent said, getting back on track, "with only lab-controlled creations, we started to see a stalemate in evolution. Our race mostly flatlined. Everything was too controlled—"

"I don't need a history lesson, son."

"Yes, sir. Sorry, sir." Trent wiped his brow, and then wiped his newly wet fingers on his suit leg. "Basically, I'm hoping to hurry along the next phase of evolution. This will all be perfectly natural. Mostly. I'm just following the natural curve already in progress, and attempting to speed it up. A tiny bit at a time."

Mr. White's shoulders rolled. "I see. And these?" He jerked his chin up, indicating the pictures on the idea board.

"Yes, those. Sir." Trent moved the image of his compound out of the way to make room for the faces and stats of the assets he'd researched. "I've gone through the breeder roster and selected brain patterns and skill sets that I think will work perfectly. All are two or three clicks above the Curve in mathematics, reasoning and logic, and analytics, with fast processing capabilities. They are strongly geared toward hands-free controlling, especially her, her . . . and him." Trent tried to *shake* the pictures with his own hands-free controlling. A blond woman and dark-haired man wiggled. The other woman jerked. The rest shimmied.

He wasn't as good at hands-free as the breeders in question.

"Based on our testing in the animal labs," Trent said, "this serum shows real promise."

"Side effects?" Mr. White asked, stepping closer.

Trent bumped against his desk to maintain distance. "We haven't had—"

"All of that is carefully detailed in the report, sir," Ms. Hutchins said, glancing out over the floor again. Faces whipped back toward their work stations. Trent's pulse sped up—meetings never lasted this long with Mr. White. Not ever. It had to mean good things, like perhaps the green light to continue on as planned . . .

"Yes, of course." Mr. White tapped the air above the blond woman. "I recognize this asset. She's the best we have in major defense systems, I believe. She's local."

"Yes, sir," Trent said. "She is my greatest hope. Driven, content in her position, and has a very low compassion rate."

"Compassion rate—what does that matter?" Mr. White looked over the other faces, his presence imposing.

Trent edged out of his work pod so the air wasn't tinged with the musky smell of the antiaging face cream that so many upper-level staffers used. They each had two different bodies housing replacement parts and organs—why didn't they just switch out their skin instead of applying that glop? Ms. Hutchins looked like her tight red bun was stretching her face beyond its capacity.

"Natural birth means the parents are subject to biology's hang-ups." Trent itched his nose. The smell wouldn't go away. His eyes were starting to water. "If a bond between parent and infant develops, there really is no telling what the parent will do. And in this situation, with three masters of defense, two specializing in weapons, and the best systems specialist in our conglomerate, possibly the world . . . well, let's just say, if they wanted to tear down this company to save their child, they could very well do it."

"Chute wash." Mr. White snorted and backed away. His lips twisted into a wry grin that was terrifyingly malignant. "The two other competing conglomerates in this world are trying to pry our prized assets out of our hands—that woman being one of them. That failing, they're trying to kill them to knock us out of the intelligence race. Hell, son, even the various governments in North and South America lost power to us during the Turn. A couple assets taking down a super power?" Mr. White chuckled, a sound like a dry wheeze. He clearly didn't laugh often. "Doubtful, but I admire your spunk. Get this in the works, Ms. Hutchins. I want more stats on my desk early next week." Mr. White shook his head and stalked away.

"Yes, sir." Ms. Hutchins gave Trent an assessing glance before turning for her office.

In his boss's wake, Trent stared at the faces spread across his screen. They all looked back with smug expressions, as if to say that Mr. White was wrong. That if they wanted to, spurred on by a hard-coded impulse only Mother Nature could program, they would tear it all down to snatch away their child. Weirder things had happened. Heck, Trent had felt those urges more than once, and that was only from a faux bond created by proximity in the child's early years.

His gaze roved over the blond woman who was three clicks above the Curve before a shiver arrested him. She knew the system front and back, along with how to create devastating weaponry and practice hand-to-hand combat. Trent would hate to see someone like that raise hell.

Possibly choosing her wasn't the best of ideas . . .

Trent waved his hand through the air, scattering the faces. He needed to stop thinking of worst-case scenarios. Everything would be fine.

Chapter 3

The delicate light fell across Millicent's brow. She fluttered her eyes open and adjusted her vision to take in the beautiful sunrise over the green fields. Bright yellow rays sliced through the deepening blue, meeting the horizon with fiery orange and pink. She inhaled deeply before stretching her arms wide.

"Good morning, Ms. Foster," said a pleasant female voice localized in the bed area.

"The sun is bright this morning," Millicent said sleepily.

"I do apologize, miss." The intensity of the sunrise faded somewhat.

"Better." Millicent swung her legs over the edge of the bed and stared for a moment, letting the beautiful tableau lighten her spirit.

"Transportation will arrive five minutes late, miss," the computer said.

"What's the delay?" She glanced at the green letters within the wall screen, reading 0636.

"Your craft has an extra passenger this morning, miss. They encountered a delay through the tech district. They apologize for the tardiness."

"An extra passenger?" Millicent frowned as she got up and pulled open the glass door to her cleaning stall.

"Yes, miss. I was given no further information."

Her frown was more pronounced when she entered the stall and closed the door. Millicent thought, *On*, and a blast of warm air pushed against her body from all sides, sweeping up her legs and stopping at her midriff. Three beeps had her closing her eyes and holding her breath. The air rushed up against her top half and face, disinfecting as it ran over her skin. She exhaled as the jets shut off and pulled back into their cavities in the wall.

"Is this a business person, or a government investor of some sort . . ." Millicent allowed for the application of lotion before exiting the stall. She stared out the computer-generated window for a moment, waiting.

"That information is classified, miss. I pushed the issue, but received no response."

Millicent took the proffered suit from the extended mechanical arm, but then paused. Slowly, she replaced the clothing. "Give me a suit with more defensive capabilities."

"Of course, miss. I apologize for not thinking of that."

Millicent waited as the suit disappeared into a slit in the wall. Pictures of clothing options cycled across the wall screen until the feed finally stopped on a bright-pink suit with flared sleeves. The conglomerate's insignia decorated the right breast.

"What else?" Millicent said.

More clothing choices cycled across the screen, pausing on various options that might fit the situation. Unfortunately, those in a darker color either had too much hardware or more complicated schematics than she wanted or were too light in both. The conglomerate wouldn't knowingly put her in danger, but she'd nearly died on three occasions from their shortsightedness. She had no idea why this civilian was being allowed to ride with her in her private craft, but it was safe to say a precautionary wardrobe was entirely necessary.

But a bright-pink one?

She sighed heavily. "Go back to the first choice."

The various attributes of the suit flashed across the screen as the horrendous item shot through the wall. Millicent squinted at the screen's image before thinking, *Enlarge.* Labeled hardware flashed larger before revolving so she could familiarize herself with the needed commands.

In distaste, Millicent removed the suit. "Who chose this color?" A pair of boots shot through next.

"Aubrey, your AI clothing specialist, took the liberty of specially making that suit for you, miss. I believe it was commissioned last spring, 2546. That color was in the height of trend."

Only half a year ago. It'd probably stay in trend for two more years. Colors that awful usually wouldn't die.

Her mind turned back to the passenger approaching in her transportation. *Her* transportation. "Since when has my transportation become a conglomerate bus?" she asked. "I should've been *asked*." She shook her head as she stepped into the suit. "At the very least, notified. This is appalling. I'll be taking this up with my higher-up."

"Of course, miss. I was assured that this was a rare circumstance. I do apologize."

Millicent bit her lip, thinking this through. She didn't like unexplained situations. They never turned out well within this conglomerate.

❖ ❖ ❖

An hour later, she sat on her bench, looking out the window, waiting. Purple numbers flashed across her wrist screen, showing her the time. Ten minutes late.

"Update," she said, trying to push down her irritation while completely ignoring her anxiety. If she was being punished for some reason, there was nothing she could do about it now. The passenger was on board. She'd have to take what came.

"Please brace yourself, miss. They are pulling up now. Have a safe journey. I'll meet you at work."

Millicent's head jerked back toward her apartment. "You won't be within the craft?"

"No, miss. No third-party AIs are permitted on today's journey."

The anxiety was a little harder to ignore as the glass wall parted down the middle. The image of a field with the sun climbing into the blue melted away into angry gray sky. Cold air rushed toward her, freezing her breath against her face. Across the chasm, another glass wall, smeared with rain, stood between her and the raging environment. A shuddering but sleek hovercraft slid into the protected bay before her, held tight to the side by guiding rails. It docked before its doors parted and a walkway extended, perfectly fitting into the groove of her landing area.

Her breath was shallow as she waited for the doors to open and the craft to stabilize, taking the few precious moments to judge what awaited her. A man in a gray bodysuit, with no conglomerate affiliation, sat near the front partition, perfectly straight backed. His eyes, a strange electric blue that looked like a breeding experiment gone wrong, flashed to her for a moment, roved her suit, and hovered on her sleeves before glancing behind her into her lodgings.

She stepped into the craft slowly, ready for any sudden movement. The usual two defensive guards who escorted her into her department each day sat as they always did, straight backed and eyes forward.

The door of the driverless vehicle slid shut behind her. Then the bay door opened, subjecting the vehicle to the travel ways of San Francisco.

As she sat, she glanced at the stranger. His right brow was a smidgen more arched than the other, and his lips seemed fuller than most men's. That cleft in his chin was in no way common.

He was a natural born!

Confusion growing, she scanned his powerful body and noticed his calloused and scarred hands.

A natural born like she was, but one who was used to heavy physical exertion. Something was definitely amiss. No natural born would travel without their own security . . .

Not to mention she hadn't had a passenger since her first day of work, half a decade ago or more.

It was then she noticed his hair. Loosely pulled back from his head, it formed a knot at the base of his skull. A rather messy knot!

Her fingers tingled, and a surge of adrenaline ran the length of her spine. Anyone employed and/or created by the conglomerate, in *any* department, had to adhere to a strict code of appearance as well as conduct. Long hair was to be properly maintained and styled or pulled into a tight bun. Short hair could be no more than four centimeters long and styled or less than one centimeter and natural. Any staff member caught breaking the rules would be reprimanded and forced to fix it before he left his quarters.

She remembered the subjects she'd tested a week ago. Each had had longer hair than was routine, not cut because the men weren't cared about.

A chill ran through her as she, once again, surveyed the strength and power inherent in this man's body.

"Are we stopping anywhere on the way?" she asked no one in particular, hoping for a different answer than the one forming a knot in her gut.

The two guards turned their heads, each with mild expressions of astonishment. She'd spoken on the way to the department as many times as she'd had a passenger.

Annoyed with the continued silence, she quirked an eyebrow, a movement that had been perfected over time to eliminate the need for her to speak.

The left guard recovered quickest. "No, miss. We are en route as usual."

Not as usual, or there wouldn't be an unexplained stranger in their midst.

As if hearing her thought, the stranger's head turned slowly until he stared at her. There was something untamed as well as unsavory in the depths of his glimmering eyes. Humor sparkled alongside a maniacal and violent light.

A ferocious powerhouse in incredibly confined quarters . . .

This couldn't be the conglomerate's answer to her demands about more thorough testing, could it?

A shiver of fear dumped adrenaline into her body. This being a test was the only logical explanation.

As if the man had heard her thoughts for the second time, his lips pulled into a smile with perfectly straight white teeth. His head turned back slowly until he was looking out the window again. Still smiling. Now at nothing.

Yes, they were testing her most recent update. It was obvious. The man was clearly deranged. Voices were probably sounding off in his head, and not from tech. He was a natural born gone wrong. She'd seen this before. The lottery ball of genes had dumped out a psychopath instead of revealing new traits that could be exploited by the conglomerates. And now he sat here, with no guards of his own, fighting against her new restrictive program.

Millicent tapped her fingers against her legs, seeing the stranger's smile burn a little brighter. The brows of the guards quirked—they'd recognized something was amiss. Hard not to—the lunatic was sitting right there, smiling at nothing. Even an engineered, Curve-hugging moron could see what was going on.

A burst of perspiration erupted along her brow. She was thankful for the suit she'd chosen.

"I need access to the console in this craft," she said primly, looking straight ahead at the plain gray partition.

The stranger started to chuckle, of all things.

"We are five minutes out, miss," the left guard said, eyes wide with disbelief.

"I didn't ask for an ETA. I told you I needed to access the console."

"Yes, of course, miss. I apologize." The left guard turned and palmed the screen next to the partition. He entered the code and then sat up straight again. "It's ready to be moved over when you access the hologram."

She nodded to show she'd taken in the info. Now she would stay unaffected until the worst case.

What is the worst case?

She eyed the smiling madman. His head sat higher than the guards, indicating he was taller and had a longer reach. With that breadth of shoulder and those arms stacked with muscle, his movements would be powerful. Fast? Probably. She had to assume the worst. A launch from those thick legs and he'd be in her lap before she knew it.

That was assuming her tech didn't work.

Stupid assumption. *It will.*

She'd made the necessary fixes and increased the muscle-freezing power. Even a man as big as the one currently sitting much too close to her should be paralyzed by it. Regardless, it would take him time to break through the invisible bindings, and in that time, she'd stab him.

Her pulse throbbing, she took a deep breath and prepared for the worst. The soft shudder of the vessel docking startled her. She looked out the window in surprise, seeing the walkway into her department, eighty-four floors from the wasteland of the ground level. When she looked back, the stranger was staring at her.

She stood slowly and braced herself. And then almost threw up when he stood as well, easily. Without flexing.

The man was huge.

Was this some kind of joke by the conglomerate?

"Ma'am." The stranger's deep rumble was like an earthquake in his chest until the words worked out, coated in velvet. It sounded like a greeting, and an awfully civilized one considering his hairstyle.

She jumped when the vessel door opened behind her. The guards edged out of the opening, leaving her alone with the stranger as they took up their posts outside.

What the hell is going on?

"Ma'am?" He smiled again. Why was anyone's guess.

The open door gaped at her back. Did she have this all wrong . . . ?

The man's continued smile said he was reading her discomfort.

She must've had this all wrong.

Feeling sheepish and desperate not to show it, she said, "Of course," in the most unaffected tone she could.

Wind whipped against her in the holding area. The stranger stepped up beside her, and the door closed behind them with a *fffuuuup*.

"Long ride, huh, princess?" he asked in a tone she didn't much care for.

The doors in front of them opened into a walkway that led along the side of the building, providing access to various departments. Staff could only get into a select few doors dictated by their pay grade. A ways in front of them was a grand entrance. Crystal-clear blue showed in the glass overhead—a delusion of fair weather. Usually she cherished the computer-generated model of Old Earth, but now it seemed like a mockery. The stranger and his enigma wouldn't let her drift into the pleasant fiction of a time when a blue sky had been possible.

Against privacy protocol, she very nearly turned to ask the man about his involvement in her morning, but a shout drew her focus away and to the right. A woman screamed, and the pounding of running feet thundered through the hollow entranceway. A man tore around the bend of the building, his clothing nothing but rags and his face covered in slime. Something metal glimmered in his hand. When he saw her small group, determination hardened his features.

For the second time that morning, adrenaline dumped into her body. Maintaining calm, she thought, *Heels.*

One of her guards sprinted toward the intruder while the other crowded in close. He rose his wrist to his mouth and yelled for the craft to reenter the bay.

Heels! she thought again. Nothing happened. *Arm stilts.*

Metal pushed out from her sleeves and clicked into her hands.

The intruder crashed into her first guard. His hand came up fast before jabbing twice in quick succession. She could barely see a knife at the end of his fist, now coated in blood. Her guard sank to the ground, his weapon unused, before being pushed out of the way.

She rammed her boot heels together, trying to jog the mechanics into working. *Heels!*

The intruder's rags flared as he started to run again, revealing a black suit of decent quality. He wasn't what he seemed. But then, she'd already cataloged that from how he worked that knife.

She leaned forward, prepared to take him out, when metal in his other hand swung into view. Her eyes opened at the same rate as her mouth. Fear choked her.

With a metallic whine of extending heels, she grew by eight centimeters.

The intruder, fifteen meters out, slowed and fell to one knee. A tube filled his hand and kept growing until it was one meter long and capable of destroying her day.

Her other guard banged on the bay door behind them, trying to shoulder it open. The craft hadn't fully docked, though. They were stuck.

She'd brought metal batons and razor-spiked heels to a rocket-launcher fight. Her morning wasn't going as planned.

Before she could switch weapons, a futile effort since nothing in her arsenal was even remotely able to handle this situation, a crowd of men and women in crisp blue suits ran out from behind the intruder.

Undeterred, he flicked a sight on the top and pushed forward a trigger guard. That model had no safety. He was hot and ready, but not altogether stable. It'd throw him back before the explosive left the barrel, which would make the explosive hit the ceiling above them.

"Let's go—we have to move! Heels, disengage!" She stepped forward to run, forgetting to put that last command into thought, but she didn't get very far. Strong fingers wrapped around her upper arm. She whipped about and promptly bounced off a rock-hard body, staggering as her ankles bent and rolled, unbalanced on the damn boots.

The intruder's finger turned white on the trigger. She tensed, waiting for the end.

Nothing happened.

The intruder looked at his rocket launcher in confusion.

Thank Holy, Millicent had chosen a suit that adequately recycled fluids, or she'd be uncomfortable in more ways than one.

A man in crisp blue dived, crashing into the back of the intruder. They spilled to the ground as more conglomerate security arrived at the scene.

Wind assaulted Millicent from behind, the guard finally getting the doors open.

Before she could process what was happening, a club smashed down onto the intruder's head. The metal tube went clattering to the ground before rolling away. Then another strike, this one crushing his skull. Blood splattered upward before starting to pool under the quickly ended struggle.

"Why didn't they use a gun?" she asked in a wispy voice.

"This way, miss!" Her remaining guard reached for her.

"That was a drill, cupcake." The stranger turned to her guard. "You're useless. You should be used for parts."

"I . . . But . . ." The guard's hand dropped in confusion.

"C'mon, time for work. You're late." The stranger, his grip still firm on her upper arm, marched her toward the entrance.

"How did you know that was a drill?" she asked. She noticed the first guard off to the side, his limbs splayed at uncomfortable-looking angles. She felt a twinge spread through her middle as she noticed the thick deep-red puddle of blood crawling along the cement. He'd been around for years, silently sitting in the craft or walking her to and from her work pod. And now . . .

She forced her features into smooth disinterest before abruptly facing front.

Her persona said she wasn't affected by such carnage. And to an onlooker, she wasn't. She designed the most heinous weapons the world had ever known. She'd seen the effects of some of her handiwork, and she'd borne it beautifully. At least, that's what her reports said. They had to, or she'd be retired to some low-level department where they'd belittle and taunt her for being a failed natural born. She'd be beaten up by jealous bosses and starved, moved from her apartment into a tiny dark dwelling with a roommate. She couldn't live like that.

They'd bred her with a job in mind, and she would do that job. No matter what it took.

She rose her chin in defiance of her discomfort. Getting back on track—and into the role intended for her—she thought, *Heels—disengage.*

Nothing happened.

"Sexy." The rumble was like a deep drum.

"What's sexy?" she asked as she stomped one boot, and then the other.

"The heels. Horribly inefficient, though."

She could feel the severe glower on her face. *Heels—DISENGAGE!*

"Flats are for running away. Heels are for running toward."

"Not sure I follow, princess."

"Stop calling me that." She unclenched her fists. "Commenting on your sexual approval of my footwear is not permitted within this organization. Surely someone covered that with you . . ."

"Do you always go into your work pod armed?" he asked, the humor dripping away.

"That's none of your concern."

"Yes, it is. Answer the question."

She scowled at his forceful tone as they neared the entranceway to her department. "I'm afraid that information is reserved for higher-level staff. Thanks for walking me, but now I must—"

"Good morning, Mr. Gunner," a raspy male voice greeted the stranger beside her, reading his retinal scan.

If he could get into this part of the building, why wasn't he wearing the conglomerate insignia?

"Good morning, Ms. Foster," Millicent's AI said.

"Since I can tell you won't give me a straight answer, excuse me, I have work to do." Mr. Gunner strode away without another glance.

She stared after him for a moment, mouth agape. He'd never answered her question regarding the drill, not that he was probably permitted to. But two men lay dead on the walk outside. Surely that deserved some kind of explanation. She felt like she was missing a large piece of the puzzle . . .

Or perhaps the entire puzzle.

She thought briefly of bringing it up with her superior, but tossed the idea away. The department gave her information as she needed it—if she made any such requests, she'd be asked why she was suddenly getting curious about matters that didn't concern her.

She stripped anything not relevant to her daily tasks from her mind—it was safer that way. Easier, too. Shaking her head, she slipped into her work pod, twelve minutes late, and immediately focused.

She was the job. Nothing else mattered.

Chapter 4

The drum of a deep voice reverberated through the open office space and clawed at her focus. Millicent frowned and rubbed her temples, willing the disturbance to fade into the background. But while the speaker was making an obvious attempt at being quiet, the rattle of his speech drew her out of the problem she was working on.

Sighing in irritation, she stood in a rush, looking over the wall of her work pod. When she saw the person she'd expected to see, she cursed the day as a complete throwaway. For the last six hours, if she wasn't bombarded by the memory of blood pooling in the little holes in the cement, she was wondering what the stranger had to do with the scene and her ride to work. She'd barely progressed on the program she wanted to finish by the end of the week, and now here he was, interrupting her yet again.

Beats of his vocal drum kept sounding off, banging away in the dimly lit interior of the spacious and plush surroundings. Heads popped up throughout the work pods, interested in the incredibly distracting new addition.

Millicent stepped out from her pod and into the hallway before heading toward the coffee vestibule. Her route would take her right by the two men, one of whom was still talking. And still drawing people's eyes and stealing their focus.

Both men fell silent at her approach. One, a lower-level security staffer, lowered his gaze out of respect. The other, Mr. Gunner, who had thankfully donned a generalized conglomerate badge, thus stripping away a tiny bit of mystery, stared straight at her from those strange-colored eyes wrapped in slightly curled black lashes.

She looked at the lower-level departmental staffer, ignoring the anomaly. "Excuse me, but this floor is a place of intense concentration, and that is nearly impossible with your loud voices."

"I apologize, Ms. Foster. We were trying to keep our voices down." The lower-level staffer bowed slightly and took a step back, out of her way.

She glanced at Mr. Gunner and then raised her chin fractionally when she saw that he was still staring back. Her eyebrow quirked as she waited for either a response of some kind—like an affirmation—or for him to respectfully clear the way, as the other man had done. The strange, uncategorized morning aside, she pulled rank on this floor. That needed to be addressed in either words or action.

He continued to look at her quietly. Like he was analyzing her.

Anger rising, she said, "Why is this person staring at me with direct eye contact?"

"Excuse me, miss," the lower-level staffer said uncomfortably, "but he is a director of security management."

"Director?" she asked in surprise. And just like that, the pieces fell perfectly into place. The unannounced ride, the hostile morning, his confidence . . . It all made absolute sense, only strange because it was the first time she'd ever been in the vicinity of a security director of any kind. "Why wasn't I told an equal-level staffer would be on my floor? Or on my morning ride, for that matter."

"Because I don't answer to you, cupcake," Mr. Gunner said with a grin. He bent at the waist, invading her space.

Arm st—

She squinted to prevent from thinking the command. The last thing she needed was to flinch and swing a baton at his head. A director of security, especially one his size, would easily catch it, making a fool of her. That was not the way to regain dominance of the floor and get him sent elsewhere.

She rose up eight centimeters. *Damn it!*

Heels—disengage.

She lowered back down.

"Anything else?" he asked, his eyes twinkling with suppressed humor.

She kept herself from glancing around, knowing without looking that this conversation was an object of scrutiny. "Yes. Will you be assigned to this department, or are you visiting?"

"You'll get official word this evening, I expect," he said as the humor dulled and his eyes took on a hard edge. A working edge, tense and dangerous. "I'm still contemplating my parameters."

"*You're* still contemplating?" She gave him an incredulous scoff. "You tell your superiors how to do their job, do you?"

"No. I tell my superiors how I will do *my* job, and expect them to make the necessary adjustments."

Millicent tsked. "I must meet your superiors someday—they sound like extremely soft individuals. Easy to push around."

"No, I'm just that hard, princess. If you want to stop by my place after work, I'll show you . . ."

Millicent opened her mouth. Closed it. She glanced at the lower-level staffer, who was staring fixedly at the ground, utterly tense. Looking back at Mr. Gunner, she saw the sparkle of humor had returned.

So. That's how it would be, would it? He'd try to push sexuality on her like a Neanderthal. He thought he could get away with the hair and the ego, so why not try sexual harassment?

"Yawn," she said dryly as she continued on her way. "Keep me updated."

"One question," he said before she'd taken two steps. She stopped without looking back. "Why don't you work in an office? You are totally exposed to the floor where you sit."

"Of course I'm exposed. I'm an upper-level staffer. It is hard to manage when you cannot *see*."

"Ah. A micromanager."

Millicent tensed in irritation. She rose eight centimeters before swearing under her breath. Ignoring her heels, she said, "If you worked for me, Mr. Gunner, there wouldn't be a question of who was harder. You would do as you were told, or you'd be used for parts. Now. Excuse me."

Heads disappeared back into their work pods. They were correct in assuming that that was a warning.

❖ ❖ ❖

Near the end of the day, Millicent stood from her work station before wiping her hand through the air. The files on her wall screen scattered, tucking themselves away into their correct folders. *Power down.*

"Lovely to work with you again, miss." Her computer powered down, and the screen blackened. Stretching, she made her way through the mostly empty floor to the restroom. When she returned, she froze and stared at her desk.

"Congratulations."

Starting, Millicent looked around to find Mr. Gunner standing three meters away, dressed in a departmental security suit. She turned her focus back to her desk. Specifically, to the white square lying on top of it.

"Is that . . . paper?" She touched the cream relic from yesteryear, feeling the strangely scratchy surface against the pad of her finger. Slipping her nail beneath it, she carefully picked it up. It was as light as a portable screen, and the way it fluttered when she turned toward

Mr. Gunner also put the seldom-used technology in mind. "They were trying to duplicate paper with the portable screens." She wiggled it and then fingered the edges. "And they did a great job."

Finally, already knowing what it said from rumors she'd heard over the years, she read the black words covering the face.

> *Congratulations! You've been selected to represent your race as a life-creation expert. Only twenty females each fiscal year are selected for this honored and prestigious role. You will be one of five women during this quarter. We are proud to have you.*
> *—Dir. Harold White*
> *Department of Creative Biology*

"I've been selected to breed," she said in a whisper, holding the piece of paper tighter than strictly necessary.

"It's your lucky day. Please, come with me." Mr. Gunner gestured for her to move toward him.

"Do you know what this means?" she asked, following him in a daze. "It means I will actually grow life within my body. I will get to have an offspring. Of my likeness!"

"Just like the humans of days past, yes. A true product of nature. In a way. This way, please." Mr. Gunner opened a door and guided her through.

Millicent looked at the words again, not hiding the smile curling her lips.

"You have a beautiful smile. Pity you communicate with snarls. Just here." Mr. Gunner stopped her in front of a foreign craft, snapping her out of her reverie.

"Where are we going?" She rose eight centimeters, this time not caring. *Arm stilts.* Batons rocketed from her sleeves and then pressed into her waiting palms. The paper fluttered to the ground.

"Uh-oh. You'll want that." Mr. Gunner, completely ignoring her defensive readiness, jogged toward the piece of paper. He scooped it up and walked back toward her, holding it out. "I hear women like to hold on to this."

"Women probably like to live more. Where are we?"

"East gate eighty-four B. We're leaving the back way. You can no longer stick to the same routine. Security is always amped up for breeders, but they are applying extra precautions this time. They don't want anything happening to you until you are ready for phase two and can be moved to a secured location. I'm in charge of the security for this building now and, specifically, for this floor. Also, those arm stilts won't help you against me. You really needn't put yourself out."

She heard what he was saying—the relevant parts. She was already important to the organization, but now she was beyond prized. They would spend a lot of money to make sure this pregnancy went well—they couldn't afford to lose her halfway through, or worse, near the end before the baby was safely delivered.

"I see. What about the other breeders?" she asked, retracting her arm stilts. She sighed when the accursed heels refused to follow suit.

"All the breeders have amped up security, but San Francisco was especially in need of restructuring. Why they hadn't done it before now is beyond me . . ."

The blue sky disappeared to reveal inky darkness. Soft light rose up, and then the craft's door opened and its walkway extended. A bolt of lightning zipped down beyond the far glass wall, followed by thunder so close it rattled the windows.

"It wasn't in the budget," she said as she entered the craft. The inside was empty. "We had some issues with a few of our weapons that ate up our reserves. Where are the . . ." She cleared her throat, pushing away the image of the dead guard staring skyward with sightless eyes. "The guards. Where are they?"

"Being replaced." Mr. Gunner stepped in behind her and sat near the door. "What's the matter? Afraid to be alone with me?" He tapped the door closed. "Don't worry, I only bite in certain situations."

Millicent rolled her eyes and clutched the priceless piece of paper. A warm glow spread through her. She'd get to have a baby!

After a while, she noticed his continued gaze, one lacking the usual spicy violence to which she'd grown accustomed. She lowered the paper to her lap. "Running after the piece of paper was a change from your normal stodgy asshole persona. What changed? I'm of more value now, so you've conceded I'm worth hearing?"

"I'm on the job, cupcake. Have to wear the right emotional uniform in the right social situations. Surely someone taught you that in all your extensive training. Or do your superiors have such little faith in you?"

She narrowed her eyes. "I'd say something witty, but all I want to do is stick something sharp in your eye to get you to stop calling me cupcake."

❖   ❖   ❖

"Yes, yes, here we go. Here we go."

Millicent sat with a straight back and dangling bare legs as a man in a white coat walked into the small exam room. A blue sheet with armholes wrapped around her front and draped open in the back, the conglomerate insignia displayed on her breast pocket. It had been a week since she'd gotten the news, and life had almost gone back to normal. Four guards now awaited her in the craft each morning, but Mr. Gunner was not one of them. In fact, other than noticing him standing off to the side in the entryway as she arrived to work, and occasionally seeing him striding through her floor with his annoyingly entrancing voice, she didn't have any interaction with him at all.

She was now in the exam room of the creation lab, waiting for the most amazing of life's miracles to happen to her.

"So, shall I explain a little of what we're doing here, or would you prefer I just go about the task?" The man in the white coat gave her a serene smile and clasped his hands in front of him.

"And you are?"

"Oh!" He laughed to himself softly. "I do beg your pardon. Excuse me. I get so excited during these times, and this is the most exciting of all. Yes, my name is Mr. McAllister, but you can call me Trent. I am a manager in the creation-synergy department and work very closely with the creation lab. I'll be working directly with you throughout this whole process. This is a very informal setting."

She nodded once. "Please take me through what you are doing and what is expected of me."

"Of course. Sure, of course. Okay." He smiled and lightly touched her shoulder, an action that had her clasping her hands in her lap tightly. She wasn't a fan of physical touch, not having had much experience with it. "We have ascertained that you are ovulating, and your body has been prepared to receive fertilization. We've had a lot of experience with this, and the success rate is ninety percent. We are very hopeful the first time will take just fine." His grin suggested a shared joke.

She frowned and shook her head. She didn't get it.

"Right. Okay." Mr. McAllister ran the pad of his finger across his forehead. He then wiped it on his pants. "So we will introduce the male fertilization in just a moment. Now, don't worry. I know that you have always taken Clarity and aren't familiar with coitus in any form. I assure you that this procedure is purely medicinal. We don't shove a male in here like a livestock breeding farm." He laughed and tapped her shoulder.

She flinched away. "A what?"

"Livestock was—never mind." He shook his head and muttered something that sounded like, "I need to stop using those jokes." His smile returned with increased wattage. "The only thing is . . . we've shown that the rate of success is higher if the female's body is active during the insemination. This means that the muscles contract, carrying the . . . male fertilization up through the—let me just get a picture." Mr. McAllister moved to the wall and brought up a picture of a female reproductive system.

"I don't need this level of detail," she said.

He paused with his finger pointing at a place she'd rather not get a lesson on. *Another* lesson, she should say. She'd had plenty leading up to puberty.

"Yes, okay, sure." Mr. McAllister's face turned red. "At any rate, you'll feel . . . sensations you may not have felt before. They are pleasant, and completely normal. I mean *natural*. I didn't mean to imply—"

"I'm familiar with what an orgasm is and how it helps the reproductive system. Please, Mr. McAllister, let's get on with it."

Muttering to himself, Mr. McAllister moved to his station.

She assumed the position all women her level knew. Health was important for someone of her status, and the conglomerate ensured that all personnel got yearly physicals.

"Just go ahead and lie—oh. You're . . . Great." Mr. McAllister's flush turned more furious. "Sorry. I've just never worked directly with someone of your caliber. You're the first one to start ovulating."

She clasped her hands and stared at the ceiling, waiting for his role in this to be completed.

"I will now inject . . . the fertilization. You'll feel some pressure."

Pressure bordering on pain flared from deep within her body, a situation usual for these types of exams. She resisted the urge to squirm uncomfortably.

"Okay, all done." Mr. McAllister moved away as the pressure released. "Now." He handed her a pair of black briefs. "Just put those on, have a seat in the comfy chair over there, or lie down right where you are, and the computer will take care of the rest. Stay as long as you'd like."

"How long does this usually take?" She slid the briefs on under her blue sheet.

"As long as you want, really. It's up to you as long as you . . . you know."

"Have an orgasm?" She felt a small buzzing from the briefs.

He cleared his throat and backed toward the door. "Yes. Excuse me."

Mr. McAllister seemed strangely awkward for a man in his position. None of this should be new to him. Although, he had said he was working *with* the lab, not for the—

A moan escaped her lips before she'd even known it was coming. The vibration grew stronger and more intense, centering on the area just above her opening. It pulsed, prompting her hips to pulse with it. Fingers clutching the exam bench, eyes rolling to the back of her head, she soaked in the pleasure. Waves of bliss spread outward from her core. Heat seared through her middle, blistering hot, achingly sweet. Her teeth clenched as everything tightened, prompting another moan. Then another. She couldn't seem to get enough air. Didn't want to. All she wanted was to keep going. Get more of this feeling. Never stop this—

"Oh Holy—!" she exalted as an explosion of sensation ripped through her body. Everything fractured, her body humming in delight. "Holy . . . shit." Breathing heavily, she looked down between her legs at the little black briefs.

Why weren't these standard issue? They were sensational!

She glanced at the numbers on the wall. She really should be getting back, but surely she had time for one more. It was helping the cause, after all . . .

Chapter 5

Millicent adjusted her jogging suit, trying to sit it around her growing belly so it wasn't so tight. By pregnancy standards, she was twelve weeks in. By real-life standards, she'd only felt pregnant for about six weeks. It was when the waves of sickness hit, cycling through the day, that she realized changes were happening in her body. Most of those changes were not pleasant in the beginning, but Mr. McAllister had assured her that once the sickness went away, things would become more exciting.

Granted, he was a man—and, come to find out, one who'd previously worked only with lab births. So he really had no idea.

Still, she chose to believe him. What other option did she have?

The guards filed around her as she left the changing pod and made her way to the exercise facility. Moving two floors down and toward the back, she tried to ignore the glances her way and the longing on many of the women's faces. Once in the facility, standing on her running mat, she waited while the system synced with her implant. A moment later, the speed increased until she was walking, and then increased further until she was lightly jogging. There it stopped.

Frowning, she thought, *Faster.*

Her pace did not change.

"This better not be like those heels," she muttered, thinking the command again.

The air shivered in front of her before those one-of-a-kind electric-blue eyes were staring at her. She was starting to hate that color.

His mouth was turned up in a smug grin. "Ah-ah, sweetheart. You can't overdo it."

"Don't call me sweetheart, and I don't plan to," she said to the hologram. "I plan to do just enough. I've spoken with Mr. McAllister on several occasions at our many checkups. He assures me that running is permissible."

"Your welfare is in my hands." He looked down in response to a muted feminine murmur. Behind him hung tubes and canisters of different colors and sizes, interrupted by the shapes of people moving around.

"Where are you? Is that a bar?" she asked in bewilderment.

His face came back up. Humor sparkled in his eyes. "Yes, it is. Care to join me?" The feminine voice sounded again. A flash of irritation crossed Mr. Gunner's features, but he remained silent.

"Not at all. Enjoy your time."

His brow furrowed. "That's it? That's your version of *hard*?"

"Good evening, Mr. Gunner." *Stop transmission.*

The air cleared. Millicent stopped the running mat before walking to a wall console. It took her fifty-five seconds to weasel into her files, change a few settings, and then erase his security influence. Mr. Gunner really needed to enlist better help if he planned to assert his dominance over her. She had nearly hacked into the "secure," higher-level system of Gregon Corp., coded by someone who would soon be regarded as the *second* best in the world. Mr. Gunner didn't stand a chance.

She stepped back onto her running mat before it started as planned. When it hit the previous threshold, it didn't stop. Soon she was at her normal speed, warming up.

The air shivered in front of her.

Stop transmission.

Her personal transmission pulsed heat on her wrist, asking permission to connect.

Denied.

She hated to ruin his night out but . . .

Oh, who was she kidding. She could think of nothing better than dousing the flame of his infallible ego.

Without warning, the whole floor went black. Emergency lights burst to life, their beams casting sharp shadows across the staggering and sweating staffers. Running mats slowed to a stop. People's chests heaved as they checked their wrists. A couple people sought consoles. Millicent put her hands on her hips and allowed herself the tiniest smile when the air in front of her shimmered to life. He'd kept power to the transmissions to rub this in her face.

It was so clever she couldn't be properly annoyed.

"I don't like when my calls aren't answered . . ." His deep voice beat against her. "Now be a good girl and go on home. I have a craft standing by."

"I didn't realize Neanderthals could work a console. Color me impressed," she said, walking away.

"I can work more than a console . . ."

"I'm really not interested in your ability to touch yourself, Mr. Gunner. Even the first humanoids had that one down." She grabbed a towel off the rack and dabbed her face as she left the facility.

Once she arrived home, she thought, *Dinner*, to get the food pouch heating and then palmed her console open. She had a state-of-the-art device, able to read her heat signature from across the room for broad-strokes commands. After choosing the option for her running mat, she waited while it slid out from the wall. Like in the facility, it activated on its own and quickly got up to speed, reading her implant. Warming up again was no fun, but under the circumstances, she'd deal with it. Mr. McAllister had said that a healthy body would recover more quickly, and considering the frightening changes already taking place in her body, the quicker the better.

As before, the mat hit a certain threshold before stalling. "Oh, really? He's going to try and dictate my home life, too?" She palmed the console and then swung her hand, moving it to the screen in front of her. From there, while running at the ridiculously slow speed, she worked into her system, traced the modifications to the source, and reset them. Then, in retaliation, she engineered a much tighter collection of controls and placed them around his apartment. Lukewarm cleansing spray, running mat too fast, weights calibrated with slightly more weight, wake-up screen just a bit too bright—nothing too extreme. Nothing that would immediately clue him in to her tampering. But all very irritating.

That done, she pushed the console away and allowed the screen to display a dirt path through a lush green forest. Scent secretions flavored the air around her, matching her olfactory senses to her visual. As her body warmed, heat pulsed on her wrist.

Frowning, she thought, *Accept.*

"Now you are interrupting my night, and since you aren't doing it naked, you need to fall in line." He looked down for a second, his shoulders twitching. Working a console, she had no doubt.

She swung hers in front of her again, eating away some of his picture, slowed her mat speed so she could work, and chose another route in this battle. One with a more satisfying victory. As the power cut out from under her, she held up her wrist, showing him the purple square that glowed against her skin.

"Stay to the speed I set you, or no mat . . . What are you doing?"

Eyes connected with his, movements purposeful, she pushed the purple square. It could've easily been done from the console, but visuals were so much more effective.

As predicted, he winced, and his ear curled toward his shoulder.

She released the button. "Uh-oh, did no one tell you that implants could be used against you?" She paused, then said, "Butt out, or I'll make that shock more intense next time."

He straightened up slowly, his eyes on fire, his face a blank mask. In the background, she heard a female voice say, "What is taking so long? I thought you only wanted me tonight?"

"You should go. You're being rude to your guest," Millicent said lightly. She touched a button on her console and started to jog. "But don't worry—I won't go too fast."

He stared for a moment. His shoulders started tweaking again, though his eyes didn't turn away. He was more apt on a console than she would've guessed.

She worked her own console, smiling as she blocked his attempts to get through her newly created security measures. He redirected, trying to go through the conglomerate system instead of her private household loop. That was just as easy to block, of course.

She rose her finger in the air . . .

"Don't you do it—"

She let the finger fall. His left eye squinted, and his jaw clenched. A vein in his temple throbbed. Those were the only indications of the intense pain he was in.

She released the finger. "How'd you like that? Hard enough for you? Or should I ram it in a little harder?" She grinned, then let the smile grow. "Beautiful smile—that's what you like? Well, how do you like it now?"

"You never asked my name," he said slowly, his voice deeper than normal.

"I know your name."

"Don't you want to know my first name?"

"Why would it matter?"

"You need my name so you have something to scream in climax."

She scoffed. "Not necessary. I never scream. It is pointless and cuts down on reaction time. Only fools scream."

"Challenge accepted." His eyes didn't turn away from hers. "Sure you don't want to come for a drink? I think the night would be enlightening."

"I hardly think your chatter would be enlightening. Sadly, the researchers' intelligence reconstructions have so far failed. Can't fix stupid."

His lips tweaked up into a grin. "I'm going to have to try. Something has to be done with you. You have too great of a rack to let it go to waste."

She set her mat to a faster setting. "I'm three clicks above the Curve. I'm about as intelligent as you can get, enhanced with an excellent array of continuous mind trainers. A lot of money went into my breeding, while you were left to drool down your chin like a dark-age Neanderthal human before the breeding projects began."

"I'm also three clicks above the Curve, princess. And I'm lethal, hilarious, and great in bed. Give me a night and it'll be you who's drooling."

"Really?" *Towel.* She grabbed the fabric off the extending arm and wiped her forehead. His shoulders were twitching again. "Your overindulgent sheet antics aside, how could you boast that intelligence while maintaining a post as a stewardess for the breeding project? Directors don't act as asset guards, in case you are new to your title. They give commands to the people who choose the asset guards. You're no better than a low-level bodyguard."

His expression wiped away, now completely blank. Malice sparkled within the blue of his eyes. He clearly did not like her pointing out the obvious. "One does wonder, yes," he said in a somber tone.

This time her smile was genuine. Point to her.

Pushing the upper hand before he could rally, she said, "Well, while one is wondering, an occupation that will undoubtedly take you decades, I will get back to my jog."

She was moving to cease the transmission when he said, "You're out of your league, princess."

Her finger marginally veered right. And then his jaws clamped shut, the pulsing shock she sent through his implant closing him down.

"Ego will only get you so far," she said. "Night-night. Cease transmission." The burning eyes and tense shoulders disappeared from her wall.

She'd probably pay for that.

It was worth it.

❖   ❖   ❖

"Brace yourself, miss. The craft is arriving."

Millicent straightened her suit after she stood and prepared herself for the cold blast to her face. It came as expected when the lovely image of prehistoric Hawaii, all large crests and slim-bodied surfers, disintegrated and the glass slid open to reveal a volatile gray day with dark patches that could only mean a violent storm on the way. The door to the craft opened. She froze.

"Good morning, cupcake. Sleep well?"

"Computer, why wasn't I informed that Mr. Gunner would be on my vessel today?" Millicent asked without stepping forward. She didn't like the knowing gleam in the man's eyes.

"I was not authorized to reveal that information, miss. I do apologize."

"Computer?" Mr. Gunner waited with a half-smile and his legs out in front of him, crossed at the ankles. "You didn't name your AI?"

Millicent fractionally raised her chin and entered the craft, stopping in front of his outstretched legs. "This is not a pleasure cruise, Mr. Gunner. Straighten up."

"You like your men erect, is that it?" He threaded his fingers behind his head, his elbows now flaring out to the sides. "Give me a minute. I can comply while sitting as I am."

The part of her anatomy that had insisted she steal the black briefs from the lab tingled in an irritating way. She counteracted it with a scowl and stepped over his legs. "How have you not been sent to the organ mines? It boggles my mind."

He tsked. "I think your throne is too prickly. You need to loosen up a little."

"Why are you here, Mr. Gunner? And don't say it's for punishment. The conglomerate would never let you harm a carrier in any way."

"You're not a carrier, Millicent," he said in an uncustomary low, grounded voice. "You are a mother."

She glanced at the guards in the craft before her eyes shot to the small ports built into her vessel, rigged for sound and sight. And even if those were down, the conglomerate could hear through the implants in each staffer. "I am a carrier, Mr. Gunner," she said with a warning, feeling the surge of joy burn up through her middle. She squished it down. That feeling was as dangerous as Mr. Gunner's words. "After birth, this new staffer will belong to the conglomerate."

"Like you?" His posture stayed light and relaxed, but his body tensed, and his eyes took on that familiar hard edge.

"Yes. Like me. And you."

His hands came away from his head and then his forearms braced on his knees as he leaned forward. "Did they choose the job you're in, or did you bounce around for a while before you landed in it?"

Confused, she shook her head. "It . . . was assigned. Like all the jobs. What do you mean bounced around?"

"You were bred for the job you are doing?"

She smoothed her hair against her scalp until her fingers hit off her tight bun, uncomfortable. "Of course. We all are."

"And you never questioned their choice? You never asked for a transfer to something . . . less violent?"

"What . . ." Her heart started to hammer. Thank Holy, she'd deadened the emotional receptors in her implant.

"You had a knife in that suit. On my first day. You never extended it. Should've a couple times, but never did," he said. Millicent swallowed under the scrutiny of that hard gaze. "When the intruder squeezed the trigger, you wanted to run. A woman in your position should've wanted to kill. Your whole job is based on killing. Yet you would've taken the passive way out."

"My job is based on protecting this conglomerate. The weapons I make are in the name of defense."

"You can scour a department on the other side of the world in a truly heinous way with minimal resources. I've seen the effects. Thousands of people dead. Thousands more disfigured for life. That isn't defense, sweetheart. That's attack. And you are the best in the world at it. Yet . . . it isn't natural for you. You are also one of the best in the world at systems analysis and coding, but that isn't your full-time gig. You get contracted out to do that . . ."

She shifted in her seat, her eyes darting between the guards and the ports. She itched to access a console to fry her chip for a moment so she could erase this damning conversation.

"Why haven't you asked to be transferred elsewhere, like systems?" he asked.

"I . . . don't know what you're talking about. Why would I do that? These questions aren't prudent. Are you allowed to breach the privacy code like this?"

"You've never questioned their ruling about your career path. You've never sat back and thought—this is who I am. This is what I like. What I don't like. A woman as smart as you, with as much as you have . . . They'd let you do whatever you wanted. Yet you've never asked. Why?"

"This is my life. I'm happy in my life. The conglomerate provides for me, and as such, I do the job I was bred to do. End of story."

He shook his head slowly. "Imagine what you could do if you actually liked your job . . ." He leaned back and crossed an ankle over his knee. "That little stunt last night caused my implant to go offline. I had a swarm of staffers interrupting my . . . activities. They'll be replacing it with a new implant today."

She could feel the confusion steal across her expression. "How long did it stay off?"

"Two hours. They found me when it came back on. For some reason, they didn't think to track the woman I was with. Just waited until I came back on the grid."

"Hmm." She bit her lip, thinking of all the reasons it might have malfunctioned for that length of time. Immediately three possibilities popped up. She pondered each, along with their longer-term implications. "Tell them to hold off on a new implant. I'm nearly ready to roll out another beta. I can add in some modifications so the issue won't happen again."

"I'd rather not. I like knowing about the holes. But it was an interesting lesson. A telling one."

"What do you mean? How?"

He leaned forward again. "You have the key to your freedom in your dainty little fingers, and yet you work diligently to strengthen the cage. I don't understand you, Millicent."

"Stop using my first name. We're not intimate. And what's the point of freedom? Where would I go? In case you've failed to read the reports, being with one of the conglomerates is the only way to guarantee a food source. It's the only way to guarantee shelter. All the credit you've built up? It only works within the conglomerate structure. Out on the street—not even in the air, since the travel-way structures are all owned by one conglomerate or another—you'd have nothing. There are no fields to plant, no forests to pillage. The dirt is contaminated, and those not employed by this company or another are starving. You're talking nonsense." She crossed her arms over her chest. "Nonsense that'll get your mind wiped. Leave me out of it."

"Comms are down right now. No one is recording this conversation."

"What?" she asked, jolting forward. She glanced out the window—the blue waterfall looked pixelated from this close up—then swiped her hand near the sensor to take down the computer image. Flashing lights on large vessels armed with smart-sighting guns hovered not far away. "What have you done?" Her hand went to her belly. To the life within. "Stop this. They only wait—"

"I know how long they wait. We have ten minutes or so."

She shot a desperate look at the guards, who were staring at nothing. "Why aren't they reacting?"

"After my night was ruined, I looked into your work. Sleek little program you're testing. I'm using the one that cuts out hearing and sight as well as movement. Pretty intense. Like putting a bag over someone's head and tying them up. Looks like it's working." He glanced at the guards. "Anyway, I wasn't thinking about freedom on this planet."

Her eyes widened. "You're a natural born with ninety percent of your grid characteristics above the Curve," he continued. "Some at three clicks, which only one percent of the population can boast. Not only that, but you're a director. Even if you weren't allowed to breed, you would be way too expensive to lose. They wouldn't let you go."

"You've done your homework. But I *am* breeding, as you know."

The words died in her throat.

He smiled, clearly recognizing her astonishment. "I've given semen on five different occasions. Women are only allowed to carry once, twice max. More is required of them, physically. But males? They can stud us out as many times as they want. It's nothing for us to produce. A pleasure. Literally. But despite having children out there in the world somewhere, I'm not allowed to be a father. I'm not allowed to see my offspring. To hold them. Or protect them. The most fundamental desire of my species has been denied to me. We are built to reproduce. Biology demands it. We have a pressing urge to continue our species, and I have a pressing urge to guard my bloodline. But I can't. And if that doesn't chafe, I don't know what does."

"But off-planet . . . It's filled with brutal savages. All the conglomerate staffers—even the various governments—have been killed. Pieces of their bodies have come back."

Mr. Gunner chuckled in a predatory way before reaching back and placing his finger over a little gray circle. A console shimmered to life in front of him. "You say you were bred for your job, and then you say things like that. So naive." He accessed a part of the conglomerate loop she hadn't rooted around in before. "It's war, and war creates savagery." His hands worked within the glowing blue light.

She sat back and clasped her hands in her lap. "All that semen might've gone into a soup to create lab borns. Did you think of that? Many of those babies have a dozen fathers. That's not natural biology."

The glimmer in his eyes dulled. He looked away. "I've thought of that. Resigned myself to it. Which is why I'm still here. There's no reason to give up a cushy, pampered life. As you know from experience."

A flare of anger burned bright, but she stifled it as her hand drifted to her belly. "I'll know the baby, but it still won't be mine. I still won't be a mother. Not really. I think your situation is probably the better one."

"Maybe." He stared at her for a moment, his eyes intense, before he pushed away the console. His sigh hinted at disappointment, but for what, she couldn't say.

"Why did you stop us?" she asked, seeing that the craft was moving again. "Why shut everything off and grill me—"

"I didn't shut everything off, Ms. Foster," he said in a loud voice, drowning out her words. "There was a glitch. Don't worry, we're live now. But this validates the concerns I raised with my superiors. These glitches are one thing with a high-level staffer, but entirely another with a breeder. We just can't have it. Which is why I really think this is for the best. You'll thank me in the end, I'm sure of it. Everyone will." His tone was back to light and teasing. It meant bad things. "I've checked you into assisted housing for the duration of your pregnancy, and devised a planned fitness routine for you. Even if you circumvent the program, someone will rush in to keep you on track. Looks like you'll have to manage from afar after all . . ."

The guards all took a deep breath and surged forward at the same time. They shook out their arms and looked around wildly. Mr. Gunner jumped up, creating a barrier between Millicent and the disoriented guards as the craft entered a large foreign bay. "Calm down, men. It was just a glitch with the implants. More proof that Ms. Foster needs to be checked into assisted housing early." He turned back to Millicent with a bright smile. "I don't like to lose, cupcake." He bent for her hand and then shook it. "This is your stop. Enjoy your time."

Chapter 6

Trent watched through the glass as Ms. Foster—she didn't like going on a first-name basis—cried out. Her expression soaked through with pain and determination, she clutched the hands of lab staffers.

"This delivery is longer than usual, is it not?" Mr. White asked, watching the scene among various other top-level personnel.

Ms. Foster fell back against the pillow. Her head rolled to the side, and her eyes stared unfixed at the window, behind which Trent and the others stood. She'd chosen a lovely green oasis for the display.

This was the third birth in the group and two weeks past the delivery date. Trent checked the numbers on the wall. Twenty hours into labor and they were down to the wire. "She's late, so the baby had more time to grow. Meaning it's bigger, so it'll be harder for it to get through the birth canal."

"Why didn't they give her a C-section?" one of the upper-level superiors asked, crossing his arms.

"We opt for a natural birth whenever possible," Trent said, checking Ms. Foster's vitals. "It is a trying time for baby and mother both, and not knowing exactly how the birth process shapes a human, we try to keep things as natural as possible. But we're monitoring closely, and if either the mother or baby is in danger in any way, we'll take that course of action."

Mr. White shifted and checked the numbers on his wrist. "What of the other infants since delivery?"

"Doing great." Trent leaned closer to the vitals for Ms. Foster. A twinge of worry niggled at him. She was fading fast. She didn't have much energy left to push, and the baby's heart rate was starting to climb. The decision would need to be made soon.

Trent glanced to the back of the viewing chamber and connected eyes with a lab tech. The woman nodded once and crossed in front of the director of security management to leave the room. The large man in charge of monitoring security for Ms. Foster shifted. He glanced at the departing woman, the screen with the vitals, and then his gaze finally came to rest on Trent.

Trent's back snapped straight. That look communicated so many things: a warning, the man's command of the room even though he wasn't nearly the highest-ranking member in it, and his unveiled threat that if something went wrong with his charge, he'd rip the limbs off Trent's body in an excruciating way.

"I wanted more information than a platitude," Mr. White said in a rough tone.

Trent snapped out of his giddy reverie. When he turned back to the scene, Ms. Foster was pushing and the baby's head was cresting. Elation lit him up. "One infant has not taken to the breast, so the female creator has been excused from further involvement. The other infant is suckling, so the mother—excuse me—the female creator is continuing to be of service."

The baby's head worked farther out. "It won't be long now," Trent said in a hush, riveted. "And there! Fantastic. I'm amazed every time I see it."

"I don't know why." Mr. White leaned toward the glass as a nurse carried the baby to the washing station. "If my department worked as inefficiently as Mother Nature, I'd be retired immediately."

"Yes, well . . . admittedly the process seems fairly arduous for the female, with a great many risks, but . . ." He really didn't have a rebuttal, so he let his voice drift away. Ms. Foster smiled, and tears came to her eyes as she watched the baby being washed.

The stats came through on the baby. As Trent looked them over, he noticed Mr. Gunner stepping forward to get a look at the mewling infant. Mr. Gunner had probably never seen one before. Which wasn't surprising, given that infants and children were protected and sheltered until they could be put into the workforce, or the clone housing areas. In the Enlightened Ages, the governments had realized the earth couldn't sustain the continually growing human populace, so they'd clamped down, deciding to engineer life only as needed.

"Okay, we're about ready to see if the baby will take to the breast. Let's all cross our fingers." Ms. Hutchins's throat clearing had Trent closing his mouth with a snap. He was getting too chatty. Excitement had a way of doing that to him.

The crying baby, its face screwed up in anger, was placed into Ms. Foster's waiting arms. The baby settled almost immediately and nuzzled into her skin to look for a food source. A nurse stepped forward to help.

"That was a fast bond," Mr. White said, stepping closer, his focus acute.

"Not abnormal. Some are faster than others. And . . . there! She's latched." Trent smiled and made a note. "Excellent. So far, so good."

"This one is a girl?" Mr. White asked, watching the interaction.

"Yes. A healthy baby girl, by the looks of things."

"How long does the baby stay with the female creator?" someone asked.

Trent glanced back in irritation. He didn't understand why novices were allowed into the viewings. They probably had no idea what they were even looking at.

Huffing, he made a few notes as he answered, "That is dependent on the baby. We want them breast fed for up to a year, if possible. Infants feed regularly, so the moth—female creator will need to be on hand fairly constantly. After that, we try to naturally separate the child and introduce them to the milestone-assessment department where they will be raised. Some breast-fed babies take longer than others to separate. Up until about two years, we indulge the child."

"Remind me how long will it take to see results of your experiment?" Mr. White said.

If he'd bothered to read any of the reports . . . "It's hard to say," Trent answered, schooling his tone to one of patience. "I would imagine about fourteen months, give or take, since these children will undoubtedly be above the Curve in many categories."

"Excellent. Great work, people." Mr. White took one last look before turning toward the door. "Let's look toward the future."

"Mr. White, I'd like a word," Ms. Hutchins said. "Mr. McAllister, with me."

"Uh . . ." Trent looked back at Ms. Foster cuddling the baby. He hated to miss this part. It was so serene. It always warmed his heart. "Yes, ma'am."

Outside in the hall, Ms. Hutchins directed Mr. White to the side. "I think it's time to let Mr. Gunner and the other specialized security staff return to their routine duties."

Mr. White's brow furrowed. "Some of the others, okay. But we might want Ms. Foster for another pregnancy. Despite the longer delivery and the many confrontations with her regarding exercise within the assisted living area, Ms. Foster handled it well. This will make her a larger target. Gregon Corp. has been chomping at the bit lately. We get offers to buy her out constantly. I want her protected, and for that I'd prefer an expert. Either Mr. Gunner or Mr. Hunt—one of the directors."

Ms. Hutchins looked at Trent.

Trent started. He'd made this comment in passing—he had no idea he'd be called on to share it with the formidable director.

After clearing his throat, he said, "With creations like Mr. Gunner and Mr. Hunt, we must consider the issue of their protection characteristic."

"I don't understand," Mr. White said in irritation, checking the red numbers on his wrist.

"Mr. Gunner is three clicks above, Mr. Hunt two," Trent went on. "They were bred with the unyielding urge to protect at all costs. Currently they are geared toward protecting the conglomerate. You can see how that works in our favor. But should they connect with something else that calls on this drive of theirs, their loyalty will shift hard and fast. Their breeding will take on a whole new dimension."

"I'm not following." Mr. White itched his nose with his middle finger. "We've always had guards on these women. After birth, we regularly have defensive managers around the female creators. One or two developed an attachment to the infants, like the female creators sometimes do, but it was easily worked around. What's the difference?"

"The difference is the level of the asset," Ms. Hutchins said. She looked at Trent again.

"Uh, yes, ma'am." Trent wiped away a drop of sweat from his brow. "We often use characteristics of the natural-born, higher-level staffers, but we keep them away from the actual offspring. It's safer that way. Their natural urge to protect in general, paired with the biological imperative to protect their descendants in particular, would create more than a mere headache. I'd presume such a staffer would stop at nothing to cause havoc. And given their training, that's exactly what they could cause." Trent couldn't help a smile as his toes tingled. "It would be a sight, though. Truly spectacular if I had to guess. Usually they are behind the action, so they can't display their awesome ability in the heat of combat, but to be a part of—" Ms. Hutchins's throat clearing ended with the sound of Trent's teeth snapping shut.

"I see." Mr. White looked at his feet for a moment. "And these assets are represented in this breeding cycle?"

"Just one . . ." Trent looked around for the nearest console, wishing he had clearance to access that type of information from his implant. He'd studied both men extensively for this project, but he tended to get them mixed up.

"One was too volatile," Ms. Hutchins said, looking at her wrist. Stats whirled by and slowed. "He is a handful to control, so we worried about a natural offspring. We use his genes in the splicing lab for factory assets. Even still . . ." Her wrist went back to skin color. "The breeder won't know it is his offspring, and he won't have contact. However, we're flirting with danger here. A human connection might be formed from something as simple as seeing mother and baby. That in itself could promote a biological response. These men are hardwired to protect, whether they know it or not. That is the danger of natural breeding. We cannot control everything."

"Yes, I see." Mr. White stared off to the side. "Keep them in the area," he finally said. "Keep Mr. Gunner working on San Francisco, and Mr. Hunt on the ground, wall, and travel-way systems. I will not sacrifice the improved structure. We once again dominate this area. We've blocked Gregon Corp.'s attempt to weasel in. The board is pleased. Once those systems are stable, you can start phasing the men out.

"With regards to the breeding, simply keep them out of the infant holding areas. Don't let them see the infants. I've heard the female creators aren't interested in coitus, nor will they look like their former selves right away—I doubt either man will be tempted to form a connection along those lines if it hasn't happened already . . ." Mr. White raised an eyebrow.

Ms. Hutchins checked her wrist. "The two female creators assigned to Mr. Hunt and Mr. Gunner, respectively, have been on the Clarity pill. There have been no sexual relationships between them."

"There. See? Crisis averted. Now—"

"It's not a sexual connection we are worried about, sir," Trent hastened to say.

Mr. White's hard brown eyes stared him down. "Men react to sex and their children. Give them neither, and they will find interest elsewhere. Do I make myself clear?"

Trent shriveled under the stare, not willing to offer his arguments regarding the inaccuracy of that statement. It was telling as to Mr. White's character and lack of imagination. "Yes, sir. Sorry, sir."

"Now. Make sure those babies are healthy, and let's push evolution along." Mr. White stalked off. Without a word, Ms. Hutchins went in the opposite direction, leaving Trent to stand alone.

Mumbling to himself, because he hadn't realized he'd be thrust between two higher-level staffers when he proposed his compound, he let himself into the viewing room. Everyone had cleared out, not interested in the sleeping mother and baby.

With a small smile, Trent looked on for a moment before he caught movement out of the corner of his eye. Jumping and clutching his hands to his chest in a useless defense, he turned toward the large silent man in the back of the room.

Mr. Gunner lowered his wrist, where soft-green numbers had been displayed.

"Oh. Um . . ." Trent gulped. This was really the opposite of the directive he'd just received. "You're . . . You should go about your duties."

In a deep voice that did strange things to Trent's flight reflex, the muscular man said, "That woman in this room is my duty. I am to maintain her safety until she is transferred to a more secure location."

"Uh . . . right." Trent scratched his chest, unable or unwilling—he wasn't sure which—to lower his hands and expose his vitals. "Well . . . maybe just wait outside."

"No."

"That's . . ." Trent slowly sidestepped to the console. "Mr. White told me to tell you that."

"Mr. White has no bearing on my decision-making."

"Well . . . that's true." Trent typed in a quick *help* message. He didn't like being in a small dark room with someone like Mr. Gunner. The man's records indicated that he had tested every rule the conglomerate had, constantly pushing against conformity. When lower-level staffers were sent to issue warnings against such behavior, they then had to be carried to the med tech with a broken nose or jaw.

Mr. Gunner clearly knew it would be too expensive for the con-glomerate to fire him for trivial rule-breaking—like the messy man-bun piled on top of his head. He also knew they wouldn't go to the trouble of mind wiping him and paying to have him trained again. After all, the problem was one of breeding, not schooling. He'd just push against authority all over again. It was only the large infractions that would demand immediate recourse that Mr. Gunner shied away from. He was arguably the best at what he did, and he knew it. The only other person who could argue with that accreditation, and often did, was Mr. Hunt. Another man who equally fascinated and terrified Trent, but one who didn't break the rules quite as often.

Trent sighed and went about his stats, ignoring the imposing pres-ence behind him as best he could until someone came to remove him. It was all he could do.

❖　❖　❖

"Here you go, miss."

Millicent blinked her puffy eyes open in time to see the lab staffer hand her the crying baby. The baby's little fists waved angrily, and her squalls pushed Millicent's panic button.

"Is she okay? What's the matter?" Millicent sat forward and winced, her lower half painfully sore. She brought the baby close to her chest and felt a warm fuzziness flower in her middle. The little creature nuzzled into her, and the crying stopped immediately.

"She's hungry. Or else she wants her . . . you." The lab staffer grimaced. "I'll leave her with you for a while. Babies like to be held and cuddled, and this one cries when we try to do it."

"But I don't know . . ." Silence rained down as the door closed behind the exiting lab staffer, leaving Millicent with the fragile little thing. She adjusted herself, and winced. Then tried to get her top open. Then adjusted the baby, and winced.

"You're doing it wrong."

Millicent jumped at the deep drum of the voice, startling the baby. Crying filled the room before she pulled the baby into her chest, completely ruining everything she'd done to get the baby situated in the first place. Huffing, she glanced up at Mr. Gunner. "Can you get the lab tech? I don't know how to hold her to get her to feed."

"They've told you three times." He crossed to the bed and leaned over for the infant.

She shrank back, stopping his progress. "Are you allowed to hold her?"

"Millicent, I'll be gentle. I'm just going to arrange her how the lab tech always does."

"Always . . . It was only a few times . . .," Millicent muttered as she straightened up with another wince.

"And you need more pain meds." His fingers wrapped around the baby, his giant, rough-looking hands such a contrast to the soft little body. Instead of pausing in midair so Millicent could adjust and take her back, his arms kept going until the baby was snuggled against his chest. He wrapped a large arm around her and was rewarded with tiny fingers curling onto his index finger. A small smile graced his lips. "She's so small. So . . . defenseless." He rocked her and bounced in that special way, obviously having watched everything the lab techs had done over the last day.

The baby girl nuzzled into his chest, looking for a nipple.

"You probably shouldn't be—"

Three people burst into the room, cutting Millicent off. Mr. Gunner jerked, shielding the infant with his shoulder and broad back. Fire sparked in his eyes, a killing edge Millicent had never seen before. The staffers fanned out, hands up, eyes wide.

"Hey now, Mr. Gunner. That's not your job." One of the staffers stepped forward slowly. "That baby is very fragile. And very expensive."

"Why don't you just hand her off to us, sir. We'll take over," another tech said.

"He was trying to help me." Millicent held up her hands to symbolically stop them. Pain pulsed up through her as she shifted. "The lab tech left me without helping to position the baby to latch. If you were worried about the baby's safety, one of you should've helped me feed her . . ."

Two of the techs turned her way, eyes still wide, but for a different reason. She was above their pay grade. They were trained to listen to voices using tones just like hers.

"Now take the baby from him and help me. Unless you'd like me to report your negligence to your superior?" She waited with hard eyes.

"I got it," Mr. Gunner said, straightening up. "I'm strong, not stupid. I know how to handle a fragile . . . item."

"Well, now, I'd be happier if you'd just let me . . ." The lab tech's voice drifted away as Mr. Gunner walked toward them with straight, wide shoulders and a vicious sort of grace. He was both formidable and nurturing, holding the squirming baby to his chest while it continued to hunt for his nipple.

A lab tech backed away quickly as Mr. Gunner rounded the bed, then bent over Millicent. With delicate hands, he placed the baby across her chest, pausing for her to painfully shift again before helping her position the head for feeding.

The door opened again and stayed that way. A sizable man, nearly Mr. Gunner's height and also stacked with muscle, entered the room with slow, powerful strides. His smooth glide bespoke a predator patrolling his territory.

Mr. Gunner tensed, waiting for Millicent to comfortably settle with the infant before straightening nearly as slowly as the other man was entering the room. Mr. Gunner's muscles rippled dramatically as he turned toward the newcomer. The same muscle display shivered up the newcomer's frame.

"Mr. Hunt," Mr. Gunner said in a voice laced with a sharp edge.

"Mr. Gunner." Mr. Hunt squared his shoulders. The lab techs scurried out of the way. "I've been alerted to a breach of security in this room. Seems you've overstepped your duties."

"I was helping my charge."

"She is no longer your charge. I'll be taking over."

"On whose authority?"

"This is no place for a territory battle," one of the lab techs said in a wavering voice.

The baby started to squirm.

Millicent lost her patience. "What the hell is going on?" she roared. Both men frowned. Uncertainty worked tension into their shoulders. "I'm sitting here, in pain, half-naked, trying to feed a small human with my body. I've got enough going on. Do not make your problems my problems. Get out of here!"

Mr. Hunt's eyes widened minimally. His eyes flicked in her direction. Neither man moved.

"Are you deaf?" Millicent pushed. "Get your asses out of here. I've had enough."

A smile curled Mr. Gunner's lips as Mr. Hunt frowned harder.

"If you think you can handle her," Mr. Gunner said as he sauntered from the room. The door shut with a loud clang.

"Yes, there is a lot of commotion—"

"You, too," Millicent said, cutting off the lab tech. "Get out. Send in my normal staffer."

"Um. Yes, Miss Foster. Sorry, miss. But if Mr. Hunt would—"

"I'm gone," Mr. Hunt said in a scratchy voice. "Our orders are to stay out of the infant facilities." He glanced at Millicent before he walked from the room.

"Oh goodie, another prickly ego to navigate." Millicent leaned back before situating the baby a little better. Sighing in contentment, Millicent rubbed her thumb across the baby's tiny arm. A feeling unlike any she'd ever experienced saturated her chest and gripped her heart, and her arms constricted. *Mine.*

Chapter 7

Her first day physically back at her department, six months after the birth, Millicent found herself walking out of the craft with a saggy stomach, giant breasts, and an out-of-shape body. She blamed Mr. Gunner for some of this, of course. Had she been allowed to maintain a more rigorous exercise schedule prior to the birth, she wouldn't be in such bad shape.

The baby was growing perfectly, at average height and weight for infants her age. What had surprised the techs was her development. She was way ahead of not only the Curve, but all the other babies in her group. Chances were the others would catch up, but the overall vibe was that Millicent's baby was the best of the bunch.

To this, Millicent replied, "Of course she is. What else would I produce?" It was usually enough to stop the constant praise that interrupted her time with her child.

Millicent smiled to herself as the bay doors closed behind her and a beautiful day welcomed her, leading up to the grand entrance of the department. A few people passed, either headed to another department or just enjoying the computer-generated scenic walk.

A movement caught Millicent's eye. Mr. Gunner stood against the wall off to the right. His gaze landed on her for a moment before darting away.

She stared straight ahead and started walking. He hadn't been allowed anywhere near her or the other infants since the day he'd handled the baby. In fact, none of the guards were allowed near them. Mr. Hunt stalked the perimeter of the infant ward and then ensured she was protected from one secure location to the next, but other than that, he was a ghost. She had no dealings with him.

Near her work pod, she caught several glances in her direction, followed by the sound of scurrying. Her lips thinned, an annoying trait that alerted others to when she was irritated. She didn't like that they saw her wrath coming.

"Mr. Arnet," she said brusquely, coming to a stop in front of her idea board. *Boot up.* The pale blue pulsed to life.

"Yes, miss." The thin man stepped up next to her station.

"It seems you haven't kept tight enough control on these premises. Care to explain?"

"Sorry, miss. We are only two days behind schedule."

"*Behind* schedule?" She faced him, schooling her face into a severe expression. And waited.

He started to pick at his suit seam. "Yes, miss. Sorry. I'll check in with—"

"Don't check in, Mr. Arnet, push. My department is known for being *ahead* of schedule. My physical presence should not be necessary to maintain this standard."

"Yes, miss. I apologize."

She faced her idea board again and accessed her files. As she opened her most recent update, a momentary flutter rippled her heart. She thought of the baby's downy-soft hair and velvety skin. Holding the baby was like holding another piece of herself. The baby's chest pressing against Millicent's was . . . the most glorious feeling in the world. So natural. So . . . right.

The memory of running her lips across the infant's sleeping brow surfaced, causing a pang in Millicent's heart. This wasn't good. She knew it wasn't. She shouldn't miss that baby. It wasn't hers. Her genetics aside, Millicent's job was almost done. As soon as she stopped feeding, Millicent would go back to her life. Her empty, lonely life.

Blowing out a breath, she tried to push the thoughts away. Then struggled to ignore the feelings of dread for the future. Of the pain she was sure to face. She tried to get back into the job.

It turned into a long, *long* day. And when it was finally over, nearly time to go back to the nursery and feed, she put on her exercise attire and sought the buzz that endorphins gave her. Maybe running so hard she threw up would scramble her head in just the right way. It was worth a shot. She had to do something.

On her running mat, she waited patiently for her implant to sync, then quickly built to warming-up speed. Before she could even break a sweat, she saw the large frame of one of the directors emerge from the clothing area. A moment later, she recognized the messy man-bun and the infallible swagger in his skin-tight sweat suit. He walked the length of the floor before stopping in front of her with his lips pulled into a smile. "Making up for lost time?"

She rolled her eyes at his mocking tone. "Your pants are absurd. I can see the outline of your dick."

"Tempted?"

"Hardly."

"I've missed our little chats. Everyone else here does as they're told, when they're told. Where's the fun? Where's the challenge?"

"They are paid to. If you want a challenge, go make eyes at your crony, Mr. Hunt."

The smile dripped off Mr. Gunner's face. "He has his duty. I have mine."

"Ah yes. The territorial pissing match. Or is it dick measuring?"

He sauntered off, his shoulders swinging with his ridiculous swagger. "No need to measure. Mine's always bigger."

❖ ❖ ❖

"Ms. Foster is here?" Trent said as he smelled the familiar flowery fragrance. He glanced up in time to see a body pass. Beyond the glass door waited the stone face of Mr. Hunt, severe and perpetually in a bad mood.

A giggle drew his attention away from the director of security management in time to see girl C raise her hands, wanting to be picked up by Mommy.

"They are both getting too attached. It's time to sever the tie." Patricia, Trent's new assistant, spoke quietly so as not to be overheard.

Two other mothers were bouncing their children with dutiful faces, not overly engaged. The babies were only mildly invested, their attention wandering. One started to fuss as Trent watched. Of these three, only Ms. Foster was keeping the infant content with her milk supply. The other two women would soon join the two before them, who'd left after their milk had dried up from problems with feeding. Of those two, only one had cried as she walked away. Neither had had any lingering effects after returning to their duties and their regular lives. The babies, likewise, were happy with the lab staffers. All would be intelligent, if the preliminary tests held true, with a couple that were exceptional.

But there was one child above them all. She was already showing brain patterns that shouldn't have developed for months yet. Yesterday, she'd made a light flicker! Without an implant!

"In addition to being four clicks above the infant Curve in two categories right now—*four* clicks!—she knows who her mother is, and her mother makes her happy," Trent said. "No one else makes her smile like that. Mr. White is over the moon about the stats, so I've heard, and Ms.

Hutchins wants things to continue progressing. Ms. Foster, right now, is helping that progression. We have until the infant turns two. We'll indulge the child until she starts to display damaging levels of separation anxiety. Let's keep our fingers crossed it won't happen before our cutoff."

"Yes, sir."

Trent had to stop himself from preening as he moved into the main room. He liked having an assistant. It meant he was moving up in the world. And if that baby kept showing promise, he'd move up right to the top; he could feel it.

"Everything going okay?" He smiled down at Ms. Foster and girl C.

"When will her eyes change?" Ms. Foster asked, scrunching her nose and making a face as she looked at the child. Girl C giggled merrily and reached for Ms. Foster's nose.

"Those are . . . probably the end result. They might change a little, but that is basically their final color." Trent stooped for a rattle and handed it to a lab tech. The infant in the lab tech's arms stopped crying long enough to grab the rattle. The item skittered across the floor a moment later. He had a terrible temper, that one.

"This is the final color?" Ms. Foster's voice had dropped into a suspicious tone.

Confused at her reaction, he studied the child's eyes for a moment. Black lashes curled up from light-blue eyes. He'd almost describe them as electric blue. Even this early in development, he could already see the hot spark of focus that would later blossom into intelligence. Just how intelligent, he couldn't wait to find out.

"No one's eyes should be this color," Ms. Foster said in an uncomfortable tone. "Did something go wrong with the breeding?"

"Oh!" Trent laughed. "No, no. On the contrary, everything went right. Blue is a recessive gene. The sperm and the egg both carry an eye-color gene. You must have a blue gene in addition to your brown. In you, the brown—or dark hazel, in your case—took over as the dominant gene, hiding the blue."

"So why isn't the blue hidden in GC?"

"GC? Cute. Well, the father must have . . ." Trent checked his wrist screen. He now had the clearance to access most of the information he needed wirelessly. From anywhere! He'd come a long way in six short months. Everything was going as planned. "Yes, the father has two blue genes. So, being a natural birth, he offered a blue gene for the baby, and you appear to also have offered a blue gene. And there you go. Blue eyes."

"None of the other babies have blue eyes."

Why this was such a big deal, Trent had no idea. But Ms. Foster was one of the prettier people he'd ever seen—as a natural born, she had minute flaws, but they only made her more exotic and rare—so he smiled down at her despite his need to be on the way to Ms. Hutchins's office. "A couple of the babies *could* have had blue eyes. But this is natural birthing! The selection is left entirely up to Mother Nature. I love it. It's so exciting. There are literally endless results that could come of a single sperm meeting an egg. Endless! Not all good, I grant you, but when it works, it really works! And now look, your baby is one of a kind."

Ms. Foster's face transformed into an expression that looked like she was going to be sick. "One of two, actually." She clutched the baby to her chest and looked away.

Trent knew that postnatal hormones had the ability to make women crazy, but . . . Well, this was just odd. He had no idea what was happening. Or what the problem was. So he just moved on. It was safer that way. Ms. Foster could be terrifying when she got her temper up and swung her weight around. He did not like matching wills with her. Mostly because he never won. He hoped that when he finally had to separate her from her baby, she'd go quietly.

Millicent stepped out of the craft with lead feet. Her stomach flipped once, twice. She almost felt like she was going to throw up.

The doors slid shut behind her and closed with a soft bump. She jumped, and then couldn't help swinging an accusatory glare in Mr. Gunner's direction. He stood as he had yesterday, against the wall, watching her make her entrance. He wasn't her guard anymore, but still he made sure she got into the building.

That was Mr. Hunt's job, and Mr. Hunt trusted she wasn't an idiot.

Is that what Mr. Gunner was saying? That she was an idiot?

Irrational anger boiled through her veins.

Did he know, she wondered? Did he know that he'd stolen her thunder? Everyone said GC looked a little like her. But she didn't. GC mimicked her, but that was it. It had taken realizing whom GC's eyes had reminded her of to see it. GC looked like her birth father. Like Mr. Gunner.

Dominant genes, my ass!

As if hearing the accusation, the man of the hour glanced her way. He did a double take, probably wondering why she was staring a hole in his head. And he could just keep wondering, because even if she wanted to accuse him of hijacking her spotlight—which made no sense and she didn't care—she wasn't allowed to. It was forbidden to discuss the infants and their development outside the creation and growth department. She'd be segregated from her daughter immediately, and Millicent was not ready for that to happen. She wanted this to last forever, and since that wasn't a possibility, for as long as possible.

She straightened her gaze and walked toward her department with purposeful strides. Out of all the people in the world, she had been tied forever with *him*. Mr. Suave. Mr. Swagger.

GC better not have any of that.

"What is your problem, princess?"

She swatted at his annoying presence, not bothering to look over when she hit his shoulder. "Don't talk to me. They might find out. Let's just keep this civil."

"Who might? What are you—"

"Good morning, Ms. Foster," the AI said pleasantly.

Millicent hurried to her station, making sure Mr. Gunner wasn't following. The only consolation was that he was extremely intelligent. And good at his job. The San Francisco office was now running like a fine machine as far as security went. They'd had no incidents in two months, or so the reports said. That hadn't happened in a long time. So if GC inherited any of his abilities, so much the better.

Something Mr. McAllister had said floated into her awareness—"There are literally endless results that could come of a single sperm meeting an egg."

What else would GC inherit from this man who fornicated with multiple women at one time and wandered around in exercise clothing that clearly defined his pecker?

She sighed and wiped her hand over her face. She was almost afraid to watch her kid grow.

That thought sank in. A tear came to her eye, a first in as long as she could remember outside the birthing room.

They couldn't take her child away. She had to come up with a way to stay in GC's life.

Chapter 8

One Year Later

"Message for you, miss."

Millicent slipped her foot into a boot. "Read it to me."

"Of course. It's from Trent McAllister. He states, 'Hello, Ms. Foster. I just wanted to let you know that Marie—we will be adopting your name suggestion—is doing great. She is really coming along, and I think we have a winner on our hands. As you know, we've asked for your visitations to continue well beyond that of the other mothers because little Marie looks forward to them. However, we are nearing our cutoff. We cannot make this any harder on Marie than it already will be. So, for that reason, at the end of this week, you will tell her you're going on a trip, and we'll give her a clean cut. I want to thank you for all your diligent work. We have entered your name into the breeding pool for the second time, and should it come up, I look forward to working with you again. Please let me know if you have any questions. All the best, Trent McAllister.'"

Millicent's hands shook where she held the zipper. Pain such as she'd never experienced tore at her heart. Without warning, her stomach gurgled and then erupted, spilling her breakfast onto the floor.

Eyes dripping, she pulled her console closer and retrieved the message before flinging it onto a larger wall screen.

"Can I help clean that up, miss?"

Millicent ignored the voice, reading the text as her world came crashing down. As her heart ripped out. As her likely death presented itself. Because there was very little chance that she would succeed. But they were giving her no choice. She'd spent the last year reading up on every effort a natural parent had made to stay in their baby's life. Appeals to the conglomerate, trespassing, trying to change jobs—everything had been tried. Every single thing. And often, the mother was either recycled or mind wiped. The conglomerate had made the line very clear—she was a product of their organization, and her brood was, too. They were all owned.

It was time for her to take her child—and then her freedom.

She hated that Mr. Gunner had been right. And that now she'd be forced to act on it.

She was quiet on the way to her department, as usual. At the bay doors, she glanced at the empty spot along the wall where Mr. Gunner hadn't stood for months. He didn't need to make sure she made it in safely anymore. Her main task was done. Or so he thought. The ape.

At her work pod, she paused. And then backed out. "Mr. Arnet."

A moment later, he was standing behind her. "Yes, miss."

"I will be in my office today. I need to concentrate. I want productivity to stay at the current rate. Do I make myself clear?"

"Yes, miss. Of course, miss."

She ignored the grateful look on his face. In her office, she resisted the urge to shut her door. People would already wonder why she'd suddenly decided to switch locations. She didn't need them thinking something was up.

To dispel their curiosity, she filled all but one wall with her pet project: the most complex systems in all the conglomerates. Some belonged to her nemesis, the staffer in Gregon who kept thwarting her attempts to crush Gregon's newest firewall. The others were her own, which she constantly had to fortify against Gregon's passive-aggressive attacks. The good news was, in addition to being a pastime that Millicent could sink into during the lonely evening hours, it had taught her some fantastic code sequences she hadn't seen before. The bad news was, she had also taught some fantastic code sequences to the Gregon staffer, who was now using them against her.

Today, though, none of that mattered. Maybe would never matter again.

Now it was time for the first iffy part of her plan. The part where she basically sucked up to Mr. Gunner and said, "You were right about freedom. Please help me attain it."

She really hoped there had been a kernel of seriousness in his questioning all that time ago, and it wasn't just her current desperation reading into it.

Millicent bit her lip and stared at the screen.

Possibly this was a terrible idea.

After a deep breath, she started to execute the first part of her plan, which was made possible by Mr. Gunner himself.

Shortly after Mr. Gunner had tricked her into going into the assisted living facility, she'd gone into the systems to analyze how he'd set up that security loop to hide his misdeeds on the craft—she hated secrets. Then, a few months ago, she'd gone in to see if she could duplicate it, only to realize it was a sort of privacy reserved for Mr. Gunner's department, accessible only to a director and higher. Of course, Millicent could take down the firewall with ease. And with enough time and effort, she could hack one of her own if she wanted, but she'd noticed that Mr. Gunner hadn't used it again. Why hack another if she could take over this one? It was just waiting for a time she might need it.

Like now, for example.

She needed help in this endeavor, and even though Mr. Gunner had definitely been trying to distract her that one day with his talk of freedom and motherhood, he'd seemed so serious. So desirous to be a father. And the way he'd held Marie—he hadn't even known the child was his, and he'd been fantastic with her. He'd had a connection; she *knew it.*

This all certainly sounded like desperation . . .

"He'll want to help," she mumbled to herself, feeling a surge of emotion at the enormity of what she was about to take on. "He will. He'll do the right thing."

She had to believe that. Because without him, she had very little chance. And against him? Next to none—she could barely hold up her side of the insult slinging. The whole plan might unravel before she thought, *Go.*

After a heavy sigh, she hacked into the security loop, added her own code, some traps, and a time-out. She buried a message like a time capsule that would display in his cleaning stall: "When I met you, one person had eyes of electric blue. But now there are two. Carpe diem."

She paused.

She had to admit that there were a few possible hang-ups. First, would he figure out what she meant about the eyes? Second, would he have any clue what *carpe diem* meant? The phrase was a relic from over a thousand years ago. He was smart, but that didn't mean he was properly educated . . .

And last, would he figure all of that out but decide, correctly, that she was treasonous? She'd consistently read him wrong from the very first time she'd set eyes on him. There was exactly one person who could distract her, use her tech against her, and then trump her by checking her into a place she couldn't check out of, all to win a dumb battle regarding the speed of her jogging. His motivations were as fuzzy to her as what went on behind those crazy-colored eyes.

And now she was putting herself at his mercy.

Was she insane?

"No. Desperate," she muttered to herself before glancing at the door just in case. Mumbling to herself was starting to be a bad habit. It didn't chase the loneliness away, but it did make her look crazy.

"Nothing for it." Grimacing, she shook her head.

She turned back to the console, uploaded the time bomb, and then paused again.

What if someone else was in the cleaning stall?

He was sexually active. People who had sex often slept in the same quarters. The message might be wasted on a Curve hugger.

Her lip hurt from how often she was biting it in thought. Coming to a decision, she retrieved his unique implant code and programmed the message to open after the implant was verified within the cleaning stall. That done, she tried to figure out a way to attach her signature without it being obvious. If cameras in his apartment caught that message displayed on the stall wall, the employees assigned to review such footage probably wouldn't figure it out. But adding a name . . .

A smile tickled her lips. She altered his cleaning stall system so it'd switch between randomly hitting his face and his genitals. Then, to make sure he recognized her hand, she accessed his closet and programmed it to only dispense a bright-pink suit. Apparently he'd followed the trend—which still lingered in the lower levels—a couple of years ago. And just like she had on the day she met him, he would be forced to show off said trend.

Chuckling despite the gravity of the situation, she closed everything down. Now she just had to hope he both washed and was smart enough to figure it out.

Also, that he didn't try to bring her in or kill her.

She cleared her mind by creating a horrible Trojan, which she slipped into the Gregon systems. That would really piss her counterpart off. That done, she moved on to a heinous device she'd helped develop. For the first time, the possibility of one conglomerate destroying the headquarters of another was a decided attraction. When they'd ever use it was beyond her. Each conglomerate—or at least the top two—needed the other to survive. It seemed like their heightened defense budget was primarily for glory's sake. If they used it, they'd destroy themselves in the process of destroying each other.

"Miss?"

Millicent jumped and turned to the woman in her doorway. "Yes?"

"Your guard is here to see you, miss."

"Where?"

"Near your work pod."

Frowning, she followed the young woman out, not sure why a guard was meeting her so early. She wasn't scheduled to see Marie for another few hours.

When she turned the corner, though, her belly flip-flopped. She put her palm to it, wondering if she would spill her stomach for the second time that day.

Electric-blue eyes stared at her out of a blank face as she approached. His arm muscles flexed, and his hands clenched into fists for a moment before everything relaxed.

She cleared her throat and thought about wiping her suddenly moist upper lip. "What are you doing here?" she asked. "I thought you were working in another department in San Francisco?"

"Mr. Hunt is otherwise engaged. I will be escorting you to the creation lab."

"The creation lab?" she breathed. "Why so early?"

"I wasn't given the particulars."

She checked the numbers on her wrist. Midafternoon. Would they give her the whole evening to visit, or would they tell her this was it? That they'd changed their minds and today was the final day?

Today couldn't be the final day. She needed more time to get ready.

"Yes—" The words stuck in her throat. She coughed into her fist. "Excuse me. Yes, of course. Let me just . . ." She glanced around her, feeling like she'd forgotten something and didn't know what. But there was nothing. She had nothing that was distinctly hers, except Marie. "Okay. I'm ready."

Mr. Gunner stepped to the side and motioned her to precede him. It felt like she was in trouble. Like he was marching her to her death.

Maybe he was.

Outside the department, her guards waited next to the bay door. A craft, different than usual, larger, waited behind the clear glass.

"That is not my hovercraft," she said with a clattering heart. It was deafening.

"I had mine on hand."

"Oh. Sure." She smoothed the hair along her scalp until her hand hit her tight bun. "I expected you to have a larger one."

"Why is that?"

"To fit all of your ego inside."

Silence met her jab. She glanced back and read the viciousness in his eyes and the hard lines of his face. A strange shock of fear made her waver.

"Have you been home recently . . . ," she asked with a strangely level voice. Strange because her whole body was shaking.

"No. In here." The doors opened, and he steered her inside.

"You've dropped some humor since I last saw you." She forced a smile. "Get it? Instead of dropping weight, you dropped humor . . ."

"I got it." He sat down near the door as the guards filed in. "Stop talking."

She didn't want to stop talking. She wanted to coax information out of him. Either that or she wanted to *run*. Something was horribly wrong, and she was on the bad side of it.

Once at the labs, she forced herself to shrug off the anxiety and the horrible tremors. She couldn't waste this walk in a cloud of fear. She had to take it all in, to pinpoint their defenses and ensure they hadn't altered anything since terminating her involvement. If she were them, she would have.

In the entrance, she noticed all the retinal scanners, cameras, and reporting devices. There were many, all of which she'd previously mapped. They hadn't put in any additional measures.

Trying not to be obvious, she noticed the control centers, mapping in her head the places that could easily be shorted out. Mr. Gunner followed her closely, not stopping at the check-in desk like he should've.

"I'm afraid you need to wait out here, Mr. Gunner," one of the lab guards said.

A large heavy hand covered Millicent's shoulder. "She's been flagged as a flight risk. Her term is ending, starting today."

Dread trickled down Millicent's spine as the guard's eyes widened. His gaze switched to her, a look holding both fear and pity. She had no idea why he'd be afraid.

"Yes, of course. I completely understand. There are no infants, so it shouldn't be too big of a problem. Just please don't touch—"

"Don't tell me my business," Mr. Gunner said in a hard voice. His unwavering gaze beat into the guard, making the man color red and shrink back.

"Yes, sir." The guard opened the door to admit them.

"Oh. Milli—Ms. Foster." Surprise etched Mr. McAllister's face as he stood within the group of children.

"Mama!" Marie toddled up with a glowing smile and hands spread wide.

"You can't call me that," Millicent said in a soft voice, hoisting the little girl up into her arms.

"And Mr. Gunner. In here. What is happening?" Mr. McAllister glanced at his wrist with a furrowed brow.

"There was some concern Ms. Foster would have a hard time letting go of this particular duty. I've been sent to observe." Mr. Gunner took a step away, back against the wall.

"Oh." Mr. McAllister's confusion crumpled into a look of understanding, bordering on pity. "I completely understand. It's been a long time. I can only imagine—"

"That'll be all, Mr. McAllister." The deep drum of Mr. Gunner's voice reverberated through the room. Mr. McAllister's mouth snapped shut. He looked down at his feet and then shuffled away.

Seizing her moment, Millicent turned Marie toward Mr. Gunner. Her little girl's eyes flicked upward, looking out from under her lashes. Mr. Gunner, his gaze focused on the toys for a moment, looked over in irritation. The gazes of father and daughter met, eyes the exact shade of electric blue, black lashes curling outward in an identical way. Same dark hair. Same strong jaw.

A shiver arrested Millicent. What of this child, besides the chin and high cheek bones, was hers? Not for the first time, the natural selection of birth blew her mind. But it wasn't her mind she was trying to entice right now, it was Mr. Gunner's. With his offspring.

Mr. Gunner walked off to join Mr. McAllister, who was standing in the corner, looking uncomfortable. "Where do those doors lead?" He pointed toward each of the three doors around the room.

"Oh." Mr. McAllister lifted his wrist. "Is this so . . ." He glanced at Millicent. "Flight risk?"

"Exactly, yes," Mr. Gunner answered in a hard voice. "I don't need to come into this room again. But I do need to station men around the perimeter, and to do that, I need the layout. Unless . . ." Mr. Gunner glanced at Millicent. "Actually, Mr. McAllister, I'd like to speak to you outside."

"Alone?" His voice warbled a little. He cleared his throat and then adjusted his collar. "Yes, of course. Yes. Sure, sure."

As they were exiting, Millicent heard Mr. Gunner say, "I want a guard in this room. Can your staff handle that, or should I include that in my plan?"

She was going up against Mr. Gunner. *Shit.*

The enormity came crashing down over her, drowning her. She was alone, friendless, and she stood in opposition to a man who was arguably the best security director the conglomerate had.

Millicent held Marie tightly, slowly rocking her from side to side. She blinked back a tear, worried about failure. Worried that moments like this one would be ripped away from her forever.

After a shuddering breath, she hardened herself.

Mr. Gunner had won the last battle by checking her into the assisted living facility, but he hadn't won the war. She was armed now. This last year had toughened her up. She knew what she was about. If he pitted himself against her again, he'd lose. And if she could, she'd rub it in his face until it choked him.

Fifteen minutes later, Mr. Gunner followed Mr. McAllister back into the room, his expression still hard, his eyes with a sharp edge. "It's time," he said, standing with his hands clasped in front of him and mostly facing the door. He couldn't see any of the children from that vantage point. If he'd recognized his face in Marie's, he'd chosen not to acknowledge it.

Anger flared within her. *So be it.*

She blew out a breath and put Marie on the ground.

"No!" Marie clutched Millicent's pants. "No!"

"Sorry, baby. Just for now. I'll come back tomorrow, okay?" She glanced up at Mr. McAllister. "I can make promises until . . . when?"

"Friday." He shrugged in a helpless sort of way. "I don't make the rules, I'm afraid."

"So I'll be back tomorrow." She kissed Marie on the forehead.

One of the staffers pulled Marie's hands away from Millicent. The little girl started screaming. Lights flickered. Metallic clicks sounded around the room.

"Wow." Mr. McAllister bent to his wrist screen.

"What's happening?" Mr. Gunner asked, turning with wide eyes.

"Mr. McAllister's tampering has worked." Millicent watched in frustrated anguish as her child was pulled away. Hating herself, but knowing she had no choice, she walked to the door. This conglomerate would pay dearly for what they were doing. Mr. Gunner had been right about another thing: war created savagery. "C'mon. It makes it worse if I don't hurry."

The screaming cut off as the door clicked shut. The heels elongated in her boots as she walked, ticking across the tiled floor. This was a new pair, too. Still the same malfunction.

Her eyes scanned the walls and flicked to the ceiling, doing a mental inventory of every security protocol in the building. They were all the same. Had been for the last year. Heavy, that was true. There was more security in this building than most others she'd been in, but beatable. She had to believe that.

"Does she scream like that every time?" Mr. Gunner asked in a low voice.

"Yes." A guard glanced their way, his eyes wary. Word had spread, and it looked like they thought her less of a flight risk than someone to fear.

"Do the other children do that with their . . . female creators?"

"Mothers? No, they don't." They stepped into the craft and waited for the doors to close. When they were on their way, Millicent said, "Breeders are chosen based on a select set of characteristics, and often those characteristics are enhanced through the implant or with drugs. Emotions are quelled. The bond between mother and child, if allowed to manifest, is hacked away. Depression is chemically introduced until the mother is stripped away from the baby. Then the mother gets mood enhancers when she rejoins society without her child."

"And they didn't attempt those things with you?"

Millicent scoffed. "They tried. But I program implants in soldiers all the time. In spies. In assassins. I know how that game is played, and wouldn't allow them to play it with me. Besides, who could they possibly get to outsmart me in that arena? There is only one, and she never outsmarts me for long—if she outsmarts me at all. What's the point? The situation is out of my control."

"Is anything out of your control?"

She gave him a level look. "One thing. I can't control other people."

If he caught her meaning, he gave no sign. "And the pills?"

"I only take Clarity. That is it. Everything else dulls my mind. And trust me when I say that dulling my mind would create a lot more problems for the conglomerate than a love for an offspring."

"You've grown into your position." The deep drum of his voice gave no coloring of meaning to the words, and she had no idea how he meant them. Or what had led him to that conclusion.

Shrugging it off, she said, "May I leave?" The craft had docked again. She stood as the doors opened. "I have work to do."

"When did you ever listen to me?" He stayed seated. "One thing, though. Why *Marie*? They said you chose that name."

She paused in the doorway as the cold air turned her breath white. "Marie Curie was a woman from way before the Enlightened Ages. She won two Nobel Prizes in a time when women were supposed to be hidden away in the home. She battled her male peers throughout her entire career, and battled women's judgments regarding her family role versus her career. She was tenacious, and she made her mark. She stuck to her inner truth, not allowing the people and environment around her to dictate her decisions. I respect that. Everyone thinks my daughter can be great. And she can. She just needs someone to show her the way."

Millicent bit her lip before she could say what she was thinking. *And for my daughter, I will be that someone. I will not let Marie—either*

Marie—down. All she had was a plan, determination, and an air of mystery. That, and a mother's love. She couldn't give away one of her advantages.

"Well then. Be a good girl, and we'll have no problems."

She huffed out a laugh. "When have I failed to give you problems?" With that, she strode away, allowing the plan to unfurl in her mind even as she checked into the department of her new enemy.

Chapter 9

"Time to go, princess. Last day. You ready?"

Millicent straightened up, wiped her idea board clean, and turned. She didn't shut it down. She'd be back today. One last time. "Of course."

"Prim and proper. What a bore." Mr. Gunner stepped to the side easily, much more relaxed since Monday, when he must've realized she wasn't the flight risk he'd expected. He still stood too close, though. Still guarded her with a meticulous eye.

If he'd accessed her message, he hadn't responded, either through the closed-circuit security loop or verbally. He'd simply watched her like a proverbial hawk. She'd even looked up the animal when that antiquated expression had come to mind.

"Did you know," she said as she walked through the department, scanning work pods as she went by. Habit. "That a hawk is a bird of prey?"

"I did know that, yes. Me learn good."

"Cute. And did you know that it is a member of the Accipitridae family?"

"Me not learn that good. Here, we're taking my craft again today." He led her to the door with a tight hand on her upper arm.

She ignored the overbearing touch. "Yes. And interestingly enough, the Accipitridae family also houses the very-much-not-extinct buzzard. So really, we could say that this week, you've been watching me like a buzzard."

"And this is why you will never get past director. Your small talk is atrocious." Once they boarded, he sat near the door, as always, and watched her with an unwavering stare.

"Do you know why you won't advance?"

"Because I won't cut my hair. Or give up women. Or give up drinking. Or bar fights. I'm not really a department-type man."

"Just a pawn."

"Not a pawn." His eyes sparkled with that killer's heat. "I've never been a pawn."

She laughed and looked out the window. The dark-gray sky pressed upon them. Snow shook down in lazy sheets. "You don't project a utopian scene in your craft. Do you in your home?"

"No. I want to know what the real world looks like. I want to know what I'm working toward."

"And what is that?"

"A better life."

She had to concede that point. She'd done some research from his closed-circuit security loop. Beyond the protection of the conglomerates, the outside world was mostly stripped bare and horribly unlivable. At least by her standards. People squatted in hovels, starving and sickly. Sores developed on their skin from the acid rain. Their life span barely reached fifty, when her life expectancy, if she used her clones, topped out at three hundred. They traded for their goods, hoping to get enough, whereas she just told her computer what she needed. She was rich, by the world's standards, in health, life, and economy. Outside the conglomerates, this world was no place for a child.

But those weren't her only two choices. Thanks to Mr. Gunner, she had a third option. From the little information she could garner, which probably wasn't totally reliable, it was risky—one in ten didn't survive the voyage, and no one ever came back—but it was her only chance. She'd already created an alias, hacked through the ridiculous security that badly needed reworking, and booked herself and Marie for a trip on the dilapidated rocket shuttle. And if they had a problem taking her for some reason, she'd make them take Marie. As long as her daughter had a better life, that's all that mattered.

"Deep in thought," Mr. Gunner said. "Dare I offer a credit for your thoughts?"

"Stop staring at me. It's annoying."

"I do like when you're feisty. Why take Clarity? I think you could have a riot without it."

She rolled her eyes. "That is the only pill that prevents a dulled mind rather than enables it."

"The sexual drive is natural, princess. You should express it."

"And let me guess. You'd be happy to give me a tutorial if I did?"

"Precisely. I might teach you a thing or two."

The craft bumped lightly as it docked. She stood when the doors opened. "How have you never gotten called in for sexual harassment?"

"It's not harassment, it's foreplay."

"I hope you also think getting stabbed in the eye is foreplay."

"Getting stabbed? No." His overbearing touch found her arm again. "You trying to stab me? Yes. I like to be the one doing the stabbing. Or prodding, in any case."

"Neanderthal." The doors opened, the same as they had for the last year and a half. Nothing had changed down the halls. The same guard was on duty, a man one click below the Curve on average, lab born, but with a good work ethic. If the system went down, a man like him would get out his torch and have a look-see. She'd disable him easily.

"Right through here." Mr. Gunner pushed her to the right, away from the normal path she took.

"Where are we going?" She glanced behind her at the usual route. There was no reason to think it had changed in any way, but she wanted to be sure. She wanted one last look.

"This is the farewell chamber."

"There's a farewell chamber?" she asked as they went down a hallway she'd never been in before.

"It's almost nap time, so they're about to head to bed for a bit. After you say good-bye, they'll shuttle her off to bed with a sedative."

Anger boiled. "Children shouldn't be given a sedative, they should be hugged and comforted so they can heal naturally."

"Careful, your hippie is showing."

"What's a hippie?"

Mr. Gunner laughed as he stopped in front of a lonely chamber in which two lab techs, one male, one female, waited patiently with Marie. "Where's Mr. McAllister?"

"Trent is avoiding the scene because he knows how it's going to go down." Mr. Gunner's tone was completely level.

Millicent knew how it was going to go down, too.

She took a deep breath and tried to shoulder her resolve, but the tears appeared, unbidden. She turned away and wiped her face quickly. This wasn't forever. She'd see her daughter again, or she'd die trying.

"Stalling won't make it easier," Mr. Gunner said.

"Keep it up, and you'll get that knife in your ribs."

"Promises, promises." Contrasting his words and tone, his hand gently landed on her shoulder. He squeezed softly. "You can do this."

She didn't want to do this.

Millicent squared her shoulders and walked through the door. Marie's eyes lit up immediately. She jumped up from the bench and hurried toward Millicent. The toddler's arms wrapped around Millicent's legs until Millicent grabbed her under the armpits and hoisted her up. She hugged her daughter tightly, feeling the tears rising again.

"Let's sit over here." Millicent situated Marie on her lap and held her close. "Have you been good for the nice staffers?"

"Yes. I play ball."

"You played with a ball?"

"Who dat?" Marie pointed at Mr. Gunner standing with his hands clasped in front of him, a block of muscle guarding the door. Another guard, half Mr. Gunner's size, stood before the other door that led into the bed chamber.

Millicent tried to see the area beyond without being obvious about it. She'd studied the map and schematics of the area, but this was the first time she'd been allowed this far.

"That's your—Mr. Gunner." Millicent winced at her near slip as Mr. Gunner's eyes, awash in malice, hit hers. So he *had* received the message. Apparently his version of "a better life" was waxing poetic about freedom while turning his back on obtaining it. He'd rather take the easy way out.

"Your guard, I was about to say," Millicent corrected herself. "But that's silly, because you don't need a guard, right?"

"Silly." Marie giggled and got off Millicent's lap. She wobbled across the room and grabbed a ball. "Play, Mama!"

"Uh-oh, we don't use that word." The male lab tech smiled.

"She is four clicks above the Curve in communications," the female lab tech said, hands clasped on her lap. "It's miraculous. We've never seen it so high before. Only one percent are three above, and only five percent are two above."

"I'm aware. Being within the one percent." Millicent took the ball from Marie.

"And her dexterity? Her coordination?" Startled, Millicent looked at Mr. Gunner, who was awaiting the answer. He smiled in a disarming way, something she'd never seen before. "I, myself, am in the one percent," he said. "I just wondered if she holds firm across the Curve or if her grid is sporadic."

"Oh." The female lab tech batted her eyelashes as she flushed. Millicent stared at her, wondering what had prompted the embarrassed reaction. "She is three above in coordination, and three in dexterity, I believe. Four in analytical capabilities, problem solving, three in logic . . . She is high in everything."

"Her intelligence follows Ms. Foster's natural abilities, then?" Mr. Gunner asked with a glimmer in his eyes.

"Oh. Um . . ." The girl's face turned a darker shade of red as she used the screen on the wall next to her.

"Actually, she is a great crossing between both gene donators," the male lab tech said as he jogged to get a discarded ball. "Some children develop more grievous traits, and Marie does have the temper and willfulness of the male donor, but we find that those traits are tempered nicely with the levelheadedness of the female breeder. Marie will lose her temper, have an outburst, and then settle down to solve the problem. Granted, the hitting is starting to become an issue. Both the breeder and donor have a dangerous inclination toward violence, but you need it in your line of work, isn't that right, Ms. Foster?" The lab tech glanced up at her with a smile.

Wanting them to keep talking, since usually they were very tight-lipped about the donors, she took a page out of Mr. Gunner's book by feigning a lustful expression. The lab tech went rigid, and a confused look crossed his face.

That wasn't what she had been going for. "You were saying?" she asked, trying to cover the moment of awkwardness.

"Oh. Um. Yes, I was saying that it's really a great pairing. One of the better ones. I think we'll try that pairing again."

"Have you ever had siblings before?" Millicent asked, feeling her face heat.

"Oh yes, a few. We don't call them siblings, of course, but we need to track such things for breeding, as you can imagine."

"Time," Mr. McAllister's voice rang out over the room's speaker.

"No," Millicent croaked out, feeling her heart jump into her throat. "Just a little longer. I was talking. I wasn't—"

"Come on, Millicent," Mr. Gunner said, taking a step toward her. "Stay rational."

Emotion squeezed up through her chest and into her eyes. She reached for her little girl, unable to speak. Unable to utter a good-bye for fear she'd never see her daughter again.

"Where go, Mama?" Marie asked, her arms squeezed around Millicent's neck.

"I have to go away, baby," she said before kissing her daughter's forehead. "I have to go away, okay?"

"See you tomorrow?"

"No, baby. I can't come back." Hot tears cut down Millicent's cheeks. "I can't come back, baby."

That's when the crying started. Millicent had no idea who was crying harder, she or Marie. Lights flickered. Her daughter's little body was ripped away, along with her persistent hands. Strong arms took their place, yanking Millicent up and dragging her toward the exit.

She probably yelled. Maybe she screamed. If she failed, this was it. This was the last time.

"Keep it together." The fierce growl rang through her ears. "They'll wipe your mind if you don't. Force your way through this."

People were yelling: "Someone get her a sedative!" "I can't get out—the child locked the doors!" "Override the locks!"

"Keep it together," she heard again, crushed into Mr. Gunner's chest. "Calm the fuck down, Millicent. They're calling Mr. Hunt. We do not want Mr. Hunt active again." His voice louder this time, he said, "Don't just give the child a sedative, give Ms. Foster something!"

A sting pierced her arm. She struggled, but couldn't get free of Mr. Gunner's strength. Then blackness.

❖ ❖ ❖

She came to consciousness slowly. Fluttering her eyes, she recognized Mr. Gunner sitting a few seats away. A lush green landscape covered the interior of the craft.

"I thought you didn't believe in surrounding yourself with a false utopia," she said with a scratchy voice. She cleared her throat, and then touched the skin over her strained vocal chords. Finally, her fingers drifted down to her chest, where something thick and heavy filled her. Something painful.

"You made a show of yourself," he said quietly, looking out the window at a fast-moving stream.

"You don't know what I'm going through."

"No one knows what you're going through. Which is why they don't understand why you acted the way you did."

"I'm not the first to react this way."

"And that's what saved you. Mr. Hunt was called off when I carried you out."

She smoothed her hair. "What is your deal with Mr. Hunt? He was fine when he monitored me. Always stayed a few paces away."

"There's a reason for that. And a reason he's forced to take Clarity. But anyway, you're good. Do you want me to take you to your apartment?"

"No." She checked the numbers on her wrist. "I have a few hours of work left." She had to close down her work station, plant a few viruses, get her wits in order, and then plan for the evening. The end had finally come. She had to keep going forward, or she'd lose her nerve like everyone had before her.

Mr. Gunner typed something into the console and settled back.

"The guards?" she asked, noticing the absence of people in the roomy cabin as the craft jostled forward. They were in a holding bay. Mr. Gunner was clearly waiting for her sedative to wear off before moving.

"They'll meet you at your department."

"Turn the screens off." She stared at the green pathway beside the stream until it blinked out of existence. A torrid gray sky greeted her. One that would kill her and Marie both if they were exposed to it for too long.

Not for the first time, a shock of doubt arrested her. She ran her palms up her arms, trying to warm up from the chill that was creeping in. "Am I doing the right thing?" she asked quietly. "What if I can't pull this off—"

"Stop talking."

She sighed. "Maybe the mind wipe—"

"Stop. Talking. You're not yourself right now. Give it some time. Let things settle down. Get back into your routine. Then reassess."

It would be too late by then. It was tonight or never.

But as the doubt grew—staring at that formidable sky and sitting next to this formidable man—she realized she had to decide. She had to really sit down and think it through.

In the face of what was before her, which was the better life . . . for Marie? By taking her away, whom was she saving? Her daughter, or herself? Because that was a big difference. And it meant everything.

Chapter 10

"Would you like something warm to drink, miss?"

Millicent stared at the sea of lights within the black night beyond her windows; no illusion hid the reality of the environment from her. Not anymore.

With each decade, developments in technology had allowed the builders to go higher and higher. As the world's companies were gobbled up by ever larger entities, peaking in the three superpowers of Millicent's time, old buildings were knocked down and super buildings created to house people and departments both. When the environment took a turn for the worst, and the heavy smog settled low, those with more status climbed to the tops of the huge high-rises, creating an elaborate travel-way system made possible by the advancing technology of automobiles. Driverless cars had come first, followed by hover cars. Now they were nearly driverless air ships in how they operated. Air ships controlled by computers. And only those who had extensive training manipulating those computers could override the controls.

She was one such person. With two hours to go.

Millicent sighed and looked down at her hands, answering the computer with, "No."

Her computer didn't respond with the usual follow-up.

A jiggling caught her awareness.

Frowning, because it sounded like the noise was coming from her restroom, she looked back. A body came out of the bay.

"Oh!" She jumped up. A knife immediately found its way into her hand. "Call for help! Intruder!"

"That call won't go anywhere." Mr. Gunner swaggered toward her in a tight gray suit. She'd cataloged him as big, but now, in her suddenly cramped space, she had a new appreciation for his size. He had obviously been bred for his job, and it showed.

"How did you get in here? This apartment is secured!" She backed up toward her small weapons bay.

"I'm security. Breaking and entering is my specialty."

"I think you misinterpreted the job description . . ."

He leisurely took the few steps to the couch and then sank in. He threw a big arm over the back. "Join me. Let's chat."

"What are you doing here? How did you close down my loop?"

"Millicent—may I call you Millie?"

"No."

"Millie, you're tense. And that's not good. When the eyes of several departments are watching you closely, you really should go back to blindly doing as you're told. Like before this whole snafu with child rearing."

She ground her teeth.

"C'mere." He patted the space beside him.

She edged across the room, knife still in hand, and slowly lowered into an independent chair as far away from him as possible. "Are you going to tell me what you're doing here? Closing down my loop will draw suspicion. I don't need any of that."

"Actually, you've already raised suspicion. Your work has taken on an edge of violent genius. Which is amazing, because you were already putting out genius, from what I understand. Now, though . . . they are as happy as a pig in shit."

"I've never seen a pig, but I doubt it is happy in shit."

"Be that as it may, the powers that be are a little worried about your ability to cope with today's situation."

"Today's situation? You mean losing my—" She clenched her jaw to keep the words from escaping. The sharp bite of her nails against her palms helped her combat the emotion.

"No one is listening to this conversation but me. Consider it a professional courtesy. You can be frank."

"Did you get my message?"

"You mean, did my apartment go haywire for the second time since I've known you? Did a place that is supposed to be secure from all forms of intrusion get broken into? Yes, I got your message. And just so you know, I've risen to the challenge with the pressure on those weights. Apparently you thought I needed more muscle?"

"And your thoughts on the message?"

"You're in over your head, princess. I shouldn't have questioned you. Said those things to you all that time ago. Those kinds of thoughts on a weak mind can—"

"On a weak mind?" She pinched the knife blade between her index finger and thumb before leaning forward in the chair.

"Please don't throw that. It would really ruin my night."

She was just waiting for a reason . . .

He watched her for a moment, completely at ease. He must've realized what was on the line, but it didn't show. "What happened today compromised you. But, Millie—"

"Stop calling me that."

"—you can't take on this conglomerate. I know you're thinking about it. I saw you eyeing the security all week at the creation lab. But I know who implemented that security. You don't have all the right assets.

If you do anything rash, you'll fail, and then you'll get a mind wipe and have to start all over."

"You've got the wrong idea. I'm enjoying my evening. And if you will excuse me, I'd like to keep on enjoying it. Alone."

"Don't be a fool, Millie."

"Better than being a hypocrite, Mr. Freedom. Mr. Dick Wagger."

A teasing grin lit up his face before he shifted and brought his arm down to his leg. "Dick wagger? I hadn't realized you kept track of my dick's movements."

Millicent stood. "Get out. This is a violation of privacy, and if you stay any longer, I'll report you."

"To whom? My superior? He directed me here. They thought I could talk some sense into you. That I had some sway."

"They were wrong. You couldn't talk me into a different flavor of food pouch."

Mr. Gunner stood slowly, the humor drifting away. He stepped closer, his eyes deep and intense. "I know all the things I've said in the past. But I've learned some things from being close to infants and children, seeing how they're handled and nurtured. It's not such a bad life. Look how you turned out. And she'll be the best. With my aversion to being dominated and your incredible drive and intelligence, she'll get whatever she wants. She'll be treated like a piece of gold. Her throne within this conglomerate will be bigger than yours, and her admirers plentiful. Think about what you are doing."

Sudden tears dripped down Millicent's face. "You believe she's yours."

"I'm positive she is. She looks just like me. Also, I looked at the files. There isn't much a one-percenter can't access if he really wants to. This is the first child that is solely mine on the male's side. The first who's a natural birth."

"And you don't want her."

"I want her to be happy."

"I'm not happy." Sobs bubbled up through her middle. "I'm not happy without her. I feel like I've lost the better part of myself."

"You need to think of her before yourself, Millie." His hands ran up the outsides of her arms, and then moved on to her back, pulling her in and hugging her close. He laid his cheek across the top of her head. "You need to protect her. And that includes taking the hard road if you have to."

For the first time in her life, Millicent sobbed. She heaved with emotion, burrowing into Mr. Gunner and taking comfort in the strong arms wrapped around her. When he leaned back, she felt his large fingers on her chin, lifting. She gazed up into his handsome face, an appearance that was entirely his own, unique in a way only a natural born could be. His electric-blue eyes roamed her face before resting on her lips. "There are other forms of love in the world, Millicent. You should let yourself feel some of those."

"Why, when they can all be ripped away at a moment's notice?"

"Not all," he whispered. "Not mine."

His lips were soft and full as they grazed hers. Her fingers clutched at his shirt when electricity zinged through their kiss. She gasped as tingles worked down her spine, but they deadened before the feeling could manifest. That's what Clarity did—it stopped intense sexual feeling. She didn't need pills to suppress other feelings—the shell she'd lived in her whole life had protected her from feeling anything.

How could that possibly be a better life for Marie than having the freedom to run and play outside, to act as a child, and to have a loving parent? To *be* a loving parent if she wanted.

Frowning, she pushed away, stepping back. His face was serious and his pleading eyes exposed his soul.

"Will I go up against you if I . . ."

"Yes, Millie. You will be a traitor. And that child is more valuable than you are. If it becomes a shoot-to-kill situation, they will not hesitate."

"But they'll shoot me. Or capture me and mind wipe. They won't hurt her."

"Correct. But if she is exposed to the elements, she might die."

"No. She'd be collected and returned to safety. There is no real danger for her."

"You don't know what kind of people walk this earth." He shook his head. "You'd have to get out of the city without resources."

Mind made up, finally, irrevocably, Millicent hardened up for the last time. And then wiped the tears from her face. Her sob-hiccup, she ignored. "I'm one of the worst people who walks this earth, and I've designed a personal arsenal that attests to it. I've had a year to do it. I've also laundered a lot of money into Standard. It's lost half its value, of course, but I had a lot of it. I can—" She snapped her mouth shut, realizing what she was about to admit.

As if hearing her finish that thought, his eyes hardened. He took a step toward the front door. "Take some time. Think this through. I'll spin this in my report as you being amenable to my advice. Consider it a friendly warning."

"Thank you, for being a huge coward and proving me superior. See you on the battlefield."

His eyes lit on fire, and his body raged with muscle. His hands clenched. Strangely, a smile came over his face. "Stop taking that pill. I'll keep you alive, and oh, what fun we'll have." He winked at her. "Take it easy, princess. I'll look forward to blocking that knife-thrust."

He walked out through the front door, an opening that hadn't been used in years. Maybe ever.

"What did I just do?" she mumbled, light-headed.

"I'm not sure, miss. Would you like that hot beverage? I didn't hear a response."

Millicent had just revealed that she intended to get her daughter while challenging the kind of man who thrived off challenges. Not to mention that she'd undoubtedly increased the size of his giant ego by kissing him.

"Something hot would be fine. I have another hour to stew in nervousness."

"I'm sorry to hear that, miss. Might I offer you some form of relaxant?"

"No. Maybe I'll just start getting ready. Show me the arsenal."

❖   ❖   ❖

The bay doors opened, allowing her craft to enter. The lights did not activate. She'd tampered with the system, going through that security loop of Mr. Gunner's but using a different tag. When they traced this docking and her upload to the outside staffer's implants, it would lead to a dead end. They'd then question Mr. Gunner, who'd set up the loop all that time ago, but he wouldn't tell them anything they didn't already know: a one-percenter had stolen her one-of-a-kind daughter and gone off grid.

The faint glow of faux moonlight fell across the walkway as she made her way to the front entrance. Once there, she applied her eye lenses and stepped through the door.

"Lovely to see you, Mr. Eshers," the computer said, perceiving her as a member of the cleaning staff.

Mr. Eshers was not a real person, of course. Another dead end.

Retinal scans accessed her details as she made her way down the corridor, and sensors read the radio signal from her implant, which had seen a makeover update before she'd left her apartment. Dead ends all day long, none of which would trip the security system.

Oh yes, Mr. Gunner, I have the right assets to ensure my freedom, she thought. *Always have had. I just never had a reason to use them. Try messing with me now.*

Her wrist glowed faintly as she accessed the map, making sure she was taking the right turn. Past the empty play area, where she'd spent so much time with Marie, then up the corridor she'd seen in person for the first time that day.

Half of her wondered if Mr. Gunner had set all this up. If he'd shown her this area and told her they were watching her only to put them on equal footing. He was a man who liked to gain the upper hand, not have it given to him.

She also wondered if he'd watch for the break-in or wait to receive word from his systems. She'd bet on the latter. He'd want to play this fair, or else the win wouldn't be as sweet.

It was aggravating how well she knew him. Or was it that she understood him? If the situations were reversed, she'd want the same things.

Pulse.

A thin rod extended from her jacket. At the moment, she was carrying around a lot of extra weight, but each weapon had a purpose. After she used those with a specific job, like this one, she'd leave them behind.

The guard waited where she'd expected him to. What she hadn't expected was to find him wearing glasses and animatedly thrusting into empty space. He was clearly engaged in an erotic game or show of some kind, probably seeing a 3-D woman or man in front of him. His implant would be feeding him sensory details as though he were really in the moment.

She tiptoed behind him and stuck the rod against his back. His body convulsed, then spasmed, responding to the charge of electricity. After she pulled it away, he crumpled to the ground.

50% charge, her wrist screen read.

Enough charge for another go.

Pulse—disengage.

She dragged his body out of the hallway and then bent to retrieve the glasses. After seeing a paused image that made her intensely curious, she dropped the item onto his unconscious body and ducked behind the guard station. She entered the sequence of codes that would indiscriminately get her into the sleep area.

Beep.

Frowning at the noise, Millicent leaned closer to the console. An error code filled the screen. Tilting her head, she attempted to work around it.

Beep.

Biting her lip, she stood back for a moment and let both the process and error run through her head. Immediately she picked up on the problem. Then rolled her eyes. *Stupid.*

Her fingers flew across the screen as she pulled up various schematics from the breeding files. Finding a good candidate who was currently on meal break, she downloaded the information to her implant and waited impatiently while the new data was uploaded to her lenses. She should've prepared for this. Precious time was ticking by.

A moment later, the door to the sleeping area clicked. Unlocked.

Millicent's back braced against the wall for a moment as she exhaled evenly. Then she stepped into the room and rolled a custom-designed deadener, nothing more than a small orb, into the center of the space. Watching the numbers on her wrist screen count down, she waited until the right moment, and then stepped into the facility. All the electronics dimmed. Not off, just computing at one-millionth speed. So slow that the monitoring computers would assume it was a glitch and go into troubleshooting mood. She had five minutes.

Running through the foyer, she ducked into a little room with five large cribs. Fuzzy little heads lay within, squishing Millicent's heart. She wished she could take more. That she could give more of them a better life.

Someday. If I survive, someday I'll return.

Sniffling caught her focus. In the last crib, a little hand wiped the most beautiful face in all the world. Marie's cheeks glistened with tears in the dim light.

"*Shhhh,*" Millicent said as she reached into the crib.

Marie's top half darted up, and her eyes widened. The pacifier fell out of her mouth as she smiled and reached up. "Mom—"

A slap of palm on mouth muffled the word. With Millicent's free hand, she put a finger in front of her lips. "*Shhhh,* baby. We're leaving."

The joy dripped from Marie's face, replaced by seriousness. She nodded slowly as Millicent took her hand away and then reached down. A moment later, Mommy and baby were running through the foyer, the most perilous part of the journey having just begun.

The door closed behind her. Fifteen seconds later, a small burst concussed the air in the foyer. Millicent knew a loud beep would follow as the computer's systems got up and running. The logs would assume the troubleshooting feature had done its job. No warnings would be triggered, so no one would bother to investigate. That was, until hell crashed down on the facility when they realized one of the children was missing. Then they'd wonder how Millicent had done it. They'd never seen this kind of tech before.

Breathing heavily from the weight of both Marie and her artillery suit, Millicent struggled down the chosen corridor and then paused. She hadn't reset the retinal scan. They'd think she was the lab tech. So if she went down corridors that techs usually didn't use, or weren't allowed to use, she'd trigger security.

Shit, she thought, looking around for the nearest console. She couldn't hack in wirelessly from her implant. The building security was closed off on a private loop, for the most part. Plus, consoles were larger and easier to navigate.

"Get down for a minute, honey, but stay close," Millicent whispered.

Marie clutched on to her leg, and she half dragged her daughter up the corridor until she found the small red circle. Hitting that, she watched the console flare to life. The light bathed the corridor, illuminating a large figure five meters in front of her.

Mr. Gunner hadn't waited to be notified, it seemed. She never could read the man.

And now she'd have to kill him.

Chapter 11

"Ten-second head start?" Millicent asked, pushing her daughter behind her.

His face was solemn. "You did a few things wrong."

"I'm still on schedule."

He shook his head. "Give me the child." He reached for Marie.

Gun—right.

A sleek little five-shot pushed into her hand. She lifted and squeezed the trigger.

His arm swung up, knocking her gun.

The blast sounded. Ceiling rained down from the bullet.

Knife—belt.

A knife pushed out, and she snatched it as she yanked her gun hand back and shot at him again. His fist chopped down on her upper arm, sending the gun clattering across the floor.

She swung with the knife, aiming for his ribs. He jerked back. The blade sailed by his chest, just missing.

Heels.

She thrust the knife, missed, then stepped back and kicked. Her foot swiped along his side, barely opening a thin line of red. Still balanced, she drew her foot back and struck again, the heel traveling toward more vulnerable flesh.

He shifted and swung his forearm down, faster than a human should be. The jolt knocked her off balance.

She used it to her advantage, leaning into the fall and punching him in the kidney. Pain vibrated up her arm from the contact—he was also harder than a human should be.

This was not going well.

She switched hands with the knife and thrust. He blocked, which she was expecting. She thrust again, no more than a feint, and then threw her weight behind a slash. The blade barely touched his pec.

Damn it.

Lights flickered through the hall. Screens pulsed. Marie was getting agitated.

So was Millicent.

Gun—left.

She kicked out, aiming that spike for his thigh. He stepped forward and bent his leg, kneeing her in the calf. *Ouch.* Refusing to register the pain for long, she swiped again with the knife, kicked, and then brought her gun up.

His hands moved so fast she barely registered them. Suddenly her gun was gone.

A hand wrapped around her throat and shoved her toward the wall. Marie screamed. Millicent's back slammed against the hard surface, and her head bounced. He reached out and trapped her gunless hand. The light blared overhead. A glimmer infused his electric-blue eyes as he claimed victory.

Knife—right.

Millicent swung up, aiming for his vulnerable armpit.

"Careful, she's going to—"

Mr. Gunner twisted at the stranger's words. The knife grazed his skin.

He jogged back, out of her reach.

Breathing heavy, Millicent leaned forward, ready to try again. This was a fight for her daughter's life, and she would do anything. Then Mr. McAllister stepped away from the wall in the bright, harsh light, holding one of her guns.

"Look at you! You might've had me there." Mr. Gunner lifted his arm and looked at the smear of blood under his armpit. A smile graced his face as he checked the other couple of wounds she'd given him.

Eyeing the weapon held awkwardly in Mr. McAllister's hand, thankfully pointed toward the ground at the moment, Millicent slowly bent to retrieve her five-shot. Once it was in her hand, she straightened quickly.

"Careful, she's going to—"

"No, no, sweet pea, I'm on your side." Mr. Gunner cut off Mr. McAllister and raised his hands. "I'm here to help. I was trying to take Marie so I could carry her for you. You're out of your league."

"What?" She aimed the gun center mass, her finger heavy on the trigger. Mr. McAllister didn't raise the gun in his hand, thank Holy.

"That's a chick gun." Mr. Gunner put down his hands. The smile dripped off his face. "We have to go. I killed all the security staff in this section, and I noticed you applied your prison program to the outside staffers, but that gunshot and this light is going to bring someone sooner rather than later."

"You killed the . . . You're on my side?" Millicent said in bewilderment, finally catching her breath.

"Yes, Millicent. Always have been. Since day one." Mr. Gunner's eyes were deep and serious.

"I'm not on your side," Mr. McAllister said. "I've been kidnapped." He glanced at Marie before holding up a pink bunny. "But I brought Bunny in case you got scared, Marie."

"Bunny!" Marie stepped forward to grab the stuffed animal.

In a move that trapped Millicent's heart in her throat, Mr. Gunner stepped forward easily and scooped Marie up into his big arms.

"No, please." Millicent stepped forward helplessly. "Please."

He leaned toward her. "I'm on your side, Millie. I wasn't lying. I want to get you and Marie to safety."

"But . . . why'd you let me shoot?" She still hadn't lowered her shaking gun.

"I love foreplay in explosive women." He grinned and looked at Marie. "Your mama is crazy." Glancing back at Millicent, he jerked his head in the direction she had been going. "C'mon."

"His quest for danger is one of the more frustrating elements of his breeding," Mr. McAllister said in a sullen voice. "We are hoping Marie doesn't develop the same attributes."

"But you warned me away from this," Millicent said as she collected her weapons and returned them to their respective places.

"I needed to know this was the best plan of action," Mr. Gunner said. "For Marie. I trusted that you would put her first, and then choose accordingly."

"What about him?" Millicent pointed at Mr. McAllister, trying to make sense of all this. Trying to ascertain if Mr. Gunner was for real. If she could trust him as she hoped.

"He's here to keep Marie alive."

"You know, humans are remarkably durable," Mr. McAllister said, inching away. "I really don't think my limited expertise in medicinal biology outside of procreation will help should anything—"

"Shut up. You're coming." Mr. Gunner shifted Marie on his hip.

Mr. McAllister's shoulders bowed. "Yes, of course. Although, it is possible that we're all going to die."

"At least we'll get to see the sights before we do. Let's go."

A moment later, they were jogging down the silent corridors.

"Turn the lights off, Marie," Mr. McAllister said in a gentle voice. "Your mommy is safe."

"Since when did you acknowledge my real role in her life?" Millicent said as she checked her wrist screen. So far, Mr. Gunner was leading them in exactly the direction she had planned.

"Since I was taken hostage by a man who wants nothing more than to end my life as soon as I say something he doesn't like. I'd also like to point out that I don't run very fast, or for very long. I'm below the Curve in athletics. It would probably be best if you just left me behind . . ."

"*Shhhh.*" Mr. Gunner held out his hand for silence as they neared the front of the building. Beyond the check-in area, a single body lay facedown halfway between Millicent's waiting craft and the entrance. Mr. Gunner waited with Marie's arms tightly around his neck, her legs wrapped around his middle. She sure hadn't waited long to trust him, even though he'd just been fighting Millicent.

"Okay, we're—what? What's wrong?" Mr. Gunner paused near a corner, looking down at her.

"Nothing. Just wondering how you won her over so fast when she should be terrified of you."

"She's not nearly as jaded as you are. Let's go." Mr. Gunner jogged around the corner and then quickly crossed the open space.

"She is a child with survival in mind," Mr. McAllister whispered as they reached the bay. "I'm not sure which of you she gets it from. But she obviously senses that Ryker is her best bet against a physical attack."

"Ryker?" Millicent asked with a quirked brow.

"Thanks for ruining the surprise, bub," Ryker said as Millicent thought, *Open.* "I wanted to whisper it to her right before I took off her clothes."

"Oh." Mr. McAllister's face turned red. "My apologies. I'd thought . . ."

"She's playing hard to get."

"I'm not playing. Your chances are stuck on impossible." Millicent moved so the others could file in.

"We're saying the same thing, sweetheart. This thing have a trough for hot beverages? Or better yet, anything with a bite to it? I've had a long day." Ryker settled Marie into a seat and put Bunny solidly in her arms.

Millicent ignored him. "Who killed that guy?" She jerked her chin toward the heap of human right before the doors closed.

"I did when I got here," Ryker said. "He was on his way to inspect your craft. You'd missed one with your program."

"The craft would've checked out just fine."

"He'll never know."

"I am astounded," Mr. McAllister said. "The ingenuity of you two, not to mention your ability to work together, is . . . exceptional. This must be why I was warned against using people of your caliber in natural births. Although, in my defense, you did create a fantastic product."

Quick as lightning, Ryker grabbed Mr. McAllister by the throat and slammed him against the wall.

Fear twisted Mr. McAllister's features, and his hands flew out to the side. "Just to be clear, am I inside or outside your new protection bubble?"

Ryker's biceps bulged as he lifted Mr. McAllister off the ground. "You're lucky I didn't kill you along with the security staff."

"Outside of the bubble," Mr. McAllister wheezed. "I am outside. Got it."

"Dada, no." Marie buried her face into Bunny's light-pink fur.

Like melting wax, Ryker's muscles relaxed, and he slowly lowered Mr. McAllister to the ground. Ryker looked over at Marie, shock and adoration transforming his features. Something soft squished in Millicent's middle.

"Yes, she called you Dada," Mr. McAllister said, licking his lips. "I have no idea where she heard the term, but she knows you are, indeed, her father. I suspect she is able to access records, although she can't read yet, so I really have no idea—unless she saw your picture next to Milli—Ms. Foster's. In which case, her deductive reasoning at age—"

"Shut up," Ryker said, pushing Mr. McAllister out of the way.

"Yes, sir. Of course, sir." Mr. McAllister sank into a chair with a pale face. "But . . . if I may . . . I did treat her better than any child has been treated in that facility. All five of the children under my care. My superiors indulged me like they have indulged Marie and Ms. Foster. Marie, directly stemming from you two, with my enhancement, is the next leg in evolution. I am nearly certain. So I was given liberties with regards to hugging, additional story and play time, and other things that they usually wouldn't get. I—"

Ryker gave Mr. McAllister a *look* that finally shut him up. Then he stalked over and pushed Millicent away from the controls.

"What are you doing?" She shoved back, but moving him was about as easy as shooting him.

"We're meeting someone who will help us." His brow furrowed as he stared at the screen for a moment. "Here, put in these coordinates." He touched his wrist and then flicked. The information slid onto the screen in front of her.

"Who is this person?" Millicent said, waiting for him to step away before tracing the point on the map.

"He works for an organization that is aiming to tear down the conglomerate structure. Most of the work is for a good cause, but they do take money to fuel their efforts. That's where we come in."

"Can we trust him?"

"Yes. The leader of the organization is wanted by the conglomerates, as is everyone who works with him. It won't be pretty if any of them get picked up, especially the leader. Unlike them, the two of us would probably be mind wiped instead of killed. Especially when they trace some of the tech you've developed specifically for breaking out of their security. That won't make the conglomerates sleep easy, I can assure you."

"What about you? What have you done to save yourself except kill people?" she asked, finally putting in the destination.

"I've guided and manipulated you, not to mention kept tabs on your efforts. I bet I'm the only one to have accomplished that." Ryker sat down with a smug air before grabbing Marie around the middle and hauling her into his lap. He hugged her close with a protective arm around her.

"Just fantastic. It is as I said. Your sphere of protection has changed, now encompassing something like a family unit." Mr. McAllister scooted until he sat opposite Mr. Gunner, staring at him with excited eyes. The man had no sense of self-preservation. "We've come a long way from our time of swinging in trees, but certain instincts die hard. Humans will protect their young at all costs." He sat back and put an ankle over his knee. "I'd love to take notes."

"I'd love to rip your arm off for constantly causing my child and her mother aggravation, whatever your claims about fair treatment." Ryker's voice hadn't raised, but malice dripped off each syllable. Marie's arms tightened around his neck, and Mr. McAllister's lips formed a thin line.

"How have you guided, manipulated, or kept track of me?" Millicent settled into a chair near the door, just in case someone tried to stop the vessel and scuttle her daughter off of it.

"That security loop you've been accessing is illegal. And I've never stopped monitoring it."

Millicent's mouth dropped open. "But I pulled up the logs." Scrunching her nose in irritation, she swiped a console into the hologram in front of her. The air shimmered as the image solidified in the aisleway. "See? It says it hasn't been in use except by people who don't exist—my creations, obviously."

"I didn't say I've been using it, I said I've been monitoring it. I have a mirror program running that alerts me when activity has been logged. Being that I could never track the users, I knew it was you. No one else can get past this conglomerate's security without raising red flags.

I can see what you do when you go in and tamper. I knew about your message before it flashed across my wall. And yes, I had to look up the Latin. Although, half the surprises in my apartment were still surprises. You use a level of finesse I've never seen before. I think you should be tested against the Curve again."

Millicent waved the thought away. What did it matter? "That was an illegal loop?" she asked, somewhat mystified. "How did I not know that was possible?"

"Because you haven't spent a lifetime learning all the tricks."

"So how did you find out about it?" Mr. McAllister asked Millicent, with confusion evident.

"I wanted a private conversation, so I showed my hand." A grin teased Ryker's lips as he watched her. "I didn't realize she'd pick up on what I'd done so fast. I didn't install the mirror program until after she'd messed with my living space."

"You deserved it," Millicent said sullenly. "So what about guiding and manipulating?"

"Would you be here if not for me?" Ryker asked in seriousness.

"I don't know," she answered quietly. "I've been researching available solutions for the past year. You made certain things easier, I will admit."

"I rest my case." Ryker shifted with a smug smile.

Millicent rolled her eyes. "Oh, really? You randomly spout your mouth off, I happened to head in that direction when I could find no other alternative, and to you that constitutes guiding and manipulating?"

He shrugged. "Whatever works, princess. I got you here, and you can still breed. So can I. We can have as many children as we want."

"Oh, interesting." Mr. McAllister rested his chin on his fist.

"You're forgetting. Without a lab at your back, you'd need coitus to procreate, and I'm not interested." She held up a finger. "And if you try to force yourself on me, I will fry your chip, use your inability to move to my advantage, and cut your dick off. That'll end your breeding days for good."

A smile curled Ryker's lips. "I like when you talk violent. It gets my blood flowing."

"Not mine." Mr. McAllister crossed his legs. His face had gone a worrying shade of white.

"How much Clarity did you bring?" Ryker asked with twinkling eyes.

She blinked in the face of that knowing stare, realizing she hadn't even thought about it. All the doses were stored in her bedside table.

"Oops. Forgot those, huh?" Ryker stroked Marie's hair and said down to her, "Mommy is going to beg Daddy to give you a baby brother or sister. What do you think about that?"

"Don't say things like that to her." Millicent got the mad urge to jab forward with a knife. Being that her daughter was in the way, she was forced to refrain. "And I'm not the normal girl you find in a bar. I think I can resist your barbaric advances."

"I'm going to wrap you around my little finger, sweetheart. You'll never want to come up for air."

"This is making me a little uncomfortable." Mr. McAllister looked out the side window.

"What can we expect from our next stop?" Millicent asked, tired of her companion's monstrous ego and infallible confidence.

Thankfully, that wiped away Ryker's grin. He looked at his wrist. "This is the last bit of comfort we'll have for a while. Things are about to get hairy. We'll be traveling through the dump the conglomerate has created. Getting myself through is no problem. Getting a woman like you through—marginally harder. But with the baggage of a clumsy weakling and a small child, we won't have an easy time of it." His hard glare hit Millicent. "I need you hardened for this. You're softer than your paperwork says, and that's fine in general, but today I need the woman they bred to glorify their defensive might. I need the woman who has kept that company impregnable from the other two conglomerates. The woman the other conglomerates have sent people to kill three times. The one who retaliated for those attempts by creating huge holes in their infrastructure."

"Trust me—I'm way ahead of you." Millicent mentally checked all the horrors she'd prepared.

"The guy at the next stop is supposed to make us invisible to the conglomerate," Ryker said.

"How?" Millicent asked.

Ryker shook his head. "They have some tech that they've proven works."

"Not to be the bad guy or anything . . ." Mr. McAllister cleared his throat. "But how long do we have before they realize Marie is gone?"

"They'll have to do a physical check, which will be at dawn." Millicent worked her console.

"We don't have much time, then, right? Because as soon as they realize their biggest prize has been stolen by two expensive assets and the creative expert that brought it all together, they'll launch the largest manhunt we've ever seen."

"I didn't need the reminder . . ."

Chapter 12

"Let's get ready." Ryker put Marie in Mr. McAllister's arms and then leaned over them. "You'll guard her while I speak to our contact and Millie watches our rear. If you do anything stupid, particularly anything to jeopardize her, I will rip your insides out, got it?"

The sound of Mr. McAllister's gulp filled the room.

To Millicent, Ryker said, "Your suit can handle the weather, correct?"

"Yes. The reports say so anyway. I've never been outside."

Ryker flinched, and a look of pain crossed his face. "We're going to have a better life, okay? All of us."

"As long as Marie does, that's all I care about. Now stop being so sensitive and let's get going."

"I've never been outside, either . . . ," Mr. McAllister said.

Ryker ignored him. "Let's go."

The door opened onto a platform deep in the thick acidic fog. They were on the twentieth floor somewhere in the middle of the city. Hovercrafts large and small flew around them, using the multilayered travel ways. Harsh wind whipped across the open space, the cold in the air biting the exposed areas of Millicent's skin. She did a quick check to make sure the baby's wrappings would stay on, and then followed Ryker out. Immediately she peeled off to the side, seeing that he'd peeled off to the other side, and provided cover as the other two exited.

"Where to?" Millicent yelled above the thrush of environment and continual roar of the passing vehicles.

Ryker pointed with two fingers off to the right, indicating a sprawling ramshackle building with a failing roof and decaying walls.

Close.

The doors to her craft glided shut. Ryker started at a fast pace. Millicent pushed Mr. McAllister in front of her and followed him, trying to watch everything at once. Out in the open like this, with vantage points all around them, relying on the measly senses of a human was a terrible idea. They'd be captured before she even knew they'd been spotted. She needed to rig something up. A halo of some sort to deaden nearby tech and hide them beneath an electronic blocking canopy or something.

Sure, get all that going while running for your life in this pit of filth, with no tools or work pod. No problem.

"Through here." Ryker pointed them into a dark tunnel made out of rubble and bent metal.

Millicent eyed Ryker warily. She was putting a lot of faith in a man she could not, for the life of her, read. She was going solely on his word. The latest word, at that, since he'd verbally changed his stance a time or two.

"He won't do anything to harm you unless he develops a new bubble of protection," Mr. McAllister called above the environment's hum.

"Be quiet, you moron!" Millicent hissed.

"I just saw that you hesitat—"

Millicent slammed her gloved hand over his mouth.

Ryker waited for silence before leading the way into the murky darkness. They came to a fork made up of twisted metal with gleaming edges, the only thing in this rubble that looked moderately new. A purple-pink glow illuminated their surroundings as he checked his wrist screen. After a quick glance behind them, he headed right.

They took two more turns at forks, all made of that same engineered metal, and then slowed when the tunnel opened up into a moderate-sized space covered with piles of debris caught in some sort of fencing.

"Knock, knock," Ryker said in a voice that sent shivers up her back.

"Who's there?" A tall, lanky man skulked in from the left, holding a large orange gun with double barrels, like a shotgun on growth hormones.

"The big bad wolf. I've got a contract with Roe's people. You Jesse?"

A beam of light clicked on, highlighting swirling particles in the air. It flashed down to Ryker's face before playing across his shoulders and down his body. "Holy sh—" The light darted to the side, covering Millicent's face next. "Wow."

Ryker shifted, a tiny action that somehow spoke volumes and brought the light back to his body. "She with you?" Jesse asked.

"Yes."

"All right, man, take it easy. Just asking." The light swept over Mr. McAllister and then quickly highlighted Marie. Back to Ryker. "You're Tate?"

"Yeah. You need ID?"

"No. You got a kid. That's enough. Ain't no conglomerate operation going to risk a kid. Come with me."

He crossed the space and stepped through a normal-looking doorway into a room that smelled like mildew and sweaty socks. In the corner, a light highlighted various tech that looked like it had been retrieved from a recycling bin a decade ago. Jesse pointed to a chair next to the desk as he adjusted the light. Ryker picked up Marie and then motioned for Mr. McAllister to take the chair.

"Why? What's he going to do?" Mr. McAllister pulled his hands toward his chest and looked over the various instruments. "Is that rust?"

"I'm going to blank out your implant." Jesse picked up a block of metal before pushing a greenish button covered in dirt and grime.

"What does that mean—blank out the implant?" Millicent asked, studying the device.

"I just send electromagnetic pulses through it to fry it. Then it's out of commission. It doesn't hurt." Jesse pushed a chair on rollers to the edge of his desk. He pointed. "Sit."

"How long have you been using that system?" Millicent couldn't help the wonder in her voice. Before Ryker's experience, she hadn't known it was possible for an implant to short out and go offline. It had simply never occurred to her.

"I don't know. Long as I been doing this. C'mon. We gotta get going." Jesse waved Mr. McAllister forward.

"No." Millicent put out a hand to stop the progress. "That's not going to work. Even if the glitch you're exploiting wasn't fixed—at least as far as your old apparatus is concerned—we can't go offline. Ry—Tate's implant shorted once, and while they waited for him to come back online that time, they logged an alert. I checked. His implant and mine going offline together, added to a birthing tech's . . . no. With my behavior this week regarding Marie—the child—they won't wait this time, I'm sure of it. They'll check it out. Not to mention we are faster and more efficient when we have use of our implants. No, this is not the best approach."

Jesse sighed dramatically and leaned his elbow against the desk. "Look. They got hundreds of thousands of workers in this area alone. They got faulty tech beeping on and off, they got people getting shocked left and right—they won't get to it for months, and by that time, we'll have it out of your head. We're fine. Trust me. I do this all the time."

"Trust *me*, your solution will shave hours off our timetable, and we're pressed for time as it is."

"Look, lady, I know this is scary, but—"

Millicent pushed an ancient decrypter out of the way and surveyed the other instruments on the table. "Can you access the net through a nontraceable source? I'll fix the issue."

Jesse's eyes widened as the light more thoroughly highlighted her face. "You're—" He spun and grabbed the light, shining it back toward Ryker. "You both are natural born, aren't you? What the Holy Divine is Roe thinking?" Jessie backed away from the desk, his hands out. "No. I can't do this. This is out of my league. They're going to be looking for you!"

A roar sounded above them. The floor and walls shook before the vehicle passed.

"I have what you lack," Millicent said. "I just need a way to access their implants. After that, they can't track us. At least not until they break through my coding."

"Can't you do it from your craft?" Ryker asked.

"That craft's console runs from the conglomerate's net. I can disguise its log-on port and change the log-on location, but all of that takes time. Time I'd rather not lose. It'd be easier if we could do it from a completely foreign source. One that is hopefully set up outside of the conglomerate's loop."

"Loop?" Jesse said.

"Intranet," she clarified.

"But they can track us here." Mr. McAllister gestured between himself and Ryker. "So what's the difference if your craft logs in? It's just another arrow pointing to us until you get it shut down."

"I already have to change your information, Mr. McAllister. Erasing your last locations will not be a big to-do. But my craft is one more entity we need to fix." Millicent checked her wrist. The numbers flashed, and anxiety pressed on her, making her movements jerky. The shift change happened in three hours, but she had every reason to suspect it wouldn't take that long. Not with all the dead bodies lying around the facility, thanks to Ryker. "Just do as you're told."

"I can get you online, but even if you shut your implants down, they can still scan for your face," Jesse said. "If they can't reach your implants, they'll have security monitor for your face."

Millicent waved the thought away. "Obviously I'll take care of that problem, too."

"He doesn't often meet people who are three clicks above the Curve, princess." Ryker's teasing tone didn't alter his stern expression. "Now let's get this done. We need to be long gone to the next thing."

"I can't be that next thing, bro-yo." Jesse pulled the heavy device into the middle of the desk. He connected a cord and then yanked a flat rectangular pad in front. He pressed something at the top. Light filtered up from the screen, creating a splotchy hologram above it. The glowing rectangle filled with little squares showing characters. "I can't help you. You'd constantly be doing this arguing shit and I wouldn't be able to keep up."

Millicent waited for Jesse to move out of the way before she took the chair and prodded the keyboard. "This stuff is so far out of date it belongs in a museum."

"See what I mean?" Jesse mumbled, snatching a device as big as his hand from the desk. "That's only ten years out. I took it before I left the conglomerate."

"How long ago did you leave?"

"A couple years. Why?"

Millicent frowned. "I wonder why they didn't install recent tech to your department. It was a waste of time having you use this."

"We're not royalty like you are."

Ryker's laughter filled the room.

"Yes, give him more ammunition for pet names. Great." Millicent let her hands fly over the keyboard, logging in through a strange network she'd never seen before. She worked around the various conglomerate firewalls.

"Holy—" Jesse leaned down next to her, his mouth dropping at the sight of the code scrolling through the air within the hologram. "Wait." His touch on her wrist had her jerking away. He did a few keystrokes, turning on the tracking feature. "Okay. Go for it. I don't think I could ever learn this, but we got a couple people who might."

"Doubtful," Ryker said. "I got a strange vibration over here." He touched the skin behind his ear where his implant was lodged.

"I'm just uploading my changes before I close your loop and disguise your signal." Unused to typing, Millicent frowned down at the rectangular tech. It was slowing her down.

The roar sounded above them before moaning down into the floor. The metal jiggled on the table. "What is that?" Millicent asked.

"Shipping vessel passing too close," Jesse said. "That's why this whole place is just a trash heap, really. Why there's no building here. One of those vessels plowed into it at one point."

Millicent glanced upward. As if they needed another reason to get the hell out of there.

"But anyway, if your implants are still giving a signal, they can track you if they get through your code," Jesse said.

"Can they break it?" Ryker asked, looking over Millicent's shoulder before checking his wrist.

She pushed harder, feeling the time drain away. "Eventually," Millicent said.

"How long?"

Millicent pulled up Mr. McAllister's information. "If they got my best people on it, they'd probably bring me down in a month, two if they didn't have someone riding them."

"They'll have someone riding them," Ryker said in a heavy tone.

"But if they're desperate, they can negotiate for the senior director of Gregon Corp. It'd be expensive, but . . ."

"That's your biggest competitor?" Ryker asked.

"Yes. She's my equal in skill. She'd hack through this in a couple days. I spent a lot of time devising cobwebs and false paths, but she's excellent. She'd break it."

"Wait." Jesse held up his hand, fear and awe warring across his face. "Are you telling me that you're Ms. Foster? *The* Ms. Foster? No." He scoffed, taking a few steps toward the door. "I don't believe this. You're . . . You are a legend." He shook his head. "No way is Roe going to help you. I'm sorry to be the bearer of bad news, but you're too high priority."

"I'm Tate. This is Joyce. That's all you need to tell him," Ryker said in a harsh tone. "We're getting off this rock, and your people are going to take our money to do it. Got it?"

"Yes, sir. Tate. No problem, sir." He picked his nail and glanced at Ryker. "Who are you, though? Just so I can say I met you . . ."

"Ryker Gunner."

"Oh shit." Jesse blew out a breath before running his fingers through his hair. "What do you need us for, bro-yo? Who can they possibly send after you?"

"Mr. Hunt," Ryker said in a low, rough tone. "And he won't want to take me alive."

"This is done." Millicent smoothed her hair, a force of habit, as she stood from the desk.

"All right, well . . ." Jesse bent to the blank glow of the clunky hologram screen. "You gotta get to Roe. He's the only one who can do this." Jesse glanced back at Millicent. She stepped forward, getting her wrist in closer proximity to the older machine. Jesse flicked his finger between the hologram and her wrist screen. A name and coordinates flashed along her skin. "Go to that spot to meet him. It's down in Los Angeles. You just gotta get yourself down there. It's on the way anyway. The rocket shuttle leaves from Old Mexico, where the weather is a bit more stable and the conglomerates don't have any departments set up."

"How would you have taken us?" Millicent asked.

"I would've loaded you into the shuttle craft going from here to Old Mexico. But one in ten times, security randomly scans the craft and catches everyone. Show's over then. Back to the grind. With you at large, they'll check everyone leaving San Francisco. Ain't no way to sneak out of the Wall if they're checking. So . . ."

"They'll be looking for your vessel," Ryker said to Millicent.

"Then let's get out of here while we have the jump on them. After that . . . we'll have to figure it out."

"Wait, you need this." Jesse handed each of them a small metal box decorated with scratches and dings. "It's for the retinal scans. Makes you invisible from the conglomerates, but it'll alert Roe's people to who you are if they're looking. Which they will be, since I'll send word."

"Invisible . . ." The lid squeaked as Millicent opened the small case. She'd changed their identities, which could still be tracked unless routinely changed, but becoming invisible to the scanners was another thing entirely. This alone had made this meeting worthwhile. "I should've known to do this. It's much more efficient in the long run."

"Can't know everything, sweetheart. That's why you need to let the big dogs help you out." Ryker darted his finger into his eye.

"And I suppose you are the big dog, hmm?" Millicent applied hers quickly and then moved on to Marie. "Are you suggesting I couldn't have gotten this far without you?"

"You would've tripped an alarm back at that lab. They had laser censors. Your rescue mission would've been over before it began." Ryker dotted his other eye.

Millicent paused in her attempt to get the eye cover on the struggling eighteen-month-old. Ryker was there a moment later, picking up the slack as Millicent processed that information, thinking back on all the careful planning that would've been in vain. "I thought I caught all their security functions."

"Don't beat yourself up. I needed you to take down the security in the sleeping area. Hold still, Marie. Hold—ow!" Ryker snatched his hand away from Marie's bite.

"At least we know where she gets that. Hold still, honey."

"I'll give you a piece of candy if you hold still," Mr. McAllister said, moving closer.

Marie's struggles lessened, and her little face peeked out from behind Ryker's large arm and looked at Mr. McAllister. "Candy?"

"You have to bribe her," Mr. McAllister said, patting himself down. "Just as soon as we get where we're going, I'll give you candy. Just hold still while your daddy puts that thing on your eye, okay? It won't hurt."

"And that's why I brought him." Ryker moved in while Marie was still.

The bribe only lasted until the apparatus actually touched her eye. She had to be held down to get the other one in. Obviously candy only went so far.

After the battle, Ryker fastened Marie's goggles and adjusted her on his hip. "Okay. We go."

"Good luck. I hope you guys make it," Jesse called as Millicent led the way out of the tunnels.

The harsh environment met them as they emerged onto the open platform. Millicent glanced behind her at the scarred and mangled edges of the building. Behind it rose other enormous high-rises, reaching into the sky with sleek lines but battered and filth-smeared sides. "It's like a different world down here."

"Just hope you don't have to go any lower. It gets worse." Ryker looked upward. Off to the east, a faint gray was bleeding through the black. "We've been too long. The conglomerate is going to—"

A siren ripped through their surroundings, ringing over the city and bouncing off the walls. It rained down on them, cutting Ryker off.

Open. Millicent ran to her vessel. *Open!* She reached the side of the closed craft and palmed open the outside controls.

Before she could make any keystrokes, she heard Mr. McAllister say in an urgent voice, "Open the door, Marie."

A moment later, without Marie so much as moving, the locks disengaged and the doors swung open.

"Is that the tsunami siren?" Mr. McAllister asked in an elevated voice as he followed Ryker and Marie inside.

"Yes." Millicent's voice, pitched for the chaotic outdoors, sounded like a yell as the doors closed. She brought up the vessel's controls. "They test it at noon on the first Tuesday of the month. Being that it's not the first Tuesday of the month, and not noon, I can only imagine they've realized three of their prized assets are gone." That word tasted bitter in Millicent's mouth. She'd created nothing more than property for the conglomerate. She *was* nothing more than property. Expensive property, sure, but a type of slave nonetheless. "When did it become acceptable for a company to breed their workers?"

"Welcome to independent thought, princess." Ryker stared out the clear window at the rolling fog. "We have to get going. This party is about to get started."

"We gave the conglomerates that power when we let them have control over the incubators," Mr. McAllister said. "Laws kept them at bay, but when their power outstripped the government's, they started making their own laws. Or *rules* as they call them. It's boiling a frog."

"What does a frog have to do with anything?" Millicent jabbed the screen. "It won't take these coordinates!"

"Move over, love, let the big dog at it."

"The old adage was that if you dropped a frog in boiling water, it would jump out." Mr. McAllister looked out the window anxiously. "But if you put the frog in warm water and gradually turned up the heat, the frog would bear it, and bear it, and before you knew it, the water would boil and it would be dead."

"Here we go," Ryker said. The vessel lightly shuddered as it drifted away from the platform.

"What'd you do?" Millicent looked around his arm at the control log.

"This is a conglomerate-issued town vessel. It's not programmed to leave city limits. Once we get to the Wall, we'll have to work the manual override."

"Another thing I should've known. It just never occurred to me . . ." Millicent stripped off her gloves, something uncomfortable settling in the pit of her stomach. "I never would've made it."

Ryker's touch on her back made her flinch before she settled, taking comfort from his firm rubbing. "We've got this," he said. "What I can't do, you can. And vice versa. We'll make it."

"It really was genius to pair you two up," Mr. McAllister said, watching them. "You fit perfectly, and nature chose for Marie perfectly. I'm definitely in line for a promotion. Assuming they don't kill me while trying to reel you two in."

"Your profile is flagged," Millicent said, her eyes drifting closed as fatigue battled her awareness. "You might have great ideas, but apparently that's not worthy of a promotion. You're as high now as you'll ever go. At least in titles. So am I. So is Ryker. Unless they boil another frog."

"No. Not boil—" Mr. McAllister rubbed his eyes. "They are taking our control little by little, and we're letting them do it because each little infraction doesn't affect us that much. Especially now that they basically own all of us. We're merely worker drones with cognitive ability. And I'm flagged? But . . . I made a huge advancement."

"Promotions aren't about advancements, they're about politics," Ryker said, his hand roaming over Millicent's shoulder. His fingers trailed across her collarbone before pulling her against his body. Tingles worked across her skin and infused in her middle before dissolving down lower. This time Clarity didn't stop the warmth that felt like a fuzzy heater right behind her rib cage, a feeling as lovely as it was annoying, given whom it stemmed from.

Before she could shrug him off, he said, "Marie, come here." He held out his hand for the little girl. She jumped off the seat and skittered across the scant meter separating them before crawling onto his lap and curling up against Millicent.

"Foul play," Millicent said, settling into the hollow between his arm and his chest. The warmth surged inside her as his arm squeezed her closer.

"Just trying to boil the frog." His deep voice rumbled low in his chest, and his heart beat against her ear.

"I shouldn't have said anything," Mr. McAllister mumbled. "I sure wish I was in that bubble . . ."

"I'm not that kinda guy, bub," Ryker said in a growl.

The vessel shook and then stopped, jerking everyone. Ryker surged up and placed Marie next to Mr. McAllister. Outside, surrounding them, were eight striped vessels, their guns bared and pointing at Millicent's craft.

Chapter 13

"How is that possible?" Millicent jumped up, trying to see around Ryker to the controls.

"Security will be boarding your vessel," a voice boomed around them. "Surrender and no one will get hurt."

"They must have some other way to track this craft," Ryker said, his hands moving rapidly. "I see that you disguised the signal, but—"

"I didn't change the recognition plates. Damn it!" Millicent slapped the wall.

"What does that mean?" Mr. McAllister raised his hands, facing the window. "Are these windows bulletproof?"

"It means that the cameras could identify us. Like face-recognition software, but for personal transport." She shoved Ryker. "We're just going to have to resort to plan B. And yes, this craft is mostly bulletproof."

"What's plan B?" Ryker asked.

Millicent didn't have time to answer. The vessel jolted and then tipped, spilling Mr. McAllister and Millicent to the floor. It yanked back up, making Millicent bounce. Ryker took two steps to the front and banged the partition button with his fist. The gray partition slipped into the wall, revealing an assortment of buttons and lights on the dash. A leather chair hulked in front of a steering column and a throttle. "They really looked after you, princess. This is a mighty fine machine."

"They didn't look after me, they slammed me into a gilded cage." Millicent climbed to her feet. "And plan B is doing what I do best— cutting out their tech and then blasting them out of the sky." Millicent braced herself as she accessed the weapons bay. "I am in the major defense systems department after all. I wouldn't represent my department very well if I allowed something as trite as the local security enforcement to hold me down."

"Attagirl." Ryker slipped into the seat. "Strap Marie in. It's about to get real."

"Put your vessel online and prepare for entry," the voice boomed again.

"How are you going to cut out their tech?" Mr. McAllister asked, rising on obviously wobbly legs. His hands were still in the air. "And what do you mean *mostly* bulletproof?"

"I may be in weapons, but I'm also an expert with systems. If there was a Holy Divine of vessels, this would be it. Hold on to your wits. We're about to show our hand." Millicent logged on.

Immediately a voice sounded within the cabin, "Please cease all activities, miss. The local security enforcement would like a word with you."

"What a lovely helper," Ryker said. "I'm ready when you are, Millie."

"We don't need to be on manual?" she yelled up front.

"I beg your pardon, miss?" the computer said.

"Humor me," Ryker said. "Now bring out the big guns."

Millicent sliced through the conglomerate's efforts to get the vessel back online, unraveled their restrictive code, and accessed their mainframe. All the security vessels were online except one, and that one was directly above them, outside the reach of Millicent's weapons.

"How could you possibly have known the crafts weren't all online?" she yelled up to Ryker.

"Mr. Hunt and I were trained in the same place. Does the *mostly* bulletproof include shock shells?"

"No. But this does." Millicent typed, "START unleash_hell.exe," then hit "Execute."

A wave of concussion smacked into the neighboring crafts. The moan of hydraulics through Millicent's craft announced the smart guns extending from the base.

"Cease and desist," they heard over the loudspeaker.

"I have been asked to tell you that you are under arrest, miss," the computer said. "I do so apologize."

"Very lovely," Ryker said, swinging the vessel around. Millicent held on to a rail, barely stopping herself from spilling onto the floor again. "There we go. Wow. Look at you! Quite an arsenal."

"You have access up there. Shoot them out of the sky," Millicent yelled, back at the console. "I'm about to send another concussion. It'll fry their guided controls, forcing them to go to manual. You need to blast holes in them before I cut their electrical power. Make it so they can't use the fossil fuel reserves to chase us when they get back online."

"Woo-wee. Mr. Hunt doesn't have a Ms. Foster on his side. I could get used to this."

"He might be a little too gleeful in the face of immediate death," Mr. McAllister muttered. "That wasn't properly relayed in his file."

"Cease and desist," they heard again.

Another pulse rocketed out from Millicent's craft, bigger this time. Harder.

Like boats in a squall, the security vessels rocked and jolted. Through the windows, Millicent watched as the men and women inside them were thrown to the ground.

A rattle of explosives sounded before streams of fire left the vessel. Dents and then holes opened up at the base of the security crafts. Smoke filled the sky.

"Go, princess. Go, go, go!" Ryker yelled. The craft dipped as a gun extended from one of the security vessels. "They've been given the order to take us down. Hit 'em now!"

"Got it." After Millicent executed the next program, she leaned to look out the window. The lights on the other crafts flickered. Another round of furious fire blasted from her vessel. And then the glow of security crafts cut out. Like stones, they dropped from the sky.

"I do not like knowing these things can so easily lose hovering ability," Mr. McAllister said in a thick tone. He rose up in his seat, clearly trying to get a better look out the window.

"Not easy. We just have a genius aboard. Now for Mr. Hunt. Hang on." Ryker's hands flew across the controls before gripping the wheel.

"Three geniuses, actually." Mr. McAllister gripped the seat tightly. Marie, next to him, clutched Bunny and dug her face into his fur.

The craft lurched forward. Millicent slammed against the wall before sliding. She fell across the seat.

"Are you running?" she asked Ryker, struggling to right herself.

"Yes. He would expect me to turn and fight. So I'm leading him on a chase."

"I would expect you to turn and fight," Mr. McAllister said through clenched teeth. "Why didn't his craft fall?"

"I don't know," Millicent said, strapping herself in and palming the console to the hologram. "It should've."

"He was already on fossil fuel. Clearly he knows what you're capable of. He paid attention when he was guarding you." Ryker's big body leaned right. The craft tilted dangerously. A horn blared as a vessel passed by the window.

"Oh shi—" Mr. McAllister closed his eyes and snatched Marie's hand. "It'll be okay, Marie. Just hang on. He knows what he's doing."

"One would hope," Millicent muttered, pulling up the rear camera. "He's gaining!" A flat gray vessel inched toward them. In the window sat a stoic Mr. Hunt, his face the normal mask of severity and his movements easy and precise.

"He's got a faster vessel, the weasel. Who'd he blow to get that?" Ryker leaned left. The corner of a building sailed five meters from the window.

"I can see their faces. Oh Holy Divine, I just saw their faces through the window. We're too close to the buildings." Mr. McAllister squeezed his eyes shut.

"I got this." Ryker leaned right. And then forward.

With a sickening lurch, they dived. The craft shook as it cut through the exhaust of a passing vessel. Another craft sped toward them. A honk, then a few more, drowned out the sound of the whining motor.

"You got anything that can pierce his armor?" Ryker called back.

The vessel tilted horribly, still pointed straight down, cutting through the travel ways.

Millicent's stomach rolled. The strap dug painfully into her hips. Somehow she kept her fingers moving. She kept blocking the attempts from the conglomerate to control her vehicle as she worked through her arsenal for the best rear gun. "I got something. How long until we hit the ground?"

"You got a couple minutes before we reach the cheaper crafts. They don't dodge debris as quickly," Ryker yelled back.

"He's referring to us as debris. This can't end well." Mr. McAllister made a circle around his chest. Millicent had no idea what organized religion that stemmed from.

"Put your big-boy pants on, Mr. McAllister," Millicent muttered as she chose something that would blow the side out of Mr. Hunt's craft. "Because we're not done yet."

"I'm going to wet my big-boy pants, actually," Mr. McAllister whined. "I hope this suit absorbs bodily fluid like it's supposed to."

"Prepare to brake," Millicent yelled. "I'm about to unleash a lot of firepower."

"Braking is for wimps!" Ryker's tone still sounded gleeful.

Millicent executed the weapon. Thunder rolled through the floor before a blast shook them. They surged forward even faster. A horn sounded right before a loud metallic scrape screeched up the right side of the craft. Ryker swore, but Millicent didn't take her eyes off the image behind her. The cartridge punched through the lower right of Mr. Hunt's vessel, distorting the metal and exposing the guts of the craft. Sparks shot out before a black streak of smoke twisted away from the gaping hole.

Millicent could barely make out Mr. Hunt's eyes widening and his mouth gaping before the craft banked hard right. The nose crashed into a building. Glass flew out in an eruption before a ball of fire spit into the travel way. The craft fell away and then teetered, lowering like a feather falling off a bird.

"I don't think I killed him." Millicent half swallowed the words as her vehicle swung left so fast it felt like her stomach fell out of her body and rolled around on the ground. The world crushed down on her as they swooped up, now climbing into the sky.

Childlike laughter competed with Mr. McAllister's screaming.

"Definitely her father's daughter," Millicent said, gripping the seat.

Like flicking a switch, all her organs were returned to her. At least, that's what it felt like when the craft pulled into the shadow of a building and idled. The dull light of the morning illuminated the gray overhead. Rain sprinkled down onto the glass windows. Heavy panting drifted through the now-quiet vessel.

"Okay." Ryker stood easily and walked toward them, acting like they hadn't just barely evaded death. "Get us offline. And then we need to steal a vessel."

Millicent, shaking with all the adrenaline pumping through her blood, took a deep breath. "I'll make sure the cameras can't recognize us. And it looks like the factory installed some sort of beacon in this thing. They really wanted to keep track of me. But just like everything else, it can be worked around."

"Until they hire that other staffer," Mr. McAllister said. He wiped the sweat off his brow, which was worryingly pale, and then wiped his glistening fingers on his pants.

"Sweating problem, huh?" Ryker covered Mr. McAllister's shoulder in heavy pats. "You made it. You're alive." He then brushed Marie's hair from her face. "How about you, little lady? Okay?"

"Yes, Daddy." She smiled.

"Okay. And how's Mommy?" Ryker looked Millicent over.

She sighed and sat back before shutting off the hologram. "Tired. Mr. Hunt is . . . tenacious."

"Yes." Ryker bent before running his fingers down the side of her face. "You're getting used to my touch. Won't be long now."

"Get"—she slapped his hand away—"off."

"They also failed to document just how sexual Mr. Gunner is," Mr. McAllister said, frowning.

"I'm in the presence of a beautiful woman." Ryker stretched, the muscles flaring down his sides. "What else am I supposed to think about?"

"Oh, I don't know, survival?" Mr. McAllister unbuckled himself and stood. He staggered across the aisle before bracing on the wall. "Can you give me back, now? I'm not cut out for this."

Ryker ignored him and looked at Millicent. "If you took out the last of the tracking on this vessel—and you're sure—do we still need to switch it out?"

"I have it covered until, like Mr. McAllister said, that other staffer is put on my tail," Millicent responded. "After that chase through the city, I bet that happens sooner rather than later."

"That's what I was thinking." Ryker glanced out the window. "What about their checkpoints leading out of the city? What will they find when they scan this vessel?"

"They'll find a craft about to be stripped down for parts because the electrical infrastructure is toast. I have a feeling that'll match the look of the outside. I doubt anyone in the lower-paid brackets will question the computers. The Curve huggers won't think the system can be hacked. If they physically look in here, though . . ."

Ryker shrugged. "They'll die, and then we'll have another shoot-out. They won't be able to properly arm themselves against this rig in just a couple hours. Nothing local is big enough. Which is why I'd love to keep it if you're certain we can hide from their tech."

"We can make it past security, but I no longer have any idea if we can make it off-planet."

"Keep the faith, cupcake. We got this." Ryker worked at the controls. "Okay. I'll set the coordinates for the exit point. Once we pass outside the city, we'll have to go manual. Now, c'mere, Millie." Ryker turned away from the console before settling onto the seat next to her. The craft drifted away from the wall, moving into the flow of traffic. "Let's get some shut-eye before the next big thing."

"I'm perfectly capable of—"

"You, too, baby." Ryker reached out to Marie. "Cuddle up. Let's go."

"A little militant," Mr. McAllister mumbled, sitting back in his seat and crossing his arms over his chest. He'd lapsed into an eternally bad mood.

Millicent prevented herself from admitting that Ryker's warmth, coupled with the strong arm braced around her protectively, was comforting. She also refused to admit that having her child curled up on his lap, snuggling into the area where Ryker's and Millicent's bodies touched, gave her the most solid, grounded feeling she'd ever experienced. And she certainly wouldn't acknowledge the soft, peaceful bliss that settled into her core as they huddled together, merging into a type of family unit that didn't exist in this world. If she did admit to any of that, she'd also have to notice the dull tingle deep in her body that felt like it was awaking from a slumber. Ryker's advances were bad enough now—if he thought she was coming around, he'd be incorrigible.

One thing did niggle at her, though. "If I can get pregnant, wouldn't it create a problem if I were sexually active?"

"Breeders who stop taking Clarity, or who develop an interest in the opposite sex, are then put on birth prevention," Mr. McAllister said as his eyes drooped. "We monitor breeders religiously. Some, like Ryker, for example, are given the birth prevention through their food—"

"What's that?" Ryker said as he tensed. His muscles pushed at Millicent's head.

"They do not realize they are infertile," Mr. McAllister continued. "And as such, do not try to thwart our efforts. That's only a select few, of course. Mostly women who would like to procreate. I think Ryker is one of only three men. Most of the time it's not a big deal. Staffers typically follow the rules."

"Which child is Mr. Hunt's?" Millicent asked, banging on Ryker's muscles to get him to relax. The bulging was uncomfortable.

"Oh no, he isn't eligible for a natural breeding. He is much too unpredictable. And quite frankly, a little ugly, if I'm being honest. No, no. We don't need another Mr. Hunt. The quest for brutality had to be scaled back after him. Although, I think they got it right with Mr. Gunner—Ryker. He's just the right amount of hard and soft."

"I'm not soft," Ryker said, his deep voice vibrating against Millicent.

"You said the word *cuddle* and you are currently holding two females in a loving-type way that does not include sexuality. Mr. Hunt would not do that. He'd snap the neck of one and force the other. Oh no, nature went badly wrong with him. He's forced to take Clarity, and is monitored anytime he is around an important staffer."

"Yet you let him near the children," Millicent said.

"Not near. He was only allowed to monitor the premises, something he is excellent at."

"Do you still use him for lab-born children?" Millicent asked.

"Despite some of the traits that went wrong, some did go right. We try to extract those, and if the offspring leans too heavily toward being a sociopath, we terminate him or her."

Bulges of muscle pushed at her again. "You are in a disgusting department," Ryker said in a level voice. "You should all be killed."

"And there's the hard side of him . . ." Mr. McAllister's eyebrows pulled tight. "It's for the betterment of everyone to terminate sociopaths. They really can create problems."

"Yet you knowingly bred one."

"As I said, he does have some good qualities . . ." Mr. McAllister shrugged helplessly.

Millicent closed her eyes and hugged Marie tight. "For now, I'm just glad I got to breed."

"For now?" Ryker whispered, his breath stirring her hair.

"What's going on can't continue. Something has to be done about the amount of power the conglomerates have."

Chapter 14

"Security screen."

Millicent huddled with Marie in the cockpit of the craft behind the closed partition. They were waiting in a line leading up to what was popularly called the Wall, a fifty-story building that crawled across the ground and reached out to the sea. It acted as a barrier between the conglomerate's staffers and the unemployed. At least, those who were unemployed by the three major conglomerates that firmly held the reins of power.

"Need to come aboard," a security staffer said over the loudspeaker as they slowed next to the guard station. "This is a visual screen. We're screening everyone." His voice sounded bored. He must've said the same words a thousand times since dawn. "Open up. We need to visibly—oh!" Surprise infused the last word. The security staffer probably recognized the build of Ryker if not his face. "Sorry, sir. Um . . . I didn't get a report that you would be coming through . . ."

"This craft is being sent to the Los Angeles office." Ryker's voice drifted through the partition. "It was caught up in that issue earlier."

"Sir?"

"You didn't hear?"

"No, sir. Our next briefing isn't until noon, sir."

"I thought this would've been pushed through. Anyway, no matter. This and that are going to the recycling yard."

"That, sir? You mean . . ."

"Yes. The male."

A pregnant pause filled the room. It seemed the staffer was hoping to get more information, and it was quickly becoming evident it wasn't going to happen.

"Okay, sir." A throat cleared. "I'll pass you through. Be careful through the barren stretch. It's gotten rougher over these past few months."

"I'm not worried about it."

"No, sir." Heavy treads sounded before the gush of sliding doors announced the man's exit.

"That was too easy," Ryker said as the Wall rose up around them. The vessel passed through and then idled. The partition opened, revealing Ryker standing before them. "Crawl back. Stay low."

"Go, go, go." Millicent got the baby scooting into the main room before crawling in after her. Mr. McAllister lay on the seat, his eyes closed but his brow furrowed. "I hope your brow wasn't furrowed the whole time," she said.

It furrowed further. "Doesn't matter, we're through. But they'll remember Ryker. As soon as they hear what happened, they'll remember this meeting. They'll know we came this way."

"Why haven't the security on the Wall been alerted to what happened?" Ryker wondered.

"Who would tell them?" Millicent saw scraping along the sides of the building as they passed. Deep grooves and pockmarks that were undoubtedly related to the many broken windows and jagged glass. This part of the Wall certainly wasn't used for offices. "The order would need to come from the director's office, right? Mr. Hunt is busy, and you're here. Who else is there? Trust me, when the boss is away, the staffers do nothing."

"Play."

"What?"

Mr. McAllister's eyes drifted open. "When the boss is away, the staffers play. It's supposed to rhyme."

"Why?" Millicent asked. "They weren't playing when I was gone. They were just idling around, useless."

"Is this a frog situation?" Ryker called from the front as a groan shivered through the vessel.

"I may not have tested as high as you two, but I certainly have some things you lack . . ." Mr. McAllister closed his eyes again.

A deep chuckle sounded from the front. Then Ryker said, "We're clear. But this craft does not like leaving the city. Maybe we should've switched out."

"Think it'll make it?" Millicent rose up off the floor. Hazy brown fog engulfed the building behind them as the craft drifted away. In their wake, the structure looked like an enormous wall, solid and forbidding.

Hence the name, she thought to herself dryly.

"It'll make it." Ryker's voice was level.

"So you're not always overconfident. Hmm." Millicent gathered Marie up and sat.

"How do you figure?" Ryker asked.

"The level voice. It's a giveaway. No tone out of you means you're unsure. You've shown your hand."

Silence from the front.

Mr. McAllister crossed his hands over his chest but kept his eyes shut. "I am so tired. And you know what, I liked my life. I had an okay thing going. Nice place to live without roommates, decent income, I got to play with children and see them grow . . . And now here I am, hungry, tired, constantly in danger, and caught in a small space with overly smart natural borns who are annoyingly street savvy, stupidly resourceful, and too pretty for their own good. Worse, my Clarity has run out. I hope I won't be as bad as Mr. Gunner . . ."

"You touch her and I will kill you with a palm and five fingers. How's that sound?" Ryker said in a voice with plenty of tone.

"Super. Now I'll be laying here trying to figure out why you specified the details of your hand when describing my death. Just one more terrifying thing to solidify this as the worst day of my life." Mr. McAllister's brow furrowed even more, if that was possible.

"I do think we broke your brain, Trent," Ryker said lightly.

Outside the city, the landscape changed drastically. Decrepit buildings hunkered down with grime coating their surfaces and piles of debris lining the base of their walls. Crisscrossings of cracked and puckered cement ran along the ground, often with metal rods sticking out at odd angles. Rectangular dwellings layered the rolling hills to the east, and fields of black and broken solar panels lined the valley.

"Oh wow, there's movement down there," Millicent said, using her vessel's cameras to look below. Hunched figures moved about on the ground, often covering themselves with a tarp or umbrella.

"The poor don't have flying crafts," Ryker said before ripping the top off a food pouch. He squeezed the container. Thick brown gel filled his mouth. "I hope you brought enough food. I'm hungry."

"I'm stocked." A large freighter passed under them, momentarily blocking her view. "How do the people get around? How do they get food?"

"Like they always have. Work and buy it from the conglomerate."

"But outside the Wall? Who do they buy it from?" Millicent watched a figure scurry into a dwelling. She was too far away to make out any detail, but the agonized hunch and stiff movements suggested a harsh life.

"I think the conglomerate has shops out here. And people can take a ferry in. You have to pay to live in the city, though, and I think a great many of these people can't." Ryker ripped into another pouch. "I think they make food out here, too. Grow it with heat lamps, maybe. I'm not sure."

"I had no idea," Millicent said quietly. "They live in hovels. Are they a part of the breeding projects?"

"They are all sterilized." Mr. McAllister's arm, thrown over his face, muffled his words. "The conglomerates control all breeding. And before you say I should die, just know that this planet can't sustain the numbers on it. Even now it can't. So if people got to breed willy-nilly, there would be mass death as everyone fought for the limited resources to stay alive."

"But why breed to create this?" Millicent asked. "These people aren't living."

"None of us are living," Ryker cut in.

"I don't think I can really complain," Millicent said, taking a warmed pouch of food from the kitchen bay. She wasn't accustomed to eating it cold like Ryker apparently was. Or maybe she just wasn't as hungry. "My life was a cushy paradise compared to the existence of those people down there."

"Some of us get lucky," Mr. McAllister said. "And some aren't needed for any job more important than packaging the food trays. It's how the world works. How it has always worked."

Millicent leaned back against the seat and watched the landscape change even more, from decrepit dwellings to places that barely cut out the harsh weather. Eventually, though, the structures dotting the ground thinned out and then nearly stopped altogether. Slushy bog spread away to the right, reflecting the harsh sky above.

Time ticked by slowly, making her eyes droop. Marie rested her head on Millicent's legs. Her hair was fine and soft, flowing through Millicent's fingers like expensive silk. She noticed Ryker up at the controls, intently directing them toward a destination hundreds of kilometers away. Strangely, with his planning ability and her fluency with systems, she half thought they'd make it. They certainly had a much better chance together than she'd had by herself.

Her head hit the back of the seat with a slight bump, and her eyes fluttered shut as fatigue dragged her under.

"Millie, wake up! Hurry!"

"What?" Millicent startled awake and clutched Marie. Ryker stood over them as the craft slowed to a stop. "What's happening?" She looked around with puffy, dazed eyes, noticing another craft through the windows off to the right. "Was I asleep?"

"I've never even heard of pirates," Mr. McAllister was saying, peering out the window with a tense body. He ducked down quickly, crumpling to the seat. "They just brought out a gun. Oh Holy Divine."

"Pirates?" Millicent said as the fuzziness cleared from her mind.

"Yes. Pirates. They plague this route." Blazing blue eyes bored into Millicent. "This is a kill-first, ask-questions-later situation. These aren't the sort of people we want to be captured by."

"Oh Holy—" Mr. McAllister squeezed his eyes tight. "There's another one. Another pirate craft just showed up. It looks rougher, too."

Shoulders back and body at ease, Ryker moved to the console. "They are derelicts who have found a way to make easy money. Since the conglomerate puts security on their vessels, these fortune hunters prey on the weak. We are not weak. It'll be a great surprise, don't you think?" He glanced at Mr. McAllister. "You'll keep that child safe. Millie and I will take care of this."

"Good news." Mr. McAllister crawled across the floor before dragging Marie down off the seat and into his lap. He scooted them backward and into the corner, where he tucked Marie behind the jutting seat.

Millicent extracted her heavy-duty jacket from the weapons bay, as well as two guns strong enough to kill but not to breach the vessel walls. "Let's switch out our craft while we're at it."

Ryker's fingers slowed across the console. The front partition closed with a thunk. He turned to her slowly, his brow lightly furrowed. "What's that, cupcake?"

The gun clicked as Millicent cocked it. She lowered the weapon, keeping it down so the pirates on the other crafts wouldn't see it.

She glanced out the windows, getting her bearings. The desolate landscape around them offered no cover or protection from the elements. If Millicent's group lost the protection of the vessel, they'd die. Without question. None of them could last long out in the open, Marie least of all. But then, neither could their attackers.

A plan formed in her head.

Suddenly taking action, she took two quick steps and shoved Ryker. He barely moved, too heavy to be easily knocked aside. Without raising a question, though, he took a deliberate step away.

Her fingers flew over the console. "Switch crafts. Trust me." She logged into the net and was immediately confronted with sloppy code a child could have put together, trying to capture her log-on and track her location. "Amateurs," she muttered, working around them. "Which of those crafts is best, and are there any more coming?"

Ryker's body bent as he looked out the windows. "The best one's on the left. Nothing else but freighter vessels out there right now. Another pirate could be hiding below, but I doubt it. Doesn't mean security won't come along, though. If they followed us out of San Francisco, which we have to assume they did, a delay here gives Mr. Hunt more time to catch us. An injury won't keep him from our trail."

"Then we have to hurry."

Ryker braced his hand against the wall to get a better view of the left-hand vessel. "Three in that craft. Shouldn't be a problem to take over."

"Here we go." Millicent smacked the "Execute" button, causing the whole vessel to shudder. A deep rumble had Ryker glancing at his feet.

He was unable to see, through the floor, the large gun mounted on the base of the craft as it extended. A loud *keh-keh-keh* announced gunfire.

The door to the craft shimmied open, blasting a gush of putrid air coated with moisture into Millicent's face. "Overtake the left craft," Millicent yelled.

She needn't have bothered. Ryker had already jumped across the two meters of open space separating them from the neighboring vessel. His hand clutched a metal ridge as he bent over their outside control panel, working to open the pirates' door.

Marie struggled out of Mr. McAllister's grasp.

"No, no. No, Marie!" Mr. McAllister dived after her.

The doors of both neighboring vessels squealed. In jerky movements that indicated a run-down system, they quivered open.

Ryker worked hand over hand, in a vertical position, until he could swing into the open doorway. A knife blossomed into his fist. It slashed quickly, moving through the air in fast, precise movements. A spray of blood splattered against the side of the door before a loud scream turned into a gurgle.

"C'mon, Millicent, get moving!" Millicent said to herself. She clapped in front of her face, an action that often jarred her out of a tired daze from a long day. She bent to the console. Her vessel swung right until the door was near the opening of the right-hand pirate craft. She stabilized her vessel and then locked it into position. Smoke drifted up from the holes her weapon had punched in the pirate ship's bottom. It dipped hard to the right as the operator tried to keep it airborne.

She leaped, trusting she was strong enough to clear the open space between the vessels, and her feet landed with a body-jarring thunk.

Gibberish assaulted her ears, the voice rough and confused. She ripped the gun out of her holster as two small thin men rushed her. She pointed and shot twice, pulling the trigger with conviction. The first pirate crumpled to the floor. A stray bullet punched through one of the windows. Another stream of environment seeped in.

Gun was too powerful after all. Damn.

A hand grabbed her shoulder.

She swung and rammed the gun against his chest. Flexed her finger.

The blast sent the pirate staggering backward.

She fired twice more, center mass, no hesitation.

His arms flung out to the sides before he tripped and fell, a surprised look on his face.

The vessel tilted wildly, knocking her into the wall.

A loud thunk hit the roof.

The vessel slanted the other way, knocking into her craft before losing altitude. Her adrenaline spiked. If this thing went down, she was going down with it, and she wasn't positive on how to work the controls to pull it out of a crash landing. Theory without practice wasn't a lot of good in an emergency.

Staggering, using the wall braces for stability, she worked her way to the cockpit.

The craft tilted and dropped before lurching forward.

Crack.

A long knife extended through the ceiling. The blade whispered by her ear, and the point stopped just above her shoulder.

"Shit!" She jerked away as the craft wildly tipped again. The floor punched her back as the soles of her feet flashed up toward the ceiling. Another knife extended down before the first pulled back up.

That was shiny new tech. It could only belong to one person besides her, assuming Mr. Hunt hadn't shown up yet.

The craft wobbled. She rolled across the floor, and her shoulder knocked into the hard side. Dull pain throbbed from the point of contact and pulsed unpleasantly through her body.

With nails clawing the grimy floor, she worked forward, moving hand over hand. The horizon rose into the windshield. Red drenched the gray suit of the controller, his head lolling down. The bullets had run through the other pirate and struck the controller. *Of all the bad luck!*

"Hurry, Millicent!" she berated herself, her heart so far up her throat it was choking her. A metallic slice sounded behind her. Then again. Ryker would be too late. They were going down fast now. This was all on her.

Her knuckles turned white as she gripped the door frame and hauled herself up. A huge shape passed to her right, their vessel barely missing a freighter. The ground, rushing for them, filled up the whole windshield.

"Oh shit, oh shit, oh shit." Millicent clutched the controller's gray tunic and yanked. The pirate half fell toward the ground. His legs were stuck!

"C'mon!" She yanked, warm blood coating her hand. Gritting her teeth, she pulled with everything she had, using the tilt of the vessel to her favor. His butt slid off the seat.

The ground was only a hundred meters away.

She surged over him and clutched the throttle and the steering column. The craft moaned and shuddered, but it only slightly veered up. She covered the rough black surface of the column with both hands and pulled with all her might. The shudder grew more intense, and the moaning became a grinding. Cracked clay and soggy patches of mud enlarged through the windshield. More pressure; she gave it everything she had, pulling strength up from her toes to curb the frantic rushing toward the ground. Something popped. Sparks fizzed up the dash. A flame licked at a faded engraving that said "ottl."

She pushed the throttle forward, cutting some power, hoping that might help . . . ? Then fell forward. The man below her rolled against the underside of the dash. Her elbow skimmed the surface. Heat seared her body. The craft surged upward while slowing. Too far upward, though.

"Crap," she mumbled, fumbling with the controls.

"Just get it stable enough to hover," she heard from the door. "Stabilize it or it'll stall."

"Got it!" She pushed the throttle forward. The engine roared. Power surged and the ancient vehicle shuddered. She flipped on the hovering capability. Immediately the craft leveled and then entered a wobbly sort of float, the sides randomly dipping before correcting. The grinding sound within the dash turned into a pop. Her breath wheezed out of her tight chest.

"Good job." Knives retracted from the side of the craft before Ryker stepped through the door, not taking any notice of the dead men at his feet. A grin covered his face. "That was something, huh? Almost met our maker on that one."

He strode forward. At the edge of the cockpit, he bent over the dead body, yanked it free of its wedged position, and threw the limp form from the craft. The body sailed through the air before dropping out of sight.

"Okay." He slapped his hands, like he was shaking off dust, before joining her in the cockpit again. "Let's get this baby back up where it belongs, shall we?"

Millicent stared at her hands, feeling an uncomfortable pinch in her stomach at the sight of the glistening red blood. With a churning stomach, she wiped them across the partition. "I haven't seen a retractable knife like that. Where'd you get it?"

"I met a chick who worked for Gregon Corp. in a bar a while back. She had these in her apartment. I traded."

"What'd you trade for?" Millicent inched away from the blood reaching for her foot.

"Sex. Even trade."

Millicent scoffed. "Why your superior hasn't put a muter on your vocal cords, I do not know. The amount of drivel you speak."

"Just keeping it level, sweetheart. Now have a seat. I need to rescue you."

"Rescue me? Is that what it's called when you wait for me to do all the heavy lifting and then waltz in after I've saved the day?"

"Precisely. I'm taking charge. Wow, this craft has seen better days. We'll be lucky to get up to the others."

Millicent stepped over a prone body and accessed the console. The unexpected look of their net fired up her brain. It was unlike anything she'd ever seen. Something that no longer surprised her. She could now freely admit she'd led a sheltered life thus far.

"Why'd you board this craft anyway?" Ryker's voice had dropped an octave. He wasn't pleased, but he was trying not to show it.

She grinned. "Why? Worried about me?"

"When everything went lopsided . . . I was, yes."

She glanced at him, slightly taken aback. That answer and the deep—heartfelt?—tone in which he'd said it wasn't what she'd expected. Shaking it off, she went back to what she was doing, pleased with the hydraulic sound behind her. She bent to the sudden opening. A storage locker, by the look of it. "Pirates pilfer things, right? At least, that's what all the stories say. They take riches. In this day and age, riches are tech. I wanted to see what they had. It could help."

She extracted a couple of items, and then analyzed two pieces of shiny new tech she'd never seen before. Without a second thought, she lifted the most precious items into her arms, bracing herself as the craft groaned. It was then she noticed the darkening stream of smoke billowing from outside the window.

"Be prepared to jump, Millie. This thing is about to bork out."

"Bork out?"

"Go down in fiery flames and kill us both."

"*Bork out* is a better term, yes." She clutched the tech to her chest as the wind whipped at her, the pressure in the speeding craft threatening to suck her toward the door. "Close the door. That'll help its flight."

"I tried. It's not responding. Whatever Marie did, it overrode the systems." He stopped talking for a moment before he said in a rough, terrifying voice, "They didn't put anything in her head, right? She doesn't have an implant?"

"No. What she's doing is all natural."

A moment later, the frenzied environment within the craft stilled as they slowed. She stepped forward as Ryker's hand flinched away from the dashboard. "C'mon, you fickle bitch," she heard him growl.

Her craft drifted into view of the open doorway. Mr. McAllister waited in plain sight, his face pale and determined, with a gun in his hand. He might not have been there voluntarily, but it was clear he would defend himself and Marie if the need arose. The man cared for the little girl, regardless of his situation. Millicent had to respect him for that.

"At least he rises to the occasion," Millicent said, feeling the craft steady under her feet.

"He must know that facing a pirate to protect my daughter is a much better option than facing me should he allow my daughter to be harmed or taken." Ryker leaned closer to the dash. "I have some sort of message coming through. You know any other languages?"

"No. I've never had to. But I'm sure I can find a translator . . ."

Ryker hesitated. He stood in a rush and then glanced at the tech in her arms. "Yes. Do it. Given that this craft showed up with another, I'd bet they have a network in place. That flashing message might be eyes we need."

Ryker bent to the body on the ground, and with quick hands, ripped fabric off the man before tying it into a series of knots, creating a makeshift sack. Millicent deposited her tech onto the ground before stepping up to the console. As expected, translating wasn't an issue, and before she knew it, she stared at the translated warning.

Then swore.

"Moxidone security craft taking travel-way three," Millicent said in a flat tone, offsetting her rolling stomach. "That's the travel way under this one. The craft is a larger one. Doesn't say who is on it or what they are after, but they're traveling at an advanced speed."

"Distance?" Ryker strung the hastily made sack over her shoulders. Her newly acquired tech went into the sack at her back before he ripped off some more fabric and anchored everything to her body.

"Doesn't say. Just says 'check anchor.' Probably a bad translation . . ."

"Or the name of their checkpoint. We're out of time, Millie. We gotta go."

Millicent followed him to the open door and stared across the distance. She registered Mr. McAllister's relieved expression from ten meters away. "Why don't we dock closer?"

"Precaution." He lifted a rope from a side bay and then tied the end around his waist. He swung it around before throwing it out the opening. The end sailed perfectly into the doorway of her craft. Mr. McAllister grabbed it in what looked like reflex, then stared at it in confusion.

"Tie it in," Ryker yelled.

"Me?" Mr. McAllister asked before gingerly holding it up. "I'm not an expert knot-tier . . ."

"You better be today . . ."

"Oh sure, pressure always helps the situation," they heard as Mr. McAllister went about following orders.

"Okay." Ryker turned to her, his fingers around the rope. "I'm going to—"

A knock, followed by an electric sizzle, cut him off. The craft pitched forward.

Ryker fell into Millicent, taking them both to the floor. The vehicle shimmied and started to groan again, wobbling in the sky. Then an explosion pushed heat against their backs and the engine cut out. The craft fell from the sky, and them with it.

Chapter 15

Millicent screamed, weightless as the floor came up and punched them. Strong arms wrapped around her, followed by legs, holding fast. Ryker curled around her right before the edge of the door slammed into his shoulder. The carcass of the craft slipped away, leaving them exposed.

Ryker's grunt punctuated their sudden halt in midair. He hung from the rope around his waist. His tight grip on her was the only thing keeping her from falling to her death.

The pack at her back pulled her toward the ground, and the environment battered her from all sides. Stinging rain scoured her face as the freezing air bit the exposed skin from the rip in her suit.

"How necessary is that tech?" Ryker's voice sounded in her ear, strain bleeding through his words.

"I don't know. Two pieces look recent and incredibly expensive. The others probably aren't as valuable."

"Can you get rid of some without the other?"

"No. I don't think so."

"Do you want to risk our lives for it?"

Millicent hesitated. The obvious answer was no, but if they ever got into an extreme situation, it might mean the difference between life and death. Should they fall to their death now, Mr. McAllister could just wait for whoever was after them. The baby would be picked up and taken back without issue. But if they were in a place without that capability, it would be much worse for Millicent and Ryker to fall victim to some accident or attack. Marie might be exposed to the horrors of the world. Millicent couldn't let that happen.

"Yes." She did not elaborate.

He did not ask her to.

His breath blew against her ear. "Okay. This is how we are going to survive. You will wrap your arms around my neck and your legs around my waist. Then you hang on with everything you have, do you understand? Everything you have."

"Yes, okay. What about you?"

"I'm going to pull us up before my arm goes dead. We don't have long."

"If your arm goes—"

"*Now*, princess!" he said through gritted teeth.

His arms released enough for her to snake her hands up between them and loop them tightly around his neck.

"Hang on tight, now. You'll only have your arms to hold you for a few moments." His arms came away, but his legs were still wrapped around her tightly. The pull of gravity and the weight at her back tried to drag her arms away from each other. "Hang on, love. You gotta hang on. Keep with me, now."

She'd ponder that tone another time.

Grunting with effort, she used her arms to crawl around his shoulders to his neck and secure herself a little better.

"Good girl. Now for the legs. This is where it gets dicey."

Ryker's whole body went stiff. He arched and grabbed the rope, bringing them vertical. Then his legs slowly came away, something that must've taxed him greatly. His muscles quivered under her as she pulled her legs up his body and wrapped them around his middle.

"Okay, here we go. Let's hope 'check anchor' is somewhere far away."

There was no way they were that lucky. Each moment brought them closer to capture. Mr. Hunt would not rest until he had them.

She ducked her head away so he could see the rope between his hands more clearly. Hand over hand, pulling up both their weight and the pack of tech, Ryker lifted them through the sky and up to the craft hovering above them. His body started to shake under her arms and legs. Red pooled through the fabric on one of his arms. Yet still he climbed, his pace even despite his body's obvious desire to let go and succumb to gravity.

When his breath turned ragged, she glanced up. They had a quarter of the distance to go.

"Almost there, Ryker, you can do it." She hoped for a smart-ass response of some kind—a comment on her using his name, perhaps, or the way she was wrapped so tightly around him. Nothing came but fast breaths and then soft grunts each time he pulled them up with the bloodied arm.

The ground was nothing more than a distant promise of death. Sweat soaked into Millicent's suit as her own body started to quiver, her arms burning. The pack pulled at her, slowly dragging her down. Her hands, slick with the rain and running out of strength, slipped. She slid down his front, her arms now hooking around his shoulders. A different set of muscles felt the new position. A weaker set.

"Hang on," he said in a strained whisper.

"I've got it," she lied as her hands slipped again. Her muscles screamed at her to let go. Her pack constantly dragged her down.

"I've got you!" A shock of relief fluttered through Millicent at the sound of Mr. McAllister's voice. Hands found her shoulders and hooked under her arms. "What the hell is on your back?"

Her hands slid farther and then slipped off. Her body dropped. For one horrifying heartbeat, she thought that was it. That she was done.

But she was moving up, not down. Her chest rubbed up Ryker's face, followed by her stomach, as Mr. McAllister pulled her into the craft.

"For a tiny person, you are so heavy." Mr. McAllister gave a final yank, scraping her face against the floor, before dropping her. Her limbs, exhausted, splatted down.

"Mama." Marie's soft wet cheek fell against Millicent's.

"I'm okay, baby. Ryker saved me."

"That's Daddy, in this situation." He heaved himself up over the edge and then plopped down on his side, clearly refusing to completely give in to his fatigue and lie with his face on the floor, like Millicent was doing. "Can't confuse the child with first names."

Millicent couldn't be bothered to put the effort into rolling her eyes.

"We have to keep moving," Ryker said after a moment. "We need to switch out vessels and get on our way. We don't have much time."

"Why not?" Mr. McAllister asked.

"With Mr. Hunt pursuing us, we'll never have much time." Ryker laid a hand on her shoulder, ignoring the way Mr. McAllister's head whipped toward the window. "How you doing, princess?"

"Wishing my royal coach had more cushions," she said, pushing herself to her hands and knees.

"Let's get everything packed and stowed." When Ryker stood, one large arm hung loose at his side. Blood covered his shoulder and dripped down.

"Is that from the door?" Millicent picked herself up and wavered. She didn't shrug off Ryker's steadying hand. Nor did she ask how the hell he was standing straight and broad after all that.

"Yeah. I think I got a good scrape. You don't have any Cure-all do you? Or a stitcher?"

"Both. Obviously." Millicent staggered over to the med bay and palmed it open.

"Yes, obviously. Just like why you jumped onto a limping craft and drove it straight at the ground. Very obvious." Ryker's body leaned against her as he looked over her shoulder.

"Exactly. Obvious. Like the pain you are in, even though you are trying to hide it."

"I'm not trying to hide it. I'm ignoring it. That's what will make it go away. Obviously."

"You are such an idiot." She grabbed the canister of Cure-all and then glanced at Mr. McAllister, sitting off to the side with tight lips. "You have medical training, right?"

He started, realizing she was talking to him. His head shook minutely. Then he shrugged. "Not exactly, but enough to patch him up."

Ryker undid the suit down his chest and—wincing—pulled it over his shoulder.

Millicent clenched her teeth as the nasty gash came into view, the scrapes deep and the skin nearly frayed at the edges. She didn't want to gasp and cause Ryker alarm. "We can fix this up in no time."

"You don't sound sure of that, princess." Ryker studied his arm. "That's not that bad. Shoot me with some Cure-all and I'll be fine."

"Should layer it with Medi-Seal," Mr. McAllister said with a hollow voice. "It'll be faster. Since he's so great at ignoring wounds, he won't be upset about the pain."

A vein pulsed in Ryker's jaw, but he didn't say anything.

Millicent laughed; she couldn't help it. She grabbed the Medi-Seal and then a sling.

"Don't need the sling. Give me a few hours and I'll be all patched up. Especially with the Medi-Seal." His voice turned rough, but he didn't glance at Mr. McAllister with the obvious accusation.

"Ryker, this is deep," she said as she took out the Medi-Seal, a very painful but effective stitching technique.

"He was bred with a superior healing and immune system." Mr. McAllister rubbed his eyes. "It was one of the great advancements of the time. Unfortunately, it only materializes in new cases an eighth of the time. It's often a crapshoot. We have no idea why."

"Enlightening." Ryker stared straight ahead with gritted teeth.

Millicent motioned for Mr. McAllister to move over before taking position in front of her console. If a Moxidone security vessel was headed toward them, it should be easy to pick it out in their loop. Most of the security department's attention would be on it, so there would be many transmissions back and forth. That would give her some idea of how much time they had.

Or didn't have, as the case may be.

Ryker sucked in a hard breath, drawing Millicent's eye. Mr. McAllister flinched away before hurriedly stepping back. The benign-looking, foamy-white medicine was merging with the seeping blood and pus of the injury. She'd heard it felt like needles piercing the wound and then layering the pain with fire. A rumor that certainly seemed true, based on Ryker's clenched jaw and determined eyes. The man didn't show pain often, but he was definitely showing it now in his muted way.

Millicent turned back to her console as Mr. McAllister kept working. A shiver ran through her when she found the security vessel and its coordinates. "We have to go!" She wheeled around in time to see Ryker cock his head, his pain clearer now. "We've got twenty minutes at his current velocity, twenty-five tops."

"Less if we stick to this travel route," Ryker said in a rough tone. "They'll see us from a greater distance."

"Here, let me finish up." She took the Cure-all from Mr. McAllister, eliciting a relieved sigh. Fear of Ryker retaliating from the pain had slowed him down. "You pack up what we'll need out of the med bay, get Marie ready, and then grab the tech and weapons."

"We need to switch crafts and drop down into the lower travel way," Ryker said in a thick voice.

"Suppose you don't want sex right now, huh?" Millicent asked, unable to keep a smile from curling her lips despite the intense pressure they were under. "Not in the mood?"

"If you give me a minute, princess, I'll gladly rock your world."

As she readied the next injection blast, Millicent braced her hand against Ryker's chest.

His large pec and the muscles down his stomach flexed dramatically. "Lower," he said in nothing more than a grunt. "The money spot is a lot lower."

Her grin grew at the effort ringing through his voice. "Hurts, huh?"

"I've had worse."

She laughed and shot him with more force than was absolutely necessary. Then, because his ego was so ridiculous, she slapped the bulge between his thighs. "There? Was that the money spot you spoke of?"

He flinched, bending at the waist. Then he grimaced and reached for his shoulder. A grin tickled his lips. "I'll remember that, princess. When you're begging for climax, I will remember this moment, and make you suffer just a bit longer."

"I do not understand you two," Mr. McAllister said as he dropped a bag next to the satchel they'd rescued. It tinkled, the items within hitting each other. He snatched up another empty bag. "You guys almost died. Just a second ago, you almost died. Twice." He spread the bag open. "First she shoots the hell out of a craft, then goes leaping onto it like a fool—"

"Be careful who you call a fool," Ryker growled.

"She left me with a child, in a vessel I don't know how to operate. And even though we have Mr. Hunt right behind us, a man hell-bent on capturing or killing us—it could go either way with him"—Mr. McAllister threw a food warmer into the bag—"you two are making sexual jokes at each other. Sexual jokes! In the height of danger. In front of a child!" Another item went into the bag. "Natural borns are crazy. That's all there is to it. Natural borns are crazy, and I'm in hell. So that's what I have going on." Another item thunked in.

The vessel issued a soft beep.

"Fifteen minutes." Dread washed over Millicent. "C'mon. Hurry."

"Remind me why we need to switch crafts?" Ryker asked. "We have more guns on this one."

"Obviously because people who constantly break the law probably have a way to get on to the net without being noticed," Mr. McAllister said as he hurriedly wrapped Marie in a large scarf. "Or if they don't, it won't matter anyway because they won't know it's Millicent. Sorry. Ms. Foster. Though why we are still using each other's last names is beyond me. We must know each other well enough for first names by now. There is no professionalism mixed up in this situation, I'll tell you that much. It's all gone tits up."

Millicent grabbed a different canister out of the medical bag, affixed a shooter to it, and pushed it onto Mr. McAllister's upper arm. She squeezed, and the tranquilizer shot through his suit and into his skin. He flinched and looked at the offending spot. A moment later, he just sighed again. "I sure hope that was a tranq, because I can't take any-more. I've never been this afraid for this long in all my life."

"I know. You are slow and clumsy. Now get her into the other craft. I'll move Ryker over."

Without another word, Mr. McAllister handed Marie off before leaping into the commandeered vessel, which hovered a mere meter away, waiting for its new owners. He staggered, then turned back and reached out his hands. "Give me Marie first, then the bags. How long before I'm sleepy?"

"I'll take the baby over," Ryker interjected.

"You'll barely be able to take yourself over." Millicent grabbed Marie, kissed her, and then handed her off. She started passing the bags over. Once done, she turned to the man whom she would never be able to stabilize if he staggered toward the side and fell.

"Don't bullshit me on this one," Millicent said for his ears alone. "If something hurts or your muscle is going to give out, let me know. Let's get you over safely."

"Yes, dear."

"I'd rather you go back to calling me cupcake if *dear* is the alternative." She took a firm hold on his good arm and walked him over to the gap in the vessels. She glanced down at the distant ground, spreading its arms wide in greeting. A shiver covered her body. Best to look somewhere else. *Anywhere* else.

"Here we go." She was getting ready to hand him over when he leaned toward her. She had a moment to wonder if he was about to stagger when his lips grazed up her neck before sucking in her earlobe. A dull throb pounded against the safe nothingness of Clarity. Clarity was starting to lose the battle.

"I am a bit unstable, beautiful." His voice, low and intimate, started a strange, electric hum deep in her body. "I'd love a bed, your body, and then a nice long sleep."

"Instead, you're going to get another slap to the groin before you're pushed over the gap. *We do not have time for this, Ryker!*"

"That's probably the right way to play it. I'm two seconds away from passing out. You need to make a move."

No more encouragement needed. She slapped his bulge, waited until he bent in that natural flinch, and then geared up to shove him.

"Now," he grunted.

She pushed with everything she had as he weakly jumped. He crashed into Mr. McAllister within the pirate craft. The two went down to the ground, the larger Ryker trapping Mr. McAllister on the dirty floor.

Millicent took a hurried look around her, found nothing more she needed to grab, and then hopped over as Mr. McAllister wheezed in pain.

"Sorry, bub. I needed someone to break my fall."

"Can you get off?"

"Was that a rhetorical or a genuine question?"

"Will it make a difference in the answer?"

"Nope. Same answer. Although, I might've thrown you a different tone."

Millicent worked the console next to the door, frowning at the error code—or *lack* of an error code, actually. Like on the other ship, the door thought it was closed.

Strange.

No time to dig deeper. With Mr. Hunt's determined face flashing through her memory, she turned to her daughter, who was curled over her stuffed animal. There were dark circles under her eyes. Millicent's heart twisted as she said, "Marie, sweetie, can you close the door?"

"Yes, Mama." The door slid shut. Nothing obvious about the code changed.

"Thank you, baby."

"Need a little help here, love," Ryker slurred. "This guy is bony."

Millicent didn't care. There was no time to lose.

She jogged to the front and then slipped into the cockpit. After glancing over the controls, she took a deep breath and flicked the switch to take it out of stationary mode. The vessel rocked before dropping a few meters. Heart lurching along with her stomach, Millicent entered the directive to descend rapidly. The vessel, not nearly as decrepit as its crashed counterpart, rapidly complied.

Too rapidly.

The craft tore through the sky, diving toward one of the larger freighters. Her pulse pounded as the nose of her craft barely missed the rear wing of the larger vessel. She dropped below it, wiggling the steering column and working the thruster to keep them from ending up in the freighter's exhaust. Barely breathing, she steadied them in the protective shadow of the mammoth moving above.

A deep rumble sounded from the rear. Ryker had said something unintelligible. She didn't have time to find out what.

Accessing the console and the net, she once again tracked the security vessel. And sighed. It was probably just coming into visibility above. They would see her craft soon, and then they'd search the area. If she could keep them on their current path, she'd buy them some time. Though how much was anyone's guess. She doubted Mr. Hunt was fooled by much. Not if he was as good as Ryker.

Chapter 16

The craft jumped and then dipped. "Huh." Millicent hit the button, labeled in a language she didn't understand, and experienced the same jump and dip. "Defensive maneuvering, maybe?"

She hit the button next to it. The vessel's right side dipped, careening. She directed them back to the mostly unused upper travel way, far enough ahead of the security craft to risk leaving the freighter's shadow. "The buttons are programmed for preplanned defensive maneuverings . . ."

"Handy."

Millicent jumped at the deep tone and glanced back to see Ryker entering the cockpit. His hair was loose and messy. He took the copilot's seat and looked over the controls. "How long was I out?"

Millicent glanced at her wrist and then clicked a button that made the craft function as close to a system-guided vessel as possible. She stretched. "Three hours."

Ryker frowned and looked straight ahead. In the distance, a thick line interrupted the sparse nothingness. Black fog condensed, hovering over what had to be Los Angeles.

"We're almost there," she said, refusing to acknowledge the flurry of activity in her stomach closely resembling fear. Fear wouldn't help. She needed to stay focused. Determined.

"Did the security vessel give you any problems?"

"No. I stuck close to the freighter until I was sure our pursuers were left behind. They won't stay back there forever, though. All we've gained is time."

"Hopefully that's all we need."

His tone was flat, which meant he was thinking the same thing she was—*doubtful.*

"How's your arm?" Millicent asked, steering the craft back into the travel way. It had a habit of drifting left.

"You learn quickly." Ryker glanced down at his injured shoulder. The top half of his suit still hung from his hips. "The skin is still fusing together, but it's better."

"Does it still hurt?"

"Like hell, yeah. But tolerable." He settled back. "You should get some sleep."

"I took an upper. I'm sufficiently wired for what comes next. Speaking of . . . What comes next?"

He ran his fingers through his hair. "We need to find the location where we're supposed to meet Roe."

"Yes, I realized that much. But how do we go about doing that? We'll have to find parking for this vessel, probably get tags for it to make it look legit . . . or we have to dump it. But if we dump it, how will we get around? Just you and I would stand out, but with Marie . . . people are going to notice us, and someone is going to ask questions."

"How many uppers did you take?" His gaze fixed on her face.

She frowned. "One. Why?"

He analyzed her for a moment longer before minutely shaking his head and directing his focus straight ahead again. "Step one, we get into the city somehow. Step two, we figure it out. Relax. I've got this all under control."

"Yeah. I can tell." Millicent guided them back to the route. "The others?"

"The baby is sleeping, and Trent is muttering to himself. His eyes are closed, though, so probably nightmares."

"That guy didn't sign up for this. He's way beyond his limit."

"I don't care."

Millicent shrugged. She glanced at his hair, which was dusting the top of his muscular shoulders. "What's up with the loose locks? Why not cut them if you're going to leave them messy?"

"I don't like the conglomerate thinking they're fully in charge of me. Sure, they control most of my life. But not all of it. It's a distinction I've tried hard to make."

"And they let you?" She rolled her eyes at herself. "I mean, of course they did. I'm just surprised is all."

"I've learned where and how hard to push. I know what I can get away with—and how to hide what I can't. It's helped me learn my value."

"You're one of the more valuable staffers. Your position should tell you that."

He leaned against the armrest. "My position tells me plenty, yes, but there are levels within the director's role."

"How do you mean?"

"For example, we are both directors, with roughly the same departmental importance, but my apartment is three-fourths the size of yours. You have the same size apartment as my superior—as yours, too, actually—but your dwelling is much more luxurious than either of theirs. Your craft is new and well kept. Your food is richer, more flavorful. You are living way above my station."

She could feel her mouth turn downward in confusion as that sank in. "But that can't be. I'm flagged. I can't get a promotion. I'm as high as I'll ever go. Or . . . you know . . . could go if I'd stayed. How could I be living at a standard above your superior's?"

His electric-blue eyes studied her. "It surprised me as well. I've never met someone in your situation. So I looked into it. They don't want you advancing because that would put you solely in a decision-making and leadership role. You churn out genius as a worker drone. Your ideas and execution are exemplary. You can't go any higher because you're more useful right where you are. Be that as it may, you are extremely valuable to the conglomerate. More so than me. If you wanted to, you, too, could . . ." He reached over and tugged at her hair. Before she could duck away, her tie gave and her hair tumbled down. It fell to her midback in a wave of gold. "On second thought, it's probably better you always pull it tight."

"Why's that?" She put out her hand for the tie. Then frowned when he looped it over his wrist next to his.

"Because you'd turn too many heads if you kept it down, and I'd be forced to kill people."

She scoffed. "A little irrational, don't you think? Give it back."

"Haven't you heard? That's part of my breeding. I protect what's mine." He pointed through the windshield. "Steer the craft."

A light touch had them back on course. "All day long."

"What's that?"

"I'll slap you in the dick all day long. Keep it up." She massaged her scalp and then ran her fingers through her hair. "It does feel good to let it loose, though."

"See?" He blew out a long slow breath. "Any chance you brought a change of clothes for me?"

"Hardly."

He nodded like he figured that'd be the answer. "Any extra material I could use? Mine is not only ripped, it's bloody. We don't need any more reasons for people to take interest."

"I brought a couple extra suits. You can cut up the pink one."

"A *couple* extra? Of the quality you have on?"

If she kept frowning, her face would freeze. "Obviously. Why would I bring substandard suits on a trip like this?"

"And here we go again. A wardrobe fit for royalty. Where is it?"

"In one of the bags Mr. McAllister packed up." She adjusted the steering. When Ryker returned, it was with a sewing laser. He got to work cutting off the arm of his suit and trying to piece enough material together to form another one. It seemed he wanted to use the least amount of that vivid pink as possible. She didn't blame him.

"Why did you learn to make clothing?" she asked, watching in mild fascination as he worked.

"I was trained for it. For situations like this. Or for stitching a body back together. We use one as often as we use the other."

Silence drifted over them for a while as the sprawling city ahead increased in size. The fluttering in her stomach was spreading into her chest now, increasing her heart rate and perspiration output.

"Unlike you and Trent, we're on a first-name basis, huh?" Ryker asked in a tone colored with humor.

"You are the father of my child. That is first-name-basis territory. Plus, you've saved my life a couple times."

"Hmm." He ran the laser over a seam. "But not Trent?"

"Mr. McAllister wants to go back to the conglomerate, with my child, and resume his work. He's still the enemy. He needs to be kept at an arm's length."

"Hmm." Ryker held up the sleeve before glancing out the windshield. "Probably half an hour, I think. I better hurry."

It wasn't half an hour. It was only twenty-three minutes and sixteen seconds. The wall loomed large, reaching into the sky, topping San Francisco's Wall in height and thickness. The stacked travel ways collapsed into one manageable stream of traffic leading toward twenty gaping entrances. Above were the city's exits, streaming vehicles out quickly.

"Let me take over, princess." Ryker pushed his hair on top of his head and wrapped a tie around it. After handing her tie back, he flicked something on the dash and then took hold of the controls in front of him. "You might want to get to the console and . . . fix shit."

"There's one right here." She did up her own hair, tight as always, before picking up a flimsy screen off the dash and placing it on her lap, out of direct sight of someone at window height. The hologram flickered to life. She braced herself. "What am I fixing?"

"We'll know in just a minute. Hang tight." He leaned back and somewhat angled his head to yell, "Trent, you up?"

They heard a weak "Yes . . ."

"Stick with Marie. The windows are heavily tinted. I'll let you know if I'll need to make them translucent."

"And then I should . . . hide, yes?"

"Probably. We'll see what happens."

"As I said," Millicent scoffed at him, "you are extremely on top of it. Your planning is really shining through." She shook her head while bringing up the city map and going over their route for the millionth time. Unfortunately, that wasn't helping her dissipate the raging panic coursing through her system.

"I'm good in a bind, cupcake. You wait and see. I'll blow your mind." As the large freighter in front of them steered over to its lane, lines shivered green in front of them, leading straight for a short time before curving to the left. "Here we go."

They followed the green pathway to the lane in the last stall. The craft slowed as they approached a large computer. Its screen whirled, flashing patterns of colors.

"What's it doing?" Ryker asked as the craft slowed to a stop.

"Trying to identify us. It can't, though. This vessel is registered in a way I couldn't identify. I didn't want to mess with it. Should I . . ." Millicent glanced up as green light shone down on them. A barrier cleared out of the way, allowing them to progress until the light beaming through the windshield turned to red. They came to a stop next to a guard facility with a dark doorway.

Ryker reached down and picked a gun off the floor. Never looking away from the guard station, he slowly slipped the weapon under his right leg. "It'd be a really bad day if I shot my nuts off," he muttered.

A short, squat figure filled the doorway. His wrist glowed green before dulling, indicating he'd just used his implant for something. Expression hard, he glanced at the vessel before staring through the window at Ryker. His gaze hit Millicent next, but no emotion or thought registered in his expression. His finger made a circle in the air before he pointed downward.

"What does that mean?" Millicent whispered, her throat constricted by the customary tightness she'd come to expect in these situations. She wasn't much better than Mr. McAllister—it was clear she wasn't cut out for a life of crime.

"Dock." Ryker hit a few buttons before making the vehicle drift close enough to be caught and then anchored.

"How is it you know how to work a pirate ship?" she asked as she found the uplinks in this security area.

"I've taken a few ships joyriding. Unlike the haircut, apparently that is a hard no with the conglomerate. And now I know." Ryker let his finger hover over a square button.

"What is that?" The words came out muffled. Speaking through a clenched jaw wasn't the best way to communicate.

"It'll blow this docking. Hopefully."

"What brings you?" a voice said over their speakers.

"Just seeing the sights. Taking the missus to see the great city of Los Angeles." Ryker's finger touched down on the button.

"LA is a great place to *meet* new friends. You got any other passengers on this pleasure cruise?" the voice asked.

Ryker hesitated, staring hard. "Two."

Millicent's fingers turned white where they were gripping her seat. She wanted to ask what the hell he was doing but didn't dare talk with the speakers active.

"They as fit as you?" the voice went on.

"The man is thinner and shorter. And a kid."

"Uh-huh." The man reached to the side and came back with a small stack of clothes. "Unexpected vessel. But it grants you more sights to see. You want to do any shopping during your holiday? Or have an inclination to sell something you found during your travels?"

Ryker sent her a quick glance. "We can buy all day long," he said to the man with ease.

"It's customary to grease the turntable when you're in a craft like that. Generosity spreads good favor. Then you can proceed as planned. You got heat. Stay low to avoid the flame."

"None of that makes any sense," Millicent mumbled without moving her lips. "What's happening?"

"Got it. Transferring now." Ryker pulled up a screen on his side, accessed some sort of electronic cache, tapped it a few times, and then swiped his finger toward the security.

The guard's eyes widened briefly. He glanced behind him before reaching to the side again. "Route coming your way. I'll pave the way as much as possible, but you gotta scratch your way through it. Best of luck on your holiday."

Ryker didn't glance at his wrist when it lit up, a purple-pink color.

"Send out your pickup tray," the voice said.

Ryker worked the dash before a mechanical sound infiltrated the silence. The guard put the fabric and a flimsy screen into the tray and then stepped back. He glanced behind him again. "We're rooting for you. Give 'em hell."

"Hear it. Out." Ryker slapped a button, and the craft drifted peacefully away from the wall. The barrier in front of them cleared, and green shone down on them again. "Hold your breath."

"What just happened?" Millicent asked, incapable of holding her breath any longer. She was about to pass out as it was.

"He must handle the admittance of pirate vessels intending to sell their spoils. Looks like he directs them into safe ports in the city to buy or sell, whatever they're after. They work in the black, away from the various conglomerate eyes in the city. Clearly that's who he thought we were at first—"

"Yes, clearly," Millicent said dryly.

"—and since we need all the help we can get, I figured we'd better take a quick look at the black-market tech, see if they have anything we might need. Why not? He had those clothes ready and waiting. But he also works for Roe. He realized who we were—probably by the eye scan—and that we're here to meet up."

"What about the other stuff? Because if there are flames, obviously staying low makes no sense."

"You are too literal for your own good, princess."

"An annoying product of her breeding," they heard from the main cabin.

Ryker smirked, then said, "Grease the turntables is a request for a bribe. Generosity goes a long way. They want you to live so you can buy them off another day. I took care of that. Heat is obviously the conglomerate looking for us, and staying low . . . well, looks like we'll be slumming it. You don't really want to know where he's sending us."

"What floor?" Millicent asked in an even voice.

"Los Angeles is not only a hugely sprawling city with all three conglomerates housed here, it is also quite a bit taller than San Francisco, as far as structures go. So when I say we are going to floor twenty-three, that doesn't mean what you think it means."

"You're right, I don't really want to know." Millicent worked through the net, getting more familiar. "Do you need me to navigate?"

"No. The ship is half guiding. This must be a normal dock point. Annoying, the veering left." Ryker dropped them into a lower travel way as soon as he could. Tendrils of brown fog licked at their windows before they dropped farther down still. And farther. It turned into thick soupy brown that obscured all but the faint glow of travel-way markers and the lights of the vessels around them.

Millicent couldn't help her lip curling in distaste. "This is worse than San Francisco."

"And three times as dangerous. There was a reason you were stationed where you were. Our . . . past conglomerate held the monopoly on that area. It was pretty easy to monitor when a different conglomerate went rogue."

"Yet I've had three attempts on my life."

"Pretty easy for someone of my caliber, I meant. The deadweights you had in security at the time weren't worth the resources they were using."

"The others certainly didn't have your ego, that's what I'd bet." Millicent pulled her hands away from the flickering hologram. "Looks like the net port is finicky. They must have software to try and keep out these ships. I can fix it . . ."

"The hanging sentence thing is you asking for an order, is it? I'll remember that."

"Boy, this knife is itching to be used. It'd fit perfectly between your ribs." Millicent didn't wait. She just got to work as Ryker lowered the ship. Brown turned to nearly black, the environment so thick and filthy it blocked out the light. Huge buildings twice the size of those in San Francisco ghosted by, nothing more than blips in the computer and strange shapes they could barely see.

"Can you turn on some lights back here?" Mr. McAllister's disembodied voice drifted up through the silence. "Marie is getting scared."

Ryker flicked something on the dash. A glow drifted through the partition.

"I transferred all the money clocked on the ship," Ryker said into the gloom. "It was a substantial sum."

"You should've transferred funds from my account so we could keep the pirate booty. It was probably less traceable." Millicent bit her lip as she analyzed some truly exemplary code within Gregon's firewall. "That little vixen is damn good. Look at this. She's raising the bar."

"I did."

"Huh?" Millicent asked absently while trying to get into the code-writer's head. It was an extremely complex grouping of systems that seemed completely random. It almost seemed like it couldn't work. But it did. Which meant Millicent was missing the through thread.

"I used mine. Yours was completely untraceable after a certain point. I tried to trace it after I decided to get you off this planet. I'd thought mine was, but in the light of what I've learned . . ."

Like a flash of light, an explosion of brilliance lit Millicent's world. "Of course! Smart. I keep learning from this lady." Millicent clapped and then bent over the hologram. With the part of her brain she wasn't eagerly using, she multitasked. "I thought it was my choice to go off-planet?"

"I got cold feet toward the end. Regarding Marie. I wanted you to choose what would be best for her. But I'd already decided to try for you. Long before you were ready to leave."

"I see. And when did you first decide to get me off-planet?"

"It was when I—"

"Shit. Sorry to interrupt, Ryker," she said absently, her mind whirling around the problem. She was only so good at doing two things at once. "But no. This won't work. I need to go straight through, not around. She's more of a linear thinker than I am. Mr. McAllister, did I have any natural-born sisters? I mean . . ." She rubbed her nose in irritation. "Not like a sibling, but someone who got the same secret sauce I did?"

After some rustling, Mr. McAllister's head popped through the partition. "What's this now?"

"Talk about engineering human beings and he's all ears," Ryker growled.

"The woman in Gregon who is as good of a coder as I am," Millicent said. "Was she in my batch?"

Mr. McAllister checked his wrist screen. "I don't have specifics without the database, so I can't be positive we are talking about the same person, but it stands to reason. She came first. They had great success with her, so they decided to use the same recipe, as it were. So yes, she is your sister. Blood sister, actually. I believe you two had the same parents. I can't be sure—what?"

Millicent's hands had stilled. She was staring at the code, but not seeing it. Thinking of her daughter, and her current situation, the enormity of what Mr. McAllister was saying crashed down onto her. She barely felt the large palm on her thigh, supportive.

"I have parents," she whispered. She blinked away sudden emotion. "This woman is my sister. My natural-born sister. I have parents . . ."

Ryker's hand squeezed. "It's a good day," he said genuinely. "It's nice to know you aren't totally alone in the world. That there are others like you who weren't made in a lab."

"Well . . . I mean . . ." Mr. McAllister rubbed his chin as he stared at Ryker. "Obviously no one is really alone. Right? Because here we are, with people . . ."

"Family is different, you half-wit. She has a family—all related. She came from somewhere." Ryker's fingers softly brushed a tear from her cheek. "We can create that for Marie, Millie. We can expand our family. And then we can invite yours to join us. Marie will know her aunt. And maybe her grandparents if we can find them . . ."

"Okay, wait a minute. I think this just got blown way out of proportion." Mr. McAllister waved his hands. "She and this other woman have the same parents, but that doesn't mean they are actually a—"

Mr. McAllister fell back with a grunt. Ryker uncurled his fist and replaced his palm back on Millicent's thigh.

"Ow," Mr. McAllister whined. "Why did you punch me?"

"It's just . . . crazy." Millicent wiped another tear from her eye and pushed away the strange fuzzy feeling that was invading her whole body. Then, with a sigh, she let herself give in for a moment. She let this sentimentality run away with her.

Her hand covered Ryker's, and then her fingers curled under his palm. The next moment, large fingers were on her chin, pulling her in his direction. His breath dusted her face before those soft, shapely lips touched hers.

A glorious tightness consumed her as he lightly sucked on her bottom lip. His lips parted, begging hers to do the same. When she did, his tongue darted in, playful. His large but gentle palm slid over her breast. She didn't recognize her moan, as full of longing as it was.

Blaring horns drowned out the buzz in her head. A siren went off right beside them. Lights flashed.

"Look out!" Mr. McAllister yelled, popping into the cockpit.

The heat was ripped away. The vessel jolted back left.

All Millicent could do was blink. Blink, and focus on the uncomfortable pounding in her core. On the consuming feeling that would take much more than those black briefs to satisfy.

"I'm losing my mind," she mumbled, not at all worried that they were dodging oncoming vehicles, but absolutely worried that her chest felt cold where his hand had been.

"Fun, isn't it?" She could hear the laughter in Ryker's voice. That would probably work out badly for her in the end . . .

Chapter 17

"I can barely see," Trent whispered in the darkness of the cockpit as thumps and grinds announced a harsh docking.

"That's probably best. I don't like the smell of this place. Millie, I assume that larger jacket back there is stuffed with weapons?" Ryker stared out the window. Weak fluorescent bulbs hung off the wall at odd angles, showering the cracked and uneven walkway with dingy yellow light.

"Yes. It's heavy, so I won't be able to run as fast, but if the worst should happen . . ."

"I'm not worried about the worst right now, which is Mr. Hunt. I'm worried about small-scale attacks in large quantities." Ryker shifted forward. "We might have a large body count by the time we get inside this place."

Until now, they'd been safely confined in one craft or another. Trent didn't know how to operate one, having never done so before, but there'd been a sense of security. Mr. Hunt was on their trail after all, so if something went wrong, it wouldn't take long before Trent and Marie were rescued.

Now, though, everything was about to change. They were stepping into unfamiliar territory in the depths of a large and brutal city. Millicent and Ryker were more than capable, but there was no telling what security systems were in place. If they went down, Trent would probably be killed, leaving Marie exposed and alone. She could be snatched up by anyone—pirates, another conglomerate—and used for ransom or as a bartering chip.

Trent clutched Marie tighter. He would not let that happen. She must be protected at all costs.

"I'll take Marie. Right?" he asked. "You guys cover us, and I'll take her. I can run fast."

"I thought you said you couldn't." Millicent swung out of her seat and then paused, waiting.

Trent cleared out of the way. "That was before things were chasing me. Can I have a gun?"

Millicent dug through the pack of new tech before analyzing the two items she'd risked her life to rescue. She connected one of them to the computer, and a flash of joy lit up her face as she stared at the screen.

"What?" Ryker asked, filling the small interior. He was immediately crowding everyone.

"Shoo." Millicent waved him out of the way—something only she could get away with. "I'm getting the hang of this pirate network. It's really genius in a way. Like an invisible intranet or something. I bet I could construct something like this . . ."

"Right now, let's just stay hidden for as long as possible," Ryker said, arming himself.

"Gun?" Trent stuck out his hand.

Ryker glanced down at Trent's palm. "You're shaking, holding my daughter, and you want me to give you a gun?"

"If you two die and I get caught, what am I supposed to do? Ask nicely for our attacker to go away?"

Ryker tilted his head, studying Trent with those crazy blue eyes. A grin flickered across his lips. "I see your balls have dropped." A moment later, a gun was thrust into Trent's hands. "If you use this against us in any way, I will—"

"Don't tell me," Trent interrupted. "I don't want to envision it. It'll probably give me nightmares."

Millicent worked at her suit for a moment before rolling her shoulders and smiling.

"What?" Ryker asked, frustration now threading through his gaze. Trent knew that look—impatience.

"The new tech," Millicent said. "It's incredibly light. Genius, really. And extremely expensive. I wonder where the pirates got it."

"Focus!" Trent said, knowing the frustration in his tone mirrored that in Ryker's gaze. He couldn't help it, though. He was terrified and also trying to gear himself up for shooting someone. It was a lot to handle.

"How much longer until they pick apart your code?" Ryker asked Millicent.

"Impossible to say. But when they do, we'll fry the implants." Millicent held up a clunky box. "It's going to really hurt, but it'll do the job. I did leave a loophole, after all."

"What loophole? What'll hurt?" Trent asked.

"Let's go," Ryker said.

"After I fried Ryker's implant, they made my department issue an update," Millicent said. "We did, but I left a few frequencies open. Rarely used electronic frequencies, obviously, because the update had to be beta tested. If I have ample time, I can hack into the system and fry our implants remotely, but . . . well, time is no longer on our side. Luckily, this gadget can mimic one of those. It'll hurt a lot, though, because this thing is horribly old."

"Why did you bring me? Seriously, I was happy," Trent whined.

"Stop being such a baby. Marie hasn't complained once, and she *is* a baby," Ryker said as he braced himself near the door, his tone light but his eyes hard and burning with malice.

"That's because she can barely talk," Trent mumbled.

"Here we go." Ryker opened the doors.

Trent quickly strapped on a holster of sorts, stowed the gun, and then squeezed Marie to his chest. He felt the strange gravity that came whenever she wrapped her arms around his neck and hugged him tight. He wasn't technically a parent, but he had been there at her conception, birth, and every day of her life. He felt he was every bit as much of a father as Ryker did—just without the insanity that came with Ryker's hyperprotective breeding.

"You got her?" Millicent asked. Trent felt Millicent's hand on his shoulder, somewhat trembling. She was hiding her fear with her ever-confident tone.

"Yes." He wasn't.

"Okay." He got a pat.

"Okay," Trent repeated in an exhale before catching Ryker's violent gaze. Then Ryker disappeared into the cold blackness.

Trent stepped onto the cracked and buckled walkway. Millicent followed him out quickly and then fanned out behind him. "Close the door, Marie," Trent mumbled.

The door closed with a rattle and shake, locking them outside on the foul-smelling walkway. Thick air shifted around them, so dense it almost felt like a physical thing brushing his exposed cheeks.

He adjusted Marie's scarf as Ryker started moving. "Keep your eyes open," Ryker said, his voice so deep and menacing, Trent shivered. He'd hate to be pitted against that man.

Without warning, a black shape surged out of nowhere. Something glinted, slicing through the air. Another shape dashed after it, phantoms in the blackness.

Ryker rushed forward to meet them. His fist, wrapped around a knife, pounded into the first assailant, poking holes as it did so. A grunt turned into a pained scream. Ryker spun, leaving a dead man in his wake, and his arm cut through the air. Knife blade dulled with blood, he sliced through the throat of the second attacker in a smooth, clean motion. The second attacker bent over in agony. His weapon went skittering across the ground before reaching the ledge of the walkway. It practically waved good-bye as it pitched over the side and fell into the nothingness.

A moment later, the owner flew after it.

"Oh!" Trent backed up, bumping into Millicent. Ryker bent to the other body, picked it up easily, and then launched it over the ledge. Limbs waved through the air as it disappeared out of sight.

Trent clutched Marie tighter. "Was that really necessary?" he asked in a strangely high-pitched voice.

"Nope." Ryker glanced beyond Trent to Millicent. Apparently satisfied, he started forward.

A swish of fabric and a hydraulic buzz preceded a gunshot. Trent jumped and spun back toward Millicent. A person collapsed to the ground behind them.

"You okay back there, cupcake?" Ryker asked.

Two more gunshots made Trent flinch.

"Think anyone monitors the cameras down here?" Millicent asked, pushing Trent onward.

"No, I do not," Ryker said.

"Then I'm doing great."

Another shape darted out from the side, diving right for Trent. "Ryker!" Trent hunched over Marie protectively. A grunt and a wet squelch sounded behind him. Followed by a death rattle.

"All clear," Ryker said. Another body went over the side.

"Someone is going to wonder why it's raining dead people," Millicent said.

They advanced again, walking down the eerily quiet walkway. "Where are all the people?" Trent asked quietly, trying to peer into the gloom for any sign of movement or human life. If something was there, he couldn't tell.

"I don't know," Millicent said, just as softly. "I've never seen a walkway so barren."

"Not natural," Ryker said. Purple-pink glowed from his wrist, an extremely odd color for a violent man like him. Trent pointed this out. "Changed it when I found out I had a daughter. Reminded me of her when I couldn't be around her. Now that she's around . . . I like that people get the wrong idea."

"Why?"

"Because they do stupid things, which means I get to teach them a lesson."

Trent shook his head, watching a vehicle slowly drift by. A loud clack, clack, clack drifted by with it, the thing barely hovering along. "You have issues."

"You create people with issues. You should be used to it."

They stopped beside a nondescript door, the surface smooth and untarnished—a complete contrast to the scarred and pockmarked walls to either side. Millicent stepped next to Trent, facing away so as to cover them from attackers.

Ryker tapped in a code of some sort, all the buttons ever-changing symbols, randomizing with each keystroke.

"This is an expensive defensive door and code combo," Ryker said, pulling the door open a crack, bracing himself for a possible attack. After a moment, he relaxed and then widened the opening. Nothing but a dimly lit interior with beige walls awaited them.

"Why put that much money into a place this far down?" Millicent asked. "Maybe this city has too much commerce to stick to the upper parts of the city."

"I don't think that's it. Not with the surroundings looking like they do." Ryker stepped to the side as Millicent brought up her gun. "What is it?"

"I see a shape," she said. "I bet it's the person who's been following us."

"Someone has been following us?"

The gunshot made Trent flinch again. A small tendril of smoke curled up from the barrel. A hand slapped the pavement within the hazy beam of light. She lowered the weapon slowly, her focus fixed on a shadowy area. "He hung back after I killed the first couple. Probably one of the smarter ones. Got him, though. Not smart enough."

"She wasn't supposed to have these kinds of aggressive issues," Trent mumbled to himself as Marie snuggled closer; he was still not able to resign himself to killing and dead bodies. It was a lot to take in.

"Survival, Mr. McAllister, is not a situation for decorum." Millicent glanced at Ryker, got a jerk of the head, and led the way into the corridor.

With a firm hand steering him, Trent followed. The door shut behind Ryker with a well-maintained click.

"There's no way a pirate could have set this up, is there?" Millicent asked as she slowly made her way down the corridor, gun held between both hands and pointed upward. She was a natural.

"I doubt it," Ryker said, passing Trent and then putting the same firm hand on Millicent to slow her down. He took the lead. "Not with this kind of money and security. This is professional, and not our former conglomerate, so I couldn't begin to guess what is kept down here."

In twenty meters, the corridor intersected another. Uniform lighting continued throughout, but no signs or directional descriptions gave them a clue as to what awaited them.

Ryker checked his wrist before hooking a thumb right. "Looks like we turn here."

This corridor was exactly the same as the other. Same lighting, same color, same size—the only difference was the direction. The next turn was the same. And the next. Without a guidance system, it would be easy to get turned around and possibly lost for a good long time.

"A lot of money went into making this place confusing," Millicent said, somehow plucking the thoughts right out of Trent's brain.

"It's cheap down here. The property, I mean." Ryker slowed and looked at his wrist before a door that looked much the same as the others. The doors inside were all constructed of the same metal they'd encountered outside.

"Still. The construction and tech alone are hefty expenses. And without a bay? Those thieves outside must make money if they're waiting around in numbers like that." Millicent looked behind them.

"That's a back way. If pirates use it routinely, I'm sure people are picked off. That's got nothing to do with the conglomerate. This place probably has a bay in the front entrance." He keyed in a code, hesitating between two symbols at one point before finally choosing one. His sigh was barely audible. Apparently that decision had been a leap of faith.

The door cracked open but didn't swing out. Just stayed where it was, asking them to do all the work.

Ryker slowly pulled it back. He glanced in quickly, and then opened the door wider. "Looks clear."

Trent hesitated before he followed Ryker in. The color changed from the stagnant beige of the corridor to a cheery yellow with warm overtones. The warm hallway was decorated with lovely paintings and relaxing or rejuvenating murals. The floor, a warm reddish-brown tile, shone from constant cleaning. This seemed like the interior of someone's home.

"I don't like this," Trent said.

"Hurry." Millicent pushed him forward.

The door closed behind them as Ryker consulted his directions. He led them left. It only took a few dozen steps for him to freeze. Trent jostled Marie as Ryker pushed them back and against the wall.

"There is an open doorway up to the right," he whispered, "with a glass viewing area beside it. Looks like an exercise facility. I saw three people entering, all wearing the same suits. We need to change." He motioned back to the door they'd come through.

Millicent paused when they reached it, and then spread her hands across the smooth surface. Her glance back at them was fraught with consternation. "One-way door. Unless Marie can open it, we're trapped."

Ryker's face closed down into a terrifying mask of calmness. People drifting away from life probably saw that expression.

He slowly turned back in the direction of the exercise facility, looking at Marie for a beat too long, and then nodded slowly. "We get dressed. If we've been set up, we'll blow this whole thing sky-high."

"Can you do that?" Trent asked as certain parts of him tingled. It was his flight reflex. He was well versed with the signals by now. Around Ryker, he experienced them constantly.

"No." Ryker pulled out the clothing he'd been handed by the city guard. "But she can." He jerked his head at Millicent.

"But you don't have any weapons that big." Trent's limbs shook as he set Marie down. He had no idea why this news was causing him uncomfortable jitters. Surely it should've been good news that this rather petite and beautiful woman could blow a building to hell with nothing but the clothes on her back. That was helpful in the short term.

Long term, he'd never want to stand near her again.

But all his thoughts shorted out as she quickly stripped out of her clothes and displayed a perfect body with high round breasts, a tight stomach, and a delicious hourglass figure.

"If you want to keep your eyes, bub, you ought to look away," Trent heard in a low growl. "That's the only warning you'll ever get."

Face burning up to his ears—because really, he had been lucky to get a warning—he inched toward the far wall and stared at a lovely picture of a fat woman holding some sort of fuzzy domestic animal with long whiskers. Since his Clarity had long since worn off, he couldn't do much about the raging problem down below. Hopefully Ryker wouldn't get the insane urge to break it off.

After the scratchy new suit was on—the pant legs riding high and sleeves not reaching his wrists—he turned around to face the others. Even Marie had a sort of suit, though its markings were different. Everyone's but Trent's fit properly.

"They got a suit to fit the giant guy, but not the normal guy?" Trent said under his breath as he took Marie's hand. "You need to walk for a little while, okay? I need a break from carrying you."

"'Kay," Marie said in her tiny little voice. She took his hand and then squeezed Bunny into her neck.

"Keep up your guard, Millie," Ryker said, an unusual type of seriousness in his voice. "I don't know what we're going to find."

"Neither do I," she said. "I can't find any consoles and I'm not registering any wireless. How do they get onto the net in here?"

Ryker's lips thinned, and a killer's edge crept into his eyes. He shook his head once, slowly, before he started forward again. They reached the doorway he'd mentioned before he stalled, but this time they turned into it. Trent followed. His jaw dropped.

The huge room was alive with activity. Running mats, weights, and fitness machines filled the space, almost all of them occupied. Shapely and fit figures, one and all, ran like they'd been doing it all their life. Moving easily, very few of them out of breath, they looked straight ahead and went about their occupation. Through a glass wall was a pool of liquid such as Trent had never seen in his life. *Water!*

Azure blue and glistening in the white light above, it was contained in a rectangle, divided into smaller rectangles—lanes, it looked like. Within them, people were slowly propelling their bodies through the liquid.

"Have you ever seen anything like that?" Trent asked Millicent. If anyone would've, it would've been her.

"No. All that water," she said in wonder, staring. "Where did they get all that water?"

"This is a recycling plant. I should've known." Ryker took Millicent's hand and pulled her along. Trent followed on numb legs. He couldn't stop staring at all that water. His tongue thickened, and an intense thirst washed over him.

"Can't drink that water," Ryker said in a low tone as he moved through the people exercising, clearly reading Trent's mind. Or possibly the longing expression that must've been on his face. "It has a lot of chemicals in it. It's treated water from outside. It causes lesions and cancers on the skin after too much contact. If they swallow it, it'll cause sickness and long-term effects."

"Then why are they in it?" Millicent asked.

"Swimming is good for you. It is a great way to keep fit. Or so I've heard." Halfway through the room, Ryker altered their course toward the southwest, cutting through the gathered people at a diagonal now. None of them so much as looked up. They stared off into space—not even at holograms or screens—and continued to move. The machines all had a stand of controls next to them, equipped with buttons. A display read the time and speed. It looked like they had to manually control their settings.

"It sounds like it's bad for you," Millicent said.

"Why don't they use their implants?" Trent wondered aloud, noticing someone at the back reach forward and push a button on the control. Her legs churned a little faster.

"Recycling plant," Ryker whispered again as they made it to the wall. He stopped by a door and consulted his wrist. "They won't be around long enough for cancer."

It dawned on Trent what he meant, and judging by the look on Millicent's face, she did, too. Clones. Or lab bred but not assigned a civic duty. Human parts used to keep the upper levels alive longer.

"I have two assigned to me," Millicent said softly as they exited the room. Her gaze lingered through the viewing glass as they walked down another cheery hallway.

Rooms were off to the sides now, mostly with open doors. The spaces were all pristine and clean, and the general vibe was some degree of *happiness* or *relaxation*. Youthful and vibrant, the decorations provided a sense of calm.

"So this is what they do all day? Just work out and relax?" Trent yanked his gaze away from one open room in which three persons were writhing against each other, all of them nude. "Among other things."

"They are staying fit and healthy," Ryker said, directing them around a corner. "Maximum life expectancy is thirty. If some part of them isn't used by then, they'll be turned loose or killed, their choice. If turned loose, they might be able to find a sector job somewhere, but someone will have to put an implant in them. That costs money."

"Why thirty?" Millicent asked.

Another large room housed various seats in which people were sitting around with portable screens, staring. Reading, probably. The next room was filled with table screens. Puzzle pieces littered the viewers.

"Calling HRK-234RZ," a voice said over the loudspeaker. "Congratulations, you can now fulfill your duty. Please report to the assignment center. Calling HRK-234RZ, please report to the assignment center. It is time to serve Gregon Corp."

Clapping echoed through the hallways, pouring out of rooms. Someone had just been chosen to die.

"I had no idea," Trent said as disgust ate away his gut.

"What'd you think happened?" Ryker asked, veering them around a dispensary of some sort.

"I . . . don't know." He blinked at a man lathering himself with lotion. The room was full of little stations for just that purpose. "I never really thought about it. I guess I just assumed we cloned some of the higher-ranked people and used those clones whenever a transplant was needed. Not that we held people in a sort of farm until we needed to harvest them."

"This is the reality of it. They think and feel, but they're treated like hosts to precious organs intended for someone like me. Like Millie. They have no life, everything they say and do is monitored, and they are kept here until needed." Ryker pushed open a door and waited beside it as the others filed past him.

"Their lives aren't all that much different than ours," Millicent said, almost to herself. "Except I did get to think for myself."

"As long as it benefited the conglomerate, yeah." Ryker pointed at a bench seat along a far wall. "Sit. We're supposed to wait here. We're a little early. Millie, get your defenses ready. I doubt they'd try to keep us here, but we still don't know what we're meeting."

"But . . ." Millicent frowned as she messed with something inside her jacket. "If they cloned me, then that . . . person would be as smart as me, right? Isn't that how it works?"

"I don't know how it works, actually," Ryker said. "I just know the outcome."

"Why don't they just clone the organs, rather than the whole being?" Millicent asked, biting her lip. Trent recognized that quirk as her attempt to figure something out.

"Cheaper, probably," Ryker said, shrugging. "Otherwise they have to fire up the systems for each transplant. This way, they can use one person for a few spare parts."

"This conversation is making me sick," Trent said, thinking about all those people he'd passed, waiting for death. Waiting to go under the knife so a piece of them could be put into someone else. Someone more important.

A pop had Ryker brandishing a knife out of nowhere. A door Trent hadn't noticed—it blended in perfectly with the wall—swung open, emitting a tall lanky man with a canvas sack. Another man, shifty-eyed and balding, followed closely behind. He was a natural born! Unless the lab in Gregon was completely useless. Trent's department had filtered out balding a long time ago.

"What are you doing here early?" the lanky man asked in a harried voice. He glanced out the far window. His upper lip was beaded in perspiration. He dropped the sack and shook his head. "We have ten minutes, tops, before someone sounds the alarm."

Millicent leaned toward the sack, surveying the contents.

"Hold on a minute, Sticks. What's this about an alarm?" Ryker asked, not looking at the exposed interior of the bag.

"These things don't got implants, you read me?" Sticks said, gesturing wildly beyond the walls. "So the guards gotta watch with their eyes. Old school." He pointed at the corners of the ceiling. "My guy was told when to cut the feed for maintenance. You're early. He didn't cut it in time. He's trying to undo that problem, but there ain't no time travel, hip to that? So we gotta do this deal, and then you gotta deal with your problem."

"What do you mean, I have to deal with my problem?" Ryker's words held a knife and a promise.

Shifty Eye stilled, his gaze drifting down Ryker's large body before returning to his face. Dawning understanding struck, and judging by his expression, it flipped his world upside down.

"Who is yous guys?" Shifty Eye asked, now looking at Marie in disbelief.

"We're your new clients." Ryker pointed a finger at them collectively. His arm flexed, and their eyes widened at the sight of his huge boulders of muscle. "You did say you were tour guides, right? That you can get us out of here without a problem?"

"I'll take these." Millicent's light and musical voice cut through the masculine threats. Everyone's eyes shifted without meaning to, unable to ignore the draw of the woman in the room.

Or at least, that's what it seemed like. Trent really missed taking Clarity. Especially around annoyingly pretty women.

"How much?" she asked, looking up expectantly.

Sticks rubbed his fingers along his chin. Ryker clearly forgotten, he pored over the items she'd pulled out from his bag. "Nah, you can't afford all o' that. Them's top o' the line. Just came out, them did. Ain't no other tech like it on the market."

Millicent scowled at him in impatience. "Don't be daft. My department put out something like this three years ago. We featured it in the keynote. How much?"

"Your department." Worry crept into Sticks's gaze. "Where you from? Why you want all this?"

"They lookin' to get out, you trekking moron." Shifty Eye crowded in to look at the merchandise. "I'll get ya a price. Here." He brought out a screen and tapped on it before pointing it toward her. He glanced nervously over his shoulder, clearly hoping Ryker wouldn't be a part of the deal.

Millicent scoffed. "No way. Half that and you got a deal. And that's overpaying."

"You got any other options?" Shifty Eye asked.

"Obviously. I'll tell my partner to kill you both. Then I'll get everything for free. But I'm the nice one. So I'm offering to pay." Millicent handed back the screen. "Half, or you pay *us* with blood. Up to you."

"Sweet freedom, *she's* the nice one?" A tiny smile drifted up Shifty Eye's face. "You looking to pirate? 'Cause we can use a pair like you. We'd be the best outfit in this area."

"We shouldn't take no part in this," Sticks said, inching toward the door. "They tryin' to get out, you say. Two natural borns, a . . . whatever he is"—Sticks pointed at Trent—"and a *kid*, bro-yo? Nah. You caught a disease of the stupid variety. No kinda heat gonna be as bad as their kinda heat. We need to walk away."

A siren blasted, drowning out their words. "Intruder! Intruder! Intruder!" boomed over the loudspeakers.

"Too late," Ryker said, grabbing Sticks by the collar. "Get your shit and lead on. You just got a new job."

Chapter 18

Millicent flung the credit transfer at the balding man with strangely wobbly eyes before collecting the items she needed and looking for Ryker. He waited by the door, holding the skinny pirate in place by the back of his shirt.

Clutching the new tech, she jogged forward as Mr. McAllister snatched up Marie and they all filed into the bland corridor.

"No, no, no!" Sticks was saying as Ryker pushed him ahead.

"Where to?" Ryker asked, yelling above the din. The door slammed behind them. The balding man had stayed behind.

"Shit! You've just trekking killed us, you resource rapers! They'll lock down these doors. We're trapped inside!" Sticks kicked the wall. Then he grunted and hopped.

"Not real bright, this one," Millicent said earnestly as she glanced down at her wrist. "The craft is back that way." She jerked her chin left.

"That dock will be on lockdown. And it's too far away," Sticks whined. "Our only chance was sticking to the outskirts in there." He slapped the wall. "But now we're trekked."

"Lead!" Ryker shoved the man forward. "Go like the doors will open."

"But they—" The man flung up his hands at Ryker's *look*. With a sigh, the man started jogging left, but took an immediate right when they could. A moment later, they were winding away from their docking point.

"Why'd we dock so far away?" Millicent asked, breathing heavy with the weight of the tech in her arms. She'd need to figure out another bag.

"Anyone who can buy our stuff can survive that dock. The first time, they gotta be tested," the man said, jogging right up to the door and poking at the screen. He turned, raising his eyebrows and hands as if to say, *See?*

"There is a communication gap between these thieving outfits, I think," Mr. McAllister said as he switched Marie from one hip to the other. His arms were starting to straighten, though. He was getting tired. So was she. "Open the door, Marie," he said, out of breath.

Marie looked at the door, and her eyebrows furrowed for a brief moment before her face lit up in a smile. She giggled, and the door cracked open.

"What the . . ." Sticks stared in astonishment as Ryker ripped open the door.

"Now close it up," Mr. McAllister said after everyone was through.

"You have to tell her?" Ryker asked as they started a fast walk.

"The kid did that?" Sticks asked. "How?"

"She's a kid. She doesn't know what's going on," Mr. McAllister said, indignant. "A kid is confronted with a door. It keeps her in until she's old enough to try the handle. Once she figures out the handle, you can no longer keep her in. With most kids, that doesn't matter because we have electronic doors. But to Marie, the electronic mechanism is her handle. She just has to figure out how it turns. Once she does, she's through." They stopped at a door that had cold air seeping out from under it. "But she is just a passenger right now, so we have to let her know when we need her help. Marie, sweetie, open the door."

There was barely a pause before the door clicked. Ryker grabbed its edge and pulled it open.

"You have to ask nicely, though, or that door won't even open with the master code," Mr. McAllister said. He sounded strangely pleased. "And she never has to figure it out twice," he went on. "She's the smartest of the bunch."

They surged outside, Sticks in the lead. Cold assaulted them. The swirling cloud of environment coated the glass of the bay, leaving the small space next to the single docked vessel a tiny bit more pleasant. Visible anyway.

"Hurry." The man barely reached his craft before the doors jerked open. He blinked at them. "She can open craft doors, too?"

Ryker shoved him in. "It's a door, isn't it?" Ryker covered the interior of the small craft in three strides. He bent into the cockpit. "It'll have to do." He glanced back. "Why doesn't the conglomerate protect this bay?"

"They will." Sticks pushed Ryker aside and climbed into the single seat. "Our guy controls this dock. He won't lock us in. Although . . . with the kid, I guess it wouldn't matter if he did."

"I don't know if she can unlock a dock," Mr. McAllister said speculatively as Millicent dropped her tech on the seat and began hunting for a bag to put everything in. "I mean, I'm sure she *can*, but I have no idea how I'd tell her to try. She'd probably have to understand the workings of the thing. The mechanics—"

"We need to get to Downtown Southeast," Ryker yelled as he looked at his wrist screen, barely heard over the sudden frantic roar of the engine. The man at the wall must've sent the coordinates for the meet-up since Millicent hadn't transferred those over to him.

"This transport can only operate in a certain area, bro-yo," Sticks said over the din. "We got restrictions. I can take yous as far as Leston Central. After that, you gotta nab a craft or wait 'n' get yours from impound. Ain't no other way."

"It's downtown. Surely we can stick within the public areas?" Mr. McAllister asked, pushed to the side so Millicent could check under the cushion on his seat.

"Nice!" she said, grabbing white canvas from the storage bay. Two straps hung from the ends. "It'll work."

"Leston is a ways from downtown," Ryker said, picking Marie up and then sitting down with her on his lap.

"I got a lock pick right here." Millicent held up the tiny green oval.

"That's second-level security grade. It's ours." Ryker grabbed it for a closer look. "How'd they get that out?"

"Curious, isn't it?" Millicent reached for it. He pulled his hand away, half a second quicker than she was. "I bought it. It's mine."

"It's stolen, princess. Finders keepers." He glanced down as he rubbed it against his chest. "Damn. No pockets."

"Hold on!" The vessel dipped and then swerved wildly. "Air-cloggin', factory-made baby stealers!" Sticks swore.

"Is he talking about us?" Mr. McAllister asked quietly.

"They got us locked. Shit!" Sticks ducked seconds before something hit the top of the craft. He looked up before yanking the wheel to the side. The craft shimmied. He jabbed a couple of buttons and then yanked the wheel again. A foul smell sullied the air, like rubber melting. Puffs of light-gray smoke billowed up around their feet.

"Time to go," Ryker said, suddenly all action. Millicent barely blinked before Marie was in her lap, her little face closed down in consternation. Ryker ripped open a cabinet at the back before yanking out various black straps. He moved through the small space, checking under seats and in a small storage bay. "How many ejector pods?" he yelled.

"Only got one. Had two, but one weren't workin'. Jimmy found out the hard way." Sticks slapped another button before jerking the wheel a third time. The craft shimmied again. A puff of darker smoke swirled around their feet. "You can try the last one. I ain't gonna. There was a reason this dang thing was retired, that's for right. Don't worry. I bet I can . . ."

The smoke darkened with each shimmy.

Ryker moved Marie from Millicent's lap to that of Mr. McAllister, who was presently groaning in consternation. Millicent felt like doing the same.

"Can you log on to that craft?" Ryker pointed up at their attacker.

"They'll be on manual with a ship like ours," Sticks said, turning a dial with a click, click, click. "I been down this road before. They know how we cut their feet out from under 'em."

"Something has got to be connected to their craft that we can disarm," Ryker said, his electric eyes sparking. "Cause 'em hell for a minute, princess. Give me cover."

"What are you doing?" Sticks yelled back.

"Problem solving," Ryker answered in a flat voice.

Millicent felt the firm hand pushing her toward the front of the vessel. Then Ryker palmed open the console and stepped toward the door. "Marie, open the door, baby."

"No, Dada. Don't go!" She started crying.

"I got it." Millicent pulled up the craft's interior controls.

"It'll only be for a minute, baby. Just for a minute. Daddy will be right back." Ryker glanced at Millicent, the fire and burn overshadowed by something else. Guilt? Regret? Before Millicent could parse that expression, the doors shimmied open and he was gone.

"What the fuck?" Sticks half fell out of his chair as Ryker disappeared. "Did he go and jump?"

"No." Millicent bit her lip as she navigated through the strange intranet before finding an entrance point into the main net. It took her only a moment to find an image of a Gregon Corp. guard locking down an alleged pirate vessel. Social media was rampant in all things related to violence. Then it was just a matter of breaking into Gregon Corp.'s extravagant intranet, way easier than it should've been, and tracking down the right department. Child's play. They weren't worried about people three clicks above the Curve when it came to town-side matters. And why would they be? Extremely smart people didn't randomly leave their duties to become pirates.

Another first in her career.

With rough strokes that tore through the firewall, she barged remotely into the console of the craft above them and hunted for something that could cause mayhem. It took one beat of her hammering heart.

The high-pitched scream of a destabilizing alarm blared above them. The cheap, and therefore stupid, vessel would assume its Curve-hugging drivers were out of control. It would fight to override the manual setting and save the craft.

Millicent tripped the fire alarm, which would also enact an override feature. Next came the altitude alarm. She couldn't locate the door locks, however.

The craft above them shook, undoubtedly jarred by a battle for control between human and computer.

"What's going on up there?" Sticks yelled, leaning against the windshield and looking upward.

"Can you open their craft door, Marie?" Millicent asked, perspiration coating her face. "Help Daddy, baby."

"Up? Up?" Marie pointed upward.

"Yes, up there. The vehicle above us. Daddy needs to get in." Millicent shook her head, not able to find the information she sought. "The exits aren't even on their command log. What the hell—"

"The information is filed in the operations area," Sticks said, craning in his seat to look back. "They move it around to hide it from us. Try operations . . ."

"That's just not practical . . ." Millicent accessed the file as a metallic scream competed with the sirens above. Footsteps pounded against the roof; Ryker was obviously trying to find a way in—possibly by breaking into a window.

"'Kay, Mommy," Marie said, squeezing Bunny. "Open. It open."

"Here—oh." Millicent scowled at the door settings. Nothing pointed to it having opened. She really needed to figure out how Marie was able to circumvent the computers and still get the command executed.

Now wasn't the time.

"Okay. Good girl, honey. Good girl." Millicent pulled up the log. Just as she'd predicted, the craft was trying to override, but the operators were already aborting the application. They were used to the practice. Damn. "Daddy might need help," she said quietly as she looked upward. A weathered ceiling with chipped paint stared back at her.

"Got another one," Sticks said, leaning way right in his chair and staring out the window.

"Yup. That's mine." Millicent darted over to the pile of tech and snatched up a square item the size of her hand. She brought out one of her moderate-powered guns and affixed the item to the end. "I've always wanted to test one of these babies."

"Ah!" Sticks jerked back as a body smacked the windshield. Sightless eyes stared in until it tumbled away, leaving a streak of red across the glass.

"One down," Millicent said, slapping the console and then taking the two quick steps to the door. She braced her hand on the side before bending her knees. A moment later, she raised her gun.

A moderate-sized craft—a bare-bones type of vessel—hovered next to them with an orange light pulsing on top. A gun on the side pointed directly at them, the type with easily enough firepower to pierce a supposedly bulletproof wall.

"They're running out of patience," Millicent said as she pulled the trigger. The gun kicked as it fired, jerking her hand. No sound came out, though.

"Lower your—" The loudspeaker cut out. The craft started to wiggle, side to side, like a large tremble. A face with wide eyes appeared in the cockpit window.

Confused—one shot should've worked—she fired again.

Her gun kicked silently, making her step back. A body flew down in front of her, hands windmilling.

She looked down at the contraption, about ready to yank it off and just fire as many rounds into the new ship as she could before Ryker was finished, when the sound of the motor cut out.

"Ah." She lowered the weapon in satisfaction. "That's better."

"What does it do?" Sticks asked, still staring out the window in shock.

"Electromagnetic pulse. Shuts down their electronic systems. These ships are rigged so that they will still hover, so I won't actually kill anyone, but—"

The explosion blew her back to the other side of the craft. She hit the wall and then tumbled down over the seat.

Sirens blared. Her ears rang. Ryker, face closed down in a blank mask, sailed past her, holding on to a black strap that was hopefully connected to something. Fire spat down at them, licking her body with heat. Ryker flew back in the other direction, still attached to that same black strap.

"Shit." Millicent staggered to her feet, staring out as a burst of flame climbed into the air. In slow motion, the ruined craft wavered. And then tipped downward.

She leaned forward, watching it gain speed as it hurtled toward the ground. A vessel veered away, the guidance systems trying to avoid a collision, but vehicles this far down were stupid. Not fast enough. The security vessel slammed into it. Flaming debris flew out in all directions. Another craft hit, the sound of crunching metal curling Millicent's toes.

Her stomach floated away from her body as the feeling of weightlessness came over her. Their craft had been released from the one above!

And it was falling!

"What are you doing?" Millicent demanded of Sticks.

"Shiiiit—" He pushed away from the window where he'd been watching the carnage and fell back into his seat. His fingers played across the dashboard as he tried to get the craft back online.

"What about Ryker?" Millicent lurched forward. She grabbed the handle by the door and leaned way out. Then looked up.

He was freefalling above their craft, body splayed out, extended knife in hand, determination on his face. He'd jumped when the craft had first started to fall. If they veered right or left, he'd miss and fall to his death. What an idiot.

Which meant she had to be an idiot to make sure he didn't die.

"What's the issue?" Millicent asked, short of breath, as she grabbed Ryker's discarded rope and straps. She didn't want to ponder why he'd left them behind.

"This thing is a piece of shit," Sticks said. "My attempts to break free flooded the engine. I shut it down. I was waiting to try again when you blew that craft up. Didn't expect them to let us go. Watch out, watch out!" He flinched at the horn blast. A vessel raced past them, way too close. "We're in some shit. We're falling out of the sky!"

"Get it going! But don't steer. Just get it hovering." Millicent wrapped the rope around her waist and then tied it to the door. It would really hurt if it went tight, which was better than the alternative of it cutting her in half.

"No promises," the man said, working at his controls. "It doesn't always respond like I want it to."

This is a stupid idea, she thought as she tied another strap around her wrist. "Here we go."

"Where are you going?" Mr. McAllister asked, holding Marie back from running to her.

"To save the day." Taking a deep breath, Millicent swung herself out of the craft. The air caught her and pushed, knocking her along the side and up. Her nails scraped against the metal as adrenaline pumped into her body. Her fingers caught the upper ridge, and her body slammed onto the top of the craft before she started floating again.

This was a really stupid idea. What did she think she'd do once she got up here?

She grabbed ahold of the air-conditioning unit as the sound of an engine rolling over assaulted her ears. Looking over her shoulder, she saw Ryker still above, but now a little off to the side. His face was closed down into a hard scowl.

The engine rolled over again.

She lifted a hand so the strap would billow out above her. Then, when there wasn't a tug, she looked up to see if maybe he couldn't reach. It was flapping right next to his face.

"Take it, you moron!" she yelled, the words ripped out of her mouth and flung away. She doubted he heard. "Take it!" The strap tapped his cheek as she shook her hand at him.

The motor rolled over again, and this time it roared to life. The craft jerked, and the metal was ripped out of her hand, jarring her shoulder. Her palms slid across scratched metal. She was dumped unceremoniously off the edge of the roof, her fingertips just barely grabbing on. Her body slowed, but didn't stop with the vessel. Her face bounced off the window, and then she was weightless.

The world careened. Dark-brown metal craft; large body. A thick arm looped around her middle. A hard blow caught her cheek—the craft, sending shooting sparks of color behind her eyelids. Gravity sucked at her. The arm held fast. Her stomach wobbled as everything stopped spinning.

"Holy fuck," she said, out of breath. When she opened her eyes, she was staring through the window at the terrified face of Mr. McAllister.

"What are you doing, Millicent?" Ryker asked in a deeper-than-normal tone, his voice clearly expressing his disappointment. One of the straps around his wrist was somehow attached to the craft. Not tied, but just . . . stuck on. The other was dangling from the arm wrapped around her. His extendable knife was secured in a holster on his hips.

She clung to the side of the craft. "I'm rescuing you. You're welcome."

"I see." With a loud grunt, he did a one-armed pull-up with the connected strap. He then dragged her up his body, grunting with the effort. Muscles bulged, completely taxed. Horns honked around them. She had no doubt she'd be plastered all over social media. So much for keeping a low profile.

"I got it, I got it," she said as she clutched on to the edge of the roof. She strained, trying to do a pull-up. She made it about halfway. "Okay, maybe just a little push. One more push."

A large hand connected with her butt before she was shoved upward. She used the momentum to crawl onto the top of the craft and then clutched on to the air-conditioning unit.

"Don't hang on to that, it'll throw off the sensors," Ryker said as he crawled up beside her. He slapped a strap down and held on to it with a fist. He passed the other one to her. "Tie it around your wrist. Then just slap it down like I did."

"We can go without air-conditioning," she said as she hastily followed his instructions.

"This isn't an apartment, princess. That's the exhaust manifold." Ryker helped her get the strap on before slapping it to the roof. "There. Don't fall off."

"Oh." She tightened her grip on the strap while Ryker glanced around them.

"We need to get out of here."

"Probably should get into the craft first . . ." She tried to pull herself closer to the strap to figure out how it worked, but before she could, Ryker had grabbed it, disengaged it some way, and then pulled her along the top of the roof.

"Hang on," he said.

"No—waiiiit—" Her body flung in an arch, sailing through the air before the tension on her strap was released. She crashed onto the floor and then bounced into the chair. Her head smacked the seat, which was much nicer than the other surfaces it had come into contact with recently.

A moment later, Ryker swung in, landing on his feet. He stood there like he'd just walked in out of a bay.

"Who the hell is that guy, Rambo?" Sticks asked, his jaw going slack.

"Who's Rambo?" Ryker asked.

"Remake of some ancient two-D." Sticks waved the thought away. "We loaded? We gotta go."

"Close her up," Ryker said to Millicent.

The doors closed before Millicent could get off the ground.

"Why'd you release their hook?" Ryker asked Sticks in a rough growl. "I wasn't done up there yet."

"Me? I thought she did it?" Sticks threw a thumb at Millicent.

"I didn't."

As one, Millicent and Ryker both turned to Marie. Mr. McAllister's face turned red. "Oh no. Was that us? I was just trying to explain the different parts of a hovercraft—you know, to try and see if she might eventually be able to affect different areas of a vessel. Who knows, right? I mean, that should be possible given the talents she's displayed so far, but you just never know what a human brain is capable of. Often it is more or less than—"

"Get to the point," Ryker growled.

"Oh. Well, I had mentioned that the bad men had us stopped because of a locking system on our roof. And explained that that is why Daddy and Mommy were afraid. She only understands simple emotions, even though—" At Ryker's impatient *lean*, Mr. McAllister gulped loudly. "Yes. Ah. So she seems to have figured out how to unlock . . . the locking system. I don't even know what it is, you see. But she seems to have figured it out. Or at least, figured out what the problem was. I have no idea how, honestly . . ."

Ryker turned away, but not before giving Millicent a look she couldn't begin to interpret. Not explaining, he leaned over to Sticks, issuing orders.

"To cut the distance to our meeting place, we have to break through the border and get as far as we can before we're stopped," Ryker said, turning back. "This craft is a marked vessel anyway. It won't matter if we break another law. When they close in, we'll crash and run. It's about to get hairy."

"It's *about* to get hairy?" Mr. McAllister said in disbelief. "What has it been up until now?"

"Normal operating procedure . . ."

Chapter 19

Ryker settled in beside Millicent as she was retrieving another upper. She stuck the white tab on her tongue and settled back.

"How close are you to dropping?" Ryker asked in a low tone, probably so the others wouldn't hear. The craft was so small, though, there wasn't much opportunity for privacy.

"The adrenaline is going to subside soon, so hopefully this kicks in by then. In which case, not close at all. About ready for a party, actually." She retied her hair into a tighter bun.

"We need to find a place to hunker down until we can get some sleep." Ryker checked his wrist. "We'll need to connect with Roe first, though. We only have a small window, and with all these detours, we're cutting it close."

"If we do miss it, can you get a message to him?"

"Before Mr. Hunt finds us?" Ryker lowered his wrist. "I don't know. The way I climbed onto the roof and invaded that security vessel will be all over. He'll know it was me even if he doesn't see the posts. But the craft blowing out of the sky? A normal staffer can't do that."

"Yeah. About that." Millicent bent forward to retrieve the device, only to fall back against Ryker's big arm. It was uncomfortable. "Move."

"Make me."

"Just . . ." She sighed and then pursed her lips when he adjusted so she was leaning heavily against him. "I'm not in the mood."

"Headache?"

"No, why?" She blinked up at him, recognizing the teasing smile. She rolled her eyes and sat forward. "This thing is just supposed to cut out the craft's ability to function, not blow it up." She pulled the device off the gun and ran a finger along its smooth surface. "This is the latest model, too . . ."

"The first time, yes, that's what it does." Ryker reached forward to push the gun away. Apparently he didn't like it pointed at his head. *Oops.* "But when the user is impatient, she won't wait for the first trigger pull to work. Instead, she'll give up waiting and pull it again. Usually it takes four trigger pulls with a smaller-caliber weapon to blow up a small craft. We use smaller caliber because it's safer.

"However, when the user considers her favorite gun as smaller, because she designs guns that'll bring down an armored vehicle, she might, say . . . blow up a craft after the second trigger pull . . . Did I get that right?"

Millicent glanced at her gun. "Any less of a gun and what's the point?"

Ryker chuckled. "Touché."

"But this device shouldn't have enough power to blow something up. Even with a high-powered firearm. I didn't see those modifications cross my desk . . ."

"It's a glitch that hasn't been spoken of outside my department. A useful glitch, when used properly. It'll get the job done, but it won't be our fault for blowing something up. Mr. Hunt would assume I did it on purpose."

"Anyone could make the mistake of pulling the trigger more than once."

"We ain't that stupid, lo-yo. No offense," Sticks called back. "You don't kill security. Then all their security chums put a notice on your head. You're as good as dead. Not caught, dead. Lucky me, they got your pictures all over that. I crash this craft, and I'm in the clear. My name ain't on this rig."

"How's our implant defense?" Ryker asked. His head dropped against the window, and his chest rose and fell in a slow rhythm. He was relaxing after a high-energy, life-and-death situation.

In contrast, her heart pounded like she was at a full-out sprint. Her mouth was dry, like cotton had been stuffed in it. Her fingers tingled, and her foot was tapping on its own. The upper had kicked in before all the adrenaline had dripped away.

"Oh, fuck me." Millicent jumped up and bounced in the aisleway. "Party in my body." She swung her arms as her head got light. "Whoa!" She fist-pumped the air for no real reason.

"That's the last one, Millie. You'll kill yourself." Ryker regarded her lazily.

"We'll see." She turned to the console and clapped, her attempt at focus. Then she clapped a few more times, kind of digging the beat. "Yow." Her shoulders shrugged to the clapping. Her body was reacting independently of her thoughts.

Good. One less thing to operate.

"So let's check out the situation. See if they've contracted my sister to block me out of my file yet." She logged on to the net, dancing with the beat of her heart. Sneaking through the security, she figuratively tap-danced into her file and then physically tap-danced in place. She clapped, making Marie smile and Mr. McAllister frown, before turning back to the console. "I'm feeling good. Really freaking happy, bro-ho."

"That's a different thing," Sticks called back.

She had a new flag on her profile—retrieve at all costs—and the correct description and image. Nothing else, though. No defense code that she couldn't unravel like a ball of yarn with a loose end. "If she's been contracted, she hasn't started working yet. I see nothing out of the ordinary—just the security department getting involved. Simpletons. I've got their smartest member with me. Boo-ya!" She fist-pumped.

"What does all that mean?" Ryker asked in calculated disinterest.

"Uh-oh, I've got him worried. Why, I wonder." She switched out her picture for that of an orangutan before muddling the profile. Why not? It was a little "get bent" from her to them.

"You haven't done much of that before, I gather?" Ryker asked.

"What's that? Uppers?" She laughed. "They froze my accounts—what's left of them. Why they never noticed I was filtering money out in huge quantities this past year, I do not know."

"Because I assigned myself to monitor that part of your profile, and I didn't put it in my report," Ryker said. "And yes. Uppers. Downers. Hallucinogens. Alcohol. Caffeine. Anything."

"Hey, you got any of that stuff?" Sticks asked.

"They didn't question you?" she asked, logging in to Ryker's profile. It was quite a bit harder because she couldn't think straight. She just wanted to run. Just run really fast. Then maybe fly. "Flying would be awesome," she said out loud.

"They question me all the time, but it's usually about my colorful life choices. I made sure to keep them on their toes while you mucked about with preparing to screw the system. Colorful life choices, but my work was pristine. That usually keeps the micromanagers away."

"Who are you people?" Sticks asked in a wispy voice.

"They're both directors, natural borns, and at the top of the Curve," Mr. McAllister said, putting his hand out to Millicent. "Can I have an upper? I'm about to pass out."

"No." Ryker's voice held a hard command that froze Millicent in the act. "You are in charge of watching my daughter and doctoring us if something goes wrong. You are the lifesaver, and as such, will remain sober. Get some rest right now if you need it."

"But she's responsible for keeping us alive," Mr. McAllister whined.

"That's my job. She is responsible for running interference and blowing things up. She can do that stoned."

"At the top of the Curve. This all makes so much more sense," Sticks said. "I got money, though. Can I buy a fix?"

"So if you weren't on my side, you would've caught me?" Millicent asked, changing Ryker's picture out for a white butt in the act of mooning the screen.

"I had reasons to watch you more closely than most. If you were just an average woman . . . I would've questioned your spending habits. That's about it, though. You excel at what you do."

"Why, thank you." Millicent fist-pumped. "You're flagged, too, by the way. I can't take it off. Not without studying how they go about flagging things. That's deeper in the security pool, and they've spent a lot of time and money fortifying it."

"Shoot to kill?" Ryker asked, not at all bothered for some reason.

"No. Bring in for questioning. Mine is 'at all costs,' though, so shooting is a possibility. Keep your head up." She sighed. The fist pump wasn't necessary. She was starting to calm down, thank Holy. On to Mr. McAllister. "He's got a questioning one, too. No shoot-to-kills among us. Not yet."

"That was before you blew up their security," Sticks said.

"Different company. They won't care," Ryker said. To Mr. McAllister he said, "You said that other coder was Millie's sister. Why did Millie end up in defense?"

Mr. McAllister shrugged. "She's great at it, right? So that's probably why. Who knows why the other one didn't. I don't have that data. She's with Gregon."

"But how are we related and working for different companies?" Millicent asked, logic telling her to sit down, but her body telling her to laugh so hard she would throw up. She settled for random chuckling. "I think this dose is way stronger than the first one."

"She *is* a novice," Sticks said.

"Buying or trading stock isn't that rare," Mr. McAllister said. "Ryker's semen was sold once. That was before they realized what an asset he was. His late teens were . . . eye opening, I think. They weren't going to breed him. Just sell his semen with the test scores. But then he leveled out, so they changed their minds.

"I think in this case, however, the mother was rented. Our lab wanted to try an enhancing serum, like we did with Marie, so they needed to have complete control from conception until birth. From the records, I was able to deduce that the serum was largely ineffective. They couldn't tell if you would've been that smart anyway. As you've realized, your sister is just as intelligent. Or nearly anyway."

"Why would they sell one of their chief assets?" Millicent's lip curled, basically calling herself an item to barter.

Mr. McAllister shrugged. "Money. Plus, there is a limited stock of extremely smart individuals. To prevent inbreeding, we need fresh gene pools. Had they known what you'd become, I doubt they would've done it. Their loss."

"Why has all of this never struck me as odd? Ha-ha-ha!" Millicent frowned with the laughter. She couldn't stop it, though.

"Sometimes it's easier not to question," Ryker said, watching her.

"Case in point, right?" Mr. McAllister said, making a circle with his finger, indicating their frantic plight. "But really, when the human race is under threat, like when overpopulation drained the resources and affected the environment, it clutches on to the first piece of driftwood it can find. From my notes, what I gather . . ." Mr. McAllister accessed his wrist. Text scrolled along his skin. "It seemed logical at the time—to allow a trusted source to try and gain control over the chaos."

He glanced up. "I did a lot of research during the times of natural birth, to try and find clues regarding developing traits and so forth." He nodded, like anyone cared, and glanced back down at his wrist screen. "In this case, the chaos was the overpopulation. The rich were purchasing lab births, but the poor were still naturally breeding, willy-nilly. At the time, the rich basically bought the laws. So their answer was to pass control to the creators and perfecters of lab births. People would need to get licenses to breed. I think . . . yes, here. Insurance companies paid for up to two children. After that, the person had to purchase a license and birth on their own. The rich could buy more, but they often didn't. The poor, those who could afford insurance, could only have two. So that was the start, from what I can gather."

"But how did we go from that . . . to this?" Millicent asked.

Mr. McAllister fingered his wrist. "Um . . . well, I mean, it wasn't any one thing. That's what I was trying to say about the frog boiling—"

"Not the frog-boiling thing again." Ryker grinned.

Mr. McAllister's lips tightened in irritation. "I'm no scholar, but I think letting large companies take control of the chaos, rather than the government, was the start of the power shift. Then, when the conglomerates came into power, they also had control of birthing, right? Among other things. Add a bunch of time and an erosion of staffers' rights . . . well, here we are."

"Huh. Fascinating." Ryker yanked out his hair tie and ran his fingers through his locks. "All that information trapped in your itty bitty head."

Mr. McAllister's wrist stopped glowing. He glowered. "Knowledge is power. With all your intelligence, you could stand to learn a little something . . ."

"Is that your expert opinion?"

Mr. McAllister crossed his arms high on his chest, over the head of Marie, who was leaning on him. "You should be nice to the man watching your daughter."

"I am being nice. Hear that? That's my nice voice."

"You don't fool me. You'd use that voice right before sticking something sharp in my you-know-where."

Ryker's brows furrowed. He tilted his head. "No. Where?"

"We're about to cross over," Sticks said. "Get ready for a little turbulence . . ."

"Millie, get him his fix." Ryker twisted and looked out the window. "We need a risk-taker."

Chapter 20

"Please be advised, this craft is approaching its defined limit," a soft voice said through the speakers in the dashboard. "Please be advised, this craft is approaching its defined limit . . ."

"Lovely. It tells you in two different nuances," Ryker said, hovering over Sticks. "*How* you say it makes all the difference. Apparently."

"And I thought you didn't micromanage," Millicent said as she stood at the console.

"I'm preparing for decision-making, cupcake," Ryker said, his gaze skimming the dashboard. "The big dog is at the helm."

"Big douche, more like." Millicent attempted to find the border maps within the complex spider web of the Los Angeles area. "I miss San Francisco. Things were much simpler when there's only one conglomerate and intranet to navigate."

"What's the situation down here?" Mr. McAllister asked, on the edge of his seat. He was clearly preparing for danger. What he planned to do if he found it was anyone's guess.

"Three conglomerates, all with extravagant intranets, the government, which has its own ridiculous and outdated intranet, and the public internet. The conglomerates are cheap, so they don't want to duplicate information, which means there is a section in each intranet the public can access, no matter what their employment. The government duplicates their efforts because it's a money pit, but their information isn't always the same, and then there's the hodgepodge of the public net, populated with random staffer opinions and a whole bunch of irrelevance."

"Forget I asked," Mr. McAllister said with a furrowed brow.

"It's a mess of information." Millicent shook her head. "A mess. But it'll make it easier to stay anonymous. I hope. At least with the other conglomerates."

"Please be advised, this craft is approaching its defined limit . . ."

"Yet another tone. Not as nice this time," Ryker said, his arms braced on the entrance to the cockpit, leaning over so he could look out the window. "How long does it generally take to respond?"

"They'll try to take over the craft first," Sticks said.

"Please be advised, you are at your defined limit. Please turn back."

"Oh, naughty girl," Ryker said.

"Please turn back now," the voice said. "Please turn back now."

"She gets annoying," Sticks said. He glanced to the side of the dash. "Here we go." A red-and-yellow button lit up. Millicent could just see the shine from around Ryker's torso. The craft's controls, which were displayed on the bottom right of her screen, mirrored the colors with two pulsing dots. A syntax error flashed across the bottom.

"Do I need to . . . do anything?" Millicent asked, having no idea what she would do if she tried. She couldn't find a reliable border map in the mess of information, which meant she certainly couldn't change anything to do with the configuration. "Who is in control of the border anyway?"

"You are outside your defined limit," the voice said. "This is your last warning. If you do not turn back now, you will face criminal charges. I repeat, if you do not turn back now, you will face criminal charges."

"Yeah, yeah. We got it." Sticks flicked a switch. "Different borders are controlled by different conglomerates. They share the cost. The perimeter is mostly government. Downtown is largely government, too, since it's mostly public areas and not departments. Conglomerates leave the government to take care of anything they don't want to, basically. The government only has what little power the conglomerates give them."

"And what kind of security can we expect downtown?" Ryker asked. "I've never been this far into LA."

"Police, not security, unless you are wanted by one of the conglomerates. Everyone has jurisdiction. Everyone can enforce their own rules, but usually only the police enforce the public laws. Unless one of the important conglomerate staffers is in danger, obviously."

Millicent shook her head. "Security sounds like a mess, too."

"It is. There are a lot of unsolved homicides of random folk, but there will be an investigation into some tiny misdeed if the victim is a high-level staffer. If you don't have your own security, which most of the humdrum don't, then it's every man for himself."

"That's nice," Ryker said.

Sticks scoffed.

"He's not being sarcastic," Millicent said in a droll voice. "He's delighted that he can kill people without drawing notice. The Divine Holy help anyone who touches my person."

"She knows me so well." Ryker bent toward the left window. "We got some sort of authorized vehicle coming our way."

"I see it." Sticks's voice sounded strained. "It always amazes me the way you upper-level staffers speak. Divine Holy? What the hell is that?

Either you believe in something or you don't. The general term of belief, without actually believing, doesn't make sense."

"Can't a man believe in everything?" Ryker asked, his tone light. He was preparing for danger as well.

"No." Sticks sighed. "Got another one. They're moving in position to apprehend us."

"This looks like Toton's guys." Ryker dropped a hand and lightly touched a strap at his belt.

"Yeah, we just moved out of Gregon's section, and now we're in Toton's."

"They're the weakest conglomerate in terms of weaponry and defense," Millicent said, watching their cruisers approach slowly. Each had a bulky gun attached to the outside of its craft. "They put more of their budget into artificial intelligence than anyone else. So far their advancements haven't been revolutionary. Either they'll come out with something, or they'll slip further, and Gregon and Moxidone will fight over the scraps."

"They are the most severe about outsiders encroaching in their area, though," Sticks said. "Even their own staffers aren't allowed to wander into the wrong areas. It wouldn't surprise me if they had something up their sleeves."

"Or are great at bluffing," Ryker said, his gaze tracking one of the vessels. "Their secrecy has kept the other conglomerates from moving in. That won't last forever. Eventually they need to show their hand, or risk the others picking them apart, like Millie said."

"What are we doing? I either need to slow down or speed up." Sticks's hand hovered over the dash.

"That upper kicked in yet?" Ryker asked.

"Yeah. This shit is great. I need to get in touch with your supplier."

"I just asked for it. The conglomerate used to supply whatever I needed," Millicent said in confusion. "Is it a higher-lever thing?"

Ryker's laughter startled her, coming out of the blue. He shook his head. "No. It is not a higher-level thing. What the princess wants, the princess gets, including extremely hard-to-find narcotics. Your stash is worth a bucket of pure water."

Millicent rolled her eyes. The man was prone to exaggeration.

"What are we doing?" Sticks asked again.

Ryker rose slowly as the craft he was watching neared them. He glanced out the opposite window. "Any at the back?"

"No. Just the two until they give chase. Then other vessels will start popping out of nowhere."

"Does this thing have any weapons?" Millicent asked, running through the craft's log for the millionth time. If she had taken inventory in the beginning, like she should've, she wouldn't be wasting time now. The drugs were fraying her brain. It was extremely distracting.

Her clap echoed strangely.

"Why does she keep clapping? Ha-ha-ha!" Sticks gunned it. "Trek it. Let's get this party started!"

"What is *trek*?" Millicent asked. Her body whipped back. She grabbed a handrail. Her body swung around and bounced off the wall. A hand grabbed her leg—Mr. McAllister trying to keep her stable.

"Trek, fuck, flay, rock, cram—whatever," Sticks shouted back. The craft nose-dived. "Hold on. We're about to push this thing to the limits."

"Have you ever done this before?" Millicent yelled.

"Twice. Made it both times. Had a better craft, though."

"Remember there is a baby on board," Mr. McAllister called out.

"Then let's keep her alive. Ha-ha-ha! Weeeew!" Sticks pulled back.

Millicent's stomach rolled as the g-force struck her. Then her body rolled as the craft swerved off to the side.

"Criminal, stop!" a harsh voice said through the speaker.

"Can you turn that thing off?" Ryker asked, his braced arms holding him perfectly steady. Millicent pulled herself off the ground.

"I need to hear the warnings." The craft swerved the other way. Millicent's eyes widened as the corner of a building passed within meters of the craft. A person glanced up from a work pod. Millicent connected eyes with that person. Then she squeezed her eyes shut as the craft veered hard left.

"Oh shit." Mr. McAllister slid across the aisle. Marie tumbled after him, her little face showing both fear and joy, in turns. She was definitely her father's daughter.

"Stop! This is your last warning!" the speaker blared.

"Getting close now." Sticks leaned again.

"Hold on!" Millicent said through gritted teeth, clutching the handrail with both hands.

Shimmering glass sparkled through the windows before the craft's reflection took over. Two meters away.

"Holy shit," Millicent gasped. Her heart had already been beating fast from the drugs, but now it was thumping madly. Her sweaty palms made holding on challenging.

Her body swung the other way as the craft rolled, nearly on its side. She hadn't known they could do that. And then, when a cough of smoke curled around their feet, she realized they probably couldn't. The whole thing groaned and started to shake. The force pulled at Millicent's cheeks. Ryker's arms flared with muscle, hanging on.

"Nearly there . . . ," Sticks said.

Something zipped by the craft. A beam of light flared in the window. An explosion sprayed glass out of a building to their side.

"They're shooting this close to their own departments?" Millicent asked, aghast.

"Only when they are certain they'll hit the craft in question," Sticks said. "Someone is going to get recycled over that one. Pray to Rossonoman this craft holds up!"

"Who?" Millicent shouted.

Her stomach rolled again as the craft straightened out and then immediately banked left. A bang reverberated, followed by a shuddering of the craft. Deep black smoke streamed up through the cracks. Mr. McAllister and Marie both started to cough. G-force dragged Millicent to the ground, her fingers sliding off the metal handle before she splatted on the floor. The walls and windows shook. The engine whined.

"C'mon!" Sticks yelled. "Yee-haw! C'mon!"

"You shouldn't have given him that upper," Mr. McAllister exclaimed, waving smoke away from Marie's face.

Another flare of light. Fire filled the air right beside them. Glass crackled against the side of the craft. Cracks popped in the windows, spreading like wild things.

"Missed us!"

The vessel dipped, lifting Millicent off the ground. And then turned her in a dizzying way. Millicent's face felt like it was melting off. She clenched her teeth and closed her eyes, holding back the bile rising in her throat. Hoping her heart didn't burst her chest open.

She probably shouldn't have taken that last upper.

The floor trembled. The engine sputtered.

"End of the line!"

"What the hell does that mean?" Mr. McAllister yelled.

"It means prepare to crash-land!" Sticks gave a whoop.

And then Marie was in Millicent's arms somehow. A moment later, Ryker was on top of her, curling around her and the baby, shielding them with his large body. "Hold on, ladies, this might get bumpy."

"Ahhh," Marie cried, squirming.

"Hang on, baby," Millicent said, bracing.

"Here we go!"

A blast went off. A roar filled the craft, and a rip opened up along its side, a slice of air and fire gusting through the corner of the craft. Then the whole contraption jumped, shaking so violently Millicent feared it would break into pieces. It ripped one way, and then another. Metal shrieked and twisted, crunched. Glass shattered. Something sliced her face. Ryker grunted over them. A metallic squeal punctuated their slide. The craft finally stopped, and silence rained down and surrounded them like a suffocating blanket.

Sucking in a deep breath, she noticed the unnatural stillness around her. Deadness.

"Marie?" she asked with a shock of terror.

The little girl wiggled beneath her. A whimper had Millicent sighing in relief.

"Ryker?" she asked next.

The heavy body above her didn't move. Didn't so much as suck in a steadying breath.

Dread punched her.

"Ryker?" she asked again, the panic sounding in her voice. Trying to rouse him with movement, she shifted. Tried to get her hands up to shake him, but she could not. So she shook her body again.

Nothing happened.

"Mama?" Marie asked with tears in her voice. There was no excitement this time.

"Yes, baby. We're okay. Ryker!" she yelled, in terror now. "Please, Ryker, please be okay. Oh Holy—Rosso . . . mat. All the gods. Please be okay." She wiggled harder, a coldness seeping into her at his continued stillness. Tears filled her eyes. Marie started screaming. "Please, no," Millicent begged, certainty now seeping in. Reality. "No . . ."

"I'm not that easy to kill, princess," Ryker groaned.

"Oh thank Holy!" Relief such that she'd never known washed through her. "Thank Holy you're okay."

Ryker's chest pushed against them as he took a deep breath, and then he was moving slowly, lifting the pressure away from them. He helped Marie up first, quickly glancing her over as Millicent painfully stretched out her arms. When he finished his inspection, he lifted Millicent to standing, the effort obvious from his strain. His electric-blue gaze ran the length of her. His thumb wiped across her cheek and then ran down a sore spot on her arm.

"Anything hurt?" he asked, his deep rumble cutting through Marie's whimpering as she clutched his leg.

The lump in her throat making speech impossible, Millicent shook her head, her glassy eyes rooted to his. To his safety. To that deep feeling she saw in his gaze, mirrored in her middle.

She reached for him, needing his touch. Needing to make sure he was okay.

His lips met hers, firm yet soft, needy, and insistent. Desire flared to life inside her as he pulled her in tighter, surrounding her with his strength and protection. He sucked in her tongue and tilted his head, the kiss intensifying until a different sort of explosion rocked her body. One she wanted to explore.

"Damn bad timing, princess," Ryker said against her lips as he backed off. "We still have to hobble out of here."

"Too bad you can't claim this victory before I come to my senses, huh?" she asked, running her palms up his body.

"You're on the hook now. I just have to reel you in." He gave her one more deep, toe-curling kiss, staving off reality for another moment. Then he backed away, but not before his palm slid down her front and cupped a breast. A thumb ran across her taut nipple, making her shiver in anticipation for things she knew would come.

"Hang on to this little one," Ryker said, peeling Marie away from his leg and gently directing her into Millicent's waiting arms. He followed it up with a dirty and bedraggled Bunny.

When he turned toward Mr. McAllister, lying in a clump, Millicent sucked in a breath through her teeth. "Oh, Ryker, we need to fix you up." Scrapes and gashes marred his back in deep bloody grooves. Shards of glass stuck out here and there, and it looked like many smaller pieces were painfully embedded. She'd need to take to him with tweezers before she could apply Cure-all. And how many stitchers would he need this time?

"The kiss was a better use of our time." He bent laboriously, the effort testimony to the extreme pain he had to be in.

"He's alive," Ryker said, removing his fingers from Mr. McAllister's pulse before flinging off a canvas bag. Glass went flying, most of it the shatterproof stuff from the vessel, but a couple of shards from when they'd crashed through on the building. Ryker had gotten most of that, but not all. "Got lucky with the canvas. But he took some cuts, and he won't heal as fast as I will. Nothing we can do about that now." Ryker shook the other man as Millicent turned toward the front of the craft. A beam from the building had sliced through the cockpit, making a mess of debris and wire. A leg was segregated from the rest of the body that lay in a pool of blood.

Millicent covered Marie's eyes as she turned away, trying to ignore the queasy feeling threatening to empty her stomach. A moan preceded Mr. McAllister's head rolling to the side.

"Nothing appears to be broken." Ryker straightened up slowly, wincing. "Millie, can you get him to wake up? I'll take Marie out of the craft. Someone'll show up to investigate shortly."

Millicent waited for Ryker and Marie to leave before she powered into action. Instead of immediately bending over Mr. McAllister, someone who wasn't totally on their side yet, she gathered up all the tech she could find. Everything she knew would help them. Thankfully, the medical bag was intact, but a few things she'd wanted to try were squashed. Once she had everything gathered in a bag, she gave her attention to Mr. McAllister.

"C'mon, get up." She lightly shook his shoulder, looking over his wounds. He did still have some glass stuck in him, but it wasn't much, and most of the wounds were shallow. He didn't have any scores through his flesh like Ryker did, probably because he had been low enough. Ryker was a large man, and he'd been braced over her and Marie. He'd put himself at a disadvantage to keep them safe. "C'mon." She shook him again.

"Hmmm." Mr. McAllister's face screwed up in pain. "Owwww." His hands came up slowly as a siren echoed through the walls.

"We gotta go," Ryker yelled in. "Looks like we're in some sort of warehouse."

"C'mon, Mr. McAllister, we have to go." She shook him again.

"Ow." Mr. McAllister's eyes blinked open. He rolled to his side, wincing.

"What hurts? Can you move?"

"Everything hurts. These days, everything always hurts." He patted himself down. When he got to his hip, he winced. "That hurts."

She felt down his side, pausing when she reached his hip. He winced again. "How bad?" she asked.

"Apparently not bad enough to make me miss Clarity." He pushed her hand away. "I don't think it's broken."

"Can you get up?"

"What's the alternative?"

"I fry your implant and leave you behind. You'll finally get to go home."

"C'mon, Millicent," Ryker yelled in. "Someone just peeked around the corner. Staffers will let their curiosity overcome them any moment now."

Millicent had to wonder why staffers weren't there already. The crash would've shaken half the building. The fact that this place wasn't swarmed with security was . . . unnerving. They couldn't be this lucky.

Mr. McAllister sighed and stared at the ceiling. She could tell he was thinking it over. Finally, he rolled back over and slowly brought his feet under him. "As much as going home appeals to me, Marie still needs me. I'll see it through until she's safe."

Millicent nodded, not commenting. "Then let's go."

Ryker stood with Marie, straight and tall as always; the only indication that he was in pain was the tightness around his eyes. In contrast, Mr. McAllister hobbled out like an old man with a twisted spine. He moaned and grunted, half dragging the leg affected by the hurt hip.

"You doing okay, Trent?" Ryker asked, his eyes glimmering with humor.

"Do I look okay?" he muttered, holding his side and straightening up with a series of winces. "I was bred to *make* people hard to kill, not to be one of them."

"You're right as rain. Just like all of us." Ryker's face cleared of mirth. "Let's get going. Millie, we need a path out of here. Our guide is indisposed."

"What, did he run?" Mr. McAllister glanced behind him as Millicent looked around.

"Ran straight to hell, yeah. Quick like. If we don't hurry, we'll meet him there."

Mr. McAllister grabbed his stomach. He gagged into the air.

"C'mon, bub, it isn't that bad. At least he doesn't have to live with the pain."

Mr. McAllister gagged again, making a retching sound as he did so. Millicent knew how he felt. She hadn't looked into the cockpit for a reason.

Around them, metal racks were bent and twisted in the craft's wake. What once had been shelves was now garbage. The rest of the large hollow space, however, did have shelves intact. Little orbs, or long pieces, made of a sleek-looking metal covered the shelves, but what they were exactly for, she couldn't say.

"Grab one or two of those pieces," she called out to the boys. "Try to get one of each size."

"Are you serious?" Mr. McAllister asked, looking around with eyes wide in disbelief. "There are sirens and people after us, and you want me—"

"Do as she says," Ryker cut in.

"If we'd stumbled into a breeding lab, you'd want a look," Millicent said, accessing a screen. Then she swore. It wanted a code to log in without a way to bypass, which wasn't uncommon, but being in a different conglomerate, she didn't have any false personas to easily get around this. It wouldn't even let her access the staffer net as a guest, which was uncommon. "Toton isn't just tight with security for outsiders, they're pretty tight with their loop as well."

"These things . . . are just blobs." Mr. McAllister turned one of the items over in his hands. "It doesn't have any power or anything. It doesn't respond in any way."

"You have the wrong implant for it, I'd bet," Ryker said. "We have no idea how they do things in this conglomerate."

Ryker had that right.

Lights flickered at the hole in the side of the building. The sound of sirens bounced off the walls. She shook her head. "I can't log in from here. There's limited access. I'm a genius, but I'm not a miracle-maker."

"Well, don't pray to Rossonoman," Ryker said, moving farther into the warehouse. "That god didn't do our driver any favors."

"Callous," Mr. McAllister said.

"I'm callous? You're the one who breeds and kills like the god that guy was praying to. Are you above mankind, Mr. McAllister? Because you certainly act like it."

Mr. McAllister's Adam's apple bobbed, and his expression wiped clear. Millicent didn't blame him for being nervous. She wouldn't press Ryker when he was in this kind of mood, either.

"What is your plan?" she asked as she fell in line, fingering the crimson making a trail over his butt. "And will you bleed out?"

"I'm not wounded enough to bleed out. This is just a flesh wound." Ryker reached a doorway and stepped up to a viewing window beside it. He pointed to the door. "Help us out?"

"So our plan is to ask the help of complete strangers who witnessed bandits crashing into their workroom and hope they don't tattle on us?" Millicent asked in a flat tone.

"Yes. Human beings are inherently good when someone is in need. You just have to ask for help. Otherwise they'll stand around gawking, waiting for someone else to do something. Doesn't hurt that we're in a lower level. People here aren't much better than worker drones a lot of the time. They don't question orders, and it usually doesn't matter who the orders come from."

"You act like you know from experience." The door clicked before sliding open. Millicent's eyes went to the guide rails before noticing the small, sleek controller beside it. A retinal scan was present, of course—a little black telltale orb—but there was also a finger scan and one she could not identify. As one of the staffers stepped through, all three lit up green.

"What floor are we on?" she asked quietly as Ryker stepped forward to greet the female staffer with a smile.

"Thirties? Forties?" Mr. McAllister shuffled closer.

"Hello there."

Millicent glanced up at the change in Ryker's tone. The deep bass thrummed from his chest, and when the words came out, they were wrapped in extra velvet. His voice fell on the ears in a smooth and very masculine way, riveting. She wanted to stare at his handsome face until drool slid out the side of her mouth.

The woman must've thought so, too, because her mouth curled into a dreamy sort of smile.

"I need to learn that trick," Millicent muttered.

"He's had a lot more practice," Mr. McAllister said. "He had all the women at the lab wrapped around his little finger. They'd literally follow him around. I slipped a few of them Clarity. I'm not kidding. I had to. He distracted the whole place."

Millicent rolled her eyes, remembering her own failed attempt at flirting with a lab staffer. She watched Ryker's body language as he spoke with the woman. He made up some sob story about trying to get the little staffer to her permanent home in level-two housing, but it wasn't the story that mattered. It was his suggestive lean and the tone he used. It was his random flexing and the way his eyes implied a sort of intimacy and the nudity that would follow.

This all changed in an instant when a male staffer stepped into the doorway. Suddenly Ryker's voice switched from liquid fire to immovable muscle, brawny and tough. His words went from soft and deep to curt and deeper, a command riding each word. A born leader who wouldn't take any crap. A guy about to kill something.

Millicent was just about to tell him to focus on the girl, who was lapping up his charm like a starved man would a tube of gruel, but amazingly, the woman's eyes were now shining with lust, heat infusing her gaze to the point of embarrassment. She liked his controlling qualities even more than the soft approach.

"I don't understand people," she said in an undertone. "I'll just stick with threatening people and let him do the manipulation."

"All you have to do is smile, cupcake, and all the boys will come running." Ryker turned back with a wink. It didn't hide a lingering tightness in his eyes. They needed to get him fixed up. "We got a ride out. We just have to make it to their bay. Sounds easier than it probably will be."

A look back said there were already vessels hovering at the hole in the building, probably trying to determine the best course of action.

It still seemed odd that a huge crash had only brought two staffers from within the department level. Warehouses typically held fewer staff, Millicent assumed, but this seemed minimal.

As Millicent passed through the door, each light turned red except for one. That one, the retinal scan, blinked yellow. Thankfully, no alarm sounded.

"We don't have much time," Millicent warned, following the others into another room filled with rows of shelving. "Did you hide those . . . things you got?" she whispered to Mr. McAllister, who was right behind her.

"Oh Hedona," the girl cried out as she caught sight of Ryker's back. "Look at you. You must be hurt."

"Take us back to your place. Maybe I'll let you fix me up." He smiled at her. The girl would have no idea he was placating her.

"Oh please." Millicent rolled her eyes and shoved the woman on. "We don't have time for your antics, Ryker. Keep moving."

They reached another security corridor. Two more red lights and another blinking yellow. This time, though, the door issued a soft click. Nothing else happened.

What did a sophisticated clicking door mean?

"I don't like this," Millicent said, feeling uncertainty pinch her gut. Her smile dwindled. Her mind was starting to get foggy, too. She was coming down off the drug, fatigue trying to steal away whatever sort of focus she might have.

"This way," the woman said. She walked through the smart door and into a strangely sterile corridor. Inside, the walls and ceiling looked like they were covered in padded white tile. The floor was cream, the same color as the walls. The door clicked again as Millicent passed through.

"No, Mama!" Marie screamed.

A rough hand clutched her hair and yanked. Millicent fell back right before the door slid shut with a soft clunk. Her teeth clattered as her butt hit ground. Ryker winced and went rigid; yanking her back had apparently played hell on his wounds. Marie rushed forward, grabbing her around the neck.

"What's the matter—" Screaming, muffled through the door, cut Millicent off.

Pounding beat on the door from the inside. The screaming rose in pitch, pushing Millicent's breath out in fast pants as she identified the primal agony inherent in that sound.

The male staffer stepped up to the door quickly. "Pauline?" His hands flattened against the surface. *"Pauline?"*

"What's happening?" Millicent asked, standing. Shaken.

"I don't know. I've never seen this happen. Heard about it, but . . . Pauline!"

An intense howl that had Millicent shivering ended in horrible silence, the screaming cut off abruptly. Millicent's heart beat through her ears.

The man banged on the door. "Pauline? Can you hear me? Pauline!"

Three clicks, like a complicated lock disengaging, made the man take two steps back, staring down at the handle of the door. He pushed it down. Nothing happened.

Millicent put her hand on the man's shoulder. "What level are you?"

He shook his head, still staring at the handle.

"We're way down in the towers," she tried again. "But you seem to have some futuristic tech here. What is your level? What is this place?"

"It's just storage." He slowly shook his head. "Just storage. I'm . . . I'm lab born. One click below the Curve in most things. I just monitor. I . . ."

The door slid open. Ryker's hand landed on her shoulder before a cold shiver of fear flash-froze her blood.

The corridor was completely empty.

No blood.

Not even a trace.

Another door, on the far side, slid open.

The corridor had sealed in the girl. But her body was gone. The cream material, which should've been soaked in blood, was pristine.

"What the hell are you people making in your labs . . . ," Millicent whispered.

Suddenly she didn't feel like the biggest monster on the planet. Toton had seemed like a company in jeopardy, but in reality it was a company lying in wait.

"Let's get out of here," Ryker said, pulling Marie away from the door.

"Is there a way out of here without going through one of these smart doors?" Millicent asked the man, whose face had gone completely white. He was staring into the room with unfocused eyes. "Hey!" Millicent slapped him across the face.

The man blinked slowly, an effort that wasn't synchronized. "Just one. Through the old service door. We were supposed to install the Vera-Tech corridor through there, too, but they sent the wrong configuration of parts. We're still waiting on one of the . . . cleaning mechanisms." His eyes slid back to where his friend had disappeared.

"Let's head that way," Millicent urged, leaving her hand on his shoulder. "Do you have a craft?"

"I . . . I take the company craft. I can't afford my own."

"Okay. Well, we'll figure it out." Millicent gave him a small shove. "C'mon. Let's head that way."

"Do you know what kind of door that was, Marie?" Mr. McAllister asked with a shaking voice.

The little girl clutched Bunny tightly, tears streaming down her face. She shook her head.

"Do you know how to open it?" he prompted, taking her hand.

She shook her head, her brow furrowing. "Lock. Too lock."

"It locks, so it can't be opened?" Mr. McAllister cleared his throat, but it didn't do much to stop his shaking limbs. Millicent knew exactly how he felt.

Marie shrugged, and then looked back.

Behind them, they faintly heard a door click.

Chapter 21

"Through here—" The man jogged, his voice harried.

"What had you heard about those doors?" Millicent asked, trying to ignore the labored breathing coming from Ryker as they ran down an aisle of silver orbs. He needed help, and soon.

"Just that . . . I heard that someone—a guy—was visiting one of his lady friends in her department. He didn't have clearance for it, but the entranceway let him in, so whatever, right? If it lets you in, you're usually fine. But when they were on their way to lunch, one of those doors locked them in a corridor. Everyone said they heard all this screaming, and . . ." He staggered and bumped off the stack. An orb bumped into another with a strange bell-like sound, not the metallic clink she would expect from that substance hitting together. "But they weren't in there when the doors opened. Nothing was . . . Nothing was left behind. I didn't believe it. Because . . . But . . ."

"It isn't a weapon, while being a weapon," Millicent said to herself, chewing her lip. She wanted to access a console in this place so bad her palms itched. "Do you have anyone in this conglomerate who is more than three clicks above the Curve?"

Breathing hard, the man turned a corner and abruptly stopped. He waved his hand, forcing everyone back. A woman was bustling by, scratching her head and muttering to herself.

"I don't want to explain you all. Or what happened," the man said. "Everyone will . . . I just don't want to explain."

"No worries," Millicent said as she watched the woman pass through a smart door. All three lights turned green. No click sounded. "Are there usually more people through here?"

"No. Our job is to keep it tidy. Keep an eye on things. C'mon." He waved them on.

"Are you in the security department?" Ryker asked with a thick voice. His ability to ignore pain was going up in flames. Another indication he was badly hurt.

"Me? No." The man opened a door the old-fashioned way, by turning a knob and then pushing it open. *This* was the type of door she'd expected so close to ground level. It went with the level of the employee and the horrible condition of the air.

That was when she realized something else. The air in here wasn't horrible at all. Quite the opposite. She was perfectly comfortable. The disgusting, brownish, foul-smelling environment on the outside did not reach the interior of this warehouse. The system installed in here created air as good as that in her old department, but in much worse conditions. This conglomerate had spent a lot of money on this warehouse.

The pinch in her gut churned her stomach. "Sir, do you have anyone more than three clicks?" she asked again.

"More than that? No, I don't think so." Their footsteps echoed off the faded walls covered in stains and peeling paint. The floor, however, had already been changed over. It felt strangely bouncy, like hard rubber.

Was it her imagination, or did faint lights glow deep within it with each step?

"I think we only have one or two that smart," he said, stopping at another door. He pulled it open and breathed a soft sigh of relief.

Stepping out after him, she echoed it. A security station stretched out before them, low-tech and fairly rinky-dink. It would probably just scan retinas. The door clanged shut behind them—no door handle on the outside, she noticed. "This leads out to the walkway into the bay. I can get you a ride with a company craft. They'll take anyone, mostly."

"So . . ." Millicent glanced back the way she'd come as the man started forward. She felt Ryker's hand on her shoulder, directing her. "The walkway is stupid. The company craft is stupid. The staffers are—" Ryker's hand squeezed. *Oops.* "Not totally necessary to this . . ." Another squeeze. She skipped it. "But they are storing some . . . things I've never seen. This doesn't add up."

"Hide your most valuable possessions in a place no one will ever think to look," Ryker said in a low tone. "Toton's got something brewing. Something big. And we best get off this world before they unveil it."

"Get off this . . ." The man blinked at all of them for a moment, his hazel eyes unfocused.

Mr. McAllister looked back the way they'd come. "This conglomerate would have to have some incredibly smart individuals to think all that up. But they don't have any reports of staffers for sale. Not even any troubled geniuses. And they don't buy stock from others—not much anyway. A few here and there. When I was researching breeder candidates, they didn't have one viable source. We only contracted one sperm donor in Marie's group. We are the leaders in human intelligence . . . or so I thought . . ."

"Human intelligence," Millicent said again, mostly to herself. "Maybe this isn't a boiling-frog situation. Maybe this is a keep-it-quiet situation, so no one can stop them from breaking the rules. Greed at its worst usually results in wanting to take over the world. It wouldn't be the first time in history."

"I agree with one thing," Mr. McAllister said. "We best get off this world before they unveil whatever they are doing. I don't want to be any part of it. Our group still has rules against killing innocent staffers, like that girl."

"Mostly." Ryker turned to the clunky craft shuddering into the bay. It docked with noisy rattling. "We pretend we do anyway. And that is far better than . . . what went on in there."

They filed into the craft, which was every bit as stupid as the man had led them to believe, and sat down, falling into silence. As it pulled away, the inside mostly empty besides two very intoxicated men and a woman chatting loudly to whoever was on the other end of her communication, the man said, "Who are you people?"

"We get that a lot," Mr. McAllister said.

❖ ❖ ❖

Millicent's eyes drooped as she extracted the millionth tiny piece of glass from Ryker's back. They had retreated to the dingy apartment assigned to Conrath—the man from the warehouse—to catch a few hours of shut-eye and get Ryker on the mend. The larger shards from the warehouse window had scored him deeply, and crumbles from the craft window littered the wounds, needing to be extracted before any sort of medicine could be applied to close him up. A normal man would've bled out, or at the very least passed out. But then, a normal man wouldn't have reacted quicker than she could blink, combatting the agony with a kiss.

She slapped her face. Clapping had long since stopped working. The drugs had worn off, and the adrenaline was long gone. She was shaky and only half-conscious.

"You should let me do it," Trent said, kneeling beside them. The baby was lying on the floor with a fluffy blanket, one of the few nice things in the tiny hovel where Conrath lived. She now knew why Ryker called her princess. Not that she would admit it. "You're poking him half the time. And it's taking too long. I know you care for him, but I'm better at this . . ."

"He's sleeping. He can't feel it. Besides, I'm almost done." To prove Trent's point, her tweezers jabbed his torn and weeping flesh. "Oops."

"Just . . ." Trent forcefully took the tweezers. "I can't kill the man with a pair of tweezers. I don't even know if I could kill him with a gun."

"How much time do we have?" She looked at her wrist, but the numbers meant nothing. "Did Ryker tell you when we're supposed to meet this Roe person?"

"No. But his urgency means we're running out of time. His breed is almost always cool under pressure. As you could probably tell."

"You talk about him like he's an animal."

"We *are* animals. Mammals."

Millicent felt the fog overcome her senses. Her head thunked off the floor, a strangely hollow sound.

"Are you okay?" she heard.

Her body was shaking worse now. Freezing. Her teeth chattered. "Trent, could you get me a blanket, please. I think I'm about to—"

The black pulled her under.

❖　❖　❖

Three beeps sounded from outside the dwelling's haze-covered window.

"That'll be the bus," Conrath said, still sitting on the edge of his bed.

Millicent, feeling like she was deep underwater, leaned against the wall as fatigue dragged down her limbs. Ryker, eyes puffy and loose hair tousled, stood straight and broad in front of the door, holding a sleeping Marie. The back of his suit was green whereas the rest was navy, the color of Conrath's favorite—and only—good suit. Being that now Conrath could buy two new suits with the price they'd paid for his used one, he didn't complain. At all, actually. He still wasn't talking much. Staring, he did plenty of.

"Trent, get off the floor," Millicent ordered, trying for her hard director's voice and ending up with something squeaky instead.

The lab staffer picked himself up slowly before rubbing his eyes. "It's a testament to how tired I am that I don't mind the flea bites."

"I bet Millie still did," Ryker said in a teasing voice.

"Do you have to be half-dead to be serious?" she said in annoyance. Because yes, she did mind the fleas.

A long beep.

"It's outside," Conrath said. "Down the walkway a little, remember? Like when we came in?"

"Got it. Thanks for your help." Ryker gave the other man a nod and opened the door. The environment blasted in, swirling his hair before reaching Millicent. The bite of the air, not as bad as in San Francisco, revived her a bit. The smell, though . . .

She pushed away from the wall and followed Ryker out, noticing the deeper glow. The sun had to be close to the horizon. "I miss my apartment."

"I would've liked to live in your apartment," Ryker said, patting Marie's back as she stirred. "It was chic. Very high-class. We would've both fit easily."

"No."

"What's that?"

"Just in case we end up back there—no."

"Always playing hard to get, huh?" He tsked. "You'd think she'd learn her lesson."

"Trent can't hear you. He's holding his head as he's walking."

"I wasn't talking to Trent."

"Then who were you talking to?"

"Never mind." The door to the employee bus slid open. The inside, shabby with hard use, held ten people, all staring down at their wrists or wearing black glasses that signified some sort of 3-D game.

Her mind flashed back to the glasses the guard in the lab had worn, what seemed like so long ago. The image on the small screen flared in her memory, followed by a tingly feeling she realized was uncomfortable arousal. And it only seemed to get worse, often prompted by ridiculous things. A while ago she'd caught sight of Ryker's upper thigh, of all things. His thigh! As if something even remotely related to the reproductive system could bring on a hot flash of desire. She didn't mind the deep, consuming feeling of Ryker as a person—that was somewhat grounded and pleasant—but this clenching, pounding, tightening thing was a distraction without any benefit.

After clearing her throat, she crossed her arms over her chest. She wondered if sex would ease it, and if so, how long that feeling would last. Because she'd knock that out right now, people or no, if it helped her get back on track.

"What's wrong?" Ryker asked, his voice low. "What do you see?"

Millicent glanced around as Trent sat next to her. One woman, on the far side of the bus, glanced up and caught her gaze. Her brow furrowed before she looked back at her wrist, hunching.

"Nothing, I don't think . . . ," she whispered. "I don't think these people make contact with each other."

"No, I meant, what's got you frustrated? What am I missing?"

"Oh." She waved him away. "Nothing. What happens now?"

Ryker glanced at the person closest to him. He minutely shook his head. "Just follow me when I get up."

The craft visited other apartment areas, all on the same level as far as Millicent could tell. None had bays, just open sidewalks without rails, the staffers braving the acidic rain and blasting wind with scarfs and rain slickers. Few had decent suits. The thin material didn't even keep out the cold, if the shivers and chattering teeth were any judge.

"Downtown next," Ryker said quietly.

The woman across the aisle glanced up, and then did a double take. Her gaze roamed his face before dipping to his shoulders and grazing his chest. She totally ignored Marie, who had her head resting on Ryker's shoulder.

Millicent sighed, lifting her eyebrows and shaking her head. "I just don't understand why more people don't use Clarity," she said. "What possible benefit could sexuality have to the masses who can't reproduce? There's no point to it when procreation is absent."

"You'll see," Ryker said ominously.

"I agree with you, Ms. Foster—can I call you Millicent now?" Trent asked. "Since you call me Trent?"

"I don't care," she answered, watching someone get in. There was no retinal scanning equipment that Millicent could see. She had no idea about facial-recognition cameras, but she didn't think so. This was just a dumb hovering transportation unit.

What was this conglomerate spending all its money on if it was eschewing such simple little devices for better security? It would cut out the need for whatever massive amounts they were spending on those killing corridors. Or maybe she was missing the point entirely . . .

"Millie?" Trent asked hopefully.

"Don't push it," she warned.

"Right. Millicent, then. Well, anyway, I agree. Clarity was great for focus. I really thought so. But then, I'm trapped with an outrageously pretty woman who is off-limits because of a homicidal man bred to kill with his hands. So our situations are a bit different, even though they lead to the same goal . . ."

"We aren't in enough danger. He's talking too much," Ryker said. "And I wasn't bred to kill with my hands. I was trained to. There's a difference."

"Not to me. It amounts to the same deadness." Trent scratched his shoulder.

"Here we go," Ryker said, leaning forward as the craft entered a large bay. Each side had a walkway. Ahead of them, another large, equally shabby transport was letting people out. Next to them, a vessel going the other way started forward, having just dropped off a mass of people.

When it was their turn to depart, they exited with five other people.

"Is that a kid?" someone behind Ryker asked as they filed out.

"Not if you want to keep your life, it isn't," he answered in a harsh tone.

"Yes, sir," the person mumbled.

Above them, as far as Millicent could see, tiers of platforms stretched up into the sky, vessels coming and going.

"This way," Ryker said, leading them through a throng of people to a dispenser of some sort. He tapped into the screen and then flung his finger from his wrist to the machine. "These are outdated, but I imagine they still work."

"Personal hover boards?" Millicent reached down and picked hers up. It resisted leaving the ground, pulling at her as she turned it over. Mostly flat until the ends, which curved up, it was not much more than a thick tech board with a few strips of tread. There was no real design and, she'd bet, no real luxury.

After stepping on, she nodded. Just as she expected. A jerky ride without a stabilizer.

"Surely there is another stand with more expensive rentals?" she said. She leaned forward. It didn't respond.

"People who can afford more wouldn't be down here." Ryker pushed his forward with his toe before stepping on. Trent did the same. "Speaking of, we need to head down another few levels."

"Down?" Millicent glanced at the space between platforms, just barely able to see down to the landing below. "What sort of meeting place is going to be lower than this?"

"Bars, probably. Not ones you should ever go to by yourself."

"Do they not have women there?" Millicent leaned forward harder, following Ryker's lead. The sound of skin slapping the grimy tiles, followed by an *oomf*, brought her up short.

Good thing Ryker was holding Marie, because Trent had tipped onto his face. His board slowly drifted out from behind him, headed away on its own. She barely contained a snort as he laboriously picked himself up and then started when he realized his board was getting away from him.

"I'd planned to leave him behind," Ryker said in an undertone, watching Trent limp after his board. "But I can't now. Not after all he's done for Marie."

"He's knowledgeable about medicine and child development. Marie's development, specifically. Even though this plight is way out of his league, he's valuable." Something occurred to Millicent. "Is this your protection bubble he was talking about? It now includes him?"

Ryker's brow dipped. He glanced at her before turning around, not commenting.

"About the bar, though," Millicent said as Trent came toward them with windmilling arms.

"They do have women, yes. Of course they do. But none like you." Ryker leaned forward gracefully, making it look easy.

Millicent tried to emulate his movements, but she had her own issues with waving arms. "This is probably why so many people are walking."

"No, it's not, princess," Ryker said, humor infusing his voice again.

"I think what he means is that you got a lot of benefits that not many other people—"

"I know what he means," Millicent snapped. Ryker's chuckling didn't help matters.

They made their way through the masses of people and took the movable platforms down, one at a time, never having to leave their hover boards. Ryker drew a fair share of looks, mostly from wide-eyed passersby. He was easily the biggest, most muscular person on this level. The only one carrying a child.

Millicent was also the subject of quick, harried scrutiny. Even though she was on par for a healthy weight, she was substantially curvier than those around her. In fact, most people were sticklike. Starved well past health. Their cheeks were hollowed, and their bones clearly showed.

"Is this what it's like in the lower areas of San Francisco?" she asked Ryker as they were waiting for the platform down.

"Near the ground level . . ." His eyes squinted in thought or remembrance. "Not as skinny but just as unhealthy. They can only afford mostly synthetic substances."

She chewed on her lip, watching as a man dropped a pouch of food. His head bent, and he stared at it for a moment before slowly bending to retrieve it. Straightening up looked physically painful.

The platform down to the next level shook to a start. The floor obscured Millicent's view as they were lowered. "One more," Ryker said as they stopped at the floor below.

"So the man with the plan hangs out in seedy bars," Trent said as he picked at his nail. "That doesn't bode well, right? I don't know what you're paying him, but I'd imagine it's a lot, right? So what is a man with a lot of credit doing at a seedy bar . . ."

"Not getting caught," Ryker murmured. He started forward as the platform stopped at the correct floor. "Stay close. Someone bothers you, kill them."

"Oh shit." Trent leaned too far forward, trying to catch up with Millicent, and started waving his hands to stay balanced. "That sort of thing goes on down here?"

Hard eyes tracked them as they passed, a greedy light in their depths. More people were taking notice now, more often of Trent than Ryker's size. They probably realized he was easy pickings, wealthy but not used to violence or killing.

"Stay close, Trent," Millicent said, ready to command a gun into her hand. She was thankful to have changed back into her suit at Conrath's apartment. Lugging all that weight around was about to pay off.

"You guys are going really fast," he said with a tight voice. Bent too far forward, he zoomed in front of her and then wobbled, his arms circling.

"Stop looking the fool," she said through clenched teeth. Large and scarred men stood against walls, watching. One guy, grizzled with salt-and-pepper hair tucked behind his ears, chewed a small plastic stick. A scar sliced across one cheek and continued over both lips. His hands twirled something in front of him. "How much longer, Ryker?"

Instead of answering, he stopped at a corner; Marie, now seated on his hip, sleepily wiped her eyes. He waited for Millicent to get closer before continuing onward. "Not long. These guys are just sizing us up. They won't engage yet. They'll want to see who we're affiliated with."

"Is this Roe person enough to keep them away?"

"I'm enough to keep them away."

"You know what I meant."

He didn't respond, which meant he probably didn't know if Roe could or not. Soon it might get ugly down here, because she hadn't made it this far to get robbed and killed. Blood might be shed, but it wouldn't be from her crew. She'd make sure of it.

Chapter 22

Ryker stepped off his hover board and then flipped it over with his foot. He toed something. The board clattered to the ground, lifeless. His eyes always moving, he turned off Millicent's board before moving on to Trent's. When he was done, he stopped beside Millicent and stared at a low entranceway four people wide.

"He's supposed to be in the back of this bar. You'll go first. Just walk in like this was your department, and keep your eyes on people's hands. Kill if you have to, but quietly. Do you know what I mean?"

"Yes. Use a knife. I got it."

"Good girl. Off you go. I've got the baby, and Trent will follow me." She felt his firm touch low on her hip, and it set off that annoying tingling again.

She commanded a knife into her hand, then walked through the entranceway and did a quick scan. Small booths lined the walls with a few people sitting and chatting in each. A wall to her left cut through the open space, closing it down into sections, more or less, probably to promote privacy.

In the middle section, there was more room for standing. People clustered around the tables, often sucking off tubes hanging from a dispenser above the table or from the wall next to it. A woman's hand drifted down to a man's stomach before lingering below. She grabbed him before barking out laughter.

Millicent threaded down an aisle and between an opening in the wall, now entering the third section and seeing another doorway for a fourth. This room was different still, filled with large couches and lounging areas. No one touched in here. They lay like dead things, limbs spilling around them or off the arms of the couches. Eyes unfocused and staring at nothing, mouths hanging open. A woman at the end was lying on the floor, her eyes staring at the ceiling, sightless.

"OD," Ryker said quietly. "Keep going."

"I hadn't planned to stop."

The door at the far end of the next section promised they had not yet reached the end. There was movement everywhere. Shaking limbs, snapping fingers, and laughter assaulted her. A man danced completely naked, his skin red—probably from the cold of the room—and his eyes bloodshot. He moved in strange ways, marching and then jumping and then dropping to the ground and rolling around.

"This is what bad narcotics will do to you," Ryker said, his hand now on her arm, steering her.

She grimaced as they went through the next doorway. Dark and still, this last section was all booths with two to four people sitting together, speaking quietly or not at all. Postures weren't tense, per se, but they weren't relaxed, either. A man at the door leered at Millicent, his eyes sparking with desire. A smile curled his lips as he leaned closer, about to say something.

Ryker's big hand slammed him back against the wall. The wall shook along the length of the bar, nothing more than a partition, but Ryker didn't seem concerned about taking it down.

"She's off-limits, bub," he said in a nightmarish voice. She didn't need to see his eyes to know there was a killer's edge to them. "Spread the word. Anyone who touches her dies. You doubt that?"

"No, bro-yo. No, sir. I'll let everyone know. Yes, sir." The man's Adam's apple bobbed, his shallow breathing audible.

"A little heavy-handed . . . ," Millicent said quietly.

"You expected anything less?" Trent's voice drifted up from the back of the line.

People glanced up as she passed. Eyes stuck. Millicent recognized the spark of intelligence and the scrutinizing assessments. These people didn't belong on this level, nor were they what they seemed. Something was amiss.

She stopped and put out her hand to Ryker, looking at the tubes hanging from the table next to her. Different colors as well as different sizes, they were each for something, but their mouth pieces were unused. No pink lipstick had rubbed off from the woman, nor fluorescent green from the man. The tubes near them, mounted to the wall, were also unused. The screens on the tables in front of the patrons glowed, their surfaces sleek, the tech nearly up to date.

"What is this place?" Millicent asked, backing up. "Who owns it?"

"Privately owned, I think," Ryker said, his hand landing on her shoulder. "We're in the right place."

"That may be, but who are these people? They don't belong on this floor."

"This floor, if any."

Millicent spun around at the gruff voice behind them. Ryker's back was to her, Marie's little arm around his neck as she straddled his hip.

It was the man she'd seen earlier, the one with the gray hair tucked behind his ears and the scar running across his lips. He still had a plastic stick between his teeth and was rolling it across his lips with his tongue. "Made it, huh? I didn't think you would." The man's eyes roved over Ryker before he said, "You're in no danger here."

"I know that," Ryker said.

The man huffed out a laugh as he passed by. His eyes swept over Millicent next, but he gave her a wide berth, humor flaring in his expression. Heavyset and with a slight limp, he made his way to the back booth.

"Do we go forward, or get the hell out of here?" Ryker asked. "Now is the decision-making time. We'll have to fight our way out if we want to go back."

"What would we go back to?" Millicent asked, looking over those working on their screens. Watching their movements, the way they interacted. They were fluent and comfortable with the tech, but didn't use it like the knowledge was ingrained. She'd guess midlevel staffers, people who could learn, but had to work at it.

Ryker's hand touched Millicent's chin, turning her face toward him. His eyes were deep and serious, though the color was mostly lost to shadow. When he spoke, his breath dusted her face, and that feeling she actually liked warmed her middle. "We would lose Marie at first, that's true. But we could easily find her again. We'd just have to wait. And we could stay together. The conglomerate would let us, I have no doubt. They'll give you anything but that child. Anything at all. You need only ask, and if that doesn't work, I'll force their hand. You had a cushy life, Millicent. As did I. As will Marie. We don't need to go any further. We don't need to risk all of our lives."

She stared up into his eyes, seeing the gravity. Seeing his seriousness. All this, all they'd been through, and if she gave the word, he'd throw it all away. For her. "Are you out of your mind?"

His brow drew tight over his eyes. His thumb paused in its stroking of her jaw. "What's that?"

"We've nearly been killed. I've taken a ton of drugs. You'll probably scar, and that's a shame because you've got a great back. And here we are, almost there, with someone who can get us off this horrible planet before Toton unleashes whatever human-killing tech they've developed, and you want to *go back*? You want to just hand back our child, our *child*, and take what comes? Which will be extreme danger, I have no doubt. That's what you're proposing?"

He stared at her, his thumb still frozen.

"Dumb ass." She pulled her face back and turned, nearly missing the delighted twinkle that lit up Ryker's gaze. "Let's get this done. And if all these people, who do not belong on this floor no matter what anyone says, try to kill us or send us back, I'll kill them first."

"Stubbornness. Huh. I don't remember this being documented." Trent bent to his wrist.

Chin held high, Millicent walked through the center of the aisle and then slid into the cushioned seat across from the grizzled man. Ryker handed the baby to her before sliding in himself. Trent stood next to Ryker, staring down. "Can I sit?"

"Who is that?" The man pointed at Trent.

"He's the lab staff who enhanced my daughter." Ryker stared at the man, not motioning at Marie in any way. "He's keeping her alive."

"Well . . . not exactly," Trent said. "As I told them, the human race is really very—"

"Shut up," Ryker said.

"Right. Sorry." Trent eyed the space next to the grizzled man.

"Jesse said you were a couple of natural borns." The grizzled man moved over a little. Trent sat down gratefully. "I didn't believe him. He didn't mention that you are so far above the Curve you're practically urban legend. And yet here you are." His hard gray gaze pounded into Millicent. "What do you do?"

"I was a director in the major defense systems department for Moxidone, but my aptitude is—"

"You're Millicent Foster. I thought as much." The man blew out a breath and leaned back. His gaze switched to Ryker. "Gunner. Jesse wouldn't give me your real names. He wanted to help you. Not hard to figure it out, though." He bent his head to Trent. "What did you say you did? Carry their belongings?"

"Um . . . no. Well . . ." Trent shrugged, his gaze swinging to Marie. "Kind of. I guess."

"Kind of. You guess." The man crossed his arms over his chest and rolled the plastic thing around his mouth.

"There a problem?" Ryker asked.

"Yeah, I'll say there's a pretty damn big problem. You are legendary natural borns. Not just in your conglomerate, in *all* conglomerates. You got a lab slave with you who can enhance humanity—that's gotten all the conglomerates' attentions, too. Including Toton, so I've heard. And you got the winning product of his proven formula with you. That little kid who has got this whole damn place up in arms. There is not one kill order out among you. That is unheard of. Know what that means? It means they are going to put out all their resources to get you back. It means that if I help you, I'll have a pretty damn big notice on my head. On my whole operation's head. Yeah. It's a problem."

"Then why go through with this meeting?" Ryker asked.

The grizzled man minutely shook his head, his gaze falling on Marie. Then Millicent. "Word on the street is, that kid is yours. As in, both of yours. Exclusively . . ."

"Yes," Ryker said.

"And she's just as smart as you are."

"Smarter. She's four clicks in a couple—"

"In most all categories—" Under Ryker's stare, Trent put down his finger and tightened his lips.

"You thinking of turning us in for a profit?" Ryker leaned forward. His large arms bulged against the table.

The man's eyes didn't waver. If he wasn't intimidated, he was the only one in the world. "They'd torture me for information if I tried to turn you in, then they might or might not kill me. No. I'm wondering if I want to brave your conglomerate to help you. We got a ship leaving in two days. Even a couple days might be too long of a window. From what I hear, they're throwing everything they can into capturing you."

"She can command electronics with her mind," Ryker said. "She doesn't need an implant to unlock a door. And Ms. Foster and I can both still breed. We plan to make more. Mr. McAllister is on hand to oversee this."

Millicent tried to hold back her annoyance at Ryker's assurance, but when the grizzled man's eyes flicked to her, his humorous response told her a scowl had slipped onto her face.

The man sobered quickly. "We don't have a lot of tech off-planet. It's a whole different sort of living. If you want to wear something, you reach into your closet and pull it out. You wash it yourself. You hang it back up. You make your own food. No hover technology. You'd be the smartest people there, but . . . your sort of intelligence might not be useful."

"I'm sure we could figure something out," Ryker said evenly.

"I could program one hell of a pirate network that you could easily install planet-side," Millicent said quickly. "I can design weapons you've never seen. I can design tech, not just work it. I've programed implants, too. Changed identities. I can hack into any system. I can work around any situation—except, maybe, my daughter's. When these conglomerates finish ruining this planet and they get more serious about colonization, where do you think they're going? You think you can hold them off forever? Not without Mr. Gunner, who dreams of security protocols. And with the two of us working together, you'll have a chance to keep them away for a little longer. Not to mention I am three clicks above the Curve, with proven success in creating a smarter, more advanced child—with the help of Mr. Gunner and Mr. McAllister, of course." A flare of indignation took over. "Are we really having this conversation? You are wondering if my crew is worth the hassle? I can run circles around anyone in this room. You want proof?"

It took her less than five minutes of silence to make a dancing fat man holding a monkey appear on all the screens in the establishment. "I meant that to be more spectacular," she mumbled. "You need to beef up your security."

"It seems so . . ." The man was frowning at her.

"And Mr. Gunner can probably kill everyone in the room, with just his hands, in the amount of time I used to cripple your systems."

"You crippled my systems?" His gaze dipped to the screen in front of him.

"Well, I mean, I can patch it up . . ." She smoothed her hair against her head. "Regardless, we've evaded them again and again, and we'll continue to evade them. We just need the location of this ship and we're good. We don't even need your guidance."

Silence descended slowly, those hard gray eyes staring at Millicent. She stared right back. If she had to, she would make Ryker torture the information out of him. She intended to leave this planet, and he would help them whether he wanted to or not.

Finally, after a long moment, the older man cracked a smile. "Your reputation does not do you justice, Ms. Foster. No wonder they want you even more than they want your daughter. You're something." He pulled a tube from the wall and sucked. After three swallows, he used it to gesture toward her. "Fancy a drink?"

"No, she wouldn't. But I would." Ryker reached over his shoulder and pulled out a tube of the same size and color. He grabbed a plastic piece from a dispenser and attached it to the end of the tube. He took a few more gulps than the man had.

"Actually, I would," Millicent said, indignation still riding high. "This can't be worse than a bunch of drugs."

"Come again?" the grizzled man said.

She took the tube from Ryker.

"You don't want your own mouth piece?" he asked with a smirk.

"I've already been in contact with your spit. I don't think this is much different."

"I wouldn't count on that."

Millicent sucked in. A bitter liquid filled her mouth. Before she'd thought it through, she swallowed it down. Fire scraped her throat and then made war in her chest. It felt like she was being pierced with needles. Finally, it hit her stomach as an acidic burn coated her mouth. Her belly rolled. Then gurgled.

"That is *horri*ble," she said, bringing the back of her hand up to her mouth. "Horrible. Why? Why would you willingly drink it?"

"I'm Roe," the man said, extending his hand to Ryker with a laugh. "I'll take you."

Trent's loud exhale drew eyes as he slumped against the seat.

Millicent beat on her chest. The flame wouldn't go out. She drew more eyes.

"I honestly didn't think you'd make it this far," Roe said before sucking down more of that horrible concoction. He held the end of the tube out to Trent, who shook his head. "That you did is impressive. I really want to say no, but it is a once-in-a-lifetime opportunity to have access to people of your intelligence."

"Then why all the rigmarole with the indecisiveness?" Millicent eyed the tubes hanging over the table. "What are these?"

"Because I need to be able to use your intelligence, not just breed it."

"Don't start talking like him," Millicent said, pointing at Trent.

"Those are various forms of narcotics and hallucinogens," Ryker said, his hand sliding over her thigh. "I wouldn't advise them."

"Roe." A woman from the next table over slid out of her seat with a finger to her ear. "We've got trouble."

Roe didn't give any outward sign that he was worried; he just stared up with a blank face, waiting for more.

"They've called in a director." The woman's gaze darted down the aisle. "Landed in the upper middle. Working his way down. Doesn't look like they have a clear picture yet, though. Just hunting."

"That'll be Mr. Hunt. His name was chosen for a reason." Ryker's hand squeezed Millicent's thigh before he took it away. "He'll find his way down here eventually."

"No one down here will talk to an upper-level staffer." Roe clasped his hands on the table.

"They'll talk to Mr. Hunt," Ryker said with a dark surety in his voice.

"Or they'll die," Trent said, his lips thinning.

Roe's eyes hit the woman before he pushed Trent out of the seat. "Give him a distraction. Half-truths. I'll get them out of here. Message me."

"Yes, sir." The woman brought a small device up to her mouth and spoke into it.

"Do they not have implants?" Millicent said as Ryker helped her out of the booth. She hefted Marie into her arms.

"No. We remove those before we go off-planet." Roe motioned them after him. "This way. I have a safe place for the night."

"Wait." Ryker stopped them. "Assume there is no safe place. It's best to keep on the move."

Roe stopped in front of a back door that blended well, if not perfectly, into the wall. "I always assume there is no safe place. That's why I'm still alive. C'mon."

Ryker hesitated for a moment before touching the hollow of Millicent's back and applying pressure. She took the subtle cue and followed Roe out the door, through a few dingy corridors—a standard at this level—and to a small craft docked in an open bay. Wind whipped at them and rain stung their faces as Roe flipped open a box that must've held the controls. Before he could touch them, though, the doors slid open.

"What—" Roe glanced up in surprise.

"We'll explain later," Millicent said, jogging into the craft with Ryker and Trent right behind her.

Roe sat in the cockpit, and Ryker positioned himself as close to him as he could, leaving everyone else to take seats in the passenger area. "How long have you been doing this?" Ryker asked.

"Since I was your age, give or take. I was two clicks above when that was exciting. It seems like each generation gets smarter."

"And more dependent," Ryker said in a hollow tone.

"For the elite, yes."

"How many times have you failed in this sort of thing?" Ryker asked.

"Me personally? A few. My people? Many. This isn't a sure thing. Nothing about this is a sure thing. We're better at getting people off-planet now, but we're not perfect. Shit happens."

The dock made a grinding noise—Millicent hoped it was the dock—before the craft started to lower through the air. She did everything she could not to push her face against the window and look down. Surely someone would be beneath them, unable to get away from the dock in time?

"We have to travel a ways to get to the ship," Roe said. "Getting out of the city is going to be the hardest part. These conglomerates have eyes and ears everywhere. We can't get past security to alter your files in any way, but I assume you have that ability?"

"Of course," Millicent said, holding Marie close and running her fingers through her soft hair.

"Of course . . ." Roe shook his head. "Used to being in command, huh?"

"Yes," Ryker said.

"I meant the girl," Roe growled. "You're just the muscle."

Trent ducked his head, probably to hide his smile.

"I'm used to getting things done," Millicent answered.

"Good." The vessel started forward before continuing to lower. "It'll take them a long time to search this low. Very little usable tech down here. When everyone is used to computers doing everything for them, they forget how to get around without them."

"I doubt Mr. Hunt would have that hang-up." Ryker threaded his fingers together and leaned his elbows on his knees.

"I get the feeling Mr. Hunt is as good as you are," Roe said. The vessel moved forward again in its now pitch-black surroundings. Shutters lowered, clearly screening the lit interior from the outside.

"He's as good as I am, but without a soul. He goes about things a little differently than I do."

"And that's saying something," Trent grumbled. "If I were in charge, I wouldn't have let someone like Mr. Hunt go through the tests."

"That's why they never would've put you in charge," Roe said. "These conglomerates breed monsters when they need them. Humanity takes a backseat the higher you advance."

"What made you get out?" Trent asked. "If you were two clicks above the Curve, you would've been treated as well as these two."

"Fell in love. Pretty standard these days. They moved her away and wouldn't let me join her. They tried to dose me with Clarity—not realizing that was just for sex, not for love. When it wouldn't work, I got a dose of something that's off the market now. It turned me into an emotional zombie, but it didn't erase the memory. I no longer gave a shit about them, only about her. I knew that when the drug wore off, I'd be fine. So did they. Their final response was to kill her."

Silence descended in the craft, finally broken with "You must've been more valuable than she was."

Ryker turned his hard look on Trent, whose lips thinned before he hunched down into himself.

"I was, yes," Roe said. "Much more so. She couldn't even breed. Lab born."

"So you devised a way out?" Millicent asked. "Like we're doing?"

"No," he said. "I burned the whole department to the ground. That crap they dosed me with left me with nothing but logic and a vendetta. That's a damn scary thing for someone who's cut off from morals and emotion. I killed over a million people, most of them just following the rules." Millicent saw one of his shoulders twitch—a shrug, maybe. "When the drug wore off, I was so sick with myself, so disgusted with their resolve, I figured out a way to get off-planet without them catching me. But where can you go to get away from yourself? It wasn't long before I came back. That's when I started all of this. I was something of a legend. People were more inclined to listen."

"Jessima Smith," Ryker said in a knowing voice. "You're still a legend. It's why I get away with so much."

"We're a special breed."

"Jessima Smith . . ." Trent took to his wrist. "You are the most bred man in history, I believe."

"They like violence for certain positions, yes." Another softer grinding sound emitted before the craft shook. They'd docked. "The conglomerates try to control everything, but they're equally excited and terrified by what they can't control. The whole system is . . ." He shook his head as he emerged from the cockpit.

"Don't tell me we're related," Ryker said into his hands.

"No, no. He wasn't approved for natural births. Too unpredictable." Trent scrolled through the text on his wrist screen.

Roe barked out laughter. "If we were, you would've gotten your good looks from your mother, 'cause they sure wouldn't have come from me."

"They haven't figured out how to quell the love emotion," Trent said, not realizing the others had stood and were readying to leave the craft. "It's an elusive thing. We don't really understand what creates it. Sex is easy enough, of course. That's chemical, for the most part, revolving around touch and pleasure and the biological need to procreate . . ."

Heat surged through Millicent's center, simmering and burning and settling deep. It urged her to step closer to Ryker. She rolled her eyes and wiped her hand across her forehead to clear the sudden moisture. "I did procreate. Why does it persist? It's the most annoying thing . . ."

Roe laughed as he stopped near the door. "Wait until you experience love, Ms. Foster, if you ever find it. That'll be even more annoying, especially when it's time to compromise over something trivial and you realize you can't walk away, no matter how much you want to."

"I have love, and I don't want to walk away." She kissed Marie on the head.

"I'm talking about a different love. Let's go." The doors slid open. Roe brandished an older-style gun with plenty of power before stepping into the pitch-black. A beam of light flared from his hand. "Best not to advertise our presence more than we must. We're not the worst thing down here, I assure you. And given all our track records, I don't say that lightly."

"We won't have long," Ryker warned.

"I know. But it'll work for tonight. You all need sleep. You look half-dead. I need you at full capacity." Farther down the platform, Roe stopped at a door, took out a small metal thing, and fitted it into the metal door handle. He turned and then pushed. The door swung open.

"Wow. Talk about no tech." Millicent looked at the contraption.

"Exactly. It is very confusing to people like you," Roe said, slapping the wall to turn on the lights. "Okay. Through there"—he pointed down a hall—"are two bedrooms. One is mine. Out here is a couch that makes a bed. Figure it out. We leave at dawn. The sun doesn't reach this far down, so dawn will be a loud alarm or my foot nudging your ribs."

"Do you have any tech at all in here?" Millicent asked as Ryker took the baby and settled her and her stuffed bunny onto the soft bed Trent had already pulled out. She was half-asleep, and she quickly curled up and closed her eyes. That she needed no more comfort than a stuffed toy was probably a testament to how tired she was. That, or how she'd been raised thus far, without someone to sing her to sleep or cuddle her through the night.

"Of course we do. How do you think we have light?" Roe pointed up at the bare lightbulbs from yester decade.

"I meant computer tech of any kind. Can I get online?" Millicent asked.

Roe's eyes sparkled as though a joke had been told. "Yeah. Got a console in my bedroom. As well as an emergency exit. No screens out here, though. No wireless."

"I'll need to check it in the morning. To see how things are going."

"Got it. Get some sleep." Roe limped away down the hall.

"At least I won't be the slowest one anymore," Trent said, watching him.

"Ryker, I should check your back." Millicent motioned for him to undo his suit. "We really need to get new suits, too. I realize they recycle fluids, but it's not tech I've ever looked into. I don't know if there is a limit . . ."

"I've definitely pushed mine further than you have," Trent said as he sat on the bed next to Marie and then fell back. He threw an arm over his eyes. "And it's still working."

"Let's take the other bed," Ryker said, stepping to the side while gesturing her forward. "You can take a look in there. A long one. Up close."

Millicent scoffed and rolled her eyes. "Fine. Let's go."

The walls seemed freshly painted, but maybe that was only in comparison to the exterior. The door was wood, and she let her fingers run over the surface before she pushed it open. "This apartment is probably a hundred years old. More. When's the last time you saw a wood door?"

"In pictures. When's the last time you saw a lock that required a physical key?"

"Never. But it's all in great shape."

"Defies logic, doesn't it?" He dropped the tech bag on the ground and stripped down his suit. He didn't stop at his waist, though. He pulled it all the way down to his feet before stepping out. His manhood stuck straight out.

The tingling turned up a notch. Her brain started to fog over, but not from fatigue.

And that's why they named the drug Clarity.

"Right then." She cleared her throat and turned him around so she could see his broad back covered in angry red flesh. "Miraculous." She traced a few of the more healed lines with her fingers. "Inhuman that you heal this fast."

"I am all human, I assure you," he said, his voice deep and coated in velvet. "One hundred percent man."

Butterflies filled her stomach. "Yes. I noticed that part of your body a moment ago."

"Impressive, huh?"

"Ugly, actually. Obviously designed by a man." Millicent applied a stitcher to a couple of places and healing gel to a couple of others. She'd save the rest of the Cure-all for the next time he nearly died. No sense speeding his healing up any more—he had some time to lie idle. "Okay, I think that'll do you. Is there any pain?"

"None." He turned to her, his eyes burning and intent. "Desire, though. Of that, I have plenty. You are a beautiful woman, Millicent Foster. And incredibly intelligent and resourceful. One of a kind."

"All natural borns are."

"No. Natural borns are unique in some ways, but usually small ways. Our characteristics are not perfectly symmetrical, a strange concoction of traits due to nature's surprise, but we're not that different from lab borns. And some of us are exactly the same as one or two clones. We're just born differently. But you . . . are just you. There is no one like you, and believe me, I've looked. I've met a lot of people. A lot of women. You are one of a kind. The conglomerate knew that before I did. And now you've created another one of a kind." His lips were soft and insistent, nibbling on hers. He tasted savory and delicious.

"I've wanted you from the first moment I saw you, Millicent. The very first moment. I'll never forget all the thoughts racing across your face on that first ride. You were trying to figure me out, figure out what I was doing there. It was interesting to watch, especially since your reactions weren't what I would've expected. Your brain works differently than mine. Than the type of brain I was taught to counteract. You're smarter than me. It's a first."

"We're on the same level, and I hardly believe it's a first." Her words came out wispy as his lips nibbled down her neck.

"I told you before that you should be retested."

"What's your point?"

His lips found hers again as his hand slid along her suit's clasp. The fabric parted. His warm palm slid across her stomach before the other joined. Together they moved upward, roaming over her breasts and against her sensitive nipples. "I wanted to get you off-planet when I first saw you. I knew in that moment that I could spend the rest of my life with you. And only you. But when I watched you cuddle your baby. Our baby—I hadn't realized she was mine at the time. When I saw that, I wanted to take you both. I wanted us to be a family. Before I even knew Marie was mine, I wanted to help raise her."

She closed her eyes and got lost in his kiss. In his confession. It tickled that deep place inside her, softening the compassion she wasn't supposed to have.

Then his thumbs stroked over her taut nipples, and suddenly all the sentiment was replaced by the tightening, pounding parts of her body that wouldn't be ignored.

"Uuuoo. That's . . . I like that." Millicent's eyes fluttered closed. "Yes, keep doing that."

His chuckle was dark. "So many things you haven't experienced, Millie. It'll be fun awakening your desires."

"Do you live with arousal constantly?"

"Around you, yes."

"Isn't it extremely annoying?"

"No. I enjoy the anticipation. It's more exciting. You'll see."

"I don't want to s—" A hot mouth encircled her nipple. Her gasp filled the room as fire blazed through her body. "I might want to see . . ." She groaned.

His hands slid over her shoulders and then down her arms, taking the suit with it. Then over the swell of her hips and down her newly trembling thighs. Her breath came faster, and everything tightened up.

"Have you done any of this before?" Ryker asked quietly, his breath tickling her navel.

"You know I haven't."

His mouth inched lower until another of her gasps filled the room. "Let me take you on a tour of your body, Millie, starting with this spot."

The suction was probably the single best thing in the world at that moment. If she could form words, she would answer in the affirmative. More heat, followed by winding so tight she gripped his hair and made unintelligible sounds, panting and moaning in the process. An explosion so glorious only those black briefs had been able to match it rocked through her body. She breathed in deeply as shivers and vibrations made a smile blossom on her face.

Ryker pulled back strange-looking sheets before scooping her up and then laying her down. The fabric was softer than it was at home. It smelled different, too, like her air freshener. That was called cotton, after a plant that had existed hundreds of years ago.

She felt the fabric again. "Do you think this comes from off-world?"

"Or maybe we aren't told all that's happening on this world . . ." Ryker settled between her thighs. His playful, teasing tongue brought the tightness back with an intensity that had her writhing under him.

"I won't stop until I hear you scream my name, princess," he said quietly, moving back up her body so he could suck in her bottom lip.

Despite his earlier ministrations, nothing prepared her for what came next. His thrust pushed all the air from her lungs. His body inside hers chased away all the thoughts, big and small. All she could do was feel.

As he continued to move, her legs drifted farther up the sides of his body before hooking over his hips. Her arms held on tight, and her swinging hips rose up to meet his downward plunges. And the *heat*, oh the glorious heat, soaked through her in a way that defied words.

An explosion of pleasure made her cry out. She bit back further exclamations just in time to maintain her dignity. Praising the divine, or worse, him, would get her teased forever. But he kept on, so intense. So consuming. It stole her will and then swept her away. When the next explosion came through, her yell of exquisite bliss probably woke the neighbors—assuming there were any.

"Not until you say my name," he said as his lips met hers again. Then his deep and sensuous kiss got the heat building inside her all over again.

One thing was for certain: the black briefs had nothing on Ryker Gunner. And if she ever admitted that out loud, there would be no craft big enough to carry his monstrous ego.

Chapter 23

Millicent came awake slowly, still gripped by sleep. Purple flashed in the dark room, highlighting the large arm wrapped around her middle. The warmth coating her back was the distinct form of a man made of solid muscle. His breath fell across her cheek evenly, indicating he was still deeply asleep.

In confusion, she blinked and then widened her eyes, trying to clear away the sandy quality. The purple glow persisted, throbbing. She brought her wrist up grudgingly.

Then bolted upright.

"Ryker, wake up!" She shoved him.

One word pulsed across her skin: *Breach!*

"Ryker!"

She shoved him again so she could jump out of the bed. Cold assaulted her, but she didn't have time to don her suit. She ripped open the bedroom door before slamming into Roe's door. The handle would only turn a fraction, the soft click-click hinting at a lock. "Roe!" She slammed her shoulder into the solid wood again.

"What's happening?" Ryker had followed her.

The door swung open, revealing a puffy-eyed Roe with disheveled hair. His hand slid along the wall next to the door. Light bathed the room. Roe's gaze swept down her body. "No, thank you."

"She wasn't offering," Ryker said in a fierce tone.

"Shut up, you two. She busted through my code. We're live." Millicent pushed past Roe. "Where's the console?"

"What do you mean you're live?" Roe asked, crossing the room and slapping a console active.

"We're traceable. What network is this?" She stared at a log-in screen.

Roe fingered a control and then stepped in front of a red dot on the wall. A red beam crossed his face up and down, side to side. The scan was as obvious as it was breakable.

She shook her head as the screen flared to life. "Your security is ridiculous."

"It's done me so far."

"You haven't had anyone worth their salt after you so far, I'd wager," Millicent said, greeted with the complex web of code. "Shit. Yeah. So I won't have time to wade through this mess. She already knows what trips me up, and she's used that knowledge plenty."

"Who?" Roe's brow furrowed as he looked at the console. "Holy shit."

"As good a god as any," Ryker said. He turned toward the other room. "Let's shut off these implants and get going. We don't have time to lose."

"I'm not sure I can access the new weapons without assistance from my implant," Millicent said as a weight of fear crushed her chest. "They're close enough, but I haven't perfected the correct thought commands. I'm used to relying on my implant."

"The new tech isn't from our conglomerate, right?" Ryker handed her suit to her, but she was too distracted to put it on.

"So?"

"So your implant wasn't helping anyway. Not with those."

She stared at the code in front of her. Its faults were easy to see—the little patches resulting from a rush job. She could easily exploit those and break her way in, but . . . what else was waiting for her? How much of this was a wild goose chase intended to keep her busy while they moved into position? Knowing that she'd want to tear down that code just to prove she was better.

It was extremely tempting. But now wasn't the time.

"Very good. She knows my personality type, all right." Millicent couldn't help but smile. "She thinks I'm a machine. Like I'm supposed to be. Like I was trained to be."

"Who thinks you're a machine?" Roe asked. "Your superior?"

"No. My sister." Millicent leaned against her knees and lowered her head, her thoughts zooming through cyberspace faster than any computer could. Solving problems and thinking through the system in a way no machine could mimic. She thought of their goal, and what the enemy—because the conglomerates were now her enemy—knew of their goal. She merged her deductions with her knowledge of how they operated.

"You know your sister?" Roe asked, incredulous.

"Blowing up a building," Millicent said, vaguely looking at Roe. A grin lit up her face. "That's a thought."

"What's she doing?" Roe asked.

If someone answered him, she didn't hear it. Instead, she accessed Ryker's old security loop, then started leaving little bombs in the form of system quirks and viruses everywhere she could easily access. Then she planted a timed bomb to fry the implants of a large tier of staffers. She couldn't reach every department and didn't bother with anything too complicated. After that, she worked into the private loops of a select few higher-level staffers and timed her prison program to affect them. That'd scare the shit out of them, and hopefully make them panicked and unfocused.

After spending more time on it than she should have, she logged out and moved on to the pirate network. Here she went nuts, logging in to any conglomerate intranet she could, hitting the government, creating multiple worms and horrific Trojans. None of this would be permanent, but it would sure be annoying until they spent time to fix it. All this would give them a few precious hours to sneak out. Hopefully.

A firm hand on her shoulder sucked her attention away from the screen. She blinked through the sudden daze—the disruption of intense focus always gave her vertigo.

Ryker, eyes tight, held a familiar device to her head. "I'm not going to lie. It hurts like a bitch."

But suddenly she couldn't even focus on the color of his eyes. Searing pain rolled through her head. Her teeth chattered until she clenched them tight. Shock waves electrified her mind and then struck her body like points of lightning.

She came to in Ryker's arms with drool running down the side of her cheek. His anxious eyes stared down at her. Marie was screaming somewhere in the room.

"Ouch," she said, licking her lip. The coppery taste of blood told her it wasn't drool on her cheek. She must've bit her tongue.

"You weren't kidding about not screaming. Ego boost for me for last night."

"As if you needed one." Millicent wiped her face with the back of her hand.

Ryker's mouth turned up into a smile. It didn't reach his eyes. "We have to go, princess. They'll be swarming us in no time."

"Half of them won't be able to operate their vehicles, actually." She let Ryker stand her up, only then noticing Trent was still sprawled out on the ground.

"Mama! Mama!" Marie sprinted forward, released by Roe, and wrapped her arms around Millicent's legs.

"That kid has got something . . . interesting," Roe said as he glanced up at the lightbulb. "Made this whole place look like a disco ball."

"What's a disco ball?" Millicent asked.

"Never mind." Roe toed Trent's side. "Get off the ground, numb nuts. You're not supposed to scream louder than the girls."

"I don't care about your antiquated man-speak." Trent picked himself up. "We all know she's tougher than me. What's the point in pretending?"

"At least you know where you rank in the scheme of things." Roe shouldered a pack. "Ms. Foster, get dressed. We need to move out."

"What do you mean, Millie?" Ryker asked.

"Please, for the love of Holy, put something on, Millicent!" Trent hunched painfully again—his hands on his knees, his head bowed.

"Here, kid. Take this." Roe took something out of his pack and handed it to Trent.

Trent's miserable expression cleared. "See? That one guy prayed to an actual god, and look how he ended up." He popped a little white pill into his mouth.

"Is that Clarity?" Millicent asked as she stepped into the suit.

"Yeah. You want some?" Roe reached into his pack.

"Or would you rather ride the beast again?" Ryker asked, strapping on a pack he must've gotten from Roe. It was thick black canvas with heavy straps. It didn't look like it would even bounce when he ran. "It'll just get better, I promise. There's a lot we haven't tried . . ."

She sniffed and dropped her hand, turning away. No sense in making a big show of it. Or acknowledging his dark chuckle.

"Here," Roe said. He grabbed a pack like Ryker's off the ground.

Nothing jiggled as she lightly shook it. "Who packed these?"

"I did," Ryker said. "I split up the smart tech from that warehouse. If one of us loses a pack, we'll still have a piece. Including Trent."

"Except for me. He didn't trust me." Roe eyed Ryker with a blank expression. His eyes hinted at his irritation, though.

"You didn't see what we did," Millicent said, jogging into the other bedroom and grabbing her jacket. "And I have a feeling it's just a small slice of what's actually going on."

"Your life is just a small slice of what's going on," Roe said. "You sure you need all that weight? We need speed."

"She's faster than me with that weight." Trent wiped his puffy eyes.

Roe stared at him for a moment. "You really do know where you rank in the scheme of things. Huh. Welp. More power to you, I say. Why try to be something you're not. Like tough. Let's go."

"I think he's more of an asshole than Ryker is," Trent muttered.

"You don't know me very well, kid." Roe pushed open a door, revealing a row of hanging clothing. He pushed the suits aside, poked a part of the wall, which clicked, and then pulled open an expertly hidden door within the dark space. "I am absolutely more of an asshole than he is."

Light flared from a globe in Roe's hand. He handed it to Millicent before turning on another one. "There are a few things I need to know should the worst happen. If I can only save one of you, who's it gonna be? And don't say the lab rat. He's of no use to me without you two."

"Holy Masses," Trent grumbled.

"Marie," Millicent said immediately. "If we are overtaken, save Marie."

"Ryker, you good with that? I can't have you trying to complicate things at the worst of times."

"Yes." That one syllable was his only response as he held the little girl.

"Are you sure you'd save her over yourself?" Roe asked Millicent. "You can make more children."

Ryker flexed but said nothing.

"She's my child," Millicent said, trying to hold back the sudden need for violence. Her face probably held the same expression as Ryker's. "I would do anything for my child."

"Including dying?"

"No one is dying," Ryker said in a flat voice.

"Sorry, He-Man, forgot you were with us for a second."

"Yes, including dying. Who's He-Man?" Millicent asked.

"Historic cartoon—never mind." Roe led them down the stairs, his limp slightly more pronounced. "I'm getting too old for this shit. I need to pass on the legacy."

Down they went, ten floors. The rank smell of urine and mildew made Millicent gag. Marie dug her face into Ryker's shoulder, whining and moaning. The ground turned slimy, as though it had been under-water at some point and never dried out.

"Ground level, ladies and gents. May your experiences with it be few and far between." Roe shouldered open a door, the metal sticking halfway. He pushed it farther, struggling. "Oh no, I got it. Don't bother helping. I wouldn't want you to pull a muscle." He jammed his shoulder into it, forcing it wider. Finally, he gave up and continued through.

Weak yellow streetlights affixed to heavily leaning poles rained down illumination on the crumbled and tiny walkway below. Equally tiny vehicles with round wheels, often metal or what looked like a soft decaying rubber, sat off to the side. Mostly without windows, the rusted and twisted frames enclosed scarred, black interiors. Spray paint covered the faded and badly scratched wall, as if whatever fires had been set hadn't burned it all away. The vessels lined the narrow concrete travel way on both sides, ground bound.

"These aren't as old as you might think," Roe said out of the blue, walking between one that was raised up on blocks and another that was so burned it was hard to tell what color it had once been. "None of this, including the apartment we were in, is as old as you might think."

"How can that be?" Millicent asked, looking at the walls barely visible through the oppressive atmosphere.

"Any new tech is always more expensive than most people can afford. It takes a long time before the poor can use it on a daily basis.

These things are old, don't get me wrong, but you live in a very different world than most people do."

"Lived. Past tense."

"Here we go." Roe stopped next to a vehicle. The glow of his light traced over the wall, highlighting freshly painted characters in yellow and blue over a dark-gray surface. At the bottom, showing clearly, was a red circle with a slash through it.

"What does that mean?" Millicent pointed at the symbol.

"Rebel Nation." Roe glanced around. Silence hung heavy around them; not even the sound of motors drifted down far enough to reach them. A drip hit a pool of water. And then again. Millicent clutched on to that sound, needing something to disrupt the foreign sound of nothingness.

"That's the name you came up with? Rebel Nation?" Ryker asked in an even tone.

Roe's brow furrowed and he leaned closer. "Your teeth are practically glowing they're so white."

"I look after myself," Ryker responded.

"Maybe a little too much. You'll probably draw eyes down here. Although, that is a perfect reason to keep your mouth shut. That'll help us both out."

"It'll help us *all* out, actually," Millicent said, edging down a ways and scanning the other writing. Some symbols appeared over and over again.

"Don't wander too far or you'll get jumped," Roe said. "This is the jungle. Violent, desperate, or risky people come down here to skirt the law. You don't want to run into any of them."

"I'll be fine." Millicent started back anyway. "But I'd rather not waste my ammo on average people."

Roe huffed out a laugh. "Average, huh? I take it you aren't as uptight as you look."

"Yes, she is. She's just a violent sort of uptight who doesn't care about consequences," Trent said, inching closer to Ryker while scanning the far side of the street.

"My kinda woman. This way." Roe walked into the middle of the street and then turned left.

"What's our plan?" Ryker asked, coming even with Millicent.

"We've got a car waiting up here, blending in. We'll take the street out of the downtown area. From there, we've got a craft available. We'll stay as low as we can. The goal is to keep your face out of the tech areas as much as possible. I have an identity masker for everyone, but it doesn't work for long without constant charging. So we're saving it until something goes wrong."

"How big of a nation do you have?" Millicent asked. A shape caught her eye.

Z-eighteen.

She opened her fingers. Nothing happened. "I'm already missing my implant."

"Think harder," Trent said quietly, staring at the same spot Millicent was. "The implant just amplified your thoughts. You didn't have to try as hard."

"I helped design them, Trent. I know how they work. It doesn't prevent me from lamenting its absence."

Z-eighteen!

The gun nudged her wrist. She sighed in irritation and pulled it the rest of the way down before untangling it from the hyperelectromagnetic holster in the jacket. On the other side of the street, a shoe merged with the black shadows.

"Are there often people down here at . . ." She glanced at her bare wrist and then sighed again. "It's early, right?"

"There is no time down here," Roe said quietly. "And yes, there are always people. With Mr. Muscles back there, though, we shouldn't be bothered."

"Would you be bothered on your own?" Ryker asked.

"Always."

"They don't know who you are?"

"Those who know me know to either help out or hide because I'll shoot them. So no, I am not troubled by people who know who I am."

"Shoot many people?" Millicent asked, keeping her gun low and her eyes open.

"Every few blocks, usually. It's the desperate you have to watch out for. They mistake people like me for incapable risk-takers."

"And people like Ryker?" Millicent asked.

"No mistaking the obviously violent. He's making my life incredibly easy right now, which will probably mean he'll make my life incredibly difficult down the road. That's how my luck always seems to land."

"It's not luck. It's your personality," Trent mumbled.

"You're a real pocket full of daisies, aren't you?" Roe swung his gun to the right, aiming at a scrawny man with sketchy eyes and jerking body parts who was slowly walking forward. "Not wise, my man. You'll be dead before you make it halfway."

"Shouldn't you look at him when you threaten to kill him?" Trent asked.

"You do you. Let me do me." Roe kept looking in the other direction. "These fuckers like to do pile-on attacks."

Proving Roe correct, a man bolted toward them, coming up on Millicent's side. Before she could even turn and fire, Ryker was there. He grabbed the man almost lazily. Two fast punches doubled him over before Ryker spun him around and wrapped two arms around his head. A loud crack rent the street, overshadowing the scrape of more feet. The footsteps slowed, and two other people hovered at the far reaches of the light.

"Looks like they got the message." Roe's finger squeezed. A gunshot blasted and then echoed off the walls. One of the men dropped to the ground, clutching at his middle. The other turned to flee. The second shot took him in the back, knocking him into the hazy yellow of a streetlight. He groaned as his clawlike hand reached back. He relaxed into the walkway as the life left him.

"I thought you said they got the message?" Trent said.

"I wanted to make sure everyone else got the message, too." Roe tucked his gun away. "Good people don't walk this street. There's no harm in cleaning up the dredge."

"We're walking this street!" Trent said, outraged.

"And how many people have you killed?"

"None. I haven't killed any. I've been guarding the child the whole time."

"You've killed plenty," Ryker said, his eyes continually moving. "Babies, all. Anything that doesn't work out gets the axe."

"There you go. Guilty. You belong down here with the rest of us." Roe slowed, glancing at the cars on his right.

"Your code is really rudimentary," Millicent said, catching more writing along the wall. It was everywhere, the code never changing. She'd read riddles written by Curve huggers that were harder to decipher.

"It's been a while since I've traveled with people smarter than me," Roe said, shining his light toward a rusted blue vehicle. "It's getting on my nerves."

"I know how you feel," Trent said, peeking into the car.

"Red, right? You're looking for a red car? With a hood over the bed? It must be a big vehicle to fit a whole bed . . . or is it a children's bed?" Millicent shined her light up the street. She belatedly realized Roe was staring at her. "What?"

"My code isn't that rudimentary. How'd you know all that?" he asked suspiciously.

She walked around him, looking for a red car. It was hard to see in the dim light from her orb and harder from the streetlights with their pale glow. "The only reason you haven't been found is because they obviously don't care about your operation."

"They care plenty."

"If they cared plenty, someone like me would've been transported down here to decipher it in less than ten minutes."

"She's right," Ryker said. He pointed at a vehicle up the way. "A bed is that platform at the back, I think. With the . . . You had *hood* wrong, but I don't know what the word is."

Roe stalked ahead.

"There have been a few advancements since you were bred," Trent said, jerking away from a car he passed. "That one had someone in it."

"Apparently." Roe stopped beside a longer car with the hood over the platform. "It's called a camper. The camper goes over the bed. See?" His tight, sarcastic smile crumpled into annoyance. "Get in."

"I can help you make a better code," Millicent said.

"You're going to have to, if even the muscle head can catch on." Roe turned a plastic handle, lifted the glass hatch, and then pulled down a metal piece. Soft flooring covered the platform, and there were benches on either side.

"Who devised it, you?" Ryker asked, helping Millicent into the back.

"Yes. And like I said, it's been fine up until now." Roe waited until they were all gathered inside the back. "And here I thought we were a thorn in the conglomerates' sides. It appears I was delusional."

"A thorn, but not a sword. If we get off this rock, Millie and I can help you sharpen that sword. Together, we'll all drive the conglomerates to their knees." Ryker held Marie in his lap.

Roe grunted a nonanswer before lifting the metal piece at the back of the truck and lowering the glass hatch. He moved around to the front and opened a door. The vehicle shook as he climbed inside.

"Can they track us in this?" Millicent asked through the glass partition.

Roe reached back and swiped his hand from right to left, opening a little window as he did so. "Track us, did you say?"

"Yes. Is there any way for them to track us?"

"No. This truck is made up of old-world parts. Its engine has a lot of computer elements, but their only applications are for operation and parking, things like that. It could drive itself if the road was in any way clear, but . . . it's not. Besides, you'd have to physically hook it up to a computer to program the controls."

"And yet, it only looks a few decades old . . . ," Millicent marveled, touching the fabric above her.

"We've found even nicer models. All kept pristine in garages. Not sure what happened to the owners, but we have a few mechanics who work on these. It's the type of machine we use off-world." The engine roared to life, and the whole thing vibrated under them with the effort of keeping it going.

"I hope it makes it," Millicent muttered to Ryker.

"This is a purr compared to some of the older models," Roe said. He moved a stick, and the vehicle went forward.

"I don't like this," Ryker said in a low tone, staring back the way they came. "You're right about that code. It was too easy by far."

"You think they'll come down here looking?" Millicent asked.

Ryker shook his head. "There's no way to know for sure." He raised his voice. "Is your craft still in its usual docking?"

"Yes. Why—" Roe cut off. Judging from the tenseness in his shoulders, he'd realized the answer to his question.

"Because without a craft, we would've had to walk out. Just like we did," Millicent said to herself, ice forming in her belly. "Since humans can't fly by themselves . . ."

A bright beam of light showered the vehicle. Two more rained down, moving over them from above. Drones.

"Your friends have arrived," Roe said in a rough voice. "And no way can we outrun them in this. Time to make some tough decisions."

"Those decisions have already been made," Ryker said, moving toward the entrance of the bed with guns in hand.

More lights clicked on, lighting up the street. Humans looking more like critters scurried off to the sides. One man walked between the cars. His shoulders were huge and squared, his hands hung down at his sides, and his face was all too familiar.

"Mr. Hunt," Ryker said in a low primal sort of growl. "Looks like he and I will finally settle the debate on who is better."

Chapter 24

"Get rid of those drones and get out of here," Ryker said as he walked out into the middle of the street, facing Mr. Hunt. "I'll find you."

"Like hell," Millicent said, fitting a device on the end of her high-powered handgun.

"I can take him, Millicent. *Go.*"

"Can't go until those drones are gone," Roe yelled out the driver's window. "We're ground bound. They'll just follow."

"I'm on it." Millicent aimed her gun in the middle of the two flying discs up the street, their spotlights too bright in the murky darkness. She squeezed the trigger as Ryker came to a stop.

It was the first time Millicent had ever seen Mr. Hunt smile. "Went too far this time, Gunner," he said.

"It's only too far if you get caught."

Mr. Hunt spread his arms, as if to say, "Here I am. You're caught."

Ryker grinned, his silent "Not likely" reading clearly.

"What are they doing?" Trent asked through the opening in the truck bed, holding Marie close.

The explosion sent a concussion of air at them, smashing into Millicent and knocking her off her feet. Fire blasted out in all directions, followed by pieces of metal. The other two drones, twenty meters away and above the truck, started to spark.

"No!" she yelled, gun pointed at the ground. "They were far enough away—"

The explosions seared her face. Fire coughed into the sky as the first two drones crashed into the ground up the street.

"Gun was too big," Ryker yelled, still facing Mr. Hunt, but with knees bent and body braced. He'd withstood the force of the blast. "Get that truck moving!"

Even as he said it, the second set of discs, nearly as big as the truck, wavered in the air before succumbing to gravity.

"Shit!" The truck roared to life. Tires squealed as Trent flung Marie out of the truck and then leaped out after her.

Millicent scrambled up and grabbed the screaming child before Trent reached them. He helped her lift Marie and carry her off to the side. The first drone roared with flame as it hit the hard ground. The second was right behind, catching the edge of the truck and knocking it to the side. Roe's body rolled away a moment later. Fire licked the truck bed.

"Run," Millicent said, pushing Marie at Trent. "Hide. A virus will hit in . . ." She checked her wrist and then swore. "Soon. Very soon. It's eating through the defenses as we speak. It won't hit the higher-level crafts, but it'll hit the lower-level ones. Our conglomerate's and the government's, both."

"What are you doing?" Roe yelled as he limped over to them, a gun out, his face an angry mask.

"Run!" Millicent shoved Trent, who was now holding a crying Marie. "Go! Save Marie. That's all that matters . . ."

Roe's eyes widened as he looked down the street.

Millicent turned. Time slowed down.

Mr. Hunt ran at Ryker. Behind him, three more drones were drifting down the street. White beams of light rained down on a host of enemies, all tough and muscular, all armed. Midlevel, probably, which meant they were adequately trained.

Mr. Hunt had ensured that she and Ryker didn't stand a chance.

Pressure pushed on her chest. Her heart quickened as a strange flopping filled her stomach. Was this what looking death in the face felt like?

She let a breath tumble out of her mouth.

It didn't matter. Her death didn't matter. As long as Marie was alive, Ryker and Millicent would live on. Marie was part of them—her life meant all their lives.

"Go," she said again as Mr. Hunt fired his gun. Ryker jerked to the side. His gun rose and fired. Mr. Hunt jerked away, dodging.

"They can dodge gunfire?" Roe said in disbelief.

"Breeding has come a long way since you," Trent said for the millionth time, this time with a slack jaw.

Mr. Hunt reached Ryker, gun raised. Ryker knocked it away, raising his own weapon. The fallen gun skittered across the concrete as a knife came out of nowhere and slashed at Ryker's middle. He jumped back, but not fast enough. The blade opened a gash through his suit. A line of red welled up as Ryker brandished a knife of his own. He struck. Mr. Hunt turned sideways, avoiding, but Ryker was already slashing. His blade cut through Mr. Hunt's arm.

Mr. Hunt didn't even react. He was already blocking the next thrust and answering with his own knife stroke.

"Go!" Millicent yelled, suddenly all action. She shoved at Trent, then Roe. "Get her out of here!"

"What about those?" Roe pointed at the other drones, which were keeping pace with the troops marching down the middle of the street.

"I'll take care of those." She glanced around, going over the various tech in her arsenal. "Fossil fuel," she breathed, half dancing through the fire to grab the bag from the truck. She dug through it until she found a sort of tube with a mechanical pump. Now she knew it as something used in bars, but it didn't matter. The principles of what she needed were the same.

She kicked a fiery piece of debris out of her way as Mr. Hunt punched Ryker in the gut. He then swung with his other hand, which held a knife. Ryker was ready—Millicent could tell he'd taken the punch so he could grab the knife-thrust. He dropped his own knife, gripped Mr. Hunt's arm with both hands, and then twirled, bringing his elbow down in the middle. A vicious crack did not illicit a scream. Instead, Mr. Hunt staggered back, arm now dangling unnaturally at his side, and yanked a gun from his holster with his good arm.

"Where is the fossil fuel tank on this thing?" Millicent yelled.

"What are you looking for?"

"I need liquid on that street. Now!"

A gunshot went off. Millicent swallowed around the throbbing of her heart.

"Fossil fuel is a terrible idea." Roe grabbed something out of the truck. "I have another idea that'll work. Then we gotta go." He ran to a protuberance on the concrete walkway. Using a thick metal tool, he screwed off part of the top.

Another gunshot drew Millicent's eyes.

Mr. Hunt staggered. His good shoulder glistened with blood. Ryker's side did as well.

Ryker punched into Mr. Hunt's side before stabbing with the knife in his other hand. Knife sliced into ribs. Mr. Hunt jerked his gun toward Ryker, firing.

Missing.

He fired again, making Ryker jump out of the way. All it would take was one lucky shot. Just one, and Ryker would go down.

"Damn it, hurry up—" A sludgy sort of liquid gushed across the curb and into the street. It washed over the ankles of both men and then spread out behind them, filling up the empty space separating them from the foot soldiers.

"What is it?" Millicent said, touching the leads of the tech together. They sparked, charged and ready.

"Once it was water. Now it's . . . this stuff." Roe limped hurriedly back to the truck. "Trent, help me get this crap away from the truck."

"Half the back is bent," Trent said.

"It's the front that makes it go. Hurry!"

Millicent waited a moment for the first line of foot soldiers to step into the liquid. Another gunshot went off. She didn't have any more time.

"Clear away," she yelled at Ryker. She bent to the liquid. "Get out of the way!"

Without looking up, Ryker stabbed Mr. Hunt, slashing through his gun hand, and then dived. He rolled away when he hit the edge of the liquid. Mr. Hunt, visibly flagging and bent, not much left in him, lifted the gun and sighted.

Millicent jammed the charge into the liquid.

Mr. Hunt's gun arm jerked. A rigid body followed. The gun blasted into the air.

The first two lines of troops froze and shook. Arms and bodies stiff, they convulsed from the electrical current.

Bodies toppled into those behind them. Someone stepped out of the puddle, pain lancing his face. The rest stopped twitching, now only jerking where they lay.

The charge was gone.

Mr. Hunt still stood, the only one upright in the puddle, bent and broken. Leaning to the side, still jerking, though no electricity ran through his body, he raised his gun laboriously.

Gun—right!

The gun filled her hand, but not before two more gunshots rang out. Mr. Hunt's arms flew back. His body crumpled to the ground.

"Don't shoot yet," Ryker said, holstering the gun and glancing at the ground. "Can I step on this?"

"Yes, the charge is dead. Why?"

"This leg of security is bred and raised to be dronelike." Ryker stared at the remaining troops facing him, out of the liquid and not affected by the charge. There were probably a few dozen in all, more possibly hidden in the shadows. "Their world is loyalty and violence. They'll follow the rules before they try to destroy us. It's how they were trained. How we were all trained. But these troops aren't smart enough to rise above the orders they're given. Or question them. So they won't shoot until we do. They'll want to take us alive. But as soon as we act defensively, they'll act aggressively."

Ryker slowly pulled out a large cumbersome gun from the pack on his back. Then another. He clearly didn't have close combat in mind. He didn't need finesse. Just killing. And the second he lowered those beasts at them, someone would fire, she didn't care what he said.

No time to lose, she spun and took a few steps toward her electro-magnetic pulse, only then realizing the others hadn't left yet!

"Get out of here," she yelled at Roe frantically.

Roe kicked a piece of flaming debris out of the way and then stamped his foot to quell the flame clawing at his suit. Sparing a glance for another large piece near the front of the truck, he nodded. "Let's go, Trent!" His glance landed on Millicent. "I'll keep her safe."

"Mama!" Marie screamed as Trent rushed her toward the truck.

"It's okay, baby. Mama will be okay." Millicent snatched the gun and device off the ground where she'd left it.

She held up the device. "Will it work as intended from this range?"

"Have to get closer." Ryker walked down the middle of the street, heading straight for the amassing troops.

"Turn yourself over to us," one of the troops said, his voice amplified, "and you will be spared."

"Turn yourself over to us," Ryker said, "and I'll kill you anyway."

"Oh good, make them even more nervous," Millicent said, cocking her gun. It was time to run toward the fight, and she needed all the weapons she could get.

Heels.

"This is your second warning," the voice said in an even tone.

"How many do we get?" Millicent asked, walking at an angle to meet Ryker in the center of the street.

"This is your last warning," the voice said, strong and firm. One of the troops at the front of the line pulled at the gun strap on his shoulder, bringing the point upward.

"That was fast," Ryker said, still walking slowly. "Millicent, I can hold them. Put those heels away and run. Run away, love. I don't need you."

"Obviously you do, you moron. You have no hope of dealing with these guys by yourself. Look how long you took with Mr. Hunt." She lifted her gun.

"Stop! I'm warning—"

Ryker's rapid fire cut out the warning shot. The man went down, followed by those around him, joining the bodies she'd already destroyed. Millicent took aim and squeezed the trigger as the truck roared behind them, probably trying to get around the debris. Marie's screams struck Millicent's heart. Determination stayed her hand. "Let's kill these fuckers!"

The drones exploded. The whole street lit up. Air rushed at them, knocking down those closest to the blast and blowing heat against Millicent's face. The drones fell, balls of flame, crushing men under them. Still there were more than forty troops, and probably more hidden in the darkness.

Ryker ran at the enemy, his guns blazing, his movements perfectly synchronized and graceful despite his wounds. Millicent lowered her gun and pulled the trigger again, no idea what would happen, before tossing it away.

Tiny explosions lit up the crowd, setting pants on fire and making men throw sparking items to the ground. Guns wouldn't be affected, though, and those came out next. Ryker barreled into the crowd, screaming at her to run, shooting everyone in front of him.

Utterly relaxed, knowing that she was protecting her child, Millicent stalked to the middle of the street. Three people were raising their weapons. At her. Others were already firing at Ryker, hitting their own men in the process. Not caring.

Millicent bent her arms, a grin tickling her lips. And then jerked her hands upward as she thought, *Fat boyz.*

Long barrels reached her hands but kept rising. Light and agile, the barrels extended fully, and she lowered her hands as the hooks near the butts secured around her elbows. Then her forearms, all electronic. The trigger guards flipped up, and she wrapped her fingers around the handles. Perfectly balanced.

Sleek personal tech with a huge impact, compliments of Gregon Corp. and the pirates who stole it. Millicent couldn't have designed it better. *Let's hope this was worth the risk.*

She squeezed the triggers. Like horizontal rain, bullets sprayed out of the weapons, pulled from the harness crisscrossing her torso. Bodies danced and jolted as they were hit with fire and forced back. Red splotches peppered bodies before they crumpled to the ground.

Ryker froze for a second, his eyes as wide as those around him. He recovered quickest. "Aim high! Get their heads!" His voice was barely heard above the firepower. "The suits farthest away will block most of the impact."

"Aim high, my ass." Walking forward, determination keeping her arms steady, she pulled at the harness to get more slack. Then bent.

Her knee planted down on the ground. Bullets spewed forth, slicing through feet and legs. Cracking bones. Men danced and then fell. Blood shot up. Heads were hit next, spraying blood across the sidewalk. "High means they could've ducked," she said into the rapid-fire blasts. "But now they're not going anywhere . . ."

Her arms jolted back rhythmically; tolerable. Ryker dived to the side yet again as her sweep went in his direction. She cut down troops who were running at her. Cut down troops who were aiming. Blood washed the street. Screaming took over the night.

And then the last bullet erupted through the gun.

Smoke curled through the streetlights. Agonized moaning accompanied the writhing of individuals who were slow to die. A handful of men staggered, holding some part of their person, staring off into the distance.

Bang!

Ryker sighted and fired again. Another man dropped. He was killing off the survivors.

The revving of a truck made Millicent turn back. Roe was just now maneuvering around the flaming debris. Marie's wails cast an eerie horror on the scene.

And then the echo of boots against the ground reached her ears. Movement at the edge of the darkness had Ryker drifting toward the line of cars in that direction.

Shadows moved in front of the dancing flames before solidifying close enough to see. Ten—now fifteen—now twenty more men and women walked out into the middle. They re-formed into lines, standing around the dead at their feet.

"Waited for us to use our first wave of ammo," Ryker said in an even tone. "Mr. Hunt never did care for the lives of his subordinates."

Millicent had already believed she would die, so this wasn't that big of a setback. "I guess those weapons weren't a lifesaver after all." She wrestled the guns off her arms. They clinked onto the ground. "Time to get personal."

She snatched out the last two remaining guns, which were different sizes and much smaller than she would've liked, before starting forward.

"This is your final warning," another voice said. Guns came off shoulders and pointed at them. "We do not wish to—"

Millicent rose her gun and fired. A patch of the man's head flapped back. He fell in a boneless slide as she charged forward. Her heels clicked against the ground. She reached the nearest troop and kicked out. The razor-sharp heel punched through his suit armor and into his sternum. She ripped it down, slicing his body, before yanking it out and whirling. She kicked through the air at an angle, slicing through a throat. Then stuck her gun up and squeezed, blasting someone in the face.

She felt absolutely not one twinge of discomfort from her stomach.

"Bring it on!" she yelled. Fire blazed through her. Adrenaline pounded. "Come at me!"

Gunfire sounded from the side as she sighted, shot, sighted, shot. Men went down, but some only faltered, their suits able to withstand the bullets.

She'd finish them off later.

She grabbed a man, shot him in the stomach, then ducked behind him as another gunshot blasted out. It hit his suit, bending him backward before he fell away. Ryker was shouting something. Trying to tell her to get clear, probably.

She ignored him. They both needed to be here to give their baby time.

Finger squeezing, she shot someone in the throat. Blood splattered her face as she whirled. Something whistled by. A bullet smacked into the back of the troop in front of her. He fell forward, surprise on his face, gun reaching for her.

She snatched the semi and lowered the point. The troop hit the ground. Her gun went off a moment later, clipping him in the head for good measure. Ducking from incoming shots, she pointed up and fired.

Two men ran in her direction. She shot one in the chest and the other in the head. Back to the first, but he was already falling. *Damn.* Hopefully he wouldn't pop back up.

"They'll overrun us. Run, Millicent. Please, run!"

Ryker just did not get it.

She popped up again, following someone running by her. A moment of confusion overshadowed her squeezing finger. She glanced where he was going, taking her focus off the battle for one moment. Then her stomach dropped.

Marie was on the ground, running toward her. A security staffer was closing the short distance to her.

"No!" *Heels—disengage!*

Trent sprinted toward the little girl. Metal glinted as he raised a gun and shot. His face a mask of cold determination, he fired three more times without flinching. The staffer jerked backward as the bullets struck. He faltered and fell.

Her heels retracted, and then she was running toward her daughter. "Get her out of here!" she screamed.

Trent reached Marie and scooped her up. Without a second glance, he turned and sprinted for the truck, where Roe was hanging out the window, yelling at Trent to hurry. Marie twisted in Trent's grasp, and a mask of pure agony peeked over his shoulder before her hand whipped out, fingers splayed.

Explosions rocked the world, shaking Millicent off her feet. Starting from the dwellings at ground level and going up, windows exploded. Fire and glass coughed into the street. Another explosion up above took out a wall, and bricks rained down on the street, pelting the troops. Ryker staggered backward, blood coating half his body, the fire illuminating his wide eyes.

Another explosion burst from the building. Something in the middle of the street exploded down the block, probably drones kept out of sight. Electrical fire zinged across wires and licked up the walls. Strange bursts of liquid fire rained down on the cars before crawling outward like lava. More explosions, farther up, probably ten floors, all alongside the host of troops.

Arm at his face to block the spewing fire, Ryker shot into the crowd, killing off those left standing. Then he was running, the only one moving, reacting quicker than Millicent could even think. He snatched her off the ground, threw her over his shoulder, and raced after Trent.

"Go! Go! Go!" Ryker yelled, pushing Trent faster.

"What the fuck just happened?" Roe asked before he disappeared into the cockpit. Trent jumped into the bed.

"My daughter saved the day," Ryker said. "Let's not let it go to waste."

Millicent's teeth chattered as her butt hit the bed. The truck roared and lurched forward, the sound of twisted metal groaning against the tires.

"Dada!"

Ryker jumped into the truck bed before turning to face the opening with his gun out, his chest heaving.

"We're going to need a miracle to get out from under those drones," Roe yelled back.

"We've got Millicent and Marie. We've got all the miracles we need," Ryker answered.

Chapter 25

"We were so concerned about her brain responding as we anticipated, we didn't expand our scans to see what else was affected." Trent stared at Marie in wonder. He could not believe what he'd seen. He had never imagined a human could be capable of that. Not so soon anyway. "I mean, we probably would've eventually, but . . . this is certainly something. This . . . and the *range!*"

The truck stopped next to a building with a big metal door, like a bay, but it was ground-side. The front door opened, and then Roe appeared at the back, gesturing for them to come out. "We just have one more hurdle to jump, caused from what just happened. We're almost there."

After jumping out of the truck, Ryker held out his hands for Marie. "She's mine. I'll take her."

"She's both of ours," Millicent said as she passed the baby out.

"You need to worry about keeping yourself alive, cupcake. Let the big boys handle the heavy lifting."

"You do have experience with heavy lifting, what with the size of your ego," Millicent said, climbing out after them.

"He's just trying to console himself," Trent said without thinking, gripping the gun he'd never thought he'd use. He started when he realized his mouth was getting away from him. "I mean, you know. He almost lost her, so—"

"I'm still in a killing frame of mind . . . Trent," Millicent said through clenched teeth, making the use of his first name clear. "I wouldn't talk about how close of a call that was."

Trent's extremities shriveled in a way usually reserved for Ryker. "And this is why you were chosen for the weaponry department, I'd wager," he mumbled, following her through a flimsy, half-rotted door at the side of the ground bay. "It was in there all along. And now we know."

"We always knew." Ryker slowed in front of them at a door. Little arms were wrapped tightly around his neck, and a blue glow surrounded his body. "Holy shit."

"Get that truck out of here." Roe's voice drifted from the room. "And someone get Mr. Gunner a basketful of Cure-all and stitchers."

"Something is going on with Moxidone," another voice drifted out. "I have no idea what. Their vessels are stalling all over the place, and several of their departments are randomly going black."

"Something's up with the government uplink. What the hell is this code . . . ?" someone else said.

"Get Ms. Foster in here," Roe yelled.

Ryker moved aside, giving Trent a view into the room as Millicent rushed forward. The space before him was huge and filled with people. Wall screens as well as handhelds illuminated people's faces as they worked with furrowed brows. Various instruments lined the shelves, some with lights blinking, many dark.

"I'll get rid of the truck," a man said as he cleared out of the way for Millicent, allowing her to sit down. He jogged from the room, only sparing a quick glance for Ryker as he passed.

"I'll grab medicine," someone else said, leaving the room out of a far door.

"This network will be transparent to their coder," Millicent said. Images and binary code flashed across her screen. She palmed a console over to her, stealing from someone who had been working with it, and then screens started changing around the room.

"Hey!" someone said.

"I need more screens," Millicent mumbled, her eyes darting all over. "What's the goal here? What are you trying for?"

"We have a craft leaving in five hours for the launch site," Roe said, standing behind her. "It's leaving from just outside the city, and it's marked as a delivery transport vessel. It's safe. All you need to do is get on that vessel without leading them to it. The problem is . . ." He pointed at a map off to the side. "The route we had picked out is compromised. They'll be checking it. We need a different route. Higher, lower, doesn't matter. Just something where they won't scan us closely."

"They've got people on all levels now," someone said, looking toward Millicent's screen. "And they have some sort of mastermind blasting your images all over. Every time we try to take them down or change them, our hackers are caught almost immediately."

"Of course they are." Millicent tsked. But didn't say anything else.

"And now their crafts are just stalling out," someone else said. "Just randomly stalling. I don't know if that's a trap, or . . ."

"That's me," Millicent said. "I bet their mastermind, as you called her, is trying to untangle that mess right now. Her superiors—my old superiors—will be flipping over it. They'll think their security is breached and that I'm trying to . . . Oh, who knows what goes through their heads." Millicent shook her head. "I can plan a route through the stalled vehicles, but we have to make good on it before my viruses are disarmed. We don't have long, and even still, they'll see us moving. They'll call in recruits, so we might have to fight our way out."

"Who *are* you?" someone asked, staring at the screen in front of him.

"Someone who wants her freedom."

"We'll lose," Roe said softly, shaking his head. "We don't have smart enough tech. The crafts that are still operational won't even have to blow us out of the sky—they'll freeze us and then just waltz right in."

"I know," Millicent murmured. "I'm trying to create a way. I just need to . . . I just need more time, that's what I need. She's anticipated me. I shouldn't have tried playing those games with her . . ."

Trent leaned against the wall, and then jumped up when half the room turned to look at him. He moved away from a screen to lean somewhere else, sighing as he looked at his shaking hands. He'd thought they were all going to die, and then he'd *known* Millicent and Ryker were going to die. And that was before he'd killed a man and the world had blown up. He'd thought that was it. He was dead.

All of it was nuts. This whole plight was insane. And for all of that, he was just as invested as Ryker and Millicent were. He wanted to stay with Marie. Even the other two. They weren't blood, but they'd become family. He would kill for that family, and had. He'd do it again.

A man approached Ryker with the various medicines, and Trent took Marie while Ryker was doctored.

He thought back to when he was choosing whom to use, and then whom to pair. He'd had to take several trips between facilities to discuss his research and choices with various superiors. He didn't have this own private vessel, like Millicent and Ryker, so he'd taken the company transport. Specifically, the crafts that Millicent had probably affected—the rinky-dink types.

"Why not just board a frozen craft before it's released?" he said without thinking.

"And deliver ourselves to them?" Ryker asked in a harsh tone. It was a pain-filled warning tone, the worst kind.

Trent cleared his throat. "No. I mean, we can board the craft, throw everyone overboard—or whatever you want to do—and then wait for the virus to be fixed. Then, can't we just . . . pretend to look for us, but actually head out? Would they know? Because I don't—"

Millicent's finger flew up into the air. She turned toward him slowly, her eyes on fire in a way that said she was problem solving. "Would they know?"

Trent looked behind him and then realized that she was, indeed, asking him. "That was my question."

Millicent turned to Ryker.

"Retinal scan upon entry for clearance reasons," Ryker said. "Then the implant connects the rider with the vessel—usually just the head personnel, not everyone in the craft. Upon leaving, the head personnel will shut it down so that it can be used by another."

"But that's not a problem because their implants are down." A smile spread across Millicent's face.

"But you have to get in somehow," someone said. "They'll probably be freaking out. They aren't going to just let anyone board."

"We've got the entrance covered," Millicent said, her focused eyes rooted to Trent in a very disconcerting way. "But what if she's freed them already? What happens if they die?"

Trent pulled at his collar. He had no idea why she was asking him.

"The vessel will automatically go to the next in command," Ryker answered. "But someone dying will be noticed by the system. Even if it's someone expendable."

"What about if they are unconscious?" Millicent persisted.

Ryker hesitated for a moment. "Gray area. Should be . . . fine. On the lesser ships. Should be . . ."

"It's worth a shot," Millicent said, turning back to the screen.

"But . . . is it?" someone asked. "If it doesn't work, you'll be caught."

"Then we'll be chased." Millicent's hands flew across her screen before pulling in information from another screen and working at code that looked like nothing more than a bunch of symbols to Trent. "If we use your way, we'll surely be chased."

"Not *surely*," the man said.

"Surely. Everyone is looking for us, radiating out from where we blew up a bunch of buildings. We could probably evade them by making our way through the dwellings in this city, but we don't have that kind of time. Unless we can stall the launch?"

"Can't," Roe said, shaking his head. "We need specific conditions."

"Then if we are flying out of this location, we'll run into a scan either there"—Millicent stood and pointed at the map—"there, or there. There is one chance in a hundred that I can time it perfectly. Since I have never been that lucky in my life, we wouldn't hit it, they'd scan us, and the chase would be on. I'd rather not land in a warehouse equipped with those homicidal smart doors. Which leaves us with Trent's idea." Millicent roamed the shelves, looking at the various devices. "Yes, taking a conglomerate craft will be the best bet. I can get us, possibly without detection, to the craft we pinpoint. There are a couple stupid vessels way higher than they should be, which means security doesn't expect us that high."

"I wouldn't," Ryker broke in. He grimaced as the stitcher was applied to his stomach.

"Right," Millicent said, snatching something off the shelf. "So we have fifteen minutes to climb the floors, maybe less, before that ship"—she pointed at another one—"circles back around to cut us off."

The room fell silent.

"So . . ." A young woman looked around. "Are we . . . doing this? Because time is ticking."

"Fuck it. Let's do it." Ryker pushed away the helper. "I assume you have a craft that doesn't require wheels?"

"Well, I mean, they all have wheels, right?" one of the guys said with a grin. "When they get worked on, they—"

"Shut up, Roger." Roe pointed at the ceiling. "There's a dock three floors up. We can shoot straight up from there. Let's go. No time to lose."

❖   ❖   ❖

"There it is." Millicent stared at the vessel, a small thing dead in the air. A man stood in the cockpit, staring down at the controls. Another stood in the window, looking at the wall, which was probably a console. She glanced at her own console, connected to the pirate's network. Her sister was steadily working through her viruses, implant malfunctions, and prison programs, unraveling them and wiping them away with the deft hand of someone who had been at this all her life. "We don't have much time. She's better than me."

"No, she's not." Ryker loaded a gun. "She's sitting in an office, in temperature control, playing coding games with you. You're running for your life in between throwing this stuff at her. If you weren't preoccupied, you'd take her, no problem."

"And if you couldn't take her, coding-wise, you could certainly pull guns out of your sleeves and shoot her," Roe said as he looked through the window. "That is an awfully small ship."

"Three-man crew. I don't see the third man, though." Ryker cocked his gun. "I'll find him soon enough."

"Let's go." Millicent entered the coordinates and then cocked her own gun. A borrowed gun anyway. Too small for her taste.

The vessel they were in moved closer, as if it were just moving along the travel way with the other vehicles. Ten or so meters away, their craft went to swerve around, the computer system trying to avoid collision. Ryker took over manually and steered them right up to the vessel.

One of the men inside stuck his head up to the window, his brows making a flat line over his eyes. He waved them on in irritated jerks of his hand.

"Open the doors, Marie," Millicent said softly, watching as another head joined the first.

"There's the third one." Ryker stepped away from the controls as their doors opened. The other craft's doors opened a moment later.

The faces in the windows glanced to their right, clearly seeking an explanation from the driver as to why the doors were opening.

Ryker launched himself in, still bleeding but not slowing because of it. He grabbed the first man and punched him in the face. The man's nose cracked. His hands came up and clutched his face as Millicent jumped in next. She slapped a coupler on the other man to quickly bind his hands and then conked him over the head with a metal tool. The man crumpled to the ground as Ryker punched his man again. Lights out.

"Can you apply your implant prison program to these men to keep them immobile, blind, and deaf?" Ryker asked.

"No," she said, out of breath. "I'd need to break into my department files, download the program—which is a huge file—then find the uplink to their implants . . . It would take too much time. I need to develop another, more mobile-friendly, program."

Ryker grabbed the man in the cockpit as Millicent turned for the others, helping Roe and Trent move Marie into the craft, and then come over themselves.

"Stash them in the corner," Roe said, pointing at the men on the ground. He threw a wave behind him, telling his man to move on. "Need the doors closed."

"Marie, can you—" Trent stopped talking as both doors shimmied closed.

Roe's vehicle moved into the natural flow of traffic.

"Did you mean to kill this one?" Trent looked up with his fingers still on the man's neck. Blood dribbled down the man's forehead from where Millicent had conked him.

She stared for a moment. "Oops."

"Mayday, mayday," Ryker's voice said from the front.

"What is he doing?" Roe brought out a gun, his eyes going fierce.

"Don't!" Millicent jumped in the way. "Don't shoot. I'm sure he's got a good explanation . . ."

"If he's calling this in, we're all fucked," Roe said, reaching out to move Millicent away.

"Dada!" Marie yelled.

Roe froze as they heard, "Headquarters, come back."

"Pirate vessel attempted to board," Ryker said in a panicked voice. "We took a gunshot. Man down, man down. Get this bird live. I repeat, get this bird live. We got a man down! Over."

"What is the state of the vessel, come back," the voice said.

"Vessel needs a refitting. It'll fly. We can still see the pirate craft. Get this bird live, headquarters," Ryker shouted into the receiver. "Over."

"Working on it, Double Twelve. Hang tight. Over and out."

Ryker tapped the comm panel and motioned for Millicent to get to the console. "Hopefully that'll explain the death."

He glanced down at his feet. "I'm going to leave that one there."

"In other words, your wounds hurt." Millicent sighed in relief as Roe lowered his gun. Marie stared, quieting.

"Cute," Ryker said, sitting slowly into the chair. "What was with the heavy artillery earlier?" he asked.

He was talking about the Gregon tech—the automatic weapons lightweight enough to fit into suit sleeves.

"I've always been told to focus on larger artillery," Millicent said, checking her code. It was being stripped away, little by little. So close.

Breathing deep, trying to keep her composure, she glanced out the window, seeing only curious passersby. "Once Gregon realized they couldn't compete, they started focusing more on personal handhelds. They've come a long way. We openly trade with them now, and I see why."

"I haven't seen those guns before. I think they would've been better off with me," Ryker said in a matter-of-fact sort of way.

Millicent huffed out a laugh. "So you could aim high and waste ammo? Yeah right. You train, but I test. I shoot more than you do."

"I doubt that, since minions test, not creators."

"You get away with growing your hair long. I get away with shooting guns and learning hand-to-hand combat." She leaned around the wall and waited until he looked back, making eye contact. "Or did you think you were a special snowflake?"

A grin tickled his lips.

"They didn't let you do those things while you were pregnant, I hope," Trent said. He startled, as if he hadn't meant to say that. He had to be exhausted again. She knew how he felt.

"No. I couldn't even run. The snowflake saw to that." Millicent's console flashed. "Online" started flashing through the controls. "Here we go."

"Double Twelve, come in," a voice over comms said.

"Double Twelve here, go," Ryker said, his hands moving over the dash.

"You're reading as live. Drop off your man, over."

"I'm on that pirate vessel, headquarters. I'll report after capture, over," Ryker said.

"Negative, Double Twelve. We need a check-in, over."

Ryker grimaced. "Well, it was good while it lasted," he muttered. Then, in a clear voice, he answered, "See you when we've got our man, headquarters, over and out." He glanced back. "Comms are muted for now. Which they will expect with a flouted command. They won't bat an eye at us going after the so-called pirate, but they won't give us much leeway, either. We have about fifteen minutes, and then they'll try to bring us in. So let's haul ass."

Chapter 26

"Looks like they're still assuming we're in the lower section of the city," Millicent said, watching the notices scroll across the screen. "The news about Mr. Hunt being down is all over the city. Private chat forums are mostly in your favor, Ryker. They thought you were better all along."

"I love when you stroke my ego, princess. Even more when you stroke other things."

Millicent sighed in annoyance as Trent said, "Ew."

"Fifty percent of the downed crafts are back online." Millicent pulled up social media across the city. "People are wondering what's going on. They think it's some kind of drill."

"A drill?" Ryker said.

"You managed to wipe out half the stupid vessels with fifteen minutes of effort," Roe said in a soft tone. He shook his head. "I wouldn't have thought it was possible. In my day, it wasn't."

"I have the right skill set, a lifetime of training, and unique info from a director of security." Millicent plotted out the Moxidone conglomerate's crafts and tried to grab what she could of the government's. Possible escape paths opened up, but then immediately closed again, their systems doing an excellent job of covering all the holes. "Plus, I've had a year to learn the inner workings of this conglomerate. I'm ahead of the game."

"A lifetime of training . . ." Roe scoffed. "Wait until you're my age."

"Being that the training stops now, I don't think it'll matter." Millicent sent a route up to the dash. "Plug that in. It should get us through."

Should was the operative word.

"I can steer us through," Ryker said. "No one is trying to stop us yet. No one's paying attention to us."

"Except your system will know you are on manual, and it'll question your strange flight pattern." Millicent pushed the route through again. "With the computer telling the humans that something is wrong, the humans are less likely to ignore us. If the computer is happy, they might leave us undisturbed for longer."

"Well, if you're going to keep nagging . . ."

Millicent let her fingers curl around the stabilizing handle so she didn't use them to grab something heavy and smack Ryker over the head with it.

"I've never heard Ryker admit he was wrong," Trent said thoughtfully. "Looks like he finally met his match."

"Did I go deaf for a moment?" Millicent continued to watch the notices, forums, and any other source of reliable info. Hopefully she'd know someone was closing in on them before the system did.

"The nagging comment." Trent crossed an ankle over his knee. "Although, it was kind of a dickish thing to say."

"He's lucky I need him for the moment," Millicent said.

"Just picking my moments, princess. And sure, you were right. Happy?"

Millicent saw Ryker's feet prop up on the edge of the dash. A glance confirmed that he was sitting back and relaxing up there.

She rolled her eyes. "If you confirmed every time I was right, you'd be talking nonstop. Just be quiet and do as you're told."

"Oh, ho, ho. Look who showed up?" Ryker laughed. "I do believe the little princess is turning diva on us."

"Always was," Trent muttered.

"Don't help, Trent. Your reports say you are well below the Curve in communications. We'd hate to prove the graph right, hmm?" Millicent pursed her lips to combat her smile as Ryker laughed harder.

A conglomerate craft changed course, their destination now in line with Millicent's. If both crafts stayed their current route, they'd meet at the same travel-way intersection in ten minutes or less. As Millicent watched the comms, though, no command to intercept came through.

She hunted through the department's private networks, found the vessel in question, and read the schematics. It was a middle-range vehicle engaged in the search. The captain in charge had been flagged to stay at the current level in his job, despite his many attempts to rise in ranks. Notices on his file indicated he often had "hunches" that led him astray and wasted company money five-to-one of coming through and getting recognized.

A cold sweat covered Millicent's brow. He was about to make good on a far-fetched hunch.

"Ryker, you're up," she said, sending another course through. "We have a cowboy."

"What's a cowboy?" Trent asked, pushing up against the window.

"It's not what she thinks it is," Roe said, standing in order to see the screen around her.

"What've you got?" Ryker asked, the joking tone from earlier dripping away. His feet dropped to the floor.

"Someone who's taking it upon himself to check it out." Millicent pushed his profile through so Ryker could look.

"Ah. One of these." Ryker's tone sounded like he'd met a few of "those" in his lifetime, and could've done without. "Looks like he got one right."

"Not like it was a huge stretch," Roe said. "Not many pirates would attack a conglomerate ship."

"Completely wrong on that score," Ryker said. "More than you'd possibly realize."

"What would be the point? The tech in here is second-class." Roe's face screwed up into disdain.

"Second-class would be an improvement over this." Millicent made a minute change to their course and sent it through.

"No way on your routing change, princess," Ryker said. "Either we wouldn't change it at all or we'd change it dramatically, like *this*." The craft banked hard, darting out of the travel way, dropping so fast Millicent's stomach shoved into her throat, and then banking again, directing them into another travel way. "We'll follow this black craft. It looks sinister."

"It looks like a government undercover vehicle," Millicent said, tapping the vehicle on the screen. She looked up its identifier and was confronted with an ironclad firewall. "Or something worse. I don't know what that is, Ryker. Get away from it."

Roe stepped forward to look through the windshield. "Just hack into the city registration."

"Yes, Mr. Enlightened, I did. And this is what I came up against." She gestured at the screen before checking in with the conglomerate vehicle. Its speed had increased and route changed again. It was trying to intercept, not chase. "There is no way he's smart enough to corral us, so he's just assuming we haven't noticed him?"

"What is that code?" Roe asked in a tone that raised the small hairs on Millicent's arms.

"He's not bright, but thinks he's above the Curve," Ryker said from the front. "Hang on."

"That's not human," Roe said, still staring at the firewall.

"Of course it's not human," Millicent said, glancing out the window. She could actually see the other vehicle now as it dropped down from one travel way to another, causing a craft to veer crazily out of the way. She shook her head and glanced back at the code.

"No, I mean, that didn't originate from a human," Roe said, pointing. "I've seen a whole lot of firewalls in my day. More than you, I can assure you. All different kinds. That is . . . not like any of them. Not the higher levels, nothing. It's . . . well, I'd say it's foreign, but these conglomerates are global. It's alien, is what it is."

That homicidal corridor briefly marched through her memory. She scoffed and waved the thought away. "You've been away from the conglomerates for a while, and you are no longer among the smartest beings on this planet. There is, undoubtedly, a lot you haven't seen."

"Just . . . do me a favor." Roe gestured at the screen. "Make a note so we can circle back. I want my people to look into it."

"I need you on deck, baby cakes," Ryker called. "Things might get hairy in a moment."

"Baby cakes?" Millicent said in distaste as she did a screen capture and logged the vehicle and access point. She prepared to download them to her implant before the realization dawned. "I can't—" Without another word, she grabbed the proffered scan drive from Roe and captured the info.

"I'll take that." Roe put out his hand.

"So a Curve hugger can muck it up and make the wrong conclusions?" Millicent sniffed and slipped the drive into her suit. "I'll take a look when I have a moment."

"There's the diva I love," Ryker said. "Now c'mon, cupcake, let's get cracking."

"Is it too much to ask that you use my given name?" she asked as she glanced out the window. A strange sound came from her throat.

Two conglomerate vehicles hovered just off the travel way, one on each side, facing the passing vehicles.

Roe sat down quickly, the growing argument dissipating immediately.

"All crafts are online, so they are actively scanning," Millicent said, finding one of the vehicles by the coordinates and checking it out. "It has firepower and a competent staffer in control. I assume the other does as well."

"Yes, I realize that," Ryker said, his tone all business. "There is no reason to assume they are looking for us."

Millicent checked the notices. "Our fifteen minutes are up, Ryker."

"I know. But they are looking for fugitives, not stupid conglomerate vehicles. They might not bother with us. *I* wouldn't bother with us."

"You were a director. They are peacekeepers . . ." Millicent held her breath as they drew close. The silent and stationary crafts drifted by slowly. The closer one had a man standing in the window with his arms behind his back. Millicent ducked to the console, but then half turned back. "Should I wave . . . ?"

"Why would you wave?" Trent mumbled, bending low with Marie in his arms.

"Brothers-in-arms . . . or something?" Millicent turned back to the console.

"You'd just look guilty," Roe said.

"I am guilty . . ." Millicent bit her lip and watched the notices.

"Shit," she heard from the front. "One is pulling in behind us. I'm unmuting comms."

"Double Twelve, come in."

Millicent's hands shook as she waited for Ryker's response.

"This is Double Twelve, go ahead," Ryker responded, his voice confident and slightly aggressive.

"We have a request to bring you in, over."

Ryker hesitated for a moment. "We hoped to find the fucker who tried to do a snatch and run, over."

"I hear ya, Double Twelve. We haven't seen anything suspicious come through here. You need to check in, over."

"Roger that. I'll change course, over."

"We'll ghost you in, Double Twelve. Out."

Ryker stepped into the partition way, his eyes on Millicent. Then his gaze swept behind her before he turned and leaned. "Any chance you can make this thing faster?"

"No," she said softly. "Especially not with all this weight. But I can help you toss people out?"

A smile crossed his lips as he looked back at the controls. He took a deep breath. "This is worse than that nitwit who is following us."

"Want an upper?" Millicent asked. His confused expression made her smile. "Like that other driver. So you can take risks?"

His smile matched hers, but it didn't reach his eyes. She was sure hers didn't, either. "Do you still have that device that blows vehicles up?" he asked.

"No. It was out of charge. I left it."

He nodded and then glanced at the controls when the buzz of the comms went active again. They were too low to hear, but it wasn't a mystery what they were saying.

"Can you think of anything else to get them off our tails?" he asked.

"I can." Roe stood and made his way to the console. "Get us to the outer sector, and I can order a unit to blow them out of the sky. Just don't get the whole fleet on our asses."

"No promises." Ryker reached for Millicent. His eyes softened as he ran his thumb along her chin. "One last sprint, huh? One last escape attempt?"

"We can do it." She put her hand to his chest. "Don't lose hope now."

He exhaled and bent to kiss her before turning back to the console. "Time to go to work."

"Double Twelve to headquarters, come in, headquarters," Ryker said into the comm system.

"Buckle up," Millicent said to the others before pulling a strap from the wall and encircling her waist. It would keep her standing through the evasive maneuvers. "Handy."

Roe sat and then brought up a hologram in front of him. Trent squeezed Marie tight.

"Double Twelve, go ahead."

"We have a lead. Going to check it out. Just one lead, and then we'll bring it in. Over."

"That's a negative, Double Twelve. Bring it home."

"I look forward to the write up, headquarters. Out." The craft fell. Plummeted.

Millicent squeezed her eyes shut while reaching for the stabilizing handle. Her hand groped through the air. The strap cut into her back as her stomach did loop-de-loops in time to the craft spinning through the air. Or maybe that's just how it felt. She might've screamed. Definitely threw up in her mouth a little. And her head bounced off the wall as they shot forward.

"What the fuck is happening?" she said, out of breath. A trickle of wetness slid down her temple. Blood from a cut, probably. With all the adrenaline, she couldn't feel a thing.

"I don't need uppers, honey buns." The craft veered again, careening to the side in a spin that shouldn't have been possible. "These vehicles are dumb as hell and weak as shit, but they can sure cut through the sky."

"We need to talk about nicknames," Millicent said through clenched teeth, holding on for dear life. The people in the back were screaming. Except for Marie, who was laughing.

The world righted. Something zipped by the craft, one meter away. "Was that an intersection marker?" Honking announced a swerving craft.

Was that screaming as the craft went by?

Surely she couldn't hear them screaming, could she?

"Get to that console, Millie," Ryker said. "Try to disable that craft somehow."

"I should've learned about their guidance systems," she muttered.

"I got it," Roe said in a gruff voice. He worked at the harness so it would let him lean forward. "Just warn me when you're going to get creative with the flying, eh, ace?"

"Are the nicknames a security thing?" Millicent asked in dismay as she brought up a mirror of Roe's screen.

"I need to know what ship I'm looking at," Roe said.

She ran through the conglomerate notices to find the right identifier, connected to the ship, and then pushed the access to the screen.

"Having you around will spoil me," Roe said, his hand flying over and through the hologram. "Fast as lightning and access I've never been privy to."

"Need you faster still. They're on our ass," Ryker warned.

"I'm on it." Roe cut the power to the pursuing ship's thrusters. The craft's system overrode the action immediately, bringing them back online.

"I got it." Millicent took control through the console and then worked at the system, disabling its programed override. "But they can just switch off the system guidance . . ."

"They'll have to switch to manual now," Roe said. "Security vehicles still give their drivers the benefit of the doubt."

"But . . . those engines are largely run with a computer. And the computer can be fooled into a glitch, causing issues with the engine . . ." Millicent looked through the other ship's schematics. It was gibberish. "We need a mechanic on board."

"Those types of things can't be changed midflight," Roe said. "Or else pirates would have a helluva lot more power. As would we."

Millicent frowned at the console. "Where there's a connection, there's a way. I have to think about this."

"Hang on," Ryker said.

The craft lurched to the side. She saw only sky out of her window before squeezing her eyes shut again. Thank Holy her stomach was empty, because if it hadn't been to start, it would be now.

They rolled the other way as an explosion went off behind them. Or was it to the side? They were moving too fast for her to gauge.

"Are they trying to wound us or bring us down?" Roe asked through what sounded like a tight throat. Marie was still laughing.

"Trying to slow us down, not bring us down," Ryker yelled over the whine of the motors. "They aren't trying to kill us. Good news."

"Ten kilometers from the outer sector," Millicent said, half wishing she hadn't opened her eyes.

"I need to work the screen," Roe said in an elevated voice. Millicent could still barely hear him.

"You'll have to do it while hanging from your ear," Ryker yelled, obviously hearing Roe through the inner speakers.

"Hanging from my *what*?"

The craft tilted. A zip of fire shot by. Buildings surrounded them on both sides, the space between them not much larger than the craft.

"Oh Holy—ahhh!" Millicent grabbed the strap and hung on as an explosion went off.

"This level of skill is above your pay grade," Ryker yelled.

The craft shot out from the tiny space and careened left. Millicent cracked an eye. The fuzzy numbers bounced around the screen. "Seven, no six! Six kilometers!"

"Running out of tricks," Ryker said. "And maneuvering fuel. This craft isn't up for this."

Something knocked the craft as a boom filled Millicent's ears. The vehicle shook, jarring her body, then shivered as Ryker yelled, "Missed."

"Missed?" Millicent said, her stomach now wishy-washy. It twisted as the numbers kept jiggling.

"They were aiming for one of the engines. They got the rear guard."

"Five kilometers. Pull something out of your ass," Millicent shouted.

"I'm not into that, cupcake, but for you, I'll make an exception." The craft rose into the sky before darting to the side, headed straight for a building. Millicent screamed and then felt her face melt off as the craft swooped upward. She hit off the wall as Ryker maneuvered again, no longer able to tell which direction he'd turned. Now just wondering when they'd hit the ground. Or a building. Or one of the many honking vessels.

"I'm . . . set . . ." Roe grunted.

"How . . . how . . ." Millicent swallowed back stomach acid and shook her head.

"How long, love?" Ryker asked.

She cracked an eye open while being squeezed painfully in the strap as she lay mostly sideways. A jiggling number greeted her. Along with more stomach acid as she threw up a little. "Three." She couldn't do much better than a groan.

"Three kilometers," Roe yelled out.

"I know. I got it up here. Just wanted her to enjoy the action. Two. Get ready, Roe. We're about to get fired on—"

Millicent groaned with the next wild career. The motors emitted a horrible grinding sound. The whole thing shook. An explosion sounded a ways off. Ryker laughed. Trent screamed—kept screaming, actually. He'd barely stopped since Ryker had gotten going.

"Ready. We're ready. We need them to be somewhat stable, though," Roe yelled out. "Get this done and we're sailing."

The motors whined again as the craft tilted. And kept tilting. Trent's scream increased in pitch. Millicent stared at the console, upside down. Bodies fell from where they'd been stashed, smacking against the ceiling. No one had thought to secure them against going upside down . . .

"How the hell are you doing this?" she yelled, the g-force tearing at her. The engines' pitch as high as Trent's.

"The craft will cut out in five . . . ," Ryker said, "four . . ."

"Cut out? Are you crazy?" Millicent screamed.

"Yes, he is!" Trent yelled.

"Three . . . two . . . Now's the time, Roe. They are about to fire. One!"

A bang. Smoke puffed up around their feet. The engines cut out. It was eerily quiet, save for Trent's screaming . . . before gravity sucked them down.

"We're all gonna die!" Trent shouted.

A rushing filled Millicent's ears as she chewed on her thumping heart. Like some sort of jet engine, it took over her awareness until she couldn't focus on anything else.

"Missiles in three . . . two . . ."

"No more counting," she begged Roe.

An explosion rattled the craft, shaking Millicent within the strap. She slid toward the ground—or ceiling, she guessed—a little more. A lovely display of fire lit up the side of the craft. It gushed against the windows and promised death.

"Now get us out of here!" Roe yelled.

The fire drifted away, silently. They were still falling. Headfirst, they were dropping out of the sky.

"On it," Ryker yelled.

The engine coughed, turning over. And over. Not catching. It coughed again. Then clicked.

"Well, that's not good," Ryker said, still sounding so confident.

"Oh please," Millicent begged, and swallowed down a horribly foul taste in her mouth. Add stomach to the list of things she was chewing on while hanging upside down with terror racing through her bloodstream.

A banging sounded from the front. Then something metallic. The next cough turned into a roar. A grinding, growling type of roar that did not sound promising.

"Here we go," Ryker said.

The vessel shook, and then flipped. Millicent struck the wall. Her head lolled. She didn't bother to right herself. She just hung there, her arms limp, as the craft steadied.

"Nothing to it," Ryker said, his tone pleased.

Millicent burped fire.

❖   ❖   ❖

"Here we go, Millie. I've got you." Millicent let Ryker slip an arm around her waist and haul her up. "C'mon, sweetie. Here we go, Marie. Okay, girls, just through here."

After limping to the edge of the city in a craft that clearly had no idea what it was capable of—much like all but one of the passengers—they exited through a gate in LA's security wall manned by one of Roe's people. They got a nod as the hobbling vehicle went through. The siren that went off was silenced.

They'd docked beside a large craft with a company's logo written on the side.

"Is this going to hold up to scrutiny? Because I need a break before I work another console," Millicent said as she wiped her mouth.

"This is a legit vessel. We have friends everywhere," Roe said, stepping to her other side. She wasn't sure if he was helping her or disguising his wobbly legs.

She decided she didn't much care.

"How is Trent fairing?" she asked. A large door was opened. They got in line with the vessel's staffers and entered without anyone raising an eyebrow.

"He fainted and hasn't yet come to. He's being carried," Ryker answered. "It's been a long couple of days."

"What comes next?" Millicent asked as they entered a large space where various-sized boxes, all with the company's logo, were being stacked.

Roe motioned them to the right, where they went through a door and then took another right, finally stopping in a small room with two rows of benches. "Now we sleep until it's time for the next leg of our journey."

"And what is that?" Millicent asked, sitting gratefully.

"The rocket. Getting off this rock."

Chapter 27

"This is it?" Millicent asked as she stared up at a giant rocket ship. Rain beat down on her hood, and the intense chill of it pushed against her clothing and the scarf covering her face. She'd seen the design long ago while researching this endeavor, a clunky vessel towering into the sky.

"This is it." Roe led them to an elevator and got in with them. "We have a half an hour until takeoff. We're cutting it extremely close."

Millicent watched out the windows as the torrid gray sky shot lightning at the barren and desecrated ground. "How does it exist? I mean . . ." She licked her parched lips. "How can you keep it operational?"

"The conglomerates don't come out here. Why would they? There's nothing." Roe held the elevator so they could exit onto a metal crate leading to a small doorway in the side of the rocket. "The rocket has specially designed tech to mask its energy and heat signature. We have people in each conglomerate and government who manually mask its trajectory through the sky. It's been a long road. We used to just race the conglomerates, making it out of the atmosphere as often as we didn't. But now . . . we should be okay."

"Should be?" Ryker growled, holding Marie.

"These rockets aren't the newest tech you'll ever see. One in a hundred still blows up. But they are as good as we've got."

After stepping out of the elevator and going through a small door, Millicent looked down at a collection of four pods. Each was a large oval with a sort of shiny beige material making up the sides and bottom. They circled and were connected to an older supercomputer, the screen blank. "And the conglomerates don't follow you up anymore?"

"They have, but the combination of the perilous journey with the high fatality rate, the loss of time, and the astronomical cost of harvesting the resources and bringing them back has stopped their progress in that direction. Not forever, I'm sure, but for a while. So our main concern is getting off-planet. Well, and getting people who can afford the trip out of the conglomerate."

"And this is?" Ryker pointed at the four pods.

"This is floor one. The other four floors are already filled. The others have been there a couple months. This is the last. You—us—we're the last." Roe gestured. "The child will need to go in with one of you."

"Let's circle back to the high fatality rate?" Trent said, picking at his nail as he looked down at the pods.

"In essence, you'll be put into a biological limbo. For ease of understanding, you'll be asleep, but you won't age. The journey takes two years, give or take. You'll go to sleep now and wake up when we're there. But some . . . haven't woken up." Roe shrugged. "This is not a guaranteed mode of travel."

"Can a child . . ." Millicent swallowed back her fear.

"We've taken children before—usually clones. Over one year of age, they are no worse off than a healthy adult. Older people, though . . ." Roe shifted.

Trent looked at the ground, an uncomfortable look crossing his face.

"And you're going with us?" Millicent asked, knowing Roe counted himself among those facing a higher fatality rate. "You make this trip often?"

"Twice. Once there. Once back." A chime filled the room. Roe glanced up at the low ceiling. Then to the pod. "But I need to train my replacement."

"Who's that?" Ryker asked with a low growl.

"None of your concern," Roe said. He motioned at the pods. "In or out. We have to go."

Millicent stared at Ryker for a long moment. And then uttered the words that ripped at her heart. "You should take her. You have a better ability to heal. If something should happen, you can protect her better than I can."

Ryker set Marie down for a moment. His strong arms crushed Millicent to his chest before his lips hit hers in a bruising kiss. "We'll be okay. I'll see you on the other side."

Tears fell down Millicent's cheeks as she nodded, not trusting her voice. She let the warmth in her heart rush through her body; that strong, deep feeling that wasn't sexual in any way. It wasn't the same as she felt for Marie, but it was just as strong. "You were right. There is more than one form of love. And you hold one of them in my heart."

"I love you, too. But this isn't good-bye." He kissed her again, deep and sensuous and confident. "We still need to make another baby, princess. I look forward to trying right after we wake up."

She ran her hand down his cheek; her eyes blurred with tears. Next she bent to her daughter and pulled her into a tight hug. "Okay, baby. Good night. I'll see you in the morning."

"Night-night, Mama," Marie said, wrapping her little arms around Millicent's neck. "See you 'morrow?"

"I'll see you tomorrow, yes." Millicent tucked Marie into Ryker's arms. The chime sounded again. A small shudder ran through the floor and then the walls.

"We have to go," Roe said.

Millicent squared off with Trent. "Glad to have you along." She hugged him, the feeling weird. She felt his awkward pats on her back.

"We'll be okay. This will be fine." Trent nodded, his shaking voice relaying his worry. "It's fine." He shrugged. "You can get in first."

She stuck out her hand for Roe, who shook it firmly. "Thank you," she said.

"I'll look forward to getting that code scan of Toton's craft back." He pointed at her suit. "And don't worry about the tech you've been carting around. It'll be stored away to meet you there."

She nodded, and then took one last look at Ryker and Marie, who were settling into their pod, before lowering herself into her own. A cover slid across, closing her in. The interior lit up, showing a beautiful picture of green meadows and a distant crystal-clear waterfall. She smiled as a strange smell affected her, making her dizzy. Before she drifted off to sleep, she felt liquid fill in around her, probably an oxygen-rich serum, high in nutrients.

Her last thought was *They forgot to take out our implants . . .*

❖ ❖ ❖

"Millie?"

Millicent blinked her eyes open slowly. The handsome face of Ryker looked down on her, his electric-blue eyes holding relief. Marie peeked into Millicent's pod a moment later, her face so angelic Millicent couldn't help laughing.

"We made it," Ryker said, reaching down to her.

"Did Trent make it?" she asked, standing. Her legs felt wobbly and weak.

"Yeah. Here." Trent was at the door of the rocket, staring out.

"Roe?" Millicent asked, allowing Ryker to wrap her up into a tight hug—Marie in the middle.

"Yes. He woke me up, and then told me to get the rest of you. His was timed. Ours was not. We've been here for a month." Ryker did not sound happy about that fact.

"You didn't hurt him too badly, did you?" Millicent walked toward the door, half-terrified to see what their new home looked like.

"He's had a month to wake his muscles up. Said he was getting ready for us. Whatever that means." Ryker waited as Millicent walked in front of him.

Trent stepped aside, allowing her to fill the door. And then her whole body went light, and she groped for the door frame. "Is this computer generated?"

"No. This is real." Trent leaned against the wall. "What you are seeing is what this world looks like." He shook his head slowly. "Incredible."

"What?" Ryker asked, trying to see around her. "Holy—"

Millicent couldn't feel her feet as she climbed from the side of the huge vessel and walked along the platform. She couldn't properly process what she was seeing as she traveled down the elevators, staring through the glass at the world beyond. She couldn't greet people who were smiling and saying hello to her. And she could only blink as Roe met them at the base of the rocket site.

"You're not a higher-level staffer here, Millicent," Roe said, grabbing her by the arm to steer her into a ground vehicle. "You aren't above anyone. They don't work for you. Granted, you are quite a bit smarter, but until you run for office, you have just as much say as anyone else. Do you understand?" He turned on the vehicle, producing a sound like an electric whine, before pulling out of the parking place and into a narrow ground-bound travel way.

"It's so green," she said to no one, watching the fields pass by the window. "So, so green . . ."

"We don't have a lot of tech, like I told you before," Roe went on. "But we would love your help developing some sort of system. They've come pretty far, but no one has your expertise. They don't have a fraction—"

"Roe. Shut up. Let this sink in," Ryker said as the car went through a group of dwellings. Behind them was wide-open space dotted with live vegetation and animals. Animals!

The silence continued as everyone stared out the windows, wide-eyed.

"Here we go. This will be your living community." Roe entered a collection of segregated dwellings, all only reaching one story off the ground. "We find it's better to live in groups."

Millicent pushed the vehicle door open and then watched her foot touch down on a sort of loose rock. She sucked in a deep breath, the lively and sweet smell glorious to her senses.

"Is that wood?" Ryker asked as he set Marie down, staring at the dwelling.

"Wood, yes," Roe said, looking around with them. "Houses are made of wood here. At least in this area. In the more rocky places, they are doing better with a type of concrete block."

"This is . . . our house?" Millicent stared at the yard—a patch of greenery with a tree at the corner. *A live tree!* Hanging from the branches was a swing.

She felt Ryker's arm wrap around her shoulders. Marie squealed and ran toward the swing.

"Yes, this is yours," Roe said.

Millicent shook her head slowly, unable to believe that she was physically standing in a setting like the ones she'd previously seen only by computer generation. She hadn't known it was possible. "I feel like I'm dreaming."

In the distance were rolling hills covered in that same beautiful green. Green stretched forever, it seemed. Little walkways were carved out this way and that, with ground vehicles moving along them, but most of the land was untouched. Untarnished. The sky above them was a blue like none she'd ever seen before, not even in computer-generated models, and harbored puffy white clouds. It was like the pictures of Earth hundreds of years ago. A beautiful place, full of magic and beauty. She couldn't stop smiling.

"What are those?" Millicent pointed at a distant group of animals.

"Cows," Roe said. "We farm here. You have a garden in back of your house. Trent, you do, too. Most people do. They—we—eat fresh food, which we try to grow ourselves."

"I get my own house?" Trent asked, staring much like Millicent was.

"Yes. I didn't think Ryker was the sort to share. Wait here." He disappeared inside the house. When he came back, he was hugging three cups to his chest. "Here. Drink that."

Millicent stared at what couldn't possibly be a whole cup of water. "I can drink this, or . . . ?"

Roe's smile cracked his face and sent wrinkles running. "Yes."

The cool liquid gushed over her tongue and moved down the inside of her body. It tasted like . . . nothing. And it was the best taste she'd ever experienced.

"You found your dream home," Ryker said, finishing his own cup of water before wrapping his arm around Millicent again. Marie laughed, a delighted sound, as Trent pushed her on the swing. The soft breeze moved her hair. "We're safe, Millie. Our family is safe. And we are free to create more children if we choose."

"We hope you do," Roe said, watching Marie with a small smile. "We love children here. They're the future, after all."

The silence settled on them then. A bird chirped, drawing Millicent's eyes. She watched in wonder as it flew away, leaving the tree branch shaking. Flowers bloomed around their yard, lovely and colorful. Real.

"Welcome home," Roe said. "Welcome to Paradise."

Epilogue

Danissa stared at the screen in a bored haze. Binary code scrolled past, presenting no interesting challenges. Her daily tasks seemed almost hollow in the absence of the Moxidone staffer.

It had been two years since Ms. Foster had dropped off the face of the earth.

Literally.

At least, that was the rumor. People said the staffer had snatched her child right out from under the conglomerate's nose and, with the help of a lab tech and a security director, forced her way to freedom.

A life of her own. What must that be like?

Danissa sighed and glanced at the left wall. The sun glimmered off the top of a bright-blue computer-generated wave before it crashed down onto snowy-white sand. What she wouldn't give to be on that beach.

The story of the staffer's escape was all hearsay, of course. Moxidone claimed they had both directors, the child, and the lab tech in custody. The adults would get a mind wipe and be back at it in no time.

Her gaze flicked back to the screen.

That had been their story for the last two years, but Ms. Foster hadn't been back online. Danissa should know. She'd searched every database out there. She'd pored over the private loop Ms. Foster had used to create all that havoc right before her log-ons went dark. Even the pirate network hadn't revealed any secrets. If Ms. Foster was on-planet, she wasn't online.

"Hey, did you hear?"

Danissa started as Puda strode into her office.

"Did you hear?" he repeated, his perfectly symmetrical smile infectious. He shouldn't have been allowed on this level, but Danissa got what she wanted, and she wanted him visiting as often as possible.

"Does this look like the face of a woman in the know?" she asked, enhancing her bored expression.

"Well . . . yes, but that's not the point." He leaned against the imagery wall. His form interrupted a wave as it crested and then crashed down around his body. "Moxidone is working on a sleek new rocket."

"Oh yeah?" Danissa couldn't help the surge of excitement, and she leaned forward. "Then she *did* get off-planet. She must have. Are they going to go get her?"

"Great heavens. Don't get so excited. If you got out of this hell-hole—" Puda winced and looked out the door. He lowered his voice, even though it would make no difference. He didn't understand how the tech in his head worked. "If you went where things like this"—he gestured at the image surrounding him—"were real, would you want to be hauled back?"

Danissa shrugged away the tinge of guilt. "We have no idea that the other planet is much nicer. Those are just rumors."

"Besides, why would you want her back?" He shifted position and crossed his arms over his chest. "She was insufferably arrogant."

Danissa shrugged for a different reason this time. She couldn't help the accompanying smirk. "She had a right to be. The woman was brilliant. She was the only one who could crack my codes. Still is. And besides—" The constant shrugging was starting to look like a tick, she was sure of it. "She's not the only woman with a reputation for being arrogant but brilliant."

"True enough. But you're prettier."

Definitely a tick. "You're a little biased." Danissa sat back and crossed an ankle over her knee. "How long do you think before Gregon starts on a rocket?"

"Not long. This will be a new space race, I guarantee it. And I hear Moxidone's rocket will be massive. They're enhancing their security, too. No more sneaking out of the conglomerate. That weird rebel group, whatever they call themselves, is dead in the water, so I hear."

"Ms. Foster still would've gotten off-planet. Paired up with that director, they were the best. It would take me and . . . I don't even know who to combat them head-to-head. Who do we have in security that could match Mr. Gunner?"

"I don't talk to those guys. I don't get guards like you do."

"Well anyway." She pulled up a map of the various solar systems and traced her finger along the path to the other planet. "Maybe they are thinking of finally colonizing?"

"Maybe. Or maybe just pillaging the natural resources. Setting up a colony would take time, and it would be difficult to oversee it from such a distance. But hauling back resources . . ."

Danissa bit her lip in thought. "Ms. Foster probably thought they were safe. That they escaped."

"You said it yourself—she was brilliant. And Gunner was legendary. No way they thought they got away. No way."

"I don't know. I feel like—" Waves of disturbance rolled over the screens. The cresting wave wiggled. Pixelated blue crashed and became fuzzy black and white.

A delighted smile crossed Danissa's face, and she motioned Puda aside. "Get out of the way."

Confused, Puda jumped toward the doorway.

Another wave crested before wiggling harder. It distorted. The coding on the other walls dimmed. A picture of lush forest and a crystal-blue waterfall didn't take the place of the ocean—a trick Ms. Foster had liked to play in the past. Instead, blackness reigned.

"This wouldn't be her," Danissa said on a release of breath, her hopes dashed.

Frowning, she turned toward her main idea board and pulled up the system logs. Confusion turned to shock, and then dread. Error codes flashed across the right screen. Alerts flared red along the top of the walls.

"What is that?" Puda asked, stepping forward.

"Ma'am!" someone shouted. "Ma'am, we have a system breach!"

Panic crept in as Danissa's gaze flew over the foreign coding that flashed across her screen, almost too fast to take in.

"I've never seen that before. Have you?" Puda asked.

"Ma'am, they are in our files! They are copying our files!" her assistant shouted from her work pod.

"Who's doing this? Moxidone?" Puda accessed his wrist screen. "What the hell—I'm locked out!"

"Ma'am, I've been kicked out!" her assistant shouted. Surprised gasps and shrieks erupted from the floor.

Cold trickled down Danissa's insides as she dived toward her console. "This isn't Moxidone. It looks like Toton wasn't crippled after all. They are fighting back."

ABOUT THE AUTHOR

Photo ©2014 Penni Gladstone

K.F. Breene is the *USA Today* bestselling author of many fantasy and paranormal romance novels, including the Darkness and Warrior Chronicles series.